# Dead Ahead

*It's hard to make a fresh start when you've got a reputation for death!*

## The Ruthless-the-Killer Mysteries

## Susan J Bruce

Beanstalk
Ink

A catalogue record for this book is available from the National Library of Australia

*In memory of Amber…*
*The best bad cat with a good heart a writer could have.*

# A Quick Guide to Aussie 'Lingo'

**AFP:** Australian Federal Police.

**Block:** A parcel of land, often with a house.

**Bogong moth:** A large, buzzy migratory moth found in southern Australia.

**Car boot:** The rear storage compartment of a car (US: trunk).

**Cop shop:** Local police station.

**Driza-Bone:** An iconic Australian waterproof coat.

**Dropkick:** Aussie slang—a foolish or useless person.

**Echidna:** A small, spiny, egg-laying mammal that eats ants and resembles a hedgehog.

**Footpath:** Paved path for walking (US: sidewalk).

**Ginger nut biscuits**: Yummy, crunchy ginger cookies (US: gingersnaps).

**Gumnut babies:** Characters from classic Aussie children's books by May Gibbs.

**Jumper:** Knitted top (US: sweater).

**Kerb:** Edge of the footpath/ sidewalk (US: curb).

**Lantana:** Fast-spreading flowering shrub with tangled branches.

**Lollies:** Small sweets or candies.

**Pre-Federation:** Before Australia became a nation in 1901.

**Ring:** To call someone on the phone.

**Roo pit:** Pit where dead kangaroos and other small animals are buried on a farm.

**Sparky:** Electrician.

**Tasmanian tiger:** A large, carnivorous marsupial native to Tasmania, but believed to be extinct. They resemble a cross between a dog and a tiger.

**Ute:** Utility vehicle with a tray back (US: truck/ pickup truck).

**Wattle:** Native tree or bush of the Acacia family, with yellow flowers.

**Yabbying:** Catching small crustaceans for bait, using a hand-pump on salt-water mudflats. You can also get fresh-water yabbies that are good to eat, but you catch these with a net.


**Ruth is an Aussie so she uses Aussie *spelling* to tell her story:**

Burnt vs burned, centre vs center, colour vs color, defence vs defense, grey vs gray, honour vs honor, jewellery vs jewelry, Mum vs Mom, practise (verb) vs practice, realise vs realize, towards vs toward, traveller vs traveler, plus **many, many more…**

# Chapter One

It's never easy to make a fresh start with a reputation like mine, especially when you believe your own bad press.

The plane pitched and rolled, my heart lurching with each thump and shudder. We weren't going down—the pilot had assured us everything was fine—but morbid thoughts still clawed through my consciousness. I tried to catch them and squeeze them back into the locked crate in my mind, but like a cranky cat they refused to be caged.

Another tilt sent my stomach into free fall.

My inner critic pounced. *You're a jinx. We're going to crash.*

*Am not a jinx!* That was my logical self.

But my childhood anxieties hissed and spat, unwilling to be reasoned with.

I loosened my sweaty grip on the armrests and took a long, deep breath. The air inside the cabin clung close as the captain's announcement blared through the loudspeaker: "We apologise that we can't serve hot drinks due to the turbulence. We'll be serving cold refreshments shortly."

A murmur ran through the cabin and two flight attendants began wobbling down the aisle with the drinks trolley. When they reached me, the fair-headed one swayed for a moment then steadied himself.

"Drink?" His smile was reassuring, and my galloping heart slowed. If he wasn't scared, I shouldn't be either, right? I'd flown on much more rickety planes than this one.

"Lemon squash, please." I hit him with my best seasoned-traveller smile. He handed me the can of soft drink, but I turned down the plastic cup and ice.

The turbulence hit again, worse than before. A bang was followed by a gasp—the trolley must have hit a seat. I swung around, my heart jangling at the flicker of fear in the attendant's eyes. He and his colleague rushed the trolley down the aisle to safety.

That was all that was needed for my childhood curse to pounce again.

*You're a jinx.*

*No.*

*Harbinger of death then…*

*NO!*

I wriggled in my seat, trying to keep away from the large, sweaty bald guy who hogged the middle armrest. At least I was next to the aisle. I couldn't have coped pressed in against the window. But this whole jinx thing was ridiculous. I've always been the kind of traveller who brings extra snacks and never forgets her neck pillow. I don't stress on planes. But a few weeks with my family and I was reliving a Grimm's fairy tale.

My adult brain knew no one on the plane was cursed because of me, and I had nothing to do with a handful of people I knew who died when I was a kid. The whole thing was made up by my cousin Karl who loved tormenting people, and thought it was hilarious to call me Ruthless-the-

Killer and blame me for everything bad that happened to my family or friends. But the reputation stuck. Even I began to believe it, although the only things I've ever truly cursed are the cacti I can never keep alive.

But logic rarely stands a chance against the ghosts of the past.

The turbulence stopped, but the fasten seatbelt sign stayed on. I sat there for a few moments then cracked open my squash and sipped directly from the can. It was cold and tart and its bubbles tickled my throat.

It would be okay. This was my new beginning. No one except Mum had died since I was a kid. My Italian ex-fiancé with Mafia ties didn't count, and I was moving somewhere far, far away from my childhood in Brisbane and my last decade in Europe. Semi-rural South Australia was beautiful, and about as far as you could escape from—anywhere. Not only was the whole 'death' thing ridiculous, but it belonged to my past. This was a different season of my life, and I was a different me.

I rummaged through my ruby leather tote bag, looking for the novel I was reading. It was fun—just the right mix of mystery, romance and suspense I needed to distract myself and relax—but I couldn't find it amidst the jangle of keys and the soft squish of my cardigan. The fasten seatbelt sign flashed off right then, so I stood, navigating my lemon squash back onto my tray table, then reached into the overhead locker for my backpack.

The bag was heavy, and it was stuck, so I yanked it hard. The man sitting across the aisle from me chose that moment to stand, at the same time as the plane lurched with another surge of turbulence. I fell back against him and somehow we both ended up in his seat—with me on top of him—our bodies and limbs tangled.

"I'm so sorry!" I tried to right myself.

His arms only came around me for a moment as he steadied me. But it was long enough for me to feel the warmth of his body and breathe in the scent of his woodsy cologne. It was also enough time to feel the thrill of electricity as his hands caught first my waist, and then my arms, as he helped me and my backpack up to my feet.

*Attraction.*

*This wasn't good.*

I stuck my arm through the backpack strap, but the plane lurched again. I was thrown off balance by the pack's weight, but managed to grab hold of the seat in front of me in time. I picked up my drink which by some miracle hadn't tipped over and slid with a mortified thump back into my seat.

The two flight attendants who had been serving the drinks hovered around us asking if we were okay. We both said yes, now safe in our seats, and waved them away.

My face burned—probably as red as my tote bag—but when I turned back to the man, his eyes crinkled with laughter.

"I can't say that's ever happened to me on a flight before. Are you okay?" He spoke with a resonant Australian drawl, mixed with another accent I couldn't quite pin down. Somewhere in the USA?

I nodded. "You?"

His face lit with an impish smile. "More than okay." He held out his hand. "Dan Rivers."

"Er… Ruth Smythe." I took his hand—there was that spark again. I let go quickly. "Sorry, I was looking for my book." I pried it out of the front pocket of the backpack and waved it in his direction.

Dan nodded at the pack. "Would you like me to put that

back up for you?" His lips twitched. "Might be safer for me if I did it."

"Ha ha!" My voice was droll. "But thanks. Although the seatbelt sign is back on."

He glanced down the aisle. "I'll be quick."

I handed him the backpack, nearly dropping it in the process, but he caught it in time and hoisted it into the overhead locker.

"I don't normally fall into the laps of men I don't know," I said.

"You mostly fall into the laps of men you do know?"

"No… I mean yes… I…" My face flushed hot again. I hadn't done *any* falling into men's laps in the past few months and I intended to keep it that way—at least until I found my bearings in my new life.

Dan laughed. "That backpack is heavy." He shot a look at the two flight attendants, who were still demurring on the drinks service. "You're lucky they let you bring it onto the plane."

"See that man up there?" I pointed to a large bloke a few seats forward who had shoulders almost as wide as the aisle. "I kept him between me and the attendants all the time when we were lining up to board."

"And pretended it was light as a feather when you had to show your boarding pass?"

His grin was infectious, and I smiled back, unable to resist the urge to eye-flirt with him. "Of course."

"So, if we crash because we're overloaded… we blame you?"

I caught my breath and focused on the cover of my book. He was joking but that was too close to my head funk of a few minutes ago.

*I am not a jinx.*

"Hey, I'm sorry." Concern washed over his face. "Hit a nerve?"

"That's okay." I picked up my book. "I'm going to read now."

From the corner of my eye, I could see Dan raise his eyebrows at the set-down. But then he shrugged, lay back in his seat and closed his eyes.

I couldn't resist letting my gaze linger on him.

He was a little older than me, mid to late thirties at a guess, with that lean muscle and easy grace that made me wonder if he was in the military. He didn't look like a gym junkie. His muscles looked real, not the boutique, artificially coiffured kind you sometimes get by ordering a particular type of protein powder you can only buy on the dark web. I knew because my last ex had used it.

He opened his eyes a slit, his mouth twitching in amusement. "Enjoying… that book?"

He knew I was checking him out. Scoundrel.

He sat back up in his seat, obviously wanting to talk.

"So where are you heading?" His warm blue eyes were encouraging, as was his easy manner.

I took a deep sip of lemon squash and winked at him. "Probably the same place you're heading." I leaned closer and spoke in a mock whisper. "And everyone else on the plane."

Dan laughed, flashing a twin dimpled smile that made my heart do a backflip. "Sorry, I get told that I often state the obvious."

He was good-looking. The above-mentioned blue eyes were set off by dark brown hair, with just the right amount of well-groomed jaw stubble. He was tall, six feet plus.

Tall, dark and handsome?

*You're such a cliché, Ruth.*

I took another sip of my squash and wished I'd asked for

something stronger. Although it was just as well I hadn't. With alcohol on board, I might not have been able to resist Dan's charms at all. And that would have been bad.

Let's just say I have a type—a type that has led to great disappointment and disillusionment over the past ten years. Dan personified that type. I couldn't deal with going there again, but semi-anonymous chatting on a plane, along with a little flirting, was okay, wasn't it? I'd wanted a distraction.

I reached for my handbag and pulled out a photo. My heart rap, rap, rapped against my ribcage when I gazed at my new home. It was more than a house—it was a beautiful old stone cottage on three hectares of land—a cottage I never realised existed until a few weeks ago.

I wasn't sure I wanted to tell a stranger where I lived, especially one whose presence made my ovaries quiver, but there was no address on the photo, and I really wanted to share it with—someone.

"This is where I'm going."

Dan leaned over the aisle to look at the image. "Nice place. Your home?"

"It will be." I handed him the photo.

"Just bought it?"

"Inherited it. From my dad."

"I'm sorry."

Dad had died a few weeks before, but a whole host of thoughts and emotions still tripped over each other whenever I thought of him. Betrayal by my sociopathic sister, ten years lost in exile, getting home... too late. The back of my eyes burned, but there were no tears. I'd wept enough over the past few weeks.

"Dad grew up in South Australia," I said. "I thought about putting the property on the market, but my friend begged me to come live there. It's in the country, ten minutes from where the river meets the sea."

There was a flicker of something in Dan's eyes. "On the south coast?"

I nodded.

"You've seen the property?"

I shook my head.

He shot me a lopsided smile. "You're brave. Some of these old homes need a lot of work." He held the image up to the light and examined it. "You don't think the roof has been photoshopped? And that wall?"

I plucked the photo out of his hand and squinted at it. Dan leaned closer, and I tried to ignore his delicious scent of warm oak with a touch of sandalwood, mixed with the fragrance of fresh-cut grass.

"See." He pointed to the roof. "There are some fuzzy pixels here. And here." He frowned and tapped the photo where the front and side walls joined.

I sat back in my seat, gazing at the image, a pang of doubt twisting in my gut. "She said it was liveable."

His expression softened. "If it's not, make sure she helps you fix it."

I smiled at that. "Shona isn't exactly handywoman material."

Dan raised his eyebrows and the same expression flickered into his eyes as before. Then his lips quirked upwards. "When was it built?"

"Sometime in the 1880s."

"That's pre-Federation."

"Yep." I studied the photo again. "Rumour has it that an old sea captain was one of the first owners and he buried treasure there."

Dan laughed. "Sounds like a rumour started by a real estate agent."

I chuckled in agreement. "Dad didn't talk much about South Australia when we were little. He studied postgrad engineering at Queensland Uni when his whole family moved north. It was strange, really. Why not talk about your childhood home?"

My question was rhetorical, but Dan shrugged and glanced down the aisle. "Sometimes you just need to move on."

I stared at the photo, pushing back memories with a wistful smile. "Like I'm doing."

Dan opened his mouth to speak, but the fasten seatbelt sign dinged off again, then a tall, blonde woman with legs so long they reached almost up to her breasts—and that was only a mild exaggeration—strode down the aisle towards Dan. He stood to let her squeeze past and she sat in the seat next to him.

She laid a hand on his knee. "Sorry, babe. With all that turbulence they made me sit up front after I went to the loo."

They were obviously together. My ovaries sighed with disappointment, but it made my job of looking the other way easier. My life was too much of a mess for me to want to hook up with someone like Dan. He had trouble tattooed over each dimple. But I didn't like the look his girlfriend gave me.

Like she was claiming a prize.

I used to have a dog who did that—our family's red kelpie, Shelby. She laid her paw on anything she wanted to call her own. My sister called it *the paw of possession.*

I gave the woman a smile more plastic than my tray table before turning back to my photo. It didn't matter. My life was about other things—like making a fresh start, finding a place to belong, and working out who I was and what I really wanted. It was about finding peace and purpose. Once I'd done that, I could look for love.

The plane shuddered and dipped once more, and the fasten seatbelt sign pinged back on yet again.

I closed my eyes and tried to imagine the plane bouncing off the clouds, with the pilots yelling, "Wheeeeee!" every time they went over a bump, like Dad used to do in the car when Sarah and I were little. A brief smile rested on my lips as I remembered. Very brief—because the plane's next bounce jolted my can of lemon squash.

"Aargh!" The sticky drink spilled all over my tray table.

"Here." Dan handed me a clean paper napkin, his fingers brushing mine. Legs-to-Breasts gave me a lethal look. I took the napkin and smiled at Dan. Not because I wanted to encourage him, but because I wanted to make his lady friend squirm.

But then guilt panged through me. I'd been in her place too many times. Not that Dan was really doing anything wrong. He was flirting a little—fair call given I'd fallen on top of him—but he was mainly being kind. But I'd known what it was like to have a guy's eyes looking elsewhere because I was too dull or too needy or too broke, or just… because.

I smiled at her again. This time it was a sister-to-sister, I-see-your-pain kind of smile. A disarming, I'm-on-your-side smile. It didn't defuse the Exocet missiles her gaze fired at me, but it made me feel better about myself.

The turbulence eased again, and I settled back in my seat, letting my mind drift to my new home. It would be perfect. A semi-rural stone cottage on the outskirts of Pelican Bay, a small town on the coast of the Fleurieu Peninsula, South Australia. A place which, according to Shona, was so safe you could leave your door unlocked at night.

"Nothing ever happens here," she'd said. And nothing was

exactly what this burned-out, grief-stricken, look-what-the-cat-dragged-in, run-around-the-world gal needed.

When the plane landed, Dan hefted my backpack out of the locker for me. I said thanks, let my eyes meet his for a moment, then worked hard to keep my gaze away. The flirting had been fun—and an even better distraction than my book—but I didn't want to cause trouble between them.

It wasn't as if I'd ever see him again.

I squared my shoulders under the weight of my backpack and lifted my head as I strode across the tarmac towards the terminal. I revelled in the familiar firmness of solid ground beneath my feet. This was my new beginning.

I wasn't a jinx, and *no one* was going to die anywhere near me.

# Chapter Two

Three months later, Shona and I were standing outside my old stone cottage, gazing up at the thoroughly blocked chimney.

I lifted my coffee, inhaling the rich aroma, then took a long, slow, satisfying, sip. The hot drink warmed me, much like the autumn sunlight on my skin, but my thoughts about the chimney were more heated. "Whatever's in there is stuck tight."

Shona tilted her head then spoke in her soft Scottish brogue. "Do you think it could be a dead body?"

I gasped, spluttered and sneezed coffee out of my nose.

"Are you okay?" Shona thumped my back a few times.

"Fine," I answered, through coffee-inhaled gasps. "How on earth would anyone fit a dead body into a chimney?"

"Piece by piece?"

I almost choked again. "There's no dead body, Shona."

"How do you know?"

I tried the sensible approach. "There'd be bones in the hearth."

"That's logical."

I giggled at the disappointment in her tone.

Her gaze became more intent. "But something is stuck in there."

We'd spent the morning trying to poke things up the chimney to loosen whatever was there, but the angles were all wrong. "I'm going to have a look from above. Push a broom down there."

"Are you sure you can do that? It's pretty high."

My inability to cope with heights was legendary among my friends.

"I'm going to try."

It was a beautiful autumn day, but the warm comfort of the sunlight couldn't stop my heart from thrumming into overdrive as I gripped the ladder.

I pulled myself upwards, the rough texture of the rungs cold against my palms. I squeezed my eyes shut, taking deep, measured breaths to try and still my racing pulse.

*You're not going to fall.*

If I looked around me, I'd see an idyllic postcard scene: rolling hills, relaxed kangaroos munching on grass and kestrels soaring high in search of prey. Anyone else might hear a symphony of magpies warbling, wombats shuffling and May Gibbs' gumnut babies singing the hallelujah chorus. But my soundtrack? Pure thrash metal—all about fear, death and hell's gates swinging wide. Just thinking about the view made my world spin, and my grip on the ladder's sides tighten.

*Don't. Look. Down.*

"You're nearly there. Just two more rungs."

I looked down.

Bad decision.

Shona's eyes brimmed with hope as she beamed up at me. But while it was good to know she believed in me, when *they* say you shouldn't look down if you're afraid of heights, *they* are right.

My vision swam. I leaned into the ladder and clutched the sides with white-knuckled force.

"Ruth?"

I clamped my eyes shut. "I'm okay."

"Breathe," my friend called.

I took a deep breath—and then another—and edged up one more rung.

"You're at the gutter," Shona called. "Focus on the roof. Once you're on, I'll hand you up the broom."

I ended up half on the roof and half on the ladder.

"My leg's cramping." My voice rose and I was breathing fast. "I need to come down."

"Okay, okay. Swing your right leg back onto the ladder."

My body froze. "I can't."

"Yes, you can." Shona's voice was soothing. "I've got the ladder. I won't let you fall."

"Okay." I sucked in an even deeper breath, squinted my eyes shut and edged my leg back over the gutter, towards the ladder.

"You're doing great."

My breathing slowed once my foot was back on the rung.

"Okay. Now come back down one step at a time."

I wobbled when my feet hit the ground.

"Uh-oh, spaghetti legs." Shona grabbed my arm before I could crumple, and I leaned against her for a moment.

"I'll be okay." I shifted to prop myself against the house.

"Just get your breath, then I can have a go."

"What?" I shook my head. "You don't have to."

"Are you kidding? I don't mind heights and I need to make sure there aren't any bodies in your chimney."

I barked out a laugh.

"You sound better. Ready?" Her eyes gleamed.

"If you're sure…"

Shona grasped the ladder. "Let's do this thing."


We stood in my living room half an hour later, frowning at the fireplace and sipping yet another hot drink. The caffeine from my double-strength macchiato surged through my veins while Shona serenely sipped black tea with milk. To my friend's disappointment and my great relief, no bodies had fallen out of the chimney, but she did lose the broom down in there.

"At least the weather's still warm," I said. "I won't need to use the fireplace for a while. Although you say it can turn quickly?"

"We're not far from the coast so it can be mild right through into June, but a storm with a strong southerly can freeze your wee toes off." Shona crouched and peered into the fireplace. "Can't you pay someone to do this?"

"I spent all my spare money fixing the roof and the wall." I looked meaningfully at my friend. We'd had this discussion before. "If you hadn't photoshopped those photos…"

"You might not have come. I really, really wanted you to come."

Shona's words tugged at something deep and raw inside me. I'd spent much of the last ten years feeling the opposite of wanted. We'd met at primary school in England. Our fathers were working on a joint Australian and United Kingdom defence project, and we went to the same school in the Cotswolds for two years. Shona was always incubating some kind of hare-brained scheme that involved me getting into trouble.

We'd kept in touch after I moved back to Australia with

my family, but reconnected when I moved to Europe. We made it our goal to have a weekend together in some famous city, three or four times a year, but a backpacking trip brought Shona to Australia. She got a job, met Joe, and fell in love with both him and Pelican Bay. It just happened to be the same small town where my dad owned property.

Coincidence?

Yep.

A good one?

Mostly.

Because Shona was getting me into trouble again.

"I probably still would have moved down here," I said. "But later, when I could afford to fix the place up properly."

Shona pouted. "But you love it here, don't you? I knew you would. You've unwound heaps."

She was right about that. Despite needing a huge amount of work, the house had the potential to be as beautiful as the location. The stonework, while decayed in places, was drizzled with character, and the view over the valley was breathtaking. Now that the roof and the hole in the wall were fixed, I'd had no problem sleeping—something I'd struggled with for the past ten years.

Working on the renovations had helped me unwind and best of all, I now had a new bathroom. After a long, hard day of repairs, I could soak in an exquisitely deep, clawfoot bath, then drive into town and take a stroll on the boardwalk and contemplate the sunset. Then I'd find a café or head to the pub and sip a glass of local wine.

Not too shabby.

"Except I've run out of money." I looked meaningfully at Shona again and tried to push away the flicker of worry that rose every time I thought about the repairs the cottage still needed.

"There's that. Forgive me?" Her eyes sparkled. She knew full well I could never stay angry at her.

I relented with a loud sigh that was only slightly exaggerated. "Yes, but never do that again."

"Of course."

I almost believed her, but the gleam in her eyes said she was promising nothing.

"Didn't you say the next part of your inheritance was coming through? You're going to be pretty comfortable, aren't you?"

"Yes, but it's been delayed. I had an email from the solicitor this morning." I shrugged. "I'm going to have to find a job soon."

Shona picked up her teacup. "In that case I think we need seconds—or is it thirds? And there's cake. It should be warm by now."

"It smells delicious, Shona." The warm fragrance of Joe's lemon myrtle and poppyseed cake made me drool. I cast one more look at the fireplace. "I think the chimney can wait."

It was late that afternoon when I parked under some giant fig trees and decided to walk the long way to the pub. There would be all kinds of festivities in town over the next week or so—thanks to a regional food and wine festival—but there was a good cover band playing tonight and Shona and Joe were meeting me there. Live music was always fun and even though I was a child of the nineties, I was an eighties rock chick at heart.

While Shona and I had failed in our quest to unblock the chimney, we'd managed to stuff our faces with warm cake served with huge dollops of organic cream. The memory of the latter dripping down Shona's chin made me smile, and I was suddenly grateful. Grateful for my friends. Grateful that I'd made the leap and moved to Pelican Bay. Grateful that I'd been accepted so quickly into the life of this quaint small town.

"Hello, Ruth." Ed, the semi-retired local veterinarian, rode by on his recumbent tricycle with Doug the cockatoo perched on a high bar behind him.

"Hello, Ruth," mimicked Doug.

"Hey, Ed. Hey, Doug." I waved at them as they rode by.

I know it's crazy—he was only copying Ed—but the fact that the town cockatoo knew my name warmed me inside.

I kept walking. Sometimes there was a strong sea breeze at this time of day, but right now it was still, and the water reflected the soft, late afternoon light. Peace settled through me and for the briefest moment I had the strange sense that my father was walking beside me.

*Thank you for bringing me here, Dad.*

I waited, as if I expected an answer, but of course there were no words. It's crazy to talk to a dead person, right? Except that he didn't feel dead. It was as if he was right there by my side. A breath away.

*I love you, Dad.*

A light breeze ruffled my hair. My imagination, of course, but that didn't stop me *feeling* his presence. It's weird what grief will do to you.

It happened from time to time. Seeing Dad in the face of a stranger. Just a glimpse out of the corner of my eye—a flicker and it was gone. Not Dad. Nothing like Dad. Just me missing Dad.

I let out a long, deep breath. It didn't matter if what I saw —or felt—was my imagination. I was here, in the town where Dad grew up, and he felt close, as if I could just step sideways and be with him.

I checked my watch. Enough of musing. I was running late for fun!

# Chapter Three

My stride lengthened as I neared the pub. Dad had often been late. A brilliant man but totally disorganised, until my sister took over as his personal assistant and IT troubleshooter. Maybe I was like him after all?

The thought made me smile.

*I wish.*

I wasn't as smart as my father, and I had enough of Mum's choleric personality to be able to mostly organise my life. But I'd always wanted to be like him.

Except I didn't like being late, so I was distracted when I barrelled through the pub door and cannoned into a man carrying two pints of beer.

"Ahhh!" I stepped back, soaked and smelling like a brewery, and looked straight up into the gorgeous but concerned face of Dan Rivers.

"I'm really sorry." Dan grabbed some napkins and tried to brush the beer from my boobs while I did everything I could to keep him away from said boobs.

It turned out that my words on the plane were prophetic. Dan *had* been heading to the same place I was.

*Exactly* the same place.

He'd moved to Pelican Bay a few months before I did, after his brother had died. Shona said it was to sort out the estate. He'd been in Brisbane for business and a short break, and he was on the way home when I'd met him on the plane.

I'd been avoiding him ever since.

"It's okay, really." I took a step back and tried not to look into his eyes in case they trapped me forever.

*Get a grip.*

Dan had a slight limp as he walked over to the counter, scooped up another handful of paper napkins, and brought them back to me. "Here." He flashed a devilish grin. "It might be better if you do it."

The limp was some kind of leg injury. No one in town knew exactly what had happened—Dan was a private guy—but the rumours went from gunshot wound, to stabbing, to tripping over a kid's skateboard and falling down some stairs. Dan worked in high-end security, so anything was possible.

I sighed to myself. I'd always had a thing for the injured hero.

"Um… thanks." I took the napkins, and this time I did look up and almost swayed towards him.

"Are you okay?" I really must have swayed because he caught my elbow to steady me.

"Yes. Absolutely. I… um… need to get clean." I didn't look back as I ran to the female toilets.

*So much for being a poised woman of the world.*

Once inside, I pulled off my top, mopped my skin as best I could, then rinsed the shirt under the tap. I was drying it under the hand dryer when Shona breezed in.

"Hey, hun. Are you okay? I saw what happened." Her eyes sparkled. "You can't stop running into Dan, can you?"

I gave her my most don't-go-there look.

But she didn't obey. "I still can't believe you were on the same flight coming down here." She tilted her head to the side, thinking. "He seems a good guy."

I inhaled deeply then let out a long, loud breath. "He probably is. And before you go there, yes, he's hot. But he's leaving in a few weeks, isn't he? You said he'd got a job somewhere in Europe. You know I don't want that."

"You could have a fling."

I flapped my shirt harder under the dryer. "I don't do flings."

Shona snorted. "What about that cop, Henri, in Paris? You said—"

"Okay." I gave her a begrudging smile. "I don't do flings *anymore*. Besides, Dan's got a girlfriend."

She looked back towards the door. "Shame."

I shot her a deadpan look. If I was honest, a teensy bit of me thought it was a shame too. Dan was gorgeous, but he could use his eyes the way a snake charmer used music. Once captured by his gaze I would be forever swaying under his influence: mesmerised, hypnotised… and most likely traumatised. I didn't want to be under that kind of power. Not again.

I shook my head and made my best attempt at a smile. "I've made too many mistakes."

"Fair enough. But it doesn't hurt to look. He's the most decorative man in this town." She caught herself. "Other than Joe, of course."

"Ha! I'll tell Joe you said that. The first bit, not the second."

"Don't you dare!"

I thumbed across the fabric of my shirt. It was dry enough

to wear and I pulled it back on over my head. "You can buy my silence with a glass of red."

"Red it is. A small price to pay." Shona's eyes danced. "Blab and I'll make sure Dan knows what you really think of him."

Right then a toilet flushed. I started. I hadn't thought anyone else was in here. On cue the door opened and out strode none other than Legs-to-Breasts, Dan's girlfriend from the plane.

My face blazed hot and my jaw dropped open in a you-have-to-be-kidding-me gape.

Legs-to-Breasts raised an eyebrow and glared at me, before stopping to wash her hands. Then she swished out of the bathroom with a sensual sway of her hips.

The front bar was buzzing both inside, and outside in the alfresco area. The upcoming local festival meant there were out-of-towners mixed in with the locals.

Shona and I pushed through the crowd towards the counter. "Hey, Bruce. It's busy tonight," Shona said.

The fair-haired publican beamed. "Always good this time of year. What can I get you two ladies?"

Bruce spoke with a clipped British accent, which sounded out of place in this very Aussie pub. Hannah, Bruce's Singaporean wife, sounded more Australian than he did. Bruce and Hannah were ex-teachers, who in their early forties decided to trade the schoolroom for their own business. So far it had worked out. They were busy but they were always smiling. That had to be good.

Shona slapped her credit card onto the counter. "Two glasses of shiraz please."

"I'll get them." Hannah set two wine glasses on the

counter and filled them. "Nice to see you again, Ruth." She smiled at me and Shona. "Are you girls coming to the self-defence class tomorrow?"

I coughed. "I… er…"

"Of course we are." Shona looped her arm through mine. "It's important to feel safe."

There had been break-ins around the local community and Dan—yes Dan—had offered to run self-defence classes for women on Saturday mornings. As I was generally trying to avoid the guy, I didn't want to go.

"I—"

"Great," said Hannah. "I'll see you there."

Armed with a glass of full-bodied red wine each, Shona and I made our way through the crowd to the booth she and Joe had reserved. Reservations were certainly the way to go if you wanted to be in this part of the pub on a Friday night.

"I don't want to go," I hissed. I'd intended to conveniently forget about the classes.

"It'll be good for you. You live on that block out there on your own. You need to be able to defend yourself if you have an intruder."

"I don't need self-defence classes."

"Every woman should know how to defend herself."

We reached our booth before I could answer. I slid into the seat, but Shona stopped and looked for Joe.

"Where is he?"

"Over there." I pointed to a table where Joe sat deep in conversation with an older couple. Paul and Donna Farrow were local dairy farmers who were essentially my next-door neighbours, but I'd met them first through Shona and Joe. Paul was tall and broad with messy salt-and-pepper hair and dark brown eyes. Donna was short and fair, with a no-

nonsense cropped hairstyle she'd said suited farm work. Both were frowning as they leaned towards Joe.

"Wait here." Shona sidled through the crowd, said a few words to Joe then pressed by people to get back to our table.

"Maybe we should have booked a table in the bistro rather than out here near the bar," I suggested when she returned.

Shona grinned as she joined me in the booth. "But it's more fun out here. And the music will start soon." She glanced at the band, who were setting up in the corner, then back at Joe. "He won't be long. Paul and Donna look like they've got something heavy duty going on." She turned back to me, sipped her wine and nodded at Dan and Legs-to-Breasts, who were sitting outside. "So, you've met Lydia then? Your face, when you saw her, was priceless."

"She was on the plane with Dan when I flew down here."

Shona snorted. "She's Legs-to-Breasts? That's too funny." I'd told Shona about meeting Dan and his tall, blonde girlfriend on the plane.

"Her name is Lydia? Why is it funny?"

"Lydia Larsen. I didn't think it could be her because they aren't together."

"What do you mean, 'aren't together'?" I ignored the small jolt of joy in my chest.

"That got your attention." Shona regarded me with a knowing smile. "As far as I know they're just friends. She hasn't been around much lately."

"She seemed pretty possessive of him on the plane."

"I think they were an item, back like a hundred years ago. Maybe they tried again. But I don't think they are now. You know she's a cop?"

I shook my head.

Shona eyed the couple. "She does have long legs." Her voice held a wistful note. "Mine are so short."

I snuck another look at Dan and Legs-to—I mean Lydia Larsen. It was true they were laughing together in an easy friendship way rather than gazing with longing into each other's eyes. "If they had babies, their children would be beautiful." It was my turn to sound wistful.

Shona snorted again, spraying red wine onto the table in a splatter pattern CSI would be proud to analyse. "You've got it bad, haven't you?" She wiped up the spillage with a napkin. "He is good-looking. You don't think he's a secret fourth Hemsworth brother?"

It was my turn to snort out wine. Dan certainly had that vibe.

"But you're pretty amazing yourself, girl," Shona added. "Your eyes are beautiful—they're a mix of blue, turquoise and gold. You've got gorgeous skin, the right amount of curves, and your dark hair gives you a European vibe. Don't sell yourself short."

I rolled my eyes and dabbed my lips with a napkin. "I'm not in her league."

Right then Dan looked up, saw me gazing in his direction and gave me a small salute. Lydia glared at me, then said something to Dan that made him laugh then look back at me again. Had she just told him what Shona and I said in the bathroom?

I held his eyes for a moment. *Stop flirting!* I looked away. I was better than this. Dan unsettled me too much.

Joe slid back into the booth beside Shona.

"Everything okay?" Shona asked.

Joe scowled and glanced back over his shoulder at Paul and Donna. "Looks like they're losing the farm."

Shona's eyes widened. "What? Why?"

"Turns out the owner is going to sell. A developer wants to buy it."

"Wait. They don't own it?" I asked.

"Nope. But they've been managing it forever," Shona said. "They're one of a handful of commercial dairies in Australia that are both organic and ethical." She saw my confusion. "By ethical I mean they keep the calves with the cows for months instead of taking them away when they are five days old. And organic means they don't use any chemicals or bad stuff. The best one I've heard about is in Scotland." There was pride in both her voice and her smile.

"Why don't all dairies keep the calves with the cows?"

Shona shrugged. "More labour intensive, I guess. And the calves drink milk so there's less yield. I think it also takes a bit of adjusting. The one in Scotland had a hard time the first year but now it's working well. Paul and Donna are similar. The cows have adjusted and are milking well. They have less disease too because they're less stressed."

"The farmers or the cows?" I couldn't help smiling.

"Both, I think."

I pondered this. I'd thought there was something different when I saw calves mooing along with their mums in the farm's paddocks, but I couldn't place what it was.

Shona put a hand on Joe's arm. "This will affect us too."

"Tell me about it." Joe glowered.

"You mean the organic ice cream?" I asked.

"The ethically sourced organic ice cream, cream and milk." Joe turned to Shona. "Where are we going to get that if the farm is sold?"

Joe and Shona sold the Farrows' yoghurt, cheese and ice cream at their café and used the products in their food. Sales had been soaring. Not everyone can get to the farm or farmers' market.

"The farm is definitely sold?" I asked. "They couldn't buy it themselves?"

"They were trying to get finance, but it's not looking good. And the land would be worth a mint." Tension oozed out of Joe. "I'm going to have a word with Aldon Rossi tomorrow."

Shona raised her eyebrows. "The PI? What's he got to do with this?"

"Apparently he's been negotiating with the owner on behalf of the developer." He paused. "From what I've heard, he should know better."

"Know better?" My curiosity was piqued.

Joe shrugged. "Let's just say there's history there."

"Small-town secrets?" I took a deep sip from my glass.

Shona winked and downed the last of her wine. "Always."

# Chapter Four

The next morning, I swung my racing-car-red Mini Cooper into a parking spot outside Joe's Café. Shona had insisted we go to the self-defence class together. I think it was her way of making sure I turned up.

It annoyed me that Dan was an issue. What was it with me? Was my ego so in overdrive that I thought this man would fall at my feet? Or was it so fractured that I was afraid he wouldn't? Dan was an attractive man. Why would I think he'd want *me*?

That thought depressed me. I had just turned thirty and there were plenty of younger and prettier women around. Did that mean I'd missed my chance at finding love? Not with Dan, but with anybody? I'd lived several lifetimes in the past ten years. The doctor said I had burnout and to give myself time. That was one big reason why I'd moved to Pelican Bay —I needed space to sort myself out. I took a deep breath in and let it out slowly, like my therapist in England had suggested. No men for now. Just peace.

"Hey, Ruth." Shona knocked on my car's window and

then opened the door. "Ready to learn how to defend the girls?"

"The girls?"

"These things." She pointed to her boobs. "We have to learn to protect them from marauders." Her Scottish accent went to town on marauders. I couldn't roll my Rs like that if I tried.

I laughed and we walked together down Main Street towards the old dance studio Dan was using for the class. Twenty-five to thirty women milled around inside the entrance of the quaint, two-storey stone building.

"Looks like the class is popular." I breathed a sigh of relief as we walked inside. There was safety in numbers, which was kind of appropriate for a self-defence class. A large contingent of local women wanted Dan to show them how to defend themselves. I wondered how many wanted to get under *his* defences. I smiled at the thought. I could hide in the back row and watch.

The room was large with mirrors along one side, reflecting the polished hardwood floor and the interlocking foam mats that would hopefully stop us from hurting ourselves.

Dan gestured for us to form a semicircle around him and began with some basic information. "What's the first thing you try to do if you find yourself in a dangerous situation and someone's attacking you?"

"Show him your left hook," suggested Bridget, Joe and Shona's barista. Her accent was a bit like Dan's—a mix of west coast USA mixed with Aussie drawl. Joe had said Bridget could start late at the café so she could come to the class.

A few of the women laughed.

"Scratch out his eyes," another answered.

"Kick him in the balls," an old woman who had to be in her eighties declared. Most of us sniggered at that one.

"Anyone else?" asked Dan.

"Use pepper spray?" This was from a slim girl with shoulder-length, straight jet-black hair. Even her goth makeup couldn't disguise her blush as she spoke.

"Who's that?" I whispered in Shona's ear.

"That's Kat Mackenzie," she whispered back. "She's had a crush on Dan since he arrived in town." Shona's eyes gleamed. "Don't worry, she's not a rival. She's too young for him."

I rolled my eyes.

"All good suggestions," said Dan. "But none are the first thing you should try to do." He scanned the room. "Anyone else?"

"Run," I muttered.

Dan's eyes lit up as he turned and looked at me. "What's that, Ruth?"

I hesitated, but I knew the answer to his question.

"Run. If you can get away, don't try to fight. Run away."

"Well done."

I hated that his approval made me feel warm inside, like Joe's chocolate raspberry brownies, heated and served with double cream and ice cream.

"Teacher's pet!" Shona whispered beside me.

I ignored her.

"Did everyone hear that?" Dan asked. "Rule number one in self-defence is don't put yourself in danger if you can avoid it. And if you are in danger and you can run away, run."

Several of the women shifted on their feet, including Shona.

"Even I know that," Hannah said to the woman next to her.

Dan must have heard her. "You'd think it would be the first thing most people would do, but have you heard of the lizard brain?"

Most of the women shook their heads.

"The lizard brain," he continued, "is part of the brain responsible for the primitive fight or flight reflex. It's called that because it's about the only brain a lizard has." A wicked gleam sparked in his eyes. "Fight, fear, feeding and fornication."

Soft laughter rippled around the room. I hated that my cheeks warmed. What was I, twelve years old?

"When faced with danger, adrenaline kicks in and makes us want to fight or run away. If our brain can't decide, we might freeze. Sometimes, you have to use your higher brain," he tapped the side of his head, "to make the right choice. When I was in Afghanistan, there were times I just wanted to hurt the mongrels who were coming at us, even if we were outnumbered. All I wanted to do was fight back. But you learn as a team leader that retreat is always an option. If you ladies are in danger, if someone breaks into your house, the first step is getting yourself to safety. You can always fight back later, but you can't if you're hurt."

"What if someone else is in danger?" asked an older woman. "And you need to protect them?"

"That's Elouise Rossi," Shona whispered in my ear.

Dan paused, his expression serious. "That's different. But you have to ask yourself if *you* really can help by fighting. It might be better to run away and get help from someone who is trained to handle the situation. I served with the US Air Force Pararescue group and there were times during a mission where we had to fight back to protect others." He gestured to himself. "But we were trained. We also had backup, radios, tactics. You girls might not have that, but you have neighbours, phones and the police. Remember, running and calling for help gets everyone safe—you and the person in danger."

"And step two?" asked Kat.

All eyes turned to her.

"You said the first step was running away," Kat continued. "What's step two?"

Dan smiled at her, and she blushed a deeper crimson than before. Even from a distance I could see her ears turn red. "Then you use your pepper spray—or some of the moves I'll show you—so you can escape and get help."

He split us into pairs, and we spent the next half hour taking turns attacking one another and using the defence tricks he showed us. That was until Shona slipped and sprained her ankle.

"I'll be okay," she said as she hobbled to her feet. I helped her over to a chair.

Dan found some ice and pulled up another chair in front of her. "Best keep it elevated."

"It's only a slight sprain. It's not broken." But she did as he said.

"Sprains can hurt." There was kindness in his voice as he wrapped an ice-filled towel around her ankle.

Then he stood to speak to the rest of us. "There's one more move I'd like to show you girls today. You don't have a partner now, Ruth." His lopsided grin made my insides tingle. "Care to help me out? You seem to know what you're doing." Mischief morphed into challenge in his eyes.

I could almost feel the air crackle as I held his gaze. My lizard brain was in overdrive. Fight or flight? My higher brain told me to run. Avoid danger at all costs. But my primal brain responded to his challenge. Fight won.

I stepped forward. After all, the only real danger was getting too close to Dan and that wasn't a danger at all. I was a modern woman. I was in control.

"Okay," Dan said. "This is the move. I come up behind

you and grab you by the throat." He put his arm around my neck and pulled me hard against him.

His warm breath in my hair made me shiver.

His arm tightened. "Then you—"

He must have triggered something in me. There was no other explanation. One minute I was Dan's sparring partner and the next I'd slammed my elbow into his bicep to break his grip, stomped on his foot, kicked my heel into his kneecap then scissor-kicked his legs out from under him. He careered onto the mat with a hard thump and a loud, "Oof." I probably ruined the effect by tripping and falling on top of him, but that's beside the point.

"Oh my gosh, sorry." I scrambled off Dan and let him up.

He rolled over slowly and groaned a little as he pulled himself to his feet.

"Are you okay?" Guilt gripped me as he limped over to get his towel. I'd kicked his injured knee. He raised his hand to indicate he was indeed okay and took a long swig from his water bottle.

The rest of the women stood wide-eyed, gaping first at Dan and then at me.

"That, ladies, is an illustration of another important concept in self-defence." He took another long drink of water, and they all waited in silence. Then he shot me a wry look. "Never underestimate your opponent. Ruth Smythe, everyone."

He applauded me and a chorus of clapping broke out around the room. Heat crept up my neck and over my face, but I couldn't help standing a little straighter.

Dan turned back to me, rubbed his knee and flashed his gorgeous, crinkle-eyed smile. "Where did you learn Krav Maga?"

• • •

We stepped out of the studio into the autumn sunshine. Unlike Brisbane, which was a sauna for much of the year, South Australia had a drier Mediterranean climate. It had been hot when I got here, like 40-degrees-celsius-for-two-straight-weeks kind of hot, but now, on this day in late March, the weather was divine. Puffy white clouds danced above us in the azure sky as we walked down the street back to Joe's Café.

"That was amazing," said Shona. "When *did* you learn Krav Maga?" She was only limping slightly, but we walked more slowly than many of the other women who were eager to replenish their energy reserves with coffee and cake in the local cafés.

"Isn't that the Israeli army martial art?" Hannah asked. Bridget had run ahead to help Joe, but Hannah had caught up with us and joined in the conversation. "I know you had adventures overseas, but I didn't think you'd joined the Israeli army."

I laughed. "There were some things that happened when I was in Europe and the UK that made me want to learn self-defence. But there are two types of Krav—the Israeli army type and the regular-human-being type. When I moved to England there was a martial arts studio down the road and the instructor taught Krav as well as Ninjutsu. I learned a bit of both, but mainly general self-defence."

"Ninjutsu?" asked Shona.

"You're a ninja!" Hannah's eyes lit up.

"You didn't tell me you were a ninja." Shona's voice was edged with hurt. "Can you throw those metal star things?"

Some of the other women caught up with us, listening in.

I rolled my eyes. "I'm not a ninja—and I've never tried to throw shuriken."

The women were digesting this when we heard shouting from the direction of the café.

"You're ruining everything," Joe yelled in Aldon Rossi's face. "You're destroying everything they've built and you're hurting us. You grew up here. Don't you care about this town?"

Rossi pushed Joe away, but Joe wrenched him around by his arm. "Go back to that developer of yours and cancel the sale."

Rossi stepped close to Joe until he was in his face. "That's not going to happen."

Joe seized Rossi by the shirt front and raised his fist as though he was going to punch the private investigator, but Shona sprinted towards them. "Stop, Joe!"

Joe hesitated long enough for the PI to pull free.

"Hit me," said Rossi, "and I'll see you charged with assault. I'll also make sure the Council shuts down this feeble excuse for a business."

Joe stood there seething, then stormed into the café. Shona limped after him, and I followed close behind, my heart rattling like a punk drummer on speed. I knew from what Shona had said that Joe could be mercurial, but I'd never seen him like this before.

He stomped out the back door of the café, and we heard a gate clanging followed by footsteps pounding. Shona stood dazed, tears welling in her eyes. She blinked them back, straightened her spine and surveyed the room. The only customers, an older couple sitting at an inside table, avoided her gaze.

Bridget, who had been wiping down the coffee machine, sidled over and gave her a quick hug. "It'll be okay."

Shona set her shoulders and limped to the front of the café. She poked her head out through the door where several women still stood outside, stunned by what had happened, seemingly unsure of what to do.

"Free coffee and cake for anyone who wants to stay." Shona came back inside and smiled at the couple. "That goes for both of you too, if you want seconds."

Soon the man and woman were each tucking into a huge slice of lemon meringue pie. But my stomach twisted when, of the women outside, only Hannah, Kat and two others took up Shona's offer. The rest made their excuses and hurried down the street, whispering to each other and occasionally looking back over their shoulder at the café.

Great.

Gossip.

Just what Shona and Joe didn't need.

Bridget took orders and I walked over to Shona, who was standing behind the counter staring into the distance. An ache twisted inside me when I saw her desolate expression. I nudged her shoulder. "How can I help? You should get off that ankle."

"It's okay, there's not many people." She hesitated. "Could you go outside and see if Joe's around? I don't want him to do anything stupid." She forced a smile. "I'll make you a coffee and save you some cake."

"Hey." I squeezed her arm. "He'll be okay. He just needs to let off some steam."

"Thanks, hun." But worry still filled her eyes.

I took a deep breath and headed for the door to look for Joe.


I strode out into the sunlight, but it didn't seem as bright as before. A huge SUV masquerading as a two-tonne truck barrelled down the street with Aldon Rossi at the wheel. Why was it that short men liked big cars? In the passenger seat beside him was a stylish woman with striking red hair, probably in her late forties. This wasn't Elouise Rossi. He wasn't taking his wife home from the self-defence class. Elouise was in her sixties, like her husband, had grey-blonde hair and was more the comfortable country type. Was this the property developer Joe was so upset about? In a moment, they were gone, and I was left with my thoughts and my search for Shona's fiancé.

I looked behind the café, then walked down the street and up the other side. No Joe. He must have gone for a walk out of town. I hurried down the street to see if I could catch up with him, but I couldn't see him anywhere. I quickened my pace, hoping he'd be around the next bend.

When I arrived back at the café about twenty minutes later, a few stragglers from the self-defence class had arrived—including Elouise Rossi—oblivious to the drama that had unfolded minutes before.

My shoulders relaxed at the happy buzz of coffee-drinking-and-cake-eating, fork-clinking chatter. Hopefully, the incident with Joe hadn't totally shattered his reputation for creating a place of welcome. His food did that anyway, and Shona's sunshine helped. I slid into a booth and Shona plonked an extra-large coffee and a huge slice of carrot and walnut cake in front of me.

"Did you find him?" She eased into the seat opposite me.

I shook my head. "Sorry. I saw Rossi drive off with some woman in his car, but no Joe."

Shona frowned.

I put my hand on her arm. "People are still here. They love you guys." I gestured to the customers now happily drinking and chatting. "And they love Joe's cakes and pastries and lunches and everything else he creates. He'll be back once he's cooled off."

Shona tried to smile. "I'm worried about him."

"I know. But Joe's smart. Dan talked about fight-or-flight today. Joe did the right thing. He wanted to fight, but he took himself out of the situation."

"After nearly punching someone." Shona wrung her hands.

"But he didn't hurt Rossi."

"He's upset over Paul and Donna's farm; it impacts us as well as them. And there's the business celebration. Joe put up his hand to cater this year, and I think he's finding it all overwhelming."

"Business celebration?"

"Once a year, after the food and wine festival, all the businesses get together for this big shindig at the community centre. This year we're doing the food. We've got the part-time servers, who helped out this morning, but we're still shorthanded." Her face brightened. "You wouldn't like some casual work, would you? You said you were short on cash. I can't offer you regular hours as we took Bridget on a few weeks ago, but we could use an extra hand next Saturday. Are you up for serving food and drink to a host of ravenous business owners?"

"Sure."

"Righty-ho. I'll tell Joe you're hired."

"Thank you!"

But my toes curled at the thought of what the simmering tensions in town might mean when all these businesspeople *celebrated* together in one room. People were hurting, while others seemed to be basking in their success, not to mention their egos. I shivered and hoped that this particular powder keg wasn't getting primed to blow.

# Chapter Five

The community centre buzzed as I whirled around balancing plates full of Joe's signature canapés. Bridget and I, along with some of the café's weekend part-timers, were run off our feet keeping the crowd fed and caffeinated, while two local wineries kept the conversation lubricated.

The event was a hit—despite Joe's grumbling in the kitchen and the near-disastrous burning smell before the party started. The kitchen accident meant Joe and Shona needed to do more cooking, rather than just serving, and they were busy chopping, dicing and plating copious amounts of finger food.

After depositing another load of plates on a table, I sagged down into a chair to catch my breath, but I couldn't help tapping my toes to the rhythm of the jazz quartet. Gauging by the bubbling conversation and tinkling laughter, the whole local business world had turned out.

No rest for the wicked, as they say—or in this case the catering staff. I pushed myself to my feet. It wouldn't do to get too comfortable.

But before I could move, Aldon Rossi appeared at my elbow, with Elouise in tow.

"Ruth, got a minute? I'd like a quick word."

Rossi and I hadn't crossed paths before—Joe and Aldon's yelling episode excepted—so what could he want with me?

I smoothed down my trendy striped apron—the café catering uniform—and nabbed the canapé plate which had mysteriously emptied in thirty seconds flat. "Let me drop this into the kitchen, first."

I squeezed back through the crowd to the kitchen, where Shona was crying over onions and Joe was sautéing something deliciously fragrant in a shallow pan over the stove.

"Mind if I take five?" I asked.

"Sure, hun." A red-eyed Shona sniffed. "You've been going nonstop."

"Thanks!" A glance at the kitchen chaos made me add, "I'll be quick."

I pushed through the crowd back to Aldon and Elouise. I was curious to see if Rossi was going to mention his fight with Joe, but I knew there was no way he'd bring up that redhead in his car. Not with Elouise present.

Aldon flashed a too-white smile. "You've met my wife?"

"Not formally." Elouise smiled warmly. "Ruth was the one I told you about, who threw Dan Rivers with some kind of judo move."

Aldon raised his eyebrows. "Impressive."

"Got lucky." Even to me it sounded lame. "I've done self-defence before."

Aldon smirked and changed the subject. "You know I knew your father?"

"Really? I thought your office here was new."

"We've been open a few months now, but I grew up in this town." He put an arm around Elouise. "We both did."

Excitement bubbled up in me and I tried to keep my voice even. "Tell me about him." I craved knowing everything I could about Dad.

"Rick was a good friend." He paused, then chuckled as he remembered. "But I suspect you got your self-defence skills from your mother."

"Oh, Aldon." Elouise nudged his arm then turned to me. "Rick was capable, but completely focused on his studies."

I wanted to ask more but Bridget pressed by us, giving me a meaningful glance as she hustled through the crowd toward the kitchen.

"He was a good man," Elouise added.

"Look, I have to get back and help, but can we talk sometime? I'd love to know more about Dad."

"As a matter of fact, there's something I'd like to talk to you about, too." He gave me a beguiling smile that reminded me of stories about spiders and flies.

The hair rose on my arms. There was something behind that smile other than friendship. I sometimes got feelings about people, feelings I found hard to put into words. I didn't a hundred percent trust Aldon Rossi.

"Is there a chance you could pop down to my office on Monday morning?" he continued.

Bridget brushed by me again and interrupted. "I'm so sorry, Ruth. Can you help? We're a bit overwhelmed."

She said it so nicely that I couldn't refuse. "Be there in a minute."

I opened my diary in my mind. Meeting with Rossi would let me put off cleaning the chimney for another day. "Sure."

"Thank you." He was definitely a smooth operator and could turn on the charm when he wasn't fighting in the street. "Shall we say ten o'clock?"

I nodded. "I can do that."

He gave me his card.

"We'll need to have you around for a meal sometime," Elouise offered. "We have a few stories about your dad. Don't we, Aldon?"

But Aldon had been distracted by the entry of the redhead I'd seen him with a few days ago.

"Excuse me, Ruth. I need to speak with my business partner." And he ran, almost panting, across the room towards her.

Elouise stood very still beside me. "The bastard." Then she turned and stalked towards the toilets.

I picked up a couple of trays and wove back through the crowd to the kitchen.

"That was weird."

"What was?" Shona clattered the knife she was holding back onto the bench.

"I was talking with Aldon and Elouise when he ran after the redhead I saw him with last Saturday."

"Claire Briscoe." Joe's face scrunched into a grimace. "She's the one buying the Farrows' farm out from under them."

I told Joe about seeing Rossi and Claire together in his car, and he harrumphed.

Shona sighed. "Poor Elouise."

"Rossi's cheating on her?"

"He had an affair with Claire a while ago, but Elouise took him back. If she's back on the scene…"

"He said she was his business partner."

Joe's jaw tightened. "He'd do anything to get in her pants."

"Joe!" Shona hit her fiancé with a hard Scottish glare.

"Well, it's true."

I pointed through the serving hatch towards the exit. "Elouise is leaving." A glance across the room showed Aldon still deep in conversation with Claire Briscoe. Elouise marched to the door, her phone to her ear, then stopped, turned and cannoned into a tall, greying, dark-haired man who was hurrying out the door with Ed, the vet.

"Watch out!" The man huffed and pushed Elouise to the side as he strode outside.

"Who was that?" My eyes followed Ed, who'd stopped to make sure Elouise was okay. "The guy with Ed. He looked a bit like George Clooney." I wrinkled my nose. "But with none of the charm."

"Don't tell me you've met George Clooney?" That was Joe.

I grinned. "I'll tell you that story later. Tell me who *that* was." I gestured in the direction of the door.

"Xavier Kingston," Shona said. "A local lawyer from a local family. Half the buildings in the town are named after his father."

I was going to ask for more detail, but Elouise had woven her way back through the crowd towards us in the kitchen. "Thank you, everyone. You've done a great job." Her tone was bright, yet brittle.

"Come in, Elouise." Shona met the older woman at the door, pulled her into the kitchen, and wrapped her in a fierce hug. "We saw."

Elouise clung to Shona for a long moment, then straightened, her face streaked with tears. "If he's at it again, I'll kill him."


Lightning strobed in the distance and the wind whipped leaves and twigs across the road as I strode through the car park. A storm was coming and after the party died down and we'd mostly cleaned up, Joe and Shona had sent me home. Flash flooding was possible.

"You don't want that little red thing you drive to float away," Joe said.

"Don't dis da Mini. The mag wheels give good corner traction."

"Not if the puddle you drive through is over your head."

I couldn't fault that logic, and I was glad to reach my car. But somewhere nearby Aldon Rossi was yelling at someone. Surprise, surprise. "You can't do that!"

The wind whipped away the reply and I couldn't work out who he was speaking to. Did it matter? That man seemed to have alienated every person in town.

The wind was cold, and I shivered as I eased into my car. I could try to suss out Rossi more on Monday when I saw him at his office. Whatever he wanted to speak to me about, I was intrigued.

The wind was even stronger when I reached home. Thunder rumbled deeply in the distance and sheet lightning flashed in the dark sky. The old gum trees near my side fence tossed jazz-hand limbs towards the inky blackness, and the old farm shed door clanged open and shut. I sighed and jogged the fifty metres or so to close the door. The shed had once been used for equipment, but right now it was holding a containerful of my old junk. Junk my sister had shipped down from Brisbane.

Originally my block had been part of the larger dairy farm, but a parcel of land that included my house had been sectioned off and sold back in the 1930s. Dad's parents had bought it back in the days before hobby farms were even a thing. The shed light had blown so I shone my phone torch around, sighing again when I saw all the boxes and crates.

My eyes fell on an old pottery wheel. Mrs J, our next-door neighbour, had bequeathed the wheel to me in her will when I was twelve. Guilt twinged inside me. Mrs J's death had put me off pottery, but I'd resolved to try again one day.

When I was ready.

I closed the door and turned the key, leaving it in the lock. As Shona said, it was safe out here and I had a talent for losing keys and having to get new ones cut. I honestly didn't mind if someone stole the stuff. It would save me from having to sort through it.

The icy sub-Antarctic wind whipped at my hair. I wrapped my arms around my body and trotted back up to the house, wishing I'd paid someone to clear the chimney after all. I was stuck with two oil column heaters which took forever to warm the place up.

The first thing I did when I scurried inside was to turn the heaters on, the second was to run a hot bath and the third was to stream some music. Post-bath, I snuggled into fleecy pyjamas, pulled on my bathrobe and slid my feet into my cosy-warm lambskin Ugg boots. The rumbling was louder outside, and I braved the elements and stepped onto my back porch to look at the lightning. I grew up in Brisbane and loved storms as a kid, but the icy wind sliced through me and I hurried back inside.

It was then that I heard the shot.

I stopped and listened, shivering in the night.

At first, I thought it was thunder, but the bang was close by and wasn't followed by any booming drum roll. Disquiet rumbled through me. The shot had come from the direction of the Farrow farm, so it was probably just Paul or Donna chasing off a fox.

I rushed back inside. It was too late for coffee, but I needed to be warmed up again, so I shuffled into the kitchen to make myself a hot chocolate. I scrounged through the cupboard for marshmallows and cocoa and frothed some steaming milk. Then I wrapped myself in a soft blanket and relaxed on the sofa, sipping my delicious, steaming drink.

My eyes closed. I really should have gone to bed, but my limbs ached and my feet throbbed from serving and I didn't want to move. I didn't know how long I was asleep before I heard the bang, bang, banging of my shed door again, mixed with the much closer grumble of thunder.

*Really?*

I thought I'd locked it.

I hauled myself off the sofa and trudged to the back door. It was just beginning to spit with rain. If I was quick, I could run to the shed and back and not get too wet.

I pulled on my brand new Driza-Bone coat over my robe, shoved some gumboots on my feet, and sprinted for the shed. I was halfway there when I realised I'd forgotten my phone. Although it didn't really matter as nearly perpetual lightning flashes lit my way.

I was just a few steps away from the shed when I heard someone call.

"*Ruth*!" The voice was urgent and full of warning.

I stopped, peering through the darkness. "Hello?" The hairs on the back of my neck prickled to attention, and a clammy chill quicksilvered through me. There was no one there… was there?

Silence.

I shook my head. I must have been hearing things.

The voice… so achingly familiar… had sounded just like Dad.

# Chapter Six

It couldn't have been Dad. My heart was raging so loud in my ears that it almost drowned out the thunder. This must be some kind of waking dream. I'd fallen asleep and only woken up five minutes ago. Was I sleepwalking?

But how could my shed door be banging? Had a fox or other animal pushed its way inside to hide?

Not likely.

I pinched myself. "Ow!" I felt awake. I *was* awake.

Lightning flashed and thunder crashed around me. It wasn't safe to be out here, so I dived for the shed door. One quick look for stray creatures and I'd lock it again.

I pulled the door open, hoping any animal would run away from me rather than towards me.

But there was no fox.

Lightning strobed again and again and again, and I could see him. A shadowed form lay face down on the floor of my shed.

I lifted my hands to my mouth. The man groaned, and I rushed forward to feel his pulse. I rolled him onto his back.

The next flash of light showed me it was Aldon Rossi, and he was bleeding from his chest.

"No, no, no!" I snatched up a rag and pressed it hard against the wound, but Rossi gasped and seized my hand, thrusting something into my fingers. Then it was as if his body deflated. I checked his pulse again—but there was no doubt.

Aldon Rossi was dead.

Bile burned in the back of my throat. I froze, not sure what to do. My gaze flickered downwards. Rossi's blood was on my hands and coat.

*Call the police…* But I didn't have my phone.

Lightning flashed, thunder growled, the wind picked up and large raindrops began splattering faster onto the dry earth. I sprinted for the house, banged through the back door, scrubbed my hands until they hurt, and found my phone. I shook so much I could hardly dial the numbers.

I clung to the phone as I finished the call to the dispatcher, my words hanging in the air, punctuated by the crashing thunder. The police would send a car shortly. They'd also send an ambulance, just in case.

I wrapped my arms around myself and sank down onto a chair, questions swirling around me. None of this made sense. Why was Rossi in my shed? Had someone stabbed him? Who had killed him?

Icy shivers prickled at the base of my neck. The killer could still be out there. I ran and locked the doors and dialled Shona.

"Where are you? Are you home?" I panted down the phone.

"Ruth? What's wrong?"

"Rossi. In my shed. Dead." I tried to squeeze out more words, but I couldn't form a full sentence.

"*What?*"

I tried again. "Aldon Rossi is dead, in my shed. I think someone stabbed him."

There was silence, then Joe swore in the background. "Hang on, hun," Shona said. "We're coming!"


It took them less time than I thought. I met Joe and Shona at the door and lead them to Rossi by torchlight in the rain.

"Rossi's dead?" Shona's eyes were wide.

I nodded and repeated what I'd told them on the phone.

Joe stepped towards the shed. "I need to check."

"There's no point."

"We need to make sure."

"Don't touch anything."

He gave me a torch-illuminated, deadpan look, then pulled the door open and entered the shed. He stumbled back out moments later. It was too dark to see his face, but I reckon it was as green as I felt.

"Let's get back up to the house." I led the way as the rain increased to another torrential downpour. We ran. My coat kept me dry, but Joe and Shona were soaked by the time we reached the back door.

Sirens wailed in the distance. For a moment I wondered where they were going and then I realised that of course they were coming to us.

"They'll probably want our clothing and shoes," said Joe.

"For forensics?" asked Shona.

"Yeah." His eyes caught mine.

"That was a lot of rain. Wouldn't it have washed off everything that mattered?" Doubt rang in Shona's voice.

I shivered as I shrugged out of my Driza-Bone.

"Maybe, but our other option was to wait in the shed." I

hung the coat in the out-room near the laundry door, leaving gumboots there too, then pulled on track pants and a warm jumper in place of my Firefly pyjamas and fleecy robe which I reluctantly put in a bag. The pyjamas looked okay, but I knew the police would want to check them for blood too. I hoped they wouldn't ruin them. I shook my head, disgusted at myself. Who was I that a man could die, and I was worried about television-themed sleepwear?

I found slippers and warm clothes for Shona, but Joe had to make do with his damp jeans and socks, and a tattered, ex-op-shop, grunge rock T-shirt I wore while renovating.

"Sit down, Ruth." Shona patted the seat of the kitchen chair next to her. "You look like you've seen a ghost." Then she realised what she'd said. "Sorry."

I waved away her apology. But then we both started to giggle. Shock? Hysteria? Soon we were falling over each other, gulping in breaths, barely able to breathe.

The police arrived with a loud wail of sirens and before we knew it, we were overrun with officers. I couldn't speak, so Joe told them where Rossi was.

One female police officer stayed inside, regarding Shona and I with deep suspicion. Our laughter had turned to real tears, but the officer still looked like she wanted to commit us for insanity. "I'm Constable Jones. Who discovered the body?"

"I did." I raised my hand, grabbed a tissue, then blew my nose. Shona recovered before me and escaped over to the kettle to make tea.

Another cop strode in, a man of medium height with brown eyes and dark, wavy hair. I'd met Gary Stone before. He gave me a speeding ticket once—then asked me out the next day. I'd said no—go figure—but right now I was glad of a familiar face.

Before I could say anything, Shona thrust a cup of tea into my hand. "Drink." She patted my shoulder, always the comforting presence.

The tea was hot and sweet, and its warmth steadied me. I'd have preferred coffee, but it was better than nothing.

Shona handed a mug to Joe then placed another two steaming cups on the table in front of Gary and Officer Jones. "It's cold and wet out there and we all need warming."

Gary blinked as if bemused by this friendly gesture, but then took out his notebook, his phone, and his need-to-take-your-statement face. "Thank you, Jones." From his tone, he obviously outranked her.

He leaned forward, his eyes bright and eager, despite the late hour. "Ms Smythe—Ruth—please walk us through exactly what happened, step by step. Every detail is crucial."

I took a deep breath and gave him as accurate an account as I could, starting from when I heard the shed door banging.

His breath hitched when I told him Rossi was still alive when I found him. "Did he say anything?"

I shook my head. "He just groaned and put something in my hand."

Gary leaned closer. "What kind of something?"

"A fifty-dollar note. I left it next to the body."

"You touched it?"

"I couldn't help it. He grasped my wrist with one hand." I demonstrated. "Then he tried to scrunch the note into my palm with the other. But then he… died." I wished the video would stop looping in my head. Channel change, please.

More cops pulled up.

"What's going to happen now?" I asked Gary.

"CSI are on their way and the detective has just arrived."

"Isn't that quick?" asked Joe. "We're well over an hour from Adelaide."

"The detective was working out of the Victor Harbor CIB this week, and they got CSI out of bed in case evidence gets washed away."

My backyard suddenly flooded with light. Men and women in blue and yellow raincoats surged through the rain towards the shed, my once quiet block buzzing like a staging area for a small-scale military operation.

I broke out in a sweat and Shona laid her hand on my shoulder again. "I'll make more tea." That was her solution for everything.

She turned to her task. Through the kitchen window I saw a tall, cloaked figure stride towards the house. That walk was familiar.

A tall, blonde woman with very long legs strode into the kitchen.

The officers stood to their feet, and Gary Stone greeted her. "Detective Larsen."

She nodded to them both, then regarded me with one raised eyebrow. "Ruth Smythe. Of course it was you." Her voice was edged with irony.

I groaned. Of all the cops, in all of South Australia, why did it have to be Legs-to-Breasts?

# Chapter Seven

It was 5 am when we rumbled back along empty roads to Joe and Shona's place. Joe was driving—we were in his twin-cab ute—and Shona sat in the front passenger seat, jiggling one of her legs up and down. I huddled in the back, too tired to speak but glad to be with my friends.

"So, what did Larsen say?" Shona stopped jiggling and turned in her seat to face me. Unlike me, she was still vibrating with excitement—probably from too little sleep and too much sugary tea. "How did it go?"

I couldn't lie. "Larsen thinks I did it." The detective had taken us each into my study to talk to us one by one.

Shona grimaced. "What possible motive could you have for killing Aldon Rossi?"

"I don't. I think that's why they didn't take me down to the station straight away. Apparently, I'm a key person of interest because he died on my property, and I found the body."

"I'll tell them you couldn't have done it."

I scrubbed my hands over my face but managed to laugh through the fatigue. "I'm sure that will sway the investigation."

It was me that swayed as Joe took the next corner too fast, his knuckles white on the steering wheel. I clutched onto the back of Shona's seat.

Shona swatted Joe's arm. "No need to get us all killed after everything else tonight. Let's get home in one piece." Her scolding felt comforting and normal. We were alive, we were together, and we had survived a difficult night.

But Joe was still upset.

He gripped the wheel even tighter. "They think *I* killed Rossi, not you, Ruth. They know about my fight with Rossi last week."

"Well, they would—it's a small town—but that also means people really know *you*, Joe." Shona patted his thigh. "Everyone knows you're a good man."

Joe shrugged off the reassurance.

"And don't forget you were with me." Shona reached up and rubbed the back of Joe's neck. "I told them you couldn't have done it."

He took another corner too fast. "They'd say you were covering up for me."

It was time for me to butt in. "If they really thought you killed Rossi, they wouldn't have let you take your car. Did they even check it?"

He shook his head and slowed the car down a notch.

"We parked on the road, not on your block," Shona said. "But maybe they messed up?"

"Maybe," I agreed. "There was a lot happening."

I'd been allowed to take some clothing but had been ordered to stay somewhere else until CSI finished their fine-tooth-combing of everything I owned. My little red Mini parked near the house was off limits. I'd thrown my bicycle in the back of Joe's ute, but other than clothing and some personal items, that was it.

I rested my head against the cool glass of the window, a mix of emotions churning inside at the thought of strangers riffling through every corner of my life.

Shona swung around to include me. "You've both seen the movies and TV shows. Police try to make everyone feel guilty to see if they crack." She gave Joe's knee a quick squeeze. "But it will be okay because you didn't do it."

"What about the knife, Shona?" Joe's voice was half an octave higher than normal.

"The knife?" I sat upright.

Shona stiffened. "I'd forgotten. I didn't think—"

"What knife?" I leaned closer, my words not much more than a whisper.

"Joe lost his best knife tonight."

"What?" I squeaked.

"I'd been using it earlier, cutting bacon for the canapés," Joe said. "I put it by the sink, but when we went to pack up, it had gone."

"We noticed just after you left. We looked everywhere," Shona said. "Bridget and I even went through the compost bin."

"People were using that corridor all night—using the wrong exit to get to the toilets," Joe grumbled. "Easy access to the kitchen as they walked by."

"We should have blocked the passage off."

"But that would have made it hard for us to get in and out with food," Shona argued. "The kitchen door is inside the hallway."

"I don't get it. Who would steal a cooking knife?" I asked.

Shona and Joe exchanged a knowing look.

"It was a great knife," Shona explained. "New and well balanced. Expensive. Sharp. Any foodie would love that knife."

I closed my eyes and let out a long, slow breath. "It sounds like the kind of knife a murderer would love, too."

Shona swivelled back towards Joe. "You told Larsen about it, didn't you?"

Joe shook his head.

"If that knife was the murder weapon…" Shona's voice rose. "That *will* make you look guilty!"

"Yeah, I know, I should have, but…"

"But what?"

"I just didn't want to go there. I was tired. I made a bad decision, okay? I'll ring her after we've had some sleep."

"Isn't there CCTV in the centre or on the street outside?" I asked. "Won't that show what time you guys left? You couldn't have got here, killed Rossi and left again before I called you."

Shona hesitated. "I'm not sure. I didn't see any cameras inside the centre. If there's any in the street, they might show us leaving. But…"

I strained as far forward as the seatbelt would let me. "But what?"

"We had left the centre well before you called. We went via the café to drop stuff off and then stopped on the way home to have a discussion. There's a lookout where we sometimes go when we need to talk things through. It's not that far from you and with the lightning the view was spectacular. That's why we got to your place before the police."

"What kind of discussion?"

"A loud one." Joe's tone was droll.

Shona half-turned to me. "It was about a small acting gig up in Adelaide next weekend." She pivoted back to Joe. "You said you'd support me taking acting jobs."

"It's not acting—you're wearing an animal suit."

"It's something, Joe. And I want to do it."

"You know we've got that huge catering job at the Kingstons' place. We need the work, and I need you to be there."

"Ruth could help." Shona turned to me again, pleading in her voice. "Couldn't you?"

"I… er… guess so." The money would be good, but I didn't want to get in the middle of a fight between my friends.

"See," she said to Joe. "Problem solved."

But his posture was rigid as we pulled into their driveway.

"As long as we're not all in jail by then." His voice was flat.

Shona patted her fiancé's knee. "They'll catch the right killer."

When we reached the house Joe helped me get my gear out of the tray and Shona ushered me inside. "Ruth, you're in the guest room that opens onto the back veranda." Her matter-of-fact tone was soothing. She liked taking care of people.

"Thanks." I hugged her. The universe may have taken a sinister turn, but Shona and Joe were still here—comforting, scolding and supporting each other as they always had—and they were both there for me.

It was only as I was drifting off to sleep that guilt flexed its claws and my childhood reputation pounced.

*What if Rossi died because of me?*

It was just a fleeting thought, but for a moment I couldn't breathe.

*Jinx…*

*No*!

It was clearly murder.

But that meant there had been a murder in *my* shed. Was Rossi their only target? Or was the murderer still out there… waiting… for me?

# Chapter Eight

Parrots squabbled in the tall eucalyptus tree above me, a bit like the thoughts that quarrelled in my head. I hadn't slept in as much as I would have liked. Joe rang the police, first thing, and told them about the knife. He also agreed to bring in his ute for CSI to check out. And now I stood outside the police station midmorning, summoning the courage to enter.

I didn't want to be here. I hadn't done anything wrong. I'd tried to save the man. I was only here because Rossi had died in my shed. I had no idea why. End of story. But here I was, about to be interviewed again by Lydia Larsen. Her piercing, blue-eyed gaze was sharper than any Valkyrie's longsword.

It was obvious she hadn't believed anything I said last night.

Deep breath in… deep breath out. If I told the truth I had nothing to fear, right?

I opened the door, inhaled deeply once more to settle my nerves, and walked inside the station.

A young officer told me where to wait. I gave him a

plastic smile and sat in the plastic chair he pointed me to, while he gave me a cup of plastic-tasting water in a plastic cup. Then he made a phone call, presumably to let Detective Larsen know I was here. They'd set up a small task force in the old art gallery across the road. At least they were looking beyond me, Joe and Shona.

Tap, tap, tap. My knee jiggled and my heel thumped the floor. I tried to still my leg as I waited for the detective. I didn't want to look nervous. I shouldn't be nervous—should I?

Every now and then you hear of people being charged and spending time in prison only to be let out later.

"Oops. Sorry. We were wrong. Pity you missed the best twenty years of your life. Oh well."

I didn't want to be that person. The other thing I didn't want was for my childhood jinx reputation to be revealed. Or the fact that the ghost of my dad might have spoken to me. I didn't believe in ghosts, and I didn't believe in jinxes. But where did that leave me?

I wriggled in my seat, trying to get comfortable. I didn't really have anything to complain about in comparison to Aldon Rossi.

Maybe Larsen had been held up? I stood to stretch my back and was about to suggest I come back later when the detective strode into the station, looked me up and down, and led me into an interview room.

I wished one of the other police officers had been interviewing—Gary would have been good—but Larsen obviously delighted in making me sweat.

We sat facing each other.

"Tell me again what happened, Ms Smythe. Why was Aldon Rossi in your shed?"

"I told you everything I know last night." I huffed out a

sigh. "I don't really know why you need to talk to me again. Do I need a lawyer? Am I being charged with something?"

Larsen sighed. "Ms Smythe, you haven't been charged, but I like being thorough. A man has been murdered and I want to know why and how. Sometimes people remember things better after they've had some sleep."

So I told her again what happened. How I'd heard the shed door banging when I was sure I'd closed it. How I stumbled over his body. How Aldon had still been alive and how I'd tried to save him. I also told her about the crumpled fifty-dollar note Rossi had pressed into my hand.

Larsen lifted a finger. "Hold on. What fifty-dollar note?"

"I told Gary. He wrote it down."

Larsen shuffled through the notes on the table in front of her. "Ah yes, here it is. He's noted that you told him about the fifty-dollar note, but no one could find it at the scene." Her gaze bored through me. "Tell me you didn't put it in your pocket."

"No." I shook my head. "I dropped it beside the body and left it there."

She said nothing, gave me an I-don't-believe-you look, and began writing detailed notes on a tablet.

I know silence is an interrogation technique and I tried to stay quiet too, but Larsen made my insides squirm.

I'd always felt guilty around the police. When I was a kid, Mum told me the police knew every bad thing I did and would arrest me if I did one more thing wrong. I once tried to hide from the officer who was doing a road safety talk at my primary school, because I was sure he knew I'd stolen my sister's lollies at recess. Or that I'd decorated a corner of the playroom wall with poster paints and Mum didn't know yet.

Guilt. Was. Real.

So there was a part of me that wanted to confess to killing Rossi—to anything—just so I could get out of there.

I broke the silence. "I didn't kill Rossi. I tried to save him. And I wouldn't have told Gary, I mean Constable Stone, about the fifty dollars if I'd wanted to keep it, would I?"

Larsen half-smiled, pleased I had broken first, as if it was confirmation of my guilt.

She waited, but I managed to keep my mouth shut.

Then she asked me the original question again. "Why was Aldon Rossi in your shed?"

"I have no idea."

She gave me *the look* again. She was good. She was the lead detective on a murder investigation, so I guess she had to be. She wasn't that much older than me. Probably mid-thirties. Around Dan's age.

I tried not to think about Dan.

"Why are you flushing, Ms Smythe?"

Fortunately, I remembered something else. "The shot. I forgot about the shot."

"What shot?" Larsen's gaze sharpened.

"After the business celebration. I was watching the lightning at home. The storm was close."

She waited.

"At first, I thought it was that first crack and sizzle you hear before the rolling part of thunder. But it was just the crack. Like a gun being discharged."

"What direction was it from?"

I thought for a moment. "I think it was from the south. Yes, it had to be because the wind was strong, and it was a southerly. I don't think I'd have heard anything against that wind."

Larsen frowned. "Any discharge of a weapon could be significant." She tap-tap-tapped the table three times. "One more thing. You said Rossi asked to see you in his office. Do you know why?"

I shook my head. "As I told you last night, he gave me his card and we made a time to talk at ten tomorrow."

"And he gave no indication as to what it was about."

I focused on a spot on the wall, trying to think. "Aldon and Elouise said they knew my dad years ago. He grew up here—they did too. But I don't think it was about him because Elouise said they were going to have me over for a meal sometime to tell me stories about Dad when he was growing up." I shrugged and shifted my focus back to the detective. "Maybe Elouise would know. Have you asked her?"

The detective shook her head and made a note. "Not yet. But we will."

"When we were driving here this morning, Shona said she thought Rossi might be going to offer me a job."

"Why a job?"

"I think it was wishful thinking on her part. Shona said he'd hired someone who had great computer skills but no people skills. I need work so she was probably projecting."

Larsen looked down at her notes. "That would be Kat Mackenzie?"

"I think so."

Larsen gave me a long look. "You've done receptionist work before?"

"I've done all kinds of things." *I just haven't stuck at any of them.*

"Have you worked for a private investigator before?"

Ah, here it comes. "You'd know if you'd done basic checks on me that I worked for an investigator for a while in England. But I was mainly doing research and making the coffee."

"But you got your PI licence and then left the job?"

I shrugged. "It didn't work out." I wasn't going to tell her about my no-good, two-timing excuse for an employer who was also my ex-lover.

"And you got a job in a plant nursery?"

"Doing dispatches. I needed some work."

Larsen gave me a long look. "I need to caution you, Ms Smythe, not to interfere in this investigation in any way."

I eyeballed her back. "I've no intention of interfering."

"Good. You are a person of interest in this investigation because the deceased was found on your property, and you were covered in his blood. You have dabbled in the same profession as the deceased and may have links to him we know nothing about. But I can assure you we will investigate those links."

The faux guilt returned.

"I didn't dabble. I was serious about it at the time."

She regarded me. "But it seems from your history those times don't last. How many jobs have you had in the last ten years, Ms Smythe? How many different things have you started? How many different places have you lived in? Our records show there have been several."

*Ow.*

"What does that have to do with the murder investigation?"

"I don't know." Larsen shrugged. "It could speak to character. Maybe you have trouble fitting in. Maybe you've done wrong things and moved on. You changed your surname twice, didn't you? Before changing it back to Smythe?"

"Yes, but there was a good reason." My muscles tensed. It wouldn't look good to storm out of a police interview. "I had personal reasons for moving on—not always good ones—but I assure you, they weren't criminal ones."

"I assure *you*, Ms Smythe, of two things. *Nothing* is

personal in a murder investigation, and we'll be verifying your history. In the meantime, I'd like to request that you don't leave Pelican Bay for the next few days. I'm certain we'll need to talk again."

With that she stood and ushered me out into the grey day.


Joe, Shona and I were sitting together on their back porch. It was late afternoon and the pattering rain had been replaced by the streaming warmth of autumn sunshine. Each of us had a glass of wine in hand. Our mission was to devour the cheese platter and the mound of leftover canapés on the plate before us. It almost felt like a regular catchup with my friends. A moment of peace amidst the crazy.

"So how did it go with the police today?" Shona topped up my glass of wine. "Did you accidentally call Larsen, Legs-to-Breasts?"

I snorted and choked on the sip of wine I'd just taken. Shona had a habit of making me inhale drinks.

Joe thumped me on the back.

"No," I finally gasped. "Don't make me laugh like that."

"You're supposed to drink it, not breathe it in," Joe said. "Didn't they teach you that in Europe?"

I laughed. It felt good to unwind with friends.

Joe and Shona hadn't opened the café that morning. Like me, they'd both given Larsen more detailed statements. Duty done, we'd finally found some time to relax.

Sam, the resident magpie, sat on the railing near us, head on the side, no doubt wondering why these humans were acting so weird, and if that meant there was a good opportunity to steal food.

I recovered enough to grab a mini vol-au-vent and bite into the cheesy pastry.

"This is delicious. No one makes vol-au-vents much nowadays, but they should." I tried not to spit flaky pastry as I talked.

"Joe's retro menu is always popular—and delicious," Shona said, closing her eyes and savouring the taste as she bit into another pastry.

"Mmmm." I took another sip of the wine. "This is great too."

She raised her glass. "As you now live in wine country, it would be criminal not to enjoy the local produce."

"Crrriminal," I echoed, rolling my 'Rs' like her. "You become more Scottish when you drink wine."

She punched my arm. "Don't mock the Scot."

"I'm not mocking. You know I love your accent."

She flicked her ponytail and grinned. "Crawler." She rolled her Rs again, in an even more exaggerated way.

We laughed together.

Joe's phone rang and he picked it up. "It's the police."

Our laughter died away.

"Put it on speaker," said Shona, but he pressed the device to his ear and walked across the porch away from us. I couldn't hear what was being said but his olive skin paled as he turned back towards us. "Right," he said. "I'll come down shortly." He walked back over, dropped into his seat, and tossed the phone onto the table with a clatter.

"What's wrong?" asked Shona.

He sat silently staring at the phone.

She took hold of his arm. "What did they say?"

"You know that knife that went missing?"

Cold prickled over my scalp and crawled down my back.

"They've found the murder weapon." His tone was sardonic as he held Shona's anxious gaze. "Guess what?"

# Chapter Nine

"No. No. No."

"Please. Please. Please." Shona swept into the kitchen like a whirlwind, scattering my protests in her wake.

"I can't. We can't."

She plonked the plate of leftovers onto the bench. "Why not? It was Joe's knife. We need to find who killed Rossi."

I fumbled the wine glasses I was carrying in from outside, sloshing the dregs onto the table. "It's not our job." I snatched up a cloth and wiped up the spill.

She huffed and pushed an errant lock of hair off her face. It fell over her forehead again—as persistent as she was. "But you're good at this stuff. Remember when we found that rare Roman coin when we were kids? You spent the rest of the summer finding out when and where it came from. You got so excited it made you study archaeology. You loved solving the mystery." She tilted her head, thinking. "And when Mr Mac at school lost his wallet and blamed poor Ahmed. He was off the football team and nearly expelled because he had three strikes against him, but you found out that Kenneth

Martin took it. Then there was Mimi in Paris, and the pick-pocketing parrot. She got her maman's locket back because of you." She smirked. "Do you ever hear from Henri?"

"No!"

Shona snorted at the vehemence in my tone. "The thing is, Ruth, you're good at this. You know what to ask. And you did all that PI stuff that you said Larsen talked about."

"I really only did research."

"But you got your PI licence, didn't you? You had to do other stuff to get that."

"Bradley only let me do the bare minimum. He never let me do any field investigating beyond what I had to do for the licence. He said I wasn't any good at it. I was mainly researching, advising on the occasional artefact theft case and getting him… coffee."

"Until you told wee Bradley to shove off and get his own coffee?" she offered.

I gave her a wry grin. "Until Bradley didn't want any more of my brand of *coffee* and ran off to make babies with his former client, Cassandra." I inflected the last word with the poshest English accent I could muster.

Shona winced. "But even with all that, you must know stuff. More than the average person."

I shook my head. "It wasn't for me."

"Why wasn't it for you? You never gave it a chance—like the archaeology. You started your master's degree, got an amazing opportunity to work for the University on a dig, but gave that up after a year to run off with Paulo. I know you guys got engaged but look how that turned out."

I ran my hands through my hair. "I messed that up, okay? I shouldn't have left my job."

Shona stood and filled the kettle. More tea therapy was on

the way. "I don't understand why you didn't go back to archaeology."

I bristled. "I moved to London after Paris and got that museum job. That was archaeological."

"Which you then left to run away with bonk-your-client-Bradley. I mean, you worked hard. Left Australia to study in Europe." Concern filled her voice.

I shrugged. "I just felt I couldn't go back."

She tilted her head to the side, regarding me. "Was it boring? Archaeology, I mean."

I must have reacted because Shona's eyes gleamed. "It was, wasn't it? All that categorising of artefacts and stuff?"

My lips twitched. "Sometimes."

"You wanted Raiders of the Lost Ark, and you got Train Trips of Europe?"

"I like train trips."

"They're fun to go on, but watching endless documentaries about them is bor-ing."

Shona's shudder made me laugh. "If you got a gig narrating one, you'd take it," I challenged her.

"I would. But I'd make it entertaining—like switching people's bags into different sleeper compartments and watching them try to work out what had happened."

I laughed again, picturing the scene in my mind. Shona would do that.

"Anyway, train trips are an adventure to be experienced, not a spectator sport. Like life. You want adventure, but when you've gone for it, you've been hurt." Shona's voice was gentle. "Then you hide."

I blinked a few times and pretended to look out of the window. Why did she have to be so perceptive?

"But even when you do hide, trouble finds you." There

was mirth in Shona's voice. "Not just with this murder. Look at Dan."

I rolled my eyes as I often did at Shona's teasing. "Ha ha."

"You can laugh it off my friend, but you two hum like a pair of high-voltage electricity wires when you're together. You like him, but you're scared."

I regarded my friend. "I'm not into—"

"Flings. I know, you said. But I'm not talking about a fling. I'm talking about getting to know the guy—at least a little. Even if he's only here for a short while, does that matter? It's not all or nothing—jumping his bones or running a mile whenever he comes near. Just because you've gone too far, too fast, in the past, doesn't mean you will now. You've told me you don't trust yourself, but maybe it's time to." She shrugged. "You're a grown-up. Your Dan might be worth knowing."

I screwed up my face. "He's not *my* Dan."

Light danced in Shona's eyes. "Not yet." She hesitated and her face became more serious. "But men aside, with this murder happening on your block, in your shed, adventure has found you again. You can hide away and leave it to the police, but what if you could help? What if it's happened this way for a reason? What if you have the key that helps solve the crime?"

"It's dangerous, Shona. It's not like some Miss Marple mystery. There's a real murderer lurking, and last time I looked, Pelican Bay doesn't have herrings, red or otherwise."

"Actually, I think there are some herring species here. And you'd look good with grey curls and pearls," quipped my friend. She tapped her chin, her eyes squinting in thought. "Nah… maybe not Miss Marple. Scooby-Doo. You can be Velma, she's the brains." She tossed her ponytail. "I can be Daphne."

I couldn't help laughing, then my voice sobered. "But it's not a story. There's a real murderer, who killed a real person, in my real shed."

We both sat in silence, staring at the canapé crumbs on the counter.

Shona spoke first. "I agree. But there's so much that's weird about this. Why was Rossi killed in *your* shed? Why was he even there? I know you didn't kill him, and you definitely didn't jinx him." She gave me a meaningful look. "But somehow this is linked to you. It could be more dangerous for you if we *don't* do anything." She pushed the lock of hair away from her face again. "And with the police... I love Joe, and I love you, and I don't want *any* of us to go to jail."

My shoulders slumped so low they were in danger of hitting the floor. "I don't want that either."

Shona's eyes gleamed with the light of impending victory and the determination of a pit bull seeking its favourite chew toy. "All I'm suggesting is that we keep our eyes open. Sometimes the police are too understaffed to do a great job. Or they get sidetracked by bureaucracy and the murderer gets away." She rested her hand on my arm. "Just think about it. Okay?"

I knew when I was beaten. "Okay."

The problem was, I couldn't stop thinking about it.

# Chapter Ten

Thanks to Shona, the mystery had taken hold in my brain like an annoying boy band song, stuck on repeat.

I'd always loved a puzzle. When I was a kid, Dad used to make up all these games. On birthdays he'd hide my presents and send me on a treasure hunt. If I solved the clues, I got the gift. I *always* got the gift. Each year, the puzzles got harder, and the gifts got better. And Shona was right. Tracking down the origin of the Roman coin we found, was a high point in my primary school life.

The other problem was that Larsen wanted me to stay away. Up until I spoke with her that morning, I hadn't even thought of doing any investigating. I'd been too shellshocked by the whole thing. But anyone who knew me, knew better than to tell me *not* to do something.

But this was a murder investigation, and I didn't want to put myself—or anyone else—in danger.

"A dollar for them." Shona nudged my arm as we neared the police station.

"What?" I emerged from thinking on the high spin cycle.

"For your thoughts. It looked like they must be worth a lot more than a penny."

I huffed out a laugh. "Just wondering what's keeping Joe."

That wasn't totally untrue. I was concerned. Two hours had passed, and Joe still hadn't come home. The wine was out of our system now, so we'd driven into town to look for him and the cop shop was the logical place to start.

It was busy when we arrived, with officers coming and going and people waiting to be interviewed. We found Gary and he said Joe had left an hour ago, but he took us in for an interview, first Shona, then me, asking us about the business dinner and the missing knife.

"Joe's probably walking off the stress." Shona's sweet face morphed into a frown when we were done. She had dark shadows under her eyes and looked as worn out as I felt.

"Coffee?" I gestured down the road in the direction of the café. "There'll be cake there."

Constable Jones ushered Hannah out of another interview room.

"Hey, Ruth. Hey, Shona," Hannah said. "Are you coming or going?"

"Leaving," Shona said. "Are you heading for the pub? We should walk together."

"Safety in numbers," Hannah agreed.

I yawned. "I'm bushed."

"So is everyone else, by the look of things." Shona paused, eyes narrowing in thought. "We should bring coffee."

"I tried some of the over-brewed stuff they have here. It's vile." Hannah made a face, then her eyes brightened. "If you guys make some at the café, I'll make some at the pub."

While I really wanted to go home and sleep for a few decades, I agreed to help Shona. Half an hour later, the three of us invaded the station with takeaway cups of coffee and tea.

We handed them out to those waiting and Gary took a tray over to the operations centre. The look of gratitude on his face was priceless.

Lydia Larsen raised an eyebrow when offered a steaming cup. "Bribing an officer is an offence."

"It's not a bribe. We want you to be working at maximum efficiency, so you catch the murderer." Shona beamed her sunny smile. "And we're happy to send you the bill if you want."

Larsen flashed her a dark look then turned and walked back into an interview room—but not before grabbing a latte.

"They can't think any of us are guilty," said Hannah as we walked slowly back down the street. "Or else they wouldn't drink our coffee."

"The murder weapon wasn't poison, or they might not have risked it," I said. Dark humour was a good go-to in times like this.

Shona ran her fingers through her hair. "I think they were desperate. I don't think many of them have had much sleep in the last twenty-four hours."

"Hey, guys. Wait up." We stopped as Bridget hurried down the footpath towards us.

"Where's Joe?" she asked as she joined us.

Shona shook her head. "Not sure. I'll try to ring him again." She pulled out her phone and rang his number, but huffed when there was no answer. "Joe, ring me please." She hesitated. "Love you!" Then she hung up.

Hannah put her hand on Shona's shoulder. "It will be okay."

"How did you go, Bridget?" I asked. "What did they ask you?"

Bridget shrugged. "Only what happened. When did I last see the knife? Who had access? To be honest I couldn't remember much, we were so busy feeding people. I told them we'd crawled through the scraps bin to see if the knife was there."

I made a face. "Sounds like I left just in time."

Bridget raised an eyebrow and regarded me with a knowing look. "Very convenient. You sure you didn't have a cooking knife in that huge handbag of yours when you left?"

I rolled my eyes. "I carry my collection with me all the time."

"She's more likely to stuff her bag full of canapés." Shona nudged me in the ribs.

"What can I say?" I licked my lips with a smack. "They were delicious."

My gut gurgled.

"Someone's hungry." Hannah beamed. "How about fish and chips on me? We all could do with some comfort food."

"I always want fish and chips," Shona groaned.

"That's because you're Scottish. Potatoes are a Scot's main food group," I teased.

"There's nothing like a good spud," she agreed with a good-natured grin.

"The Scots are definitely onto something there." Bridget's hungry-seagull smile made me giggle.

We all murmured in 'spud' and 'Scot' appreciation.

Bridget's face fell. "I just remembered. My nutritionist said I'm not supposed to eat nightshades."

"Dietary restrictions are officially cancelled during murder investigations," Shona said.

"If you put it like that, I'm in!" Bridget's eyes darted to something on the ground. She bent and picked it up. "Hey, I just found ten bucks. None of you girls dropped it?"

We all shook our heads.

She stuffed it in her pocket. "Must mean good luck. Waste not, want not."

Hannah spoke. "I'll get the cook to make us up a take-away pack and we can go down to the river and eat. There's a sheltered spot near the boardwalk."

"Isn't that dangerous?" asked Bridget. "If there's a murderer around…"

Hannah shook her head. "It's well lit, we're in a group, and we have super-Krav-master-ninja Ruth to look out for us."

I rolled my eyes at her this time. "Ha ha! In that case we're all doomed."

"We can eat in if you like."

"Normally I love the crowd vibe," Shona said, "but…"

"Outside is fine," I said. "As long as the midges stay away." The small, biting insects could be a real pest.

"They haven't been bad this week," Shona offered.

"Okay then," said Hannah. "I won't be long."

I looked up at the sky as we waited for Hannah in the pub's alfresco area. The sun had set a while ago, and I loved South Australia's long twilights. But even as we sat there, the clouds rolled in and the sky darkened. It wasn't long before a chill wind whipped through our shelter and small drops of rain splattered onto the ground nearby.

Hannah beckoned to us from the pub door. "Looks as if the boardwalk is out. Come on. I'll find us a table."

It was busy inside, but Hannah pointed us to a cosy corner booth, then Shona and I left to get jugs of lemon squash and cola. We'd had enough wine at lunchtime.

While we were waiting, my friend elbowed me in the ribs

with the subtlety of a sledgehammer. "Now would be a good time to practise."

"Practise what?" I had no idea what she was talking about.

"Investigating."

I squeezed my eyes shut for a moment. Now that Shona had put the idea in my head, part of me itched to investigate, but the other exhausted-within-an-inch-of-my-life part just wanted to sit down and become one with our cosy booth and never move again. It had been a long twenty-four hours.

"These are our friends," I countered. "None of them have any motive other than to eat fish and chips without being interrogated again." It was a motive I could get behind.

Shona rolled her eyes so hard I was surprised it didn't make her dizzy. "Even I know you need background information when working a case. Who did what, when and where. You build up a picture of what happened."

She was right, but... "Can we think about this tomorrow?"

"But background information is important."

"Shona..."

She held up her hands. "No citizen's arrest, I promise. But we can snoop around a little. We might find out something we can give to Legs-to-Breasts that will get us all off the hook."

"We should stop calling her that. It could slip out by mistake."

We both chuckled at that mental image.

"Don't call who, what?" Dan said from behind us.

We both jumped and turned. Guilt was etched over Shona's face, but she recovered with a quip. "If we told you we'd have to kill you." Then she realised what she'd just said. "Oh my gosh, I'm sorry."

The light sparkled in Dan's eyes when he laughed. "I'm going to tell Lydia you threatened me."

"Please don't," said Shona.

All levity left me at the tone of her voice. "Did you know they found the murder weapon?" I asked Dan.

He shook his head.

"It was Joe's knife," said Shona. "He identified it. We lost it at some stage during the Saturday celebration."

"Crap." Dan glanced around the pub. "Where's Joe now?"

"Not sure. Off for a walk, we think." I glanced towards the door. "He'll get wet."

"He does that when he's stressed," Shona added. "Walk, I mean."

Dan frowned. "He didn't tell you where he was going?"

Shona shook her head.

"I'll keep my eye out for him on my way home."

"Thank you." I was truly grateful. Shona and Joe were each other's alibi, but their 'discussion' on the way home meant they could have had time to kill Rossi. That didn't just implicate them—it implicated me as well.

I rolled my shoulders and they crackled with tension. Shona's idea of doing background work on Rossi's death wasn't that bad. Curiosity burned through my fatigue. It could help Joe, it could help Shona, and it could help me. Self-preservation was a powerful motivator.

We slid into the booth and deposited the jugs of soft drink onto the table, just as Hannah brought out two huge platters of fish and chips.

We descended on the food like ravenous gulls, but when we slowed down enough to breathe, I surveyed my friends, and plunged right in. Like Shona, subtlety wasn't my strong point.

"So… who do you think killed Rossi?"

# Chapter Eleven

I ate another chip and watched the faces of my friends. Hannah opened her mouth to say something, and Bridget's jaw worked in a similar way, but both held back.

When Hannah finally spoke, she chose her words carefully, as if she were defusing a bomb. "It's hard to answer that question without implicating..." She paused, her eyes pleading with the rest of the group not to make her finish that thought. "If the murder weapon was Joe's knife and he had it halfway through the evening, then it had to be someone at the celebration who took it." Her face paled, and her voice became hushed. "But it couldn't be, right? You really think it could be one of... our friends?" It felt like she'd nearly said *one of us*.

Right then, the group behind us erupted into loud, cackling laughter. I turned to see five women with Vivien, the ringleader of the local ceramics club, Gone Potty, squeezed together in the booth. The bottle of prosecco on the table was obviously lubricating their lack of volume control.

Shona's smile met mine as more laughter shrieked behind

us. I mouthed the word, "Loud," before turning back to the women in our own booth. Hannah was right. It had to be someone we knew.

"I don't know anything right now, other than I need caffeine and aspirin." I closed my eyes for a moment and rubbed my temples. The thought that someone we knew could be a killer made my head throb. "I'm just worried about Joe."

"Because of his run-in with Rossi the other day?" Bridget shifted in her seat. "I guess that doesn't look good."

"Exactly." Shona's words rushed out of her. "But I was with him for the whole time last night. I told the police, but I'm not sure they believe me." Her bright blue eyes implored us. "Joe didn't kill Rossi."

Hannah reached over and gave Shona's hand a brief squeeze. "Of course he didn't."

I butted in. "If we can put together a timeline of what happened last night, it might help Joe." I glanced at Shona. "We know the police will do their job…"

She breathed out her greatest fear. "But sometimes even the police get things wrong."

Hannah and Bridget nodded.

"Joe had the knife at the beginning of the evening, didn't he?" I directed the question to Shona and Bridget.

"Yes," said Bridget. "I told the detective. Joe used the knife to chop the salmon and prosciutto for the canapés."

"What time was that?" I asked.

She chewed her lip, deep in thought. "Not sure. Around eight thirty? Then he chopped more bacon."

Shona pushed a stray hair out of her eyes. "We did most of the work beforehand, but we needed to make more." She shrugged. "The centre's oven is touchy and burned some of the hot food, so we needed more finger food to feed the hordes."

"When was the last time anyone saw the knife?"

Bridget frowned. "I washed it several times, but we didn't notice it was missing until we were packing up. I can't really remember—the whole night was a blur."

"Who had access?" asked Hannah.

There was another round of shrieks from the Gone Potty group behind us. We shared eye rolls and smirks of amused suffering.

Shona waited until the noise died down. "All of us had access." She gestured to me, Bridget and herself. "Tara, Joanie and Kym were in and out of the kitchen too."

Bridget pursed her lips. "Some of the guests wandered in. The centre's loos are accessed by the back courtyard, and there are two hallways leading outside. The exit they were supposed to use was at the other end of the room, but people kept sneaking past the kitchen door. That electrician guy. What's his name?"

"Jim Stephens?" Hannah offered.

"He staggered in blind drunk at one point. Joe had to help haul him out."

"Anyone else?"

Shona ran her hands through her hair. "Elouise popped in for a hug after Rossi started panting over that property developer tart. And Paul Farrow wandered in at some point too."

"Paul and Donna were both pretty upset at Rossi," Bridget said.

Shona frowned. "They didn't kill Rossi."

"Was Donna there? I can't remember seeing her." I yawned, searching my foggy memory. The carb fest had finished me off. I desperately needed sleep—or high-strength, intravenous caffeine.

Hannah shook her head, stifling a yawn as well. "I heard she had a bad migraine and stayed home to sleep it off."

"Paul couldn't—I mean wouldn't—kill Rossi." Shona's voice quavered at the suggestion.

I leaned my arm against hers for a moment. "We're just trying to work out where everyone was right now. Who had access. Who has motive. We can evaluate everything later."

"You sound like you know what you're talking about." Bridget eyed me closely.

"Ruth used to work for an investigator in London." Shona's tone brimmed with importance.

I shook my head. "I made the tea and coffee and did some background checks."

"So, you're a PI?" asked Hannah, her eyebrows raised. "Like Rossi? You are full of surprises."

I shook my head. "I finished the training, but I lost my appetite for the whole thing."

"You didn't enjoy it?" Hannah raised her eyebrows.

I tried to be as nonchalant as I could when I shrugged. "It wasn't for me." I didn't want to tell them my boss thought I was hopeless at investigating, or reveal my ruinous romantic history. Like Larsen, they didn't need to know.

"But Ruth's always liked discovering things." Shona told them about the Roman coin I'd found as a kid and how I discovered it was rare. Once again, I felt the pang of running away from my archaeological degree. I wish I didn't feel so *lost*. There had been a time when I'd been sure of who I was.

"And," Shona continued, "Ruth once helped a girl in Paris find a valuable necklace when a parrot stole it. She broke open an organised pickpocket ring."

"It was a locket, and Henri made the arrests."

"Who's Henri?" Hannah's eyes twinkled.

"Don't ask!" Shona and I both answered—and laughed— at the same time.

"Another of Ruth's romantic liaisons gone wrong." Shona winked at Bridget and Hannah.

I narrowed my eyes at my friend and changed the subject before the others could question me further. "Anyone else drop in for a visit?"

Shona ate a chip, then another, then paused and took a small handful.

Bridget answered. "There was that lawyer dude who looks like George Clooney. He was there."

"Xavier Kingston. We're—Joe's doing the catering for his daughter's engagement bash next weekend." Shona spoke through a mouthful of chips which, along with her accent, rendered her nearly unintelligible. "He popped in to hit Joe with a million questions about the party."

I looked at the others. "Anyone else?"

Bridget and Shona shook their heads.

"I spoke to Rossi and Elouise for a few minutes," I said.

Bridget's gaze sharpened. "You looked pretty pally with him. Do you know what he wanted to talk to you about? I mean, why was he in your shed?"

I shook my head and spread my hands wide. "Your guess is as good as mine. He wanted to make a time to see me tomorrow." Sorrow twanged inside me. How could a life end that quickly?

I stifled another yawn as I turned to Hannah. On the one hand I hoped she had more to offer, but on the other I wanted to finish this, and escape to caffeine.

"You and Bruce got there early, didn't you?"

She nodded. "I didn't notice anything much. Only that Elouise got upset later in the night, like Shona said." She flashed a smile. "We were having a good time. We don't often get a night off."

Bridget frowned. "Does Elouise have an alibi?"

"I don't see Elouise killing anyone," argued Shona.

"Did she come into the kitchen before or after you last saw the knife?" I asked.

Shona thought for a moment. "It might have been after…"

I surveyed the table—each woman was quiet, seemingly caught up in their own thoughts. "Anything more you can think of?"

They shook their collective heads. We were all flagging.

"I do remember something," I added after a moment. "Rossi was ranting to someone outside, just when I was leaving. I didn't see or hear who he was talking to. Anyone know who it was?"

The others shook their heads, again.

"It wasn't Joe." Shona made a grimace. "Not this time."

"I don't think Rossi was popular with anyone this week. I saw Paul Farrow jostle him hard at the pub on Friday." Hannah shrugged.

"Rossi was helping sell their farm out from under them," Shona said. "But they couldn't have killed Rossi. They're too gentle for something like that."

I smiled to myself. Shona saw the good in everyone. That was why I liked her so much more than someone like Lydia Larsen. Although to be fair, Lydia's personality made her a far better detective.

"I can't think of anything else." Hannah glanced at Bridget. "You?"

The brunette shook her head.

"Okay then, coffee and dessert anyone?" Hannah asked.

"Yes, please." Shona's enthusiastic response was echoed by

all of us, although I opted just for coffee. Hannah slid out of the booth to speak to the kitchen staff.

Caffeine at last!

Hannah had been gone for a couple of minutes when my phone rang. I recognised the number and cancelled the call immediately.

"Spam?" asked Bridget.

"Worse. My sister." I put the phone's ringer on silent.

"Still not talking to her?" Shona nudged my arm.

"Would you?" It wasn't the best question to ask. Shona probably would still talk to a sister who'd betrayed her. But Sarah had systematically built a wall between me and my family. They'd believed I'd rejected them, and I'd believed they'd exiled me. Even Shona couldn't forgive something like that. Could she?

The phone lit up again, buzzing on the table like a dying blowfly. All three of us stared at it.

"You're not going to answer? It could be important." Shona's tone was gentle but insistent, like a mother urging her shy child to say 'hello' to a new grown-up. "Something could have happened. Someone could be hurt."

The phone stopped buzzing and lay still, a link to a world I no longer wanted to be part of.

"When did she last try to call you?"

"She hasn't, but—"

"So, it could be important?"

Shona was right. I hated that she was right.

The phone buzzed again and I reached for it with a scowl. "What do you want?"

Sarah said something, but it was drowned out by Hannah

returning and another eruption of cackles from the Gone Potty women behind us.

"Hang on, I can't hear." I stood to go outside, but then realised rain was hammering down. I wouldn't be able to hear out there either, so I flopped back into my seat and turned my phone on speaker at top volume.

I waited a moment until the Gone Potty giggles died down, then held the phone a little away from my ear so it wouldn't give me a brain tumour or make me deaf. "Why are you ringing, Sarah?"

"Ruth, I know you don't want to talk to me, but I need to talk to you about Dad's business. Did the solicitor call you?"

I glanced at the phone. There was a missed call from yesterday. "He sent me an email the other day. Is there something wrong?"

"Did you take any of Dad's stuff with you when you moved?"

"No, why?"

"Are you sure? No mementos? Nothing from his office?"

"Why would I? All I have are the things I stored in the shed before I went to Europe. And *you* sent all that down to me."

Sarah's sigh was very loud and very real. "That's not good."

"Why? What's going on?"

"Well, there are things missing. Some plans. And a prototype. It was part of the business' IP. It was why the business was valued so highly."

"I'll take your word for it." I knew Dad was working on some cool stuff, but I'd taken no notice. My sister had blocked me out of his life for ten long years. Why was I talking to her now? "Look, it's loud here and hard to hear. I'm with friends—"

"Ruth, listen. The value of the business was the last main

part of Dad's estate. If we can't find the plans and prototype, we can't sell. And if we can't sell, there's no more money. The rest of our inheritance is on hold until someone works out what's happened."

I hesitated at that. "Uncle Bob can't help?" Bob Hawthorn wasn't our real uncle—he'd been a family friend for years and in the last few years had become Dad's business partner.

"Nope. He has no idea. You know his interest was mainly financial. He wasn't hands-on."

"Yeah." Dad had always had the brains, but Bob had invested the money to help make Dad's tech a reality. It was some kind of compact energy generator. I didn't understand how it worked, only that lots of people wanted it. The plan was to sell the business to a Fortune 500 company who would take Dad's ideas to the next—very lucrative—level. Bob was happy—he'd be rich—and so would Sarah and me. A win-win for everyone.

"Anyway," said Sarah. "If you can think of anything or remember anything… if you've accidentally taken anything of Dad's—"

"I haven't." My voice was terse. "I told you that."

"Okay, already."

The conversation was degenerating. I should go while we were still talking civilly.

"How are you anyway, Ruth? I saw on the news there'd been a murder down there. The crime scene looked like it was in a country area. Anywhere near you?"

What? My sister was asking about me? Showing interest in me as an actual human being. Was it possible?

Nope.

"It's not the jinx thing, is it?" Sarah continued, laughter in her voice. "The Ruthless-the-Killer curse?"

"Sarah…" My heart nearly stopped, and my voice was a

tight-throated squeak. Why I didn't hang up right then, I didn't know. Post-trauma shock? Misplaced politeness? Train-wreck stupidity?

"Well, the solicitor nearly died when you were here. Now someone's been murdered. You don't know the victim, do you? Did you jinx them?"

I think Sarah was trying to be funny—she wasn't really wanting to be mean. And she obviously didn't know that Rossi had died in my shed. But with Sarah, being a lousy hagfish of a sister came naturally.

"You'd better warn everyone down there," she teased. "Tell them to watch out."

"I've gotta go." I hung up quickly. Bridget, Hannah and Shona were staring at me, and the Gone Potty booth had become strangely silent.

Crap. Crap. Crap.

# Chapter Twelve

When the kid saw me, he dropped his ice cream, hid his face against his mother's skirt, and cried.

It was the next morning and I'd received an early call from the police to say that they'd finished with my property. I could go back home. Yes! I loved Shona and Joe, but I could only take so much of the it-doesn't-matter-if-the-town-knows-about-your-past or the who-would-believe-the-jinx-stuff-anyway? streams of encouragement from my friends. A reputation could stick like chewing gum to a shoe. My Ruthless-the-Killer rap had ruined my life at school and beyond. It could be a huge problem.

But I didn't know *how big* until I began wheeling my bicycle along the footpath away from Joe's Café. Shona had offered to drive me back to my place, but I needed some exercise, so I suggested they take me and my bike into town. I could help them in the shop through the busy part of the morning, then ride home at lunchtime. I had a small backpack with me, but Shona and Joe said they'd drop the rest of my things off later.

But the shop was dead. No one wanted coffee, no one wanted Joe's famous jam-and-organic-double-cream scones, no one even wanted to gossip. So, I left early only to find the other cafés full, and every second person skirting to the outside of the footpath, so they didn't have to walk near me.

And then there was the kid. He was about five years old, but when he saw me, his cherub face crumpled.

You know that saying, the straw that broke the camel's back? That was the final straw in a huge haybale of grief that totally crushed the camel.

Tears streamed down my face as I mounted my bike and sped off down the street. I'd expected whispering and strange looks, but not scared kids. All I wanted was to start again and to *belong* somewhere. I thought I'd finally locked my reputation away in the zoo of weird life curiosities, but it was very much alive, free and stalking me with the stealth and strength of a Tasmanian tiger.

Ironic. Tasmanian tigers were supposed to be extinct, like I would soon be in Pelican Bay. I loved this quaint town of weirdos. I fit right in. But how could I stay?

I had to stop, blow my nose and wipe my eyes.

"It's not fair. It's not!" I began riding again, pumping the pedals as hard as I could. In Europe I'd ridden my bike everywhere and had found it helped when my life went wrong. It wasn't as safe in Australia—we didn't have as many bike paths here—but I still loved the challenge and rhythm of the exercise. It put me into a kind of zen—a welcome zone of peace.

A few kilometres down the road, the tears dried up. Half a hill climb later, hope tugged on my shirt, asking if it could come home. One wild descent later, with the wind whipping through my clothing, I said, "Yes, you can."

Endorphins ruled!

Until I took the last turn too wide and saw the Jeep coming right at me.

The driver swerved. I swerved. Somehow, we missed each other. My front wheel skidded into the gravel then hit a rock. One slow-motion moment later I was flying over the handle-bars headfirst into a dense wattle bush.

Someone was yelling. I tried to scramble out of the bush, but it hooked in my clothes and backpack. I shrugged out of the latter, wincing where the branches scraped me.

"Are you okay?" The driver of the car sprinted towards me.

"Yeah." I pulled myself the rest of the way out of the bush, but my knees wobbled and I sank onto the grass by the side of the road. There was a large rock next to me. It must have been what my bike hit.

The driver reached me, crouched beside me and touched my arm. "Are you hurt?"

I squinted up at him. "Dan?"

Running into him was becoming a really bad habit.

"Are you okay?"

"Yes, I think so. The bush broke my fall."

"Sit still for a minute. Does anything else hurt? Your head? Neck?" He ran a practised gaze over me.

I moved my head slowly from side to side and took off my helmet. "I didn't hit my head. I'm okay."

I flexed my arms and checked out my legs. I had large tears in my jeans, some deep scratches on my legs and arms and gravel rash on my knees and hands. I tried to stand, but Dan put his hands on my shoulders and gently pressed me back down onto the grass. Then he took his phone from his pocket and shone it into my left eye.

"Hey!" I pulled away from the bright light.

"Just checking you for concussion." He flashed the light into my other eye.

"I'm fine." I pushed his hand—and the light—away.

"Your pupils are even. That's good. How many fingers am I holding up?"

I sighed. "Three."

"What day is it?"

"Tuesday."

"Who is the prime minister of Australia?"

I told him.

"What's your phone number?"

"0439…" I looked up, saw the laughter in his eyes, and stopped. "Ha ha. Good try."

"You'll do." A wide grin spread across his face, his blue eyes crinkling at the corners. "If you'd given me your number, I would have called the ambulance right away, the way you've been avoiding me." He rose and offered me his hand, pulling me to my feet. Then he glanced down at my bike. "Although you keep running into me, too. Why is that?"

"A strange and macabre twist of fate." My voice was dry, but when I saw the amusement in his eyes, I couldn't stop myself from smiling, too. "You ran into me this time."

"Uh-uh! You were on the wrong side of the road."

"Only a little. You were going too fast."

"I was under the speed limit." He grimaced as we both took in the mangled frame of my bike. Then he held me gently by my shoulders and looked me up and down again. "You sure you're okay?"

I tried not to shake as I held his blue-eyed gaze. "I was lucky."

"I'm glad." His voice gravelled as he reached out and pulled a twig from my hair. My rotten heartstrings gave an annoying twang, and when the back of his hand 'accidentally' brushed my cheek, a frisson of electricity zinged through me.

I looked away, gathered myself and focused on something other than his nearness.

"I better go. My bike… and my things!" I began to reach for the contents of my backpack, strewn along the roadside. A warm flush flared on my cheeks. Why did there have to be tampons?

Dan's lips quirked up at the corners when he saw my embarrassment, but his expression was kind. "I'll pick them up, and then I'll take you home."

"I can walk." I tried to say more, but my lower lip wobbled, and a tremor invaded my voice. No. No. No. Not reaction.

"Ruth." His voice was gentle. "Come sit in the car. I'll get your bike and your things."

I wanted to resist but all the fight had left me. He eased his arm around my shoulders and guided me to the front seat of his Jeep. I slid inside and wrapped my arms around my body, trying to stop shaking. It wasn't just the accident—that was just the catalyst. It was the past thirty-six hours. A man had been killed in my shed. The police were suspicious of both me and my friends, and my rotten reputation meant that little boys' faces crumpled when they saw me. The more I tried to hold the grief back, the more it broke. I couldn't stop either my shaking or my tears.

Dan touched my arm and handed me a box of tissues. "Here you go." His voice was gruff.

I grabbed several and blew into them with a loud trumpet, then he dropped a soft rug around my shoulders. He gestured to the back seat. "Hope you don't mind that it smells of Frank."

"Frank?"

Something whined behind me, and I spun around to see a small, cream-coloured dog quiver with barely restrained excitement in the back seat. It had a slightly squashed-in face, large brown eyes and the prettiest, fluffiest, feather duster tail I'd ever seen on a dog. Part Pomeranian, part pug?

I reached out to pet him. "Oh, you're a darling." Frank whined again and licked my hand. I made sure the door was closed before I released him from his seatbelt.

Dan was still by the roadside, examining my bike. He was taking his time—I guess to give me space to get myself together. When he lifted his head, I could see the furrow in his brow and the deep concern in his eyes.

Frank clambered between the seats onto my lap and tried to lick away my tears. I pushed him back and he leaned into me, snuffling and snorting and wagging his fluffy tail in circles. Then he leaped up, getting in several kisses before I could push him away with a tear-spluttered laugh.

He wiggled with delight as I held onto him.

Frank yapped and I turned to see Dan standing outside the car with a strange half-smile on his face. Then he opened the back of the Jeep, threw in my mangled bike, and closed the hatch.

He moved with easy grace around the front of the car, handed me my backpack and slipped into the driver's seat beside me. "You like dogs then?"

Before I could answer, Frank leapt at Dan with a yelp and plastered a frenzy of licks on his face. "Back in your seat," Dan ordered with military authority.

To my surprise the little dog obeyed, hopping between the seats to sit in the back.

"I'm impressed, Frank." The dog was still quivering with excitement, but he was doing what he was told.

Dan reached through the seat, ruffled Frank's ears, and hitched him up to his seatbelt. "Good lad." Then he turned to me. "Okay. Let's get you home."

# Chapter Thirteen

Dan sat me down in my kitchen while Frank scurried through the house, exploring. He stopped and sniffed everything… which was fine until the little fiend started to lift his leg against my kitchen doorpost. Before I could speak, Dan's command rang out.

"No, Frank!"

Frank stopped on command again. Impressive.

Dan stood. "Hang on. I'll take him outside."

"I'm okay now anyway. You can go."

But Dan disappeared out the back door following his little dog. I could see them outside through the window. Frank ran rings around Dan then stopped in his tracks to smell something, then off he went again with his nose to the ground, zigzagging across the yard. I turned my attention to the heels of both my hands. They stung. There was still dirt in the left one, and my right knee and elbow burned. I must have skidded as I landed in the wattle bush.

Frank shot back inside. Dan followed close behind and

opened the first aid kit he found on top of my kitchen cupboard.

"Let me look." He held out his hand for mine.

I held it away from him. "I'm okay."

"No, you're not. Those wounds could get infected."

"I'm fine."

He gave me a deadpan, you're-talking-crap look. "Ruth…" His voice had a frustrated, growly edge. "I'm just trying to help."

I was just about to say that I didn't need his help when Frank trotted over, sat at my feet and pawed at my knee. He blinked up at me with his big brown eyes. Why was I such a sucker for eyes?

"Did you teach him to do that?"

Dan's lips twitched in amusement. "Nope. But did it work?"

The little dog pawed my knee again and let out a soft whine.

"Okay." I held out my left hand. "But only because Frank asked."

Dan chuckled. "Are you okay with this?" He held up a small bottle of disinfectant.

I nodded and he poured some in a bowl, topped it up with warm water and scooped up some cotton swabs to clean my hand.

"Ah!" I hissed and pulled back when he washed the wound. You know how I said Dan's touch made me shiver, just a little? This disinfectant was the antidote to that. All his touch brought was pain. Especially when he picked up some tweezers and flicked out a small piece of gravel that was stuck in my skin. I tried to pull away again, but the scoundrel held on.

"Hurts!"

"Nearly done." He finished washing the wound with the diluted disinfectant then let me go.

I glared at the disinfectant. "Have you swapped that for hydrochloric acid?"

He laughed out loud. "You're worse than some of my men."

I bit my lip, trying to hide my smile. My last boyfriend had been an ultra-sook in the man-flu kind of way. Maybe it was spreading to girls?

*Woman up, Ruth. You're tougher than this.*

"Now your elbow." His eyes twinkled. "You want some leather to bite down on?"

"Ha ha." But I let him clean my elbow and only flinched twice.

He disinfected my knee without me reflex kicking him in the you-know-whats, then unfolded his long legs and stood.

"Thanks, Dan. I'm sure you have things to do, I'll be fi—"

"Kettle."

"What?"

"Once wounds are decontaminated, tea is required."

"You sound like Shona."

Dan's eyes danced. I wanted to flirt with those eyes—and do more than flirt with his lips—but it would be a bad move. "They taught you that in the military?"

"No. But it would have been good advice if they had. My gran taught me that when my brother Jake and I got into scrapes at her place."

"Tea for kids?"

"It was mainly milk and tons of sugar." His face softened. The laughter lines around his eyes were mixed in with something else harder to explain. They were the eyes of someone who had seen—and maybe lost—too much. "Jake often faked an injury, so she'd give us milk and sugar."

"Did it work?"

"All the time. I'm sure she saw through it, but that didn't stop her." He gazed out of the window, his lips quirking upwards at the corners. "We thought she couldn't resist our charm, but she was just being kind."

"I'm sorry about your brother. I should have said so before, but—"

"You were too busy avoiding me?"

I chuckled. "That's proved difficult."

It was becoming more difficult, too. Shona was right. I was discovering I liked Dan. Not just because of our flirty sexual chemistry, but because he was a genuinely good human being. Although I wasn't going to admit that to him.

"Seriously, I am sorry about Jake. It can't be easy to come back and finalise his estate. How did he—"

Dan turned away from me to pick up the kettle. "It was a… boating accident." Emotion roughened his voice, and I wanted to hug him, just a little.

"I'm sorry, I shouldn't have mentioned him."

He turned back and gave me a laconic, lopsided smile. That did send a spark through me—the good kind that warmed every part of me. "No, thank you for talking about him. Sometimes people don't know how to deal with grief, so they ignore it. All that feels is weird." He hesitated. "Sorry, I'd guess you'd get that too."

He didn't know the half of it. "It's better when they don't know. That's one of the reasons I moved down here as soon as I could. And to get away from my sister."

Dan's eyes lit up. "And then we met on the same plane, heading to the same place."

The boys may have practised charm on their gran when they were kids, but Dan also knew how to wield it as an adult. His eyes were the colour of the ocean on a bright summer day, and they sparkled with promised adventure. But I'd been shipwrecked by similar gazes in the past. I needed my defences up. What did they say in Star Trek? *Shields at maximum, Captain.*

I coughed. "The world is full of undeniable irony."

He snorted, filled the kettle and found the teapot. Then he searched the pantry. "All I can see is green tea. You got any of the proper stuff?"

"I keep some for Shona. I'll get it." I stood a little too quickly then sat down again. I pointed. "Up there. Top shelf."

Within five minutes I was drinking a very sweet and milky tea for the second time this week. I wished I could say it was disgusting—I normally hate sugar in tea—but it helped. I felt less shaky, which was good because I could now get Dan out of my house and—

Frank burst back into the kitchen dragging one of my Ugg boots in his mouth.

"Frank!" Dan ran after the little dog, who looked so pleased with himself. "Leave it!"

This time Frank didn't obey. He was having too much fun. He ran out of the room dragging the boot, which was almost as big as he was, and did some pretty cool manoeuvres to keep out of Dan's way. But he miscalculated and found himself wedged in the corner between the sofa and the TV in the living room.

Dan snatched up the Ugg boot. "Sorry. Where can I put this?"

"There's a stool in the laundry. I can take it." I attempted to stand again.

Dan shook his head. "Stay!" It was the same voice he used for Frank. But he found the other boot, put both in the laundry, and closed the door.

Frank ran over to me, his eyes sparkling with as much

mischief as Dan's a little earlier. I scratched him behind the ears, and he licked my hand. "Ow!"

Then he jumped on my lap, rested his head against my chest and wagged his tail. Charm—or incorrigibility—ran in the family.

Dan shot me a sheepish smile. "He steals things to get attention."

"Like hearts?" I muttered under my breath.

"Sorry?"

"He's got a good heart."

Dan grinned. "A good, yet evil, manipulative heart." He sat down next to me and patted his leg to call the little dog to himself.

Frank leapt from my lap straight onto Dan's, wagging his feather-duster tail in delighted circles as he tried to lick his owner's face.

"Shouldn't you have a Rottweiler or something?" I nodded at Frank. "He's not the kind of dog I thought an ex-military type would have."

"He was Jake and Vanessa's. She's in Colorado now."

I didn't ask. Some people around town said that Jake didn't die in the boating accident. He took his life because his wife left him.

"But Jake was in the military too," Dan said. "You didn't know?"

I shook my head.

"He left the Air Force a couple of years before I did. Vanessa had chosen this little beast to keep her company when he was away. But she left him with Jake when she went." He ruffled Frank's fur. "I think Jake was happy to have a dog that didn't remind him of the military."

"Who's going to look after him while you're away? You're going to Europe soon, aren't you?" I picked at a tear in my jeans and tried to keep my voice casual. I didn't want him to think I was eager for him to stay, or anything. "Or are you leaving long term?"

"Four or five weeks. And my neighbour is taking him."

His lips curved into a half-smile.

"I'm not sure how long I'll be away for—it could be up to six months—but I'll be back." The warmth and certainty in his tone made my heart beat faster.

"That's good," I said, a little too quickly.

"Indeed." His half-smile spread into a wide grin as he eased to his feet and tilted his head towards the door. "Mind if I take a proper look out the back?"

I shrugged.

"Better still, feel up to showing me the shed?"

"Sure." I eased myself to my feet, and this time managed to stand without any wooziness. Revisiting the scene of Rossi's death was the last thing I wanted, but I'd showed enough weakness for the day.

I took a deep breath and lifted my head high. "Let's do this."

# Chapter Fourteen

The sweet tea had done its work, but my left ankle was tender when I put weight on it. Funny how you don't notice some things straight after an accident. I twirled it in circles. It didn't hurt enough to stop me walking, but I'd be sore later.

The wind blasted in our faces as we walked across the backyard and looked over the valley. It really was the change of seasons.

"Lovely spot," said Dan, surveying the view.

"It's kind of lost its shine." I pointed to the police tape that flapped in the breeze across the back part of the property. "Yellow and black isn't my thing."

We walked down to the shed at the far end of the house block.

"Mind if I have a look?" He must have seen my hesitation, because he added, "You don't have to come in."

Like I was going to let him win that one. I squared my shoulders and tried to push away the image of Rossi dead on the floor. "Follow me."

I don't know what I was expecting when I opened the door. Police tape everywhere? Boxes and crates strewn around the place? Rossi's blood?

Everything looked… normal.

Dan scanned the interior. "They've cleaned up well." He walked a few paces into the shed, skirting around the old pottery wheel, and scuffed his foot against the concrete floor. "If you'd had the original wooden flooring you might have had to replace it, but concrete is good."

"How do you know that?"

He said nothing, but raised an eyebrow and gave me an are-you-kidding-me glance.

"Right," I said. "You were in the military in war zones."

"Where did you find him?" he asked.

I swallowed then pointed to where the body had lain on the floor. "About there." I sniffed the air. "Can you smell blood?"

Dan regarded me. "No. But sometimes our brains trick us into thinking we can smell things just by seeing them again." He paused. "We can go back outside if you like."

"I'm okay." I hid my small shudder.

He scanned the room. "What's with all the boxes? Still to unpack? I hadn't picked you as a hoarder."

"Hey! My house is neat inside."

He grinned. "Sensitive, much?"

"My sister sent all this down from Brisbane. Most of it's from before I went overseas, and some…" I pointed to some crates in the corner. "Some is from the UK."

"That was nice of her."

"Ha! She just wanted more space at home and insisted I take it."

He nodded to the boxes at the back. "It's good you've got the space to store it. But I see you've opened some of it."

"Where?"

Dan pointed towards the back corner of the shed.

"I haven't touched anything back there." I pushed past several boxes to reach the crate. "Someone's opened it." My mouth ran dry. "Would the police have done this?"

"If it was opened, they'd look through it. What's in it?"

"Mainly books, some artwork and ceramics."

Dan pressed his lips together, his brow furrowing. "I'll check with Lydia." He ran his finger along the edge of the crate. "It looks like someone's used a crowbar. Can you see the splinters? The cops wouldn't usually be as rough. They might have wanted to make sure you weren't smuggling drugs or weapons."

I wanted to laugh but then I saw he was at least half serious. I tried to keep it light. "Not that I know of, but then my sister Sarah packed my things." I wrinkled my nose as I said her name.

"That doesn't sound like a good relationship."

I hesitated. How much of this should I tell Dan? I hardly knew the guy. But he was willing to listen and my secret was already out. And there was something about him—a genuineness that went beyond the good looks and easy charm.

"Dad withdrew after Mum died. I blamed myself for her death—or should I say others in my family blamed me." I whooshed out a deep breath. "I was grieving and so were they. As a kid I'd had this reputation…"

"The jinx thing?"

"I see you've heard." I shrugged my shoulders to loosen them. "I'd thought I'd buried that rep years before…."

"Buried?" Dan's eyes twinkled.

"Ha! I make no apologies for the pun. But there was so much crazy stuff around it as a kid. It became part of me, you know?"

His gaze softened. "The things we experience as kids can be hard to shake."

"I was running away, I guess, but my sister thought it was the ultimate opportunity to cut Dad and I off from each other."

"Let's go back outside," Dan gestured towards the door.

We found a sheltered spot out of the wind, and I drank in the sun's warmth.

"Why would she do that?" he asked. "And how? That's almost impossible in the digital age."

I told him the sorry details. "Mum and I never got on and Dad and I had always been close. I think he was trying to make up for Mum." I gave a half-shrug. "Family dynamics are weird. Sarah was jealous. In her grief she decided that as I'd taken Mum away from her, she would take Dad away from me. As to how… Sarah worked as Dad's PA and handled all his communication. She told him I wanted nothing to do with him—and she told me he wanted nothing to do with me. She gave the rest of the family wrong contact details as soon as I left, so when I didn't answer, they all thought I'd cut myself off."

"But didn't you have the other family members' numbers? Couldn't you have called or emailed a cousin or something? Social media?"

"Yeah, but Sarah was convincing. I was just nineteen at the time. I believed her and so did they. Even my Aunt Izzy who is pretty clued-in was duped. Sarah was brilliant at IT and set herself up as the family expert. So, if modems needed installing or computers needed troubleshooting, or new phones needed sourcing, she was their gal. She secretly blocked my number on their phones and my profile on their social media accounts. She knew my email addresses and blocked them all. She also spoofed emails to and from family.

I got emails from family members that said, 'don't come home', and they got ones that said, 'I don't want anything to do with you'. I lived in Europe and then England, so it wasn't like I could drop in on them and say hello."

Dan let his breath out with a whistle. "That's borderline psycho…"

"Psychopathic, I know. And not so borderline. For ten years I thought my family, especially Dad, had rejected me completely." My wry smile was back. "And deep down, a part of me still blamed my 'curse'. I think that's one of the reasons it's so hard for me to shake all the feelings that come with it."

Dan touched my arm. "Ruth, I'm really sorry."

My voice quavered. "I didn't find out until after Dad died and I came back home for the funeral and the reading of the will. The solicitor gave me a whole pile of letters Dad had sent me that had been marked 'returned to sender'. Sarah had consistently given him the wrong postal address."

"Oh, Ruth." Dan wrapped his arms around me and drew me into a hug. He was warm and strong and solid. I let myself feed off his strength for a few seconds before pulling back, the scrapes on my face stinging with the salt of my tears.

"I'm okay. It's all water under the bridge now, anyway. Right?" I put on a too-bright voice and wiped my face with the back of my hands.

"And Sarah is in Brisbane?"

I nodded, pulling out the tissues he had given me only a short while before and blowing my nose.

"I see why you left. And it was Sarah who rang you and let your secret reputation out."

"Yes, the one and the same. You're not scared?" I shot him a crooked smile. "Your life could be in danger just being here."

He laughed. "I'll take my chances." He studied my face and asked me the same question Shona had. "You don't believe it, do you?"

"Of course not." I cast my eyes downwards before gazing up at him again. "But I think the whole town must know by now." I told him about the kid and his ice cream. "That's why I was so distracted riding home. It's like history is repeating itself."

He looked as if he was going to hug me again, but I bent down and rubbed Frank around the ears. "Who's a good, good boy then?"

Frank wagged his fluffy tail, spun in a circle, then stood on his hind legs asking to be picked up. I hoisted him up but winced as he licked at a scratch on my neck. But it felt safer to have a barrier between me and Dan.

He gave me that funny half-smile again, like the one on his face when I was cuddling Frank after the accident. As if he was remembering something.

Then he frowned. "I'm not comfortable with you staying here all on your own."

"I'll lock the doors. I'll be fine."

"Ruth…"

"I don't need protecting."

"There's a murderer out there."

My face flushed hot. I get that Dan was concerned, but that morning Joe had insisted that he and Shona stay out here with me if I came home. He wouldn't let up about it and Shona had to tell him to stop.

"Neither you nor Joe are staying here to protect me. I'm not some helpless female. I showed you I can look after myself the other day in your class, remember?"

He laughed. "I had no intention of offering to stay here

with you, attractive though it may be. I was thinking of a security system."

"Oh." My face flamed and I turned my focus to the small dog wriggling in my arms.

"I've been doing some freelance security work while I'm in Pelican Bay and I've got some equipment left over. You've got an up-to-date laptop?"

"I… yeah."

"Because I could wire up some surveillance cameras outside, and an alarm too." It was his turn to shift from foot to foot. "So you can check if anyone is there. You can also access it from your smart phone."

Conflicting emotions swirled inside me. A security system was a wonderful idea, but I couldn't afford it. "I've no money, Dan." I told him about the delayed inheritance and my need for a job.

Dan scratched the back of his neck. "Let me put in the system. I'm not out of pocket—most of it was left over from another job. You can pay me later."

"I… can't. I might not be staying, anyway. How can I live somewhere where I'm a pox to be avoided?"

"You are not a pox." He clamped his lips together, clearly trying hard not to laugh. "It will blow over once they find the murderer."

"Maybe." I bit my lip.

His eyes narrowed. He must have heard the hollowness in my voice. "Look," he changed the subject, "even if you do leave, you need to be safe for now. Stay at Shona and Joe's again tonight, and I'll come round tomorrow to put the system in. There's a murderer around, and he or she killed someone in your shed. They could come back." I swallowed at the seriousness of his gaze. "You can pay me when you can.

And I'll only charge cost price. I'm good for money at the moment."

I bit my lip again. His offer seemed genuine.

"I don't want you to get hurt. And I want to help." He spread his arms in an open-handed shrug. "I can give you a call and meet you here in the morning and install the system. Even if you eventually sell up and leave, you still need to feel safe in your own home until you make that decision. That's all. Okay?"

A bit of police tape broke off in the strong breeze and slapped hard across my face. I snatched at it, my hand stinging as I scrunched the tape in my grazed fist. Dan was right—I needed time to think. This would give me that time.

I took a long, deep breath. "Okay. Thank you."

"You're welcome." Mischief flashed in Dan's blue eyes. "I guess that means I'll need your phone number after all."

# Chapter Fifteen

When Dan dropped me back at Shona's place and she saw my limp and my scratched arms and face, her first reaction was open-mouthed shock. Her second reaction was to make tea and ask me to tell her what happened. Her third reaction—when she realised it was Dan who had knocked me off my bike, and that I was basically okay—was to let out a loud guffaw and declare that it was fate.

I laughed it off, but even I was beginning to wonder. I was determined not to fall *for* Dan, but I kept falling onto, into or in front of him. He was turning me into the worst version of clumsy.

Before I could think any deeper into that conundrum, Shona rubbed her hands together. "Now, are you up to visiting?"

"Where? Who?"

"I thought we could go to the Rossi's place. To talk to Elouise."

Excitement vibed through me. I ached in places I didn't know you could ache, and I really needed to soak in a hot tub for a few thousand years, but I did want to know more. I needed to know more. "Will she see us? She's just lost her husband."

Shona nodded towards a huge cooler bag on her kitchen bench. "We have food. Food cooked by Joe." She smiled in a determined way, like a crouching tiger sizing up its prey. "She'll let us in."

"Then I'm *in*." I didn't really want to move and start again —*again*. And the only way to stop little boys being scared of me was to help the police catch the real killer. I wasn't sure I *could* help, but I had to try.

I slid into the passenger seat of Shona's car. She put the cooler bag in the back seat, jumped in behind the wheel and gunned the ignition, swinging the car too fast out of the driveway.

"LTB came into the shop again this morning," Shona said after a moment. "I'm still worried about Joe."

"LTB?"

Shona grinned sideways at me. "Legs-to-Breasts. It can be our code name for her."

"You're going to call her that to her face one day."

"No one but us will know what it means if I do. It could stand for 'Larsen's the best'." She giggled, caught up in her own attempt at humour.

"Or 'Larsen's totally barmy'."

Shona snorted. "The possibilities are endless."

I must have still looked doubtful.

"Relax," she said. "Okay. We want *Detective Larsen* to solve her case, don't we?"

"Yes."

She glanced sideways at me. "You want to do this now?"

My lips twitched. "Yes."

"Ha!" she said. "I knew it! So how would you approach it, Sherlock?"

I thought for a moment. "They say that in a murder, the spouse is always the first person they suspect."

"And she has a motive. But she's not going to confess in front of us."

"We can't assume she's guilty just because Rossi was cheating on her. But she was there at the celebration. Even if she didn't do it, she may have seen something."

"Which she would have told the cops." Shona pointed out.

"Maybe, but I'm curious about how she's dealing with her husband's death."

"We're here." Shona pulled up at the kerb nearest the Rossi house. It was a large Federation-style cottage. The front of the home looked freshly rendered and was framed by red roses.

Elouise met us at the door and, after a moment's hesitation, invited us in. We were immediately welcomed by two large golden retrievers, who wagged their whole bodies and leaned against our legs, letting out excited keening sounds: "Eeee-eee-eee!"

"Whisky. Soda. Get back!" Elouise pushed the dogs away from us but they both zeroed in on Shona's cooler bag, ramming their noses hard against it.

Shona pivoted to hold the bag out of the way, then handed it to Elouise. "Joe made some meals and some cake."

"Thank you so much," Elouise said over the din of the dogs. "Whisky. Soda. Bed!" She pointed to two large dog beds in the corner of the living room. Both dogs stood there, certain their owner didn't really mean it. But Elouise pointed again. "Bed!"

Both dogs continued to stare, large pink tongues lolling out of the side of their mouths.

"Bed!"

The larger and darker retriever, Whisky, was first to give in. Soda stared at Elouise, then at Shona and me, for another few seconds then did as she was told. Both dogs circled three times then sank down into their beds. Their heads drooped over the edge of each bed, watching our every move, before they let out almost synchronised sighs.

"Sorry about the dogs." Elouise beckoned to the sofa. "Please sit down. I'll just pop this in the kitchen." She gestured to the cold pack. "Thank you so much. Would you like a cup of tea? I've just boiled the jug."

We both said yes, then, when Elouise left the room, Soda crept out of her bed and wiggled her way towards us. She pressed her side against our legs, thumping her tail and insisting on pats.

I caressed her soft, silky ears. "Who's a beautiful girl then? But you're going to get in trouble."

As soon as Elouise walked back into the room Soda took one look at her and crawled back into her bed. Life was tough as a dog.

"Nice place." I gazed around the living room. Elouise's home was beautifully renovated with polished floorboards and tasteful, contemporary country decor. Large wooden double doors opened onto a sunny backyard and a hint of French vanilla essence filled the air. I'd like my home to look—and smell—like this. One day…

"Thank you." She placed the tray bearing the teapot plus three fine china cups and saucers on the table. "Milk?"

We both nodded and she poured the tea and handed us each a cup.

I sipped on my tea, suddenly at a loss for what to say. This woman's husband had died in my shed just a couple of days ago and here we were sitting in her home, not just paying our respects but wanting to quiz her about what had happened. It felt all kinds of wrong.

Shona broke the silence. "We're so sorry for your loss."

Elouise nodded. She had dark circles under her eyes and her makeup was smudged. She regarded me with sad brown eyes—an expression not unlike her bed-banished dogs. "You found him." It was a statement, not a question. She dabbed at her eyes with a tissue. "I heard he was still alive…"

"Yes." My voice cracked. "I'm so sorry, I tried to save him." Shona rested her hand on mine.

Silence again.

"Did he say anything?" Elouise asked.

I shook my head, reliving the moment. Rossi reaching out to me with the fifty-dollar note then… dying. "He tried, but it was garbled."

Elouise shook her head and looked at the floor.

"I'm sorry. I wish I'd been in time." I stumbled over the words.

She looked up at me. "The police said the knife nicked his aorta. There's nothing you could have done."

More awkward silence, then Elouise spoke again.

"Do they know what happened? Why Aldon was in your shed?"

"I've no idea."

Shona leaned forward. "Did you see him after the celebration?"

"Some celebration. *She* was back." Elouise spat the words out and turned to Shona. "You saw what happened. I couldn't handle it after he ran fawning after her. I went to the bathroom then bolted for the exit, but cannoned into that Kingston jerk and then came and said goodbye to you." She inclined her head towards Shona. "You hugged me and then I left."

"Did the redhead and Aldon have history?" I knew this already from what Shona and Joe had said, but I wanted to hear what Elouise was willing to admit.

"That Briscoe tart? More than history. They had an affair. It went on for about six months before I found out."

"That really sucks," said Shona. "But you stayed together?" It was both a statement and a question.

"More fool me." Her words cut through the air, bitter and sharp. "Aldon begged for another chance, and I was stupid enough to say yes. That was part of the plan of moving back here. To get away from Briscoe. But she turned up here, too." Her hand trembled as she brought the cup to her lips, but there was hope in her voice when she added, "do you think she could have killed him?"

Shona and I glanced at each other, then shrugged, almost as synchronised as the dogs' sighs earlier.

"Why would she kill him?" I asked.

Elouise rubbed her hands over her face. "Aldon was a PI. He knew people's secrets. Maybe she had secrets? Or she could have rejected him." Her tone was more hopeful as she sat upright and continued. "If it wasn't that cow then it could have been someone he upset, like those dairy farmers." She regarded Shona. "Joe made it clear in front of everyone that he didn't like what Aldon was doing to them."

Shona shot to her feet. "Joe didn't kill him. I was with him." I gave her a reassuring nod. She took a deep breath and eased back down on the sofa again. "Sorry, Elouise."

"I don't think Joe killed Aldon either," Elouise said. "But Aldon was involved in the sale of the farm to Briscoe. The Farrows didn't like that. I hadn't realised at the time *she* was the interested buyer." She spat out the word 'she'.

"Why was a PI involved in a sale negotiation anyway?" asked Shona. "I wouldn't have thought that was a PI thing."

"Aldon and Xavier Kingston go—went—way back. Kingston's parents owned the property and made the original agreement with the Farrows. The Kingstons pay them a wage and Paul and Donna share in some of the profits. Xavier basically inherited everything about eighteen months ago when Brian Kingston died. The mum is still alive, but she has dementia and needs round-the-clock care. Kingston has power of attorney and manages the family trust, so the decision is basically his."

I dived in. "You said Aldon knew people's secrets. Could he have had something on Kingston to force him to sell?"

"Blackmail, you mean?" Elouise sat back in her chair. "It's possible. Aldon kept files on all the people he dealt with."

"Files?" Shona sounded hopeful.

"The police took all that from his office."

I glanced at Shona. "It's Kingston's daughter's party that Joe's catering for on Saturday, isn't it?"

"Yep." She nodded. "Fiona's engagement."

I turned back to Elouise. "Did you see Aldon or Xavier Kingston after you left?"

Elouise shook her head. "I smashed into Kingston as I was leaving, like I said, but then I came back here to eat chocolate and be with my dogs." She patted her leg and both animals bounced out of their beds and bounded over to her. "It's not the greatest alibi, is it?" She rubbed the dogs' ears. "I know I said I wished Aldon was dead. And to be honest, part of me isn't sorry he's gone. But I didn't kill my husband."

Whisky put his front feet on Elouise and wriggled onto her lap. "Oomph, you're too heavy." But she didn't push him off. Soda tried to squeeze onto Elouise's lap, too, but could only get her front paws up. "There's a good boy and girl."

Elouise hugged the dogs and strained around both to look at us. "Stick with dogs, ladies. Forget about men. Dogs won't let you down and they'll always love you."

"Dogs are great." I couldn't help but smile at the small woman being drowned by her two large pets.

"By the way," Elouise added, as Soda licked her hand twice. "I've heard what the town is saying about you, Ruth, and I don't believe in any of that stuff."

My eyes burned. "Thank you." The first sign of kindness from the townspeople and it came from the murdered guy's wife. Go figure.

Shona squeezed my hand.

"I knew your dad, as I said the other night," Elouise continued. "We even went on a couple of dates together." Her eyes sparkled. "He was a good kisser."

A strong *eww* shuddered through me.

Shona saw it and coughed, trying to hide her laugh.

"I meant what I said the other night at the party, Ruth. I still want to have you over for a meal sometime. Your dad was one of the good guys."

My eyes prickled again. "I'd like that." The more I knew about Dad, the more I could pretend he was still with me.

"But with curses—I don't think they're a metaphysical thing, but I do think people curse themselves by what they do —including Aldon. My husband had lots of enemies." There was a flicker of steel in her eyes. "I didn't kill him, but I'll bet someone he was investigating did."


"What do you think?" Shona asked, as she pulled out from the kerb. "She didn't do it, did she?" She hesitated. "I don't want her to have done it."

"I really like her, but we can't rule her out. She had motive and opportunity." I let out a long breath. "And no alibi other than her dogs."

"But she's too nice. She loves dogs—and they love her."

I said nothing.

"Dogs are good judges of character," Shona offered.

I laughed. "Can you see her retrievers being called as character witnesses in a court of law? The judge asks, 'Is Elouise a good person?' 'Woof,' says Whisky, wagging his whole body. 'Can you vouch for the character of the victim?' 'Woof. Woof.' Then Soda rolls over for a belly rub."

Shona giggled. "I get your point. Hardly reliable witnesses when they're such big bundles of hairy joy."

"Exactly."

"This is going to be hard," she sighed.

"We don't have the resources to do this properly, you know. We really should be leaving this to the police."

"I would if it wasn't for Joe. They asked me again if I was with him the whole time. What would you do if the police were harassing someone you loved?"

My tone softened. "I'd try to find out everything I could." I glanced sideways at my friend. "I want Joe to be cleared— and you—and me. I don't want little kids to freak out because they think I'm the boogey-monster. But we can't guarantee that whoever did this isn't someone we know and like. People can do terrible things when they're pushed." I regarded my friend. "And that makes this dangerous. We can snoop around. But at the first sign of danger, we go to Legs-to-Br—" I caught myself. "We go to Larsen—LTB. Okay?"

"Okay." Shona nodded.

"Right then, are you up to more investigating?"

"Of course!" Her eyes sparkled. "This is like old times." She paused. "But are you? You must be sore after your bike crash."

I glanced at my grazed hands. "I'm okay if I keep moving." I thought for a moment. "Elouise mentioned Paul Farrow and he did have motive. You know them better than I do. Could we drop in on them?"

"Absolutely. And when you meet Paul, you'll know he couldn't have done it." She chuckled. "You're good with dogs. How are you with cows?"

# Chapter Sixteen

I let out a small groan as I swung my legs out of the car. We were at the Farrow farm—my next-door neighbours—and despite my bravado, my muscles were stiffening big time after this morning's crash.

"You good?" Shona was walking normally now. Her small ankle sprain from Saturday had completely healed.

"Yeah. But I'd kill for a hot bath right now." I interlocked my fingers, grimacing as I stretched my hands above my head, first to the left and then to the right. "Maybe 'kill' isn't the best word to use today."

"You can have a bath at my place later." Shona began to stride towards a large farm shed, her feet crunching on the crushed-limestone gravel. The green corrugated iron shed stood directly to the front and a little to the right of the large parking area. It had a regular-sized door that looked like it led to an office, and large, wide-open sliding doors that gave a glimpse of farm machinery inside.

Donna waved to us from a path that led up from what I assumed was the milking area.

"Shona! Ruth!" She half-jogged towards us. Cows and their calves mooed contentedly in the paddocks behind her, as if wondering why the rush.

"To what do I owe the pleasure?" Donna gave Shona a huge hug and the dazzling smile she saved for her favourite people. She always welcomed Shona like a daughter.

"We were out and about, and thought we'd drop in and say hi," Shona said.

"Sure. You've timed it well. Let me get cleaned up and we can have a cuppa."

"Great." Shona beamed her sunny smile. "How's Paul doing?"

Donna gestured towards the house. "That Valkyrie cop's here again." She checked her watch. "She's as persistent as a randy bull trying to break into a paddock of cows on heat."

Shona and I both laughed, then we waited as Donna sprayed down her boots with a hose and peeled off her overalls. We all walked up to the house just as the detective was leaving. Larsen gave us a cool nod and slid gracefully into her car.

My lips twitched. I wasn't the only one who likened Larsen to a Valkyrie. I could see her with raised sword and horned helmet, leading invading forces to defeat the enemy. In some ways that was what she was doing now—invading our lives, ransacking our secrets, conquering the enemy of deceit. I wished I had her self-assurance and aura of authority. She was a woman who knew who she was.

We all washed up and sat down at the large, wooden kitchen table. The house wouldn't have made the front page in the latest country magazine, but it had a welcoming charm, like a well-worn armchair that's shabby around the edges but is so comfortable you never throw it out.

Donna served the coffee and tea in ceramic mugs the colour of eucalypt leaves and wattle.

"These are nice." I lifted my mug to admire it.

"Someone from the pottery group in town made them," said Donna. "I can't remember who."

"I told Ruth she should join Gone Potty," Shona said. "She used to be good at ceramics."

"When I was a kid," I corrected her.

Donna laughed. "You know that's not their real name."

"But it's more fun than the Pelican Bay Pottery Club," Shona quipped, stretching back in her chair.

"I'm pretty sure they were the ones who spread the rumours about me." I gave a small shudder. "They were at the table next to us when my sister rang."

"What rumours?" Donna's eyes narrowed.

"You must be the only one who hasn't heard." I filled her in.

"I'm sorry, Ruth. That sucks." Donna grimaced. "I haven't been into town since Saturday, when I went to the chemist to pick up a script." Her voice softened. "Are you okay? It must have been awful to find Aldon… like that. And then for this to happen." She squinted at me and slipped on a pair of wire-framed glasses. "What happened to your hands and face?"

Shona jumped in and told her how Dan had knocked me off my bike and tended to my wounds *and* was going to install a security system tomorrow. Pro bono.

"Didn't I see you run into him in the pub the other day?" Donna pursed her lips and gave a knowing nod.

"She did," Shona answered for me.

"And didn't you meet him on the plane when you were moving down here?"

"Yes, she did." Shona answered on my behalf again, a gleam in her eye. "Fell on top of him."

"Does everyone know every detail of my life?" I tried to keep my voice even, but my exasperation broke through.

"It's a small town," Shona teased. "Of course we do."

A wide grin spread across Donna's face. "Not mere coincidences then."

Shona raised both hands, palms upwards, in an exaggerated shrug. "I keep trying to tell her, but she won't listen."

Donna shook her head. "A man doesn't install a security system in a girl's home for free just to be kind. And if he did, he'd be a real catch." She grinned wickedly. "A smouldering hot catch."

"Donna!" Shona put her hand to her chest, feigning shock.

"What? I may be in my sixties, but I'm not dead."

"I'm going to pay him," I blurted out.

Both Donna and Shona laughed.

"Why is that funny?" I asked.

Shona came to my rescue for once. "I think Dan's genuinely worried about Ruth's safety. We all are."

Donna regarded me. "You've no idea why Rossi was in your shed?"

I shook my head. "None at all. I saw him at the business celebration, and he made a time to see me on Monday."

"What about?"

"No idea." I hesitated, then shrugged off my doubts and tackled Donna and Paul's alibi head on.

"You weren't at the party, were you?"

Donna wrinkled her nose. "I had a migraine. Stayed home and bombed myself out with medication. I vaguely remember surfacing and looking at the clock when Paul came home about eleven thirty."

Paul walked in right then and stood behind his wife. She almost purred when he began to massage her shoulders.

"That feels wonderful," she said.

"She's a hard worker, my Donna. It takes its toll."

"Would you guys like us to go?" Shona winked at Donna. "Don't want to cramp your style."

Donna's eyes sparkled. "You girls sit right there and have another cup of tea."

Paul patted his wife's shoulders then slid into the seat beside her as she poured him a hot drink. He was tall and broad whereas Donna was small and wiry. His salt-and-pepper grey hair stood out at crazy angles, and he had large, kind brown eyes, a bit like the cows he loved so much.

I pressed on. "What about you, Paul? Did you see anything suspicious at the party? Did you see anyone threaten Rossi?"

"Other than me, you mean?"

"Paul." Donna rested her hand on her husband's arm.

"It's okay, love." He patted her hand with his, then turned to me. "Rossi and I had words. Again. You probably know he was acting as an agent to sell the farm out from under us."

I nodded.

"I'd had enough of his treachery."

"Treachery?"

"I know we shouldn't speak ill of the dead, but the man was an ars—" He caught his wife's eye. "He cheated and lied. We were friends a long time ago. Not now."

"What happened?" asked Shona.

"I don't really want to go into it." He ran his fingers through his hair, making it stand up at even more crazy angles. "When he came back to Pelican Bay, he said he wanted to patch things up, but then he went and got involved with that Briscoe woman and her mob connections."

"Mob connections?" I shivered. That was too close to home.

"We don't know that any of that's true, honey," Donna said. She shifted her gaze back to Shona and me. "But we do know she's greedy. She wants to develop all this." She waved her arms around. "So that city folk with no idea can escape to a country life on land that no longer produces anything."

She realised what she'd said, and softened her gaze. "Not you, love. You're part of this town. Your dad lived here, and he was a good man." She sat back in her chair. "But look at this place. Dairy land is being lost all over the country to development just because someone wants to make a dollar. And farmers sell because there's not a lot of money in milk. Not everyone can find a niche market like we've done. Thing is, we found that market and now it's being taken from us."

There was one more key thing I needed to ask. "Will the sale still go through, now that Rossi is dead?"

Donna and Paul regarded each other. "We don't know." Paul turned back to Shona and me. "We're trying to find out if the contract has been signed but Kingston hasn't answered our calls. We're hoping we can still get him to cancel the sale."

"Why would he do that now?" asked Shona.

They exchanged another glance. "We think Rossi had something over Xavier Kingston," Donna said. "There was no hint that he had any desire to sell the farm until about three months ago."

"Rossi had dirt on lots of the businesspeople in town," Paul added.

I met Shona's eyes. Elouise had said something similar. "When I first moved here, I thought you guys owned the property."

"We've been managing it for almost forty years. Built everything up ourselves, including the decision to go both organic and ethical in our farming methods. The Kingstons were happy as long as we were making a profit—and we have been. We don't own the land but we've a small share in the profits of the dairy side of things and the shop is ours. We've put some money aside, but we've nowhere near the kind of cash we'd need to outbid a developer."

"We know we can't do this forever," Paul added. "The work is hard on Donna especially, but we wanted to transition."

"We've farm hands that help with milking and maintenance," Donna said. "And Curtin Davis…"

"He's studying agricultural science, like I did." Paul finished her sentence. "But he's interstate on a practical this month."

"Our plan is—was—to take him on," Donna continued. "We'd do less of the hard work and one day we'd sell him our share of the business. The shop here." She waved in the general direction of the farm's shop. "But Paul would keep on with his breeding program."

"But with the land sale…" Her words tapered off into bleak nothingness.

"That's a lot to lose," I said.

"I'm not sorry Rossi is dead," she blurted. "He was a dishonest bully. But we didn't kill him."

"We should go," I said, standing and stretching my stiff arms behind me, and bumping a box of tablets off the benchtop. A sealed foil strip of tablets fell out. "Sorry." I bent and picked them up and put them back in the box. The name of the prescription medicine was familiar. "Mum used to take these." I handed the tablets back to Donna. "For your migraines?"

Donna reached out, took them from me and stuffed them in her shirt pocket. "Yeah. Thanks."

We walked towards the door then Paul rested his large hand on my shoulder. "Just give us a holler if anything doesn't seem right, Ruth. We're just down the road. You're always welcome."

"Our door is always open for you, love." Donna wrapped me in a large, but gentle bear hug. "But if you come here at dawn you're helping with the milking."

"Ha!" said Shona. "This is Ruth we're talking about. It's hard to get her out of bed any time in the morning."

"Not true," I countered. "Well, not anymore. I'm a changed woman since moving to Pelican Bay." I grinned hopefully at Paul and Donna. "I'd love to help with milking one morning."

"No worries, love, just give us a call." Paul's eyes crinkled. "Any time you want a taste of farm life, we're more than happy to put you to work."

"Better make it quick." There was a deep sigh in Donna's voice as she slipped an arm around her husband's waist and gazed out at the land she loved. "We don't know how long we've got."

Shona and I walked back to her car in silence. When she closed her door she slumped forward, rested her forehead on the steering wheel and breathed out a shuddering sigh. "Paul has motive and opportunity, doesn't he?" When she sat back her eyes were red. "Is it wrong to pray that Xavier Kingston killed Rossi?"

I'd never met Kingston, but I had similar sentiments.

# Chapter Seventeen

Two days later I was still moving with the fluidity and grace of a long-term aged-care resident, but my scratches were healing and the cloud of exhaustion was lifting. In true Ruth Smythe style, I decided to challenge myself and do some cooking.

My chosen dish was Italian beef Wellington. Italian because I'd lived there for four years, and beef Wellington because it was simple and tasty enough to be pretend gourmet. Not even I could wreck it.

I didn't mind cooking; I'd just lived a chaotic kind of life where I'd done lots of other things instead. If I did cook, I liked to take my time and make it a contemplative experience.

The main difference from regular beef Wellington was substituting prosciutto for the pâté and using Marsala in the sauce. The meal would go beautifully with a bottle of local red.

My goal was to say thank you to Shona and Joe— and Dan.

While I didn't want to encourage Dan romantically, I

was incredibly grateful for the state-of-the-art home security system he'd installed. He hadn't quite finished—he needed to get in another couple of sensors and some more cabling—but I could now monitor the front and back of my house, right from my computer. He'd even installed a panic alarm in my kitchen. The sheds would be online tomorrow. There was a zoned alarm that was triggered if anyone went inside them unannounced. The system had animal sensors, which meant that future pets or present rats and possums could gallop through the sheds or the roof without setting off the alarm.

When Dan showed me how the system worked, I'd wanted to hug him again, but decided to invite him to dinner instead. As I also wanted to thank Joe and Shona for all they'd done for me, I invited them as well. This way I could be friends with Dan without being tempted to jump his bones. There was safety in numbers. Dan didn't seem like the kind of man who would try anything a girl didn't want. I just didn't trust my own heart and hormones.

I had to avoid being alone with him.

Simple.

Amusement played on my lips.

And stop colliding with him every second day.


I slapped the tenderloin down on the bench and tied it up with cooking twine, just as the recipe book said, and turned the stove on to heat the oil and brown the beef. Then I began organising the garlic, sage and mushroom for the duxelles. I was just about to sear the meat when my phone rang.

It was my sister.

*You've gotta be kidding me.*

I pressed the reject button. Not this time. After her great

reveal the other night she could go and stick her phone up her—

My phone rang again.

Once more I declined the call.

It rang a third time. Couldn't she understand that I didn't want to talk to her? Ever. Not after everything she'd done over the past ten years. And not after she told half the town about my history.

On the fourth round my sense of responsibility guilted me into answering.

"What do you want?" I took the direct approach. This was no time for niceties.

"You cut me off the other day."

"Yes, for good reason. Do you realise half the pub overheard you?"

"Ruth, listen."

"What if I don't want to listen?" I could be a scumbag too if I wanted.

"I need to ask you one more time if you have any of Dad's stuff."

"I told you I don't."

"They're saying someone may have stolen it."

"Stolen what again?"

"I told you. Plans and a prototype of his energy generator. The initial assessment was that everything was there. But it's not now. Either someone made a mistake earlier on, or the plans could have been taken after he died."

"What about the patent office? Dad would have lodged the tech details there."

"Gone."

"What do you mean, gone? There's no record?"

"Nope."

"How could that be?"

"No idea."

"So, the police are investigating?"

"They are now. They'll probably want to talk to you at some stage."

My gut churned. Being part of two police investigations was all I needed.

"Are you there, Ruth?"

The oil sizzling in the frying pan spat out a sharp, hot droplet that hit my cheek, jarring me out of my funk. I turned the heat to a lower setting and wished I could dial down my anxiety. The first step was getting off the phone to my sister. "I gotta go."

"There's one more thing."

"What? Earthquake? Famine? I'm going for best-case scenarios here."

"You need to look at the news."

"What? Why?"

"Just do it."

"No. Wait." But the phone pinged at the sound of her disconnecting.

I stared at it for a moment then opened my phone's browser and searched for today's news.

There was a report in a South Australian feed. 'Local woman linked with suspicious deaths in her past.' There was my photo—an old, fuzzy, demented-looking one someone must have taken off the internet—labelled for all the world to see with the headline, 'Ruthless-the-Killer?'

"No. No. No." I remembered the silence of the Gone Potty crew in the booth behind me, after Sarah blurted out my history. Now it wasn't just the town who knew my secret —the whole world did.

This couldn't get any worse.

I seized the knife and pounded it into the meat on the

wooden chopping board in a stabbing frenzy. Again, and again, and again, I stabbed the meat so hard that the knife lodged deep in the board. I braced the chopping board with one hand and tugged with the other—once, twice, three times before yanking it out with a jarring force that lifted it high above my head.

It was only then that I heard the cough and realised I was no longer alone in the kitchen.

I was still wielding my knife high in my right hand when I turned to face the intruder. Lydia Larsen stood there, taking in the whole blood, sweat and gourmet nightmare.

"Put down that knife, Ms Smythe."

An alarm started bleep, bleep, bleeping as the oil hit smoke point in the frypan.

I'd turned the heat up instead of down.

# Chapter Eighteen

Larsen mustn't have thought I was a major threat, or she would have drawn her taser, but her hand twitched in that direction. I put down the knife and turned off the stove, but I was still shaking when I asked her to sit at my kitchen table. I offered her a cup of coffee and used the rhythm of grinding, counting the drips and frothing the milk, to try to regain some composure.

My voice was almost steady when I spoke. "Sorry, I got a phone call from my sister."

Larsen raised a sardonic eyebrow. "Must have been some phone call."

"Have you seen the news?"

She nodded, something unfathomable in her eyes. Was she sorry for me? "Not information you wanted the world to know, Ms Smythe?"

I gave her a latte, then sagged down into the chair opposite. "It's not true, you know. I mean my family members... my friends... who died. I had nothing to do with it." The last words came with a rush, as if—as usual—I was trying to convince myself.

"It is an unusual set of coincidences." Larsen's left eyebrow arched again. It seemed to have a life of its own.

"Call my family." But not Sarah. "They'll tell you."

"We have, Ms Smythe. We spoke to your sister and your Aunt Isobel."

My shoulders relaxed a little. Aunt Isobel—Izzy for short—was Dad's sister and one of my favourite people in the whole world. She was a smart, sassy, successful psychologist who worked in a partnership with her husband in a high-profile practice in Brisbane. She would have set the police straight.

Larsen continued. "Your aunt made it very clear that the Ruthless-the-Killer thing was, in her words, a 'load of rot' and typical of childhood teasing gone wrong. Is that what happened? I'd like to hear how you got the reputation, in your own words."

She waited as I reached inside me for composure. I was a grown woman, thirty years old. Why did this hurt so much?

I took a deep breath then let out my words with a whoosh, telling her about my demented family. "It started when I was a little kid. Mum took my sister Sarah and I to the zoo. I was about six years old, and Sarah was seven and a half. I was naughty and threw my hat into the meerkat pen. A keeper had to go in and retrieve it. The next day I heard Mum talking to her friend Daisy, saying that Sarah was such a good girl, but I was the bad child. Then a week or so later my cousin Karl—he loved tormenting people—said his school trip to the zoo was cancelled because some of the meerkats had died of stress. His obvious implication was that I had killed them."

I blinked back tears and swallowed hard.

"The kids at school all called me Ruthless-the-Meerkat-Killer. No one would come near me as I had 'death-germs'. We soon found out the meerkats were fine, but kids never let the truth get in the way of a good excuse to torture their schoolmates."

Larsen nodded. "True."

"The name morphed to Ruthless-the-Killer. Then Grandpa had a fall after he'd taken Sarah and me yabbying. The steps back up from the beach were slimy and he slipped as he reached back to help me up. He broke his hip. He was supposed to be okay, but he got a blood clot after surgery and died. Mum blamed me, especially when Grandma died six months later from what Mum said was a broken heart."

Larsen winced.

"Then there was my friend Cathy. I thought I'd done something bad to her when I hit her with a softball, but it was hepatitis that killed her. And Mrs J—our neighbour—died of a heart attack. I was there but couldn't save her."

"Your aunt said you left home after your mother died."

I told her what I'd told Dan. "We had a fight and later that day she had a stroke. Dad withdrew. I thought he blamed me for Mum's death. I thought everyone blamed me." I shrugged. "The Ruthless-the-Killer thing became larger than life."

"So you went to Europe and never came back. Why?"

"Aunt Izzy, I mean Isobel, didn't tell you?"

"No, she said it was to do with your sister and I should ask you."

I hesitated a moment, then told her what I'd told Dan about how Sarah blocked all contact between me and my family. "I think she wanted all Dad's love for herself and to punish me for Mum's death." I shot her a wan smile. "I guess once Sarah started, she couldn't easily stop."

Larsen winced again. Maybe she had a heart after all.

I looked the detective in the eye and told her about the letters Dad had sent me. "He died thinking I'd rejected him completely."

"I'm sorry, Ms Smythe. That must have been painful. But…" She frowned. "You also changed your name twice. That wouldn't have helped people stay in contact with you."

I bit my lip and tried not to give an embarrassed laugh. "I did that to… avoid certain people."

"You mean the family of your fiancé who disappeared?"

I caught my breath. I should have expected Larsen to be thorough.

"We've spoken with Interpol," she said. "We know about the Mafia connection."

There was a small, strangled snort behind us. Dan stood at the door with an electric drill in one hand, a roll of wiring in the other, and a gazillion questions in his eyes. "Mafia?" The word squeaked out of him.

I thought Lydia Larsen's eyebrows were going to crawl off her face when she saw him.

"Lydia." He nodded in her direction, his voice resuming its regular deep and resonant programming.

I jumped in. "I… er… Dan is putting in a security system for me."

"I can see that." Larsen's eyebrows had returned to normal, but her eyes narrowed, and her voice was edged with something else. Jealousy? I did not need that.

"I just wanted to tell Ruth I'm done here for now." He turned to me. "What time is it tonight again?"

"Tonight?" asked Larsen.

"I invited Dan to dinner tonight to… um… say thank you. Shona and Joe are coming too." I rushed the words, wishing my floor had a trapdoor and a basement I could hide in.

"Is that dinner?" Larsen grimaced in the direction of the battered beef Wellington, sitting limp and bruised on the bench. A blowfly buzzed in circles above the meat, then landed right on top.

We all gazed at the sorry piece of repeatedly stabbed beef. I attempted an upbeat smile. "Maybe we should have pizza instead?"

I sat with Larsen in my living room, well away from the kitchen disaster zone. Dan had wasted no time in disappearing and she wanted to ask more questions.

"I'd like to explore this Mafia connection further."

"There is no Mafia connection. Not with me, anyway. I had no idea that Paulo had a Family connection. Not until after he disappeared."

"Did you blame yourself when he disappeared?"

"Not when I found out he'd been two-timing me with the daughter of a rival drug lord."

Larsen shot me a meaningful look. "Some would think unfaithfulness is a good motive for murder."

"I had no idea until afterwards. The police confirmed that. He'd swindled another family in a financial deal, too." I locked eyes with her. "As you would know."

"I only know what people tell me, Ms Smythe. Whether it's true or not is another thing entirely." She paused. "Why did you change your name?"

"I didn't want to end up at the bottom of a river or buried under concrete, too."

"They never found the body. Why do you think he's there?"

"Because that's what both the Polizia and Carabinieri said. That's what his family do to people they don't want around anymore. The investigating officer suggested I leave Italy and lie low for a while."

"But you changed your name back again?"

"It had been a few years. I hadn't swindled anyone, and I figured I wouldn't be worth the trouble to either of the families. I'd already decided to come back to Australia before Dad died. I wanted to return from exile and face my demons—in every way. To do that I needed to be Ruth Smythe again. But I was too late." I blinked back tears. "Dad died before I got here. I lost my chance."

Larsen sat still for a long time. I wanted to say more—to fill the space with words—but I kept silent. Why give her more ammunition?

"Your sister said some intellectual property has disappeared from your father's business in Brisbane. Do you know anything about that?"

"I'll tell you what I told Sarah. I have no idea."

Larsen went silent again, as if willing me to say more. "One more thing, Ms Smythe. You said that Rossi had asked to see you at his office on Monday morning. You still can't think why?"

I shook my head.

"We discovered something today." She paused, as if for dramatic effect. "Are you aware that before he died, your father hired Aldon Rossi to find you?"

# Chapter Nineteen

Thoughts buzzed through my head like blowflies around a barbecue. I'd consigned the beef Wellington to the fridge in case Dan would like to give it to Frank, then driven back into town to get some pizza ingredients. I'd make the beef Wellington another time.

Larsen's news was perplexing. Why had Dad asked Rossi to find me, and why was Rossi in my shed when he died? There was no easy answer to either question, but they had to be related… didn't they?

I'd told Larsen about the open crate in my shed, but all she did was write copious notes on her tablet and say nothing.

I huffed out a sigh, and consigned the mystery to the shelf in my mind where I kept puzzles that had no answer. My focus right now was on dinner.

I could have ordered in, but I wanted to do better than that. There wasn't much time, so I needed to make something easy and yummy. Italian gourmet pizza, served with salad, was simple and delicious.

I parked my Mini and began striding down Main Street,

on a mission to find the freshest ingredients this town could offer. Despite the visit from Larsen and the culinary stabbing debacle, I was looking forward to tonight.

Shona and Joe had been good to me. And Dan… If I was totally honest with myself, the thought of seeing him this evening gave me a warm, chocolate-brownie glow. But as I didn't like to be that honest, I shoved that thought back onto the mental shelf next to the Rossi mystery and set off down the street.

It was a gusty day, and it only took a moment for any inner warmth to be blown away. My exposure on national news sites had borne fruit. It was even worse than the other day.

Len, the butcher, ducked back into his shop as soon as he saw me. When I passed a group of people enjoying cake at an alfresco café, their laughter dissolved into silence, every eye fastened on me as I walked by. Three teenagers drinking cola gave me a wide berth as they swept past. I heard a giggle and turned to see one girl looking back over her shoulder at me, running her finger across her throat in a slicing motion.

There weren't any little kids, which was just as well, or I wouldn't have held it together.

I headed into a pizzeria. Joe's friend Nick sold pre-rested pizza dough and I'd rung to ask him to put some aside for me. It was the best in town—much better than the stuff you could buy in the supermarket. Nick was normally chatty and fun, but today he was silent and gave me a suspicious look, as if I was going to suddenly shapeshift into a werewolf and eat him.

*I don't belong here anymore.*

The thought took the strength from my legs, the breath from my lungs and the hope from my heart. What was I going to do? I thought I'd found my home here in this sleepy small town, but my past had followed me.

I went to other stores, bought some of the ingredients I needed, and finished shopping for veggies at the greengrocers. The old Italian nonna who ran the store gave me a welcoming nod.

"Molte grazie," I said, when I paid at the checkout. *Many thanks.*

"Prego, caro." Her warm, wrinkled smile echoed her words. *You're welcome, dear.*

I knew her reception might be different when she saw the news tonight, but her words made my eyes burn. She clasped my hand. Her grip was strong, and her fingers cool and leathery, but her gaze blazed with kindness.

"It will be okay," she said in thickly accented English.

I stammered, "Grazie," and fled back to the car before anyone could see me cry.


A couple of hours later, my eyes were stinging for a different reason—onions. I hated peeling onions, even the salad ones which weren't as strong.

There was only forty-five minutes before my guests were due to arrive. I stowed everything in the fridge and was heading to the bathroom to repair my makeup when the front doorbell rang.

My heart gave a small jolt. Not many people used the front door. My driveway curved around to the back of the house, so people mostly came in through either the back door, or the side patio door that led into the dining room and kitchen. Dan had rigged up cameras at each entrance so I could see who was outside. I could either use the small panel on the wall or the feed on my laptop. The laptop was closer, and when I opened it, I burst out laughing. A large koala stood at the door, waving up at my CCTV camera.

I opened the door to my friends.

The koala squeezed through the hallway then pirouetted into the living room. "Surprise!" The muffled voice came from deep within the costume. "What do you think?" The koala took off its head and revealed a ruffled-looking Shona.

A laugh guffawed out of me. "I think it's amazing—and so are you. Is this for Saturday's acting job?"

"Acting?" Joe muttered and rolled his eyes, but they still held a sparkle.

"Cool, huh?" said Shona. "We came in by the front door so I could make more of an entrance."

I hugged her hard, fake fur and all. "Thank you." I pulled back and wiped the laughter-tears away. "I mean it. It's been a hell of a day." I stepped back and gestured to the koala suit. "This. Is. Brilliant."

"See?" Shona beamed at Joe. "I'm an entertainer. Lifting people up is my superpower. I can even do it in a koala suit."

For some weird reason that made me snort three times and giggle so hard I had to lean against the wall for support. I loved my friend.

Joe grinned and handed me a large container when I'd recovered enough to breathe. "Dessert," he said.

I lifted the lid to see a black forest cake. "Yum." It was going to be carb central tonight. Exactly what I needed. "This is *your* superpower," I said to him.

"Hang on," said Shona. "Let me get the whiteboard inside."

"Whiteboard?"

I stared as a koala-clad Shona jogged down my front path to a huge, wheeled whiteboard. She dragged it into the house and manoeuvred it into my living room.

I could only get one syllable out. "Why?" I pointed to the board.

Joe shrugged and pointed at Shona. "It was her idea."

"All investigators need a whiteboard." She beamed her sunshine at me then raised up a handbag. "I've brought whiteboard pens too. And some spare magnets. I'll put them on your sofa for now?"

I nodded silently. There was no point arguing. She was obviously pleased with herself. She sidled over and nudged me. "Come on, we both need to freshen up and change." Her eyes twinkled. "Dan will be here soon, and you can't invite him in looking like that!"

I opened my mouth to argue, but before I could say anything, she hooked her arm through mine and towed me towards the bathroom.

# Chapter Twenty

I had to admit I was having fun. Shona had turned up with a koala outfit and a whiteboard. Joe turned up with dessert and a wry smile at the antics of his fiancée. Then Dan arrived with some local red wine and his trademark charm.

They were sympathetic when I told them about Sarah's phone call, but they fell about in hysterics when I recounted the events surrounding Larsen's visit.

"Let me get this straight. You were stabbing the meat when Lydia arrived?" Dan had tears in his eyes and was desperately trying to hold it together.

"No… and yes. Sort of. I'd stabbed the meat again and again after Sarah's call, but the knife got stuck in the block. I had to use all my strength to pull it out and it ended up like this." I held my knife high above my head, as if I was going to plunge it into another victim. "She walked in right then."

That brought another round of laughter. Shona got the hiccups and had to rush and get a glass of water.

"You're lucky she didn't taser you." Dan's eyes danced. "Great control on Lydia's part."

"I did see her trigger finger twitch."

Joe raised his glass of wine. "In memory of beef Wellington. May it rest in peace."

I turned to Dan. "I kept the meat in the fridge. You can take it if you think Frank would like it. It's a bit beyond human consumption."

"Thanks—but I saw it on your bench. Frank's fussy. He might not like meat that's the product of crime."

It was Joe's turn to snort and Shona's hiccups started again. When they recovered, Joe took another slice of pizza. "This is great, by the way," he said, with a half-full mouth. "I'm impressed."

"Thanks. Coming from you, that's high praise."

"I agree," said Dan. "I haven't tasted flavours like that since I was in Naples."

I was surprised. "You were in Italy?"

He nodded. "Rome. Milan. Venice. Parts of Tuscany. Naples. Sorrento. Amalfi. I've had a few security contracts in Europe."

"The south is beautiful, isn't it? I lived just outside of Amalfi for two years after I left Rome."

"Have you walked Positano's thousand steps?" he asked.

"Several times."

"Up or down?"

"Ha! Down mainly. Up once. I gather you have? And the Walk of the Gods?" I asked.

Dan pulled out his mobile phone, searched his photos and showed one to Shona and Joe. "Breathtaking views up there."

Shona sighed. "You're making me jealous."

I beamed at her. "Italy is beautiful, but our beaches are better." I lifted my glass and took a sip of the smoky shiraz. "As is our wine."

"You're right there." Dan raised his glass and clinked it with mine. "But the Italians wouldn't agree." He turned to Shona and Joe. "You two should go there for your honeymoon."

Joe shifted in his seat and muttered something about being incredibly busy.

Shona shook her copper-coloured curls and for once her smile didn't reach her eyes. "We haven't set a date yet." Her voice was a half-tone off.

I hadn't realised this was an issue for her and I made a mental note to talk to her about it later.

Dan nodded then turned to me. "So, what's this about the Mafia? And a dead fiancé?" Intense curiosity flickered in his eyes.

"Mafia? What Mafia?" Shona's breath caught. "Paulo was in the Mafia?"

"I… Paulo's family were… are."

"You never told me! Why didn't you tell me?"

I shot a look at Dan, who didn't look the least bit apologetic. His gaze was open and expectant as he waited for my answer. I groaned inwardly. Shona wouldn't let me not tell now.

I turned to her. "I told you about Paulo disappearing and the police assuming he was dead, but I couldn't tell anyone about the other bit. Not then. I didn't know if his family were going to come after me so I had to keep things as quiet as I could."

"Is that why you changed your name?" Shona asked. "I knew he'd disappeared and that something had scared you."

I took a deep breath and nodded. "I nearly came home to Australia then." I paused. "I wish I had. I would have seen Dad and discovered Sarah's sabotage. But I moved to France, then England. I guess they could have found me if they'd really wanted to, but I obviously wasn't that important to them."

"Thank God you weren't." Dan's voice held real concern.

"What happened to Paulo?" Shona interjected.

I told her what I'd told Larsen. "As you know, he went missing. I looked for him for weeks but there was no sign. Eventually the Carabinieri said they had intel his Mafia connections had disposed of him. But they never found the body."

"That must have been hard." Dan's gaze was steady and his voice warm.

"It was, but less so when I found out he was two-timing me with the daughter of a member of a different Mafia family."

Dan made a face.

"And someone killed him for it." Joe whistled out his breath. "That sucks."

"I can see how that wouldn't look good to Lydia," Dan said with a half-chuckle. "But the Interpol report satisfied her?"

"It was pretty conclusive that he died at the hand of the Family." I sighed.

Shona rested her hand on my arm. "I'm sorry."

"It was awful." I swallowed hard, remembering. "I was scared at the time—and heartbroken—but now I'm just annoyed that I gave up my job to go off with him."

"What was your job?" Dan asked.

"Archaeology. I studied at the University of Rome and worked part-time on a dig."

"I didn't know you were an archaeologist." His tone said he was impressed.

"I'd need to do my PhD before I could really call myself that. Or have a hope of getting a decent research job."

Joe leaned forward, his eyes flashing with interest. "Would you? Do more study? Is the same course offered here?"

"I don't know." I shook my head. "That was a few years ago now. I'm not sure if it's still my passion. And the focus in Australia is more on indigenous culture. My speciality, if you can call it that, was Greco-Roman archaeology." I bit back the deep sigh that welled up whenever I thought about my future.

"Do you still write for that magazine sometimes?" Shona offered a supportive smile.

"Not much now." I turned to the others. "The mag is called *Roaming the Ruins*. It's an archaeological magazine for ordinary people. Have you heard of it?"

Everyone looked blank.

I laughed. "That's the usual response I get."

"Could you do it again?" Shona suggested. "It could bring in some income."

"I should look into it." I couldn't keep the lack of enthusiasm out of my voice. "But I'm away from all the action here in Pelican Bay."

"Well, I'm glad you're here," she said.

"I hope I can stay."

"What do you mean?" Joe asked.

I told them all what had happened when I went into town that afternoon. "It's getting worse. I came here to make a fresh start. How can I stay if everyone hates me?"

Shona's eyes moistened. "They don't hate you. They're just scared because someone was murdered, and they've got no one to blame." She squeezed my arm as if to urge me on. "You said the other day that if we could find Rossi's killer, they'd stop blaming you."

Dan frowned. "Find Rossi's killer?" His voice had an edge.

"Yes." Shona laid both hands firmly on the table and pressed herself up. "One minute they're saying it's Joe. The next it's Paul Farrow. And now the town thinks Ruth is a killer." She swung towards me. "A few days ago, you told me that you loved it here. That's still true, isn't it?"

"Yes, but that was before—"

"You need to fight this, Ruth. Your dad grew up here. This is your home." She sank back down into her chair. "Do you want to leave?" Her voice was hollow.

I lifted my eyes to hers. "I want to stay."

"Okay, then. Woman-up. You're the investigator. Help us investigate." She turned to the men. "Joe, it's time for dessert. Ruth, let's make tea and coffee. Dan, head to the living room."

Amusement danced in Dan's eyes as he glanced at Joe and gestured towards Shona. "Is she always so bossy?"

"Yep." Joe's grin said he wouldn't have it any other way.

By the time the evening was over we'd consumed copious amounts of cake and talked through everything we knew about what had happened on the night Aldon Rossi died. I managed to avoid using the whiteboard myself. I asked the questions and Shona acted as scribe and wrote down every-thing. We must have been on sugar highs because it only took us five minutes to gather the names of everyone on the guest list that night. Whoever took Joe's knife must have been at that party. We also mapped out the motives and alibis—the ones we knew, anyway.

Dan rubbed his chin, as if deep in thought, and stretched his other arm along the back of the sofa next to me. He was far enough away that he didn't touch me, but his presence was disconcerting, his long legs and well-fitting jeans making it hard to focus. Then he raised his hand and we all stopped to listen.

"I wasn't there, okay. But from what you've said there was a room full of people who could have stolen the knife. Only the police can sift through all their stories."

I nodded. "True."

"So, I don't want to put a dampener on everything, but what's the point of doing this? Lydia's no fool—she's a good cop. I don't think she'd arrest the wrong person. And you don't have access to all the information."

He leaned forward, palms upward and open, and turned to me. "A man has died, in your back shed. You need to be careful, Ruth. You can't mess around with this stuff. What if the killer comes back?" His blue eyes, which usually twinkled with humour, were shadowed with concern.

"She's got a state-of-the-art security system now," Shona said.

Dan acknowledged that with a half-smile, but then his face became serious again. "No security system is perfect. A determined person who knows what they're doing could get around it."

The first sensation was the cold that prickled over my arms and my back. The second was the feeling—somewhere between curiosity, determination and desperation—that ignited in my belly and flamed hot in my chest.

"I didn't want to do this either, but the police have limited resources and sometimes someone will say something to a regular person that they won't to a cop. It's worth a try. And Larsen might get to the right answer, but it could take a long time. In the meantime, there's a shadow over good people." I glanced at Joe, then Shona. "And there's still a murderer out there somewhere. It's not lost on me that Rossi was killed in *my* shed. I didn't kill him, but why was he here? Was the killer looking for me?"

My heart fluttered, my fists tightened and my voice held

the smallest quiver. "I don't want to leave, but the only way to stay is to find out what's going on. If I can show that I had nothing to do with Rossi's death, then maybe I'll be accepted again."

Everyone sat silently, all eyes on me. It wasn't as simple as that. Small towns could be fickle, and my reputation could stick. But I was so, so, so tired of running, of always moving on to something else. I had to take a stand. I had to try.

"Okay." Dan nodded. "I get it. But don't do anything stupid. Don't put yourself in dangerous situations, and if you get into even a hint of trouble, call me." He must have seen my hesitation. "I mean it." He turned to Shona. "Both of you." A half-smile played on his lips. "It's what I do for a living. Keep people out of trouble."

Joe coughed into his hand, and I heard a faint, "Good luck with that."

A little later, everyone rose to leave. Joe turned to me. "So, lady detective, what's on the agenda for tomorrow?"

"I've just had a thought." Shona hit her forehead with the heel of her hand. "Why didn't I think of this before? Kat Mackenzie did some work for Aldon Rossi. She'd be a great place to start." She turned to me. "She's a computer… er… expert. I'll give you her number. I can't go because Bridget has a day off tomorrow."

"But what if she won't talk to me? What if she thinks I'm cursed? Or a murderer?"

The men grinned at each other.

"What?" I asked.

"I think that would make her like you more," Joe said.

"I hope you like cats," Dan murmured.

Before I could ask why, Shona lunged in and hugged me. "I'm glad you want to stay."

I hugged her back, hard, then hugged Joe. Then I turned to Dan, hesitating for a moment. Amusement flickered in his eyes, then he bent over and gave me a soft, chaste kiss on the cheek.

"Thanks for dinner, Ruth."

"You're welcome." I kept my voice light, but the warmth of his lips, the brush of his stubbled cheek on mine and the tingle of his breath on my skin gave me thoughts that were the opposite of chaste.

Dan was right in what he said earlier. I needed to take care—but in more ways than one.

# Chapter Twenty-One

I wasn't sure what to expect when I walked up to Kat Mackenzie's door, but a young woman yanked the door open before I could knock. She had dyed black hair, dark brown eyes rimmed with dark eyeliner, and pale makeup, and she wore a long black dress covered with silver and white ghost kittens.

"Kat?" I'd seen her before at Dan's self-defence class, but that had been from a distance.

"Do people really die around you?" Her abrupt words took me aback.

"I… um… no."

Her face fell, but she just shrugged her shoulders and asked me to follow her inside.

A tabby and white cat wove its way around my ankles as I sidled into her hallway. Shona had mentioned cats, but the spicy waft of several felines in one small home hit me hard as I entered.

According to Shona, Kat was some kind of child prodigy

computer genius with a dysfunctional family life. She had two loves—computers and cats—and they'd combined to get her expelled from three high schools. The last time was two years ago, when she hacked into the school's online portal and set every person's image to a different type of cat. It might have gone down as a prank except she'd somehow also managed to alter the principal's Zoom account so that he appeared as an old, manky Persian cat in an important online meeting.

Kat was expelled again and initially charged with hacking, but Gary Stone had stepped in and got her into a youth rehabilitation program that was linked with the AFP. She did some supervised community work and helped a small network of private schools strengthen their IT security. They hadn't had a problem with data theft or online cheating since.

Kat was currently studying some high-level computer degree, and she was employed by the schools part-time. Rumour had it that the Australian Signals Directorate was courting her to come work for them after uni. But right now, all her money and focus went to her other passion: rescuing stray cats.

Now she ushered me into a tiny living room where a large white cat with no ears lounged on the sofa.

She gently lifted the big feline off the seat. "You can sit here." She brushed white fur from the cushion and gestured for me to sit. I relaxed onto the sofa, hoping I was meeting expectations so far. "He's not a Scottish Fold, he had skin cancer on his ears."

"Oh! Poor boy."

"You like cats?"

Shona had told me Kat would ask that question and I was to say yes, even if it meant lying through my teeth. Kat would accept me if I was a harbinger of death, but she'd have nothing to do with me if I didn't like cats. Fortunately, I liked all animals, although I was more of a dog person.

I nodded, smiling, as a young grey and white puss dived onto my shoelaces. "He's cute." The kitten purred and shimmied up my jeans leg to settle on my lap. His small claws kneaded my jeans and I rubbed his soft, pink ears.

Kat's smile was radiant, as if she was purring, too.

I'd passed the first test.

"On the phone I said I wanted to talk to you about Rossi. You worked for him?" I asked Kat.

She nodded but then was distracted by a loud yowl coming from the next room. "I'll be back in a sec."

There was some hissing and spitting and then she walked through holding a half-grown, sandy and white cat with grey flecks through its fur. The cat took one look at me and wiggled out of Kat's arms and dashed through the house.

"I guess some days you just don't want to be hugged," I offered.

Kat sat back down. "She's shy today—part moggy, part British shorthair."

"She's lovely. So is this little lad." The kitten had stretched out on my lap, belly up to the world, displaying his crown jewels for all to see. "He knows how to relax."

Kat reached over and tickled his belly and he stretched out even more before curling up and making a half-hearted grab at Kat's hand.

"About Rossi…" I began.

"My rescue cats need homes." Kat gave me a meaningful look. "Do you have any pets?"

I smiled and shook my head. "Not yet. I will when I get properly settled."

"Every house needs a cat."

I recognised the danger. "Um… I'm not really ready."

Kat frowned. "When people say that, it means they don't like cats."

The kitten started purring again and threw his head against my hand so I could rub his ears.

"But I can see that you like cats. And Bernie likes you."

"Bernie, is it?" I tickled the kitten behind the ears, then looked up at Kat again. "Can I ask you about Rossi?"

"I worked for him."

"Yes, Shona told me."

"And I did some online searches for him that might not have been totally legal."

"Okay. Right." How should I respond to that? "I promise I won't tell anyone..." My voice trailed off.

"I have a price for the information."

"Price?" My insides twisted. I had no money.

She looked meaningfully first at Bernie then at the big white cat with no ears. "Will you take a cat?"

"What?" I bit back a laugh. "You're serious?"

"Will you adopt one of my cats? I rescue them and find them homes."

The world had become absurd. A goth computer expert was telling me that the price for information she might have was... cat adoption? I felt as if I'd fallen inside Alice's looking glass—a bizarre Cheshire-cat-centred universe where a dozen evil-eyed felines sat winking at me with grins on their faces, yowling, "Take me home!"

"Let me get this straight. Your price for telling me what you know is to... adopt a cat?" It felt totally weird saying that sentence out loud.

She regarded me with pleading eyes. "They all need *good* homes. Please say yes."

I eyed her carefully. She was serious. I looked down at the

ball of fluff on my lap as my brain tried to catch up with the situation.

"What if I make a bad cat owner?"

"You won't make a bad owner. Please. I can't afford to feed them all and people bring them, and I can't turn them away. See old Fluff over there?" Kat pointed to an ancient-looking ball of scrawny ginger fur sitting on a chair near the window. The cat's long, pointy canine teeth jutted out from his bottom jaw at weird angles. "He has bad teeth, but his kidneys are messed up. He needs an anaesthetic to take the teeth out, but he needs fluids and other special treatment. And now Rossi's dead, I don't get paid."

"I'm sure Elouise can cover the wages you're owed."

"But I didn't finish. I was relying on at least three weeks more work so I could pay for his procedure." She picked up the old ginger fluff-ball and lay her face against his. The cat purred and nuzzled her back.

"I might not be staying," I confessed. "In Pelican Bay, I mean. It could be hard to have a cat if I'm on the move."

"Is that because people think you cursed Rossi?"

"I… yeah."

"If you take a cat, I'll help you find out who killed him and clear your name. Then you can stay. Please—you'd be a great cat owner. I can tell."

I glanced down at the kitten on my lap. Bernie was pretty cute. He'd curled up in a ball, his pink nose now hidden by his fluffy tail. Maybe it was my dormant maternal instincts, but I had a sudden yearning to have a cute little fluff-ball to cuddle up with on a cold night. Or to help keep the rats down in the sheds.

But mostly it was the dual realisation I'd do almost anything to stay here in Pelican Bay and to belong again. And

Kat wasn't going to give me any information until I agreed to her… blackmail.

Against my better judgement I said, "Okay. I'll take h—"

Before I could finish, she launched herself towards me and hugged me. The small cat jumped from my lap and capered off through the house.

"Now," she said. "Come and see what I know."

# Chapter Twenty-Two

I stood behind Kat, gazing over her shoulder at the information on the screen.

"Just about everyone was on Rossi's radar." Her fingers danced over the keyboard as she spoke. "The big players were the Farrows and Xavier Kingston. There was also Rossi's wife, his... er... mistress, and... um..." Her eyes flicked up to me. "You."

"Because of my dad, right? Larsen mentioned he brought Rossi on to find me."

"There's a massive file on you from before my time."

"Have you read it?"

"Me? No way." But her eyes dodged mine as her fingers became a blur on the keyboard.

"What did it say?"

A hint of a smile touched her lips. "Sorry."

I figured hackers lived on curiosity. And I'm not sure I could resist digging into people's secrets either, but knowing she'd sifted through my life made me feel exposed.

"Was there anything in there about why Rossi might have been in my shed?" That was the biggest mystery.

"Nothing I've seen that's conclusive." Her tone said there was more to the story.

"But?"

"He might have been looking for something."

"Looking for what?"

She flicked open a file on her screen and pointed.

"About six months ago your dad asked Rossi to find you. There was a flurry of emails. You were in Europe then?"

"England. My sister was Dad's PA and IT expert. She cut off all contact and fed him and my family all the wrong information so they couldn't reach me. She even spoofed emails."

Kat's face twisted in sympathy. "That's brutal."

"Tell me about it." My voice dripped with sarcasm.

Her eyes scanned the screen. "Did you know that your dad and Rossi knew each other when they were kids?"

"Rossi and Elouise said they knew him when I spoke with them at the dinner."

"Not long before he died?"

I nodded. "He asked me to see him in his office on Monday, but I don't think it was about that."

Kat tapped the keys again. I waited, jiggling my leg, half holding my breath.

"Looks like Rossi found out your sis was messing with your emails. Your dad was super stressed."

I leaned in, reading the email flurry over Kat's shoulder. This all happened a week before Dad's heart gave out. My fingers curled into fists so tight that my nails dug hard into the into the flesh of my hands. Did he confront Sarah? Did the stress cause his heart attack?

Kat stopped typing and her face creased into a frown.

"Rossi kept the file on you open. There's detail here on your move to South Australia, and about your inheritance."

A wave of cold seeped through my bones. "Exactly when did Rossi and Elouise come back to Pelican Bay?"

"About six months ago. Around the time your dad asked him to find you." Kat typed some more. "Something went missing from your dad's estate?"

"That's what my sister said."

"You don't have whatever it is?"

I shook my head. Even if I did, I didn't know Kat well enough to talk about this.

"Could he have been looking for it?" she asked.

"I don't know why. I have nothing of Dad's other than his old house." And the sense that he was still with me.

I ran my hands through my hair. Very little of this made sense. I needed to know who Rossi was investigating. Did the fact that he was looking for something I might have, make me more of a suspect in the eyes of the police?

"There's more." Kat hesitated. "Rossi was getting threats."

I straightened. "Death threats?"

She nodded. "The first ones were emails from an untraceable source."

"How can emails be untraceable?"

"You'd be surprised at what can be done with VPNs and the latest tech. Look at what your sister managed with you. Even I couldn't find their source. Then the written notes began arriving."

"What did they say?"

She showed me a photo on her phone. It was like one of those creepy cut-and-paste letters you see in the movies. "The emails were similar. They knew what he'd done, and he was going to pay."

"He didn't go to the police?"

"I think he thought he could handle it himself. He was an experienced investigator—and he wasn't exactly honest. He didn't want the cops getting too close to his activities. But he either underestimated his assailant's ability or overestimated his own."

"Do the police have these letters now?"

Kat nodded. "I did take photos of them. When I couldn't find out where the emails came from, Rossi had me do research on various people who'd lived in the town for years."

"What kind of research?"

She glanced around the room, as if someone could be listening. "Hacking. All the people I mentioned above... and you."

"Because of this stuff with Dad?"

She shrugged. "Nearly everyone else had known Rossi for years."

I shifted on my feet.

"Then there was the cyber-attack. It was one of the reasons Rossi took me on. I locked down his security, but it was too late. It's possible some information is missing—deleted."

"Did they get the information about me?" I felt as if I was having one of those dreams where you're walking around naked and can't do anything about it.

"Possibly, if that was what they were after." She pursed her lips.

"Bloody hell." My back ached, and a wave of weariness turned my legs to spaghetti. I sank onto a fluff-covered chair beside Kat. It was bad enough that some creep-o could know all this stuff about me, but it also left me wide open to identity theft. Rossi had details as personal as my UK driver's license. But discussing this with the police wasn't an option without revealing how I knew about it.

Crappity, crap, crap, crap.

"The hacker could have accessed any of the information Rossi had," Kat continued. "But the stuff I found later is safe. I told Rossi what I discovered, but the only copy is on my servers. I didn't want my skills being discovered."

"So… the police know Rossi was checking out people in this town, including me. They know he was sent threatening letters, but they don't know about your research." I used air quotes to emphasise the last word.

"Correct. They don't know I cloned Rossi's drive and they, um… don't know I hacked into people's email, or else they'd be on my doorstep with a warrant." She shot me a meaningful look. "I want to keep it that way."

Then she abruptly changed tack.

"I like your social media. You'll make a great pet parent. You share lots of dog and cat vids, so you must like animals."

There were no words, so I smiled sweetly at Kat and moved on.

Kat pressed onwards. "I did find a hidden, encrypted file on Rossi's drive, but it's locked down tight. The hacker might have used it as a vault for more documents. Stashed the files as they found them and planned to swing back later to download them when it's safe."

"Could the police crack the encryption?"

"They have the people and the equipment, but it could take a while." Her eyes lit up. "But I bet I'm faster."

"The data you found—the emails. Can I have them?"

She squirmed in her seat. "I can't give them to you. I told the police I worked as a researcher for Rossi—and I did—but they can't know I did some hacking too. I've covered my tracks online, but I can't share the evidence. I can't go to jail. My cats need me."

As if on cue, the large white, earless cat sauntered into the room and claimed Kat's lap as his own. She indulged him with a chin scratch, and he rumbled a deep, contented purr.

I was ready to beg. "Once I look, I'm guilty too, right? Invasion of privacy. I'm in this with you. I need to find out who did this."

There was a long pause as Kat stared, deep in thought, at some point on the wall, then a small smile formed on her lips. "Will you take two cats?"

# Chapter Twenty-Three

I managed to convince Kat that I only could cope with one pet for now, as I was still renovating the house. To my relief, she agreed. But she still wouldn't give me the hacked files. It was too dangerous.

"I promise I'll look and let you know if I find anything," she said.

I rubbed my hands over my face as the energy drained out of me. "Can't I help?"

She lifted an eyebrow. "You'd only slow things down."

"But—"

"Look, I have to do some uni stuff now. Come back tonight. If you buy me pizza, we can work on this. I'll show you anything I see that seems important, and you can say if it is or not. Deal?"

After last night I was all pizza-ed out, but desperate times called for desperate measures. "Okay."

"Could you get something to drink too? Cola or ginger ale?"

I laughed as I remembered my student days when a free

meal of junk food and cola was the highlight of my week. It wasn't that long ago really, but it felt like an eternity. "Sure."

Kat tapped away on the keyboard then she handed me a small USB stick. It was yellow and shaped like a cat. "I'll trust you with this. It's a copy of the threat letters and pictures I took of Rossi's desk appointment diary."

"Rossi kept a paper diary?"

"Yeah." She shrugged. "Old people." She pointed to the USB. "It's only a copy but keep it safe. If anyone finds out you have it, I'll say you stole it."

I laughed. "Okay. Thank you. One thing… I get that you don't want anyone to know you used your hacking skills. But what if we find out who the murderer is?"

She thought for a moment. "We'd need to find another way to prove they're guilty." Her sweet smile made her look younger and prettier. "Aldon Rossi wasn't the most honest man, but he was kind to me. I want to find his killer too."

I nodded, wrapping my fingers hard around the USB drive. At least it was *something*.

Kat's face lit up again. "Wait in your car. I'll go get your cat."

She returned a few minutes later with a large cardboard box, taped up, with holes punched in the side. My leg jiggled and my stomach clenched. Pet ownership was a major responsibility and I regularly killed house plants. Could I do this?

Blood rushed to my ears as Kat eased the box onto the front seat of my Mini. If I wanted her to help me, I didn't really have a choice. But if I was going to belong in this town, and be a responsible pet owner, I needed to solve this murder soon.

Kat ran back inside and returned carrying a beat-up looking litter tray, half a bag of cat litter, an old food dish and a couple of tins of cat food.

"Can I get these back in a few days? Not the food, but the other stuff. You can get most of what you need from the supermarket or pet shop."

"Sure," I said. "That's a big box for a tiny kitten."

She didn't answer, but pointed to the USB. "Remember. Don't tell anyone I gave it to you."

"Thank you for trusting me."

She was helping in more ways than I could imagine. I wasn't about to tell anyone.

I don't know when I first realised something was wrong. It might have been the louder than expected mewing from the box in my passenger seat. It might have been the violent scrambling coming from inside the box. But when I picked up the cat-in-the-box to take it inside, it was obvious that it wasn't Bernie.

My breath hitched. I'd spent the drive home getting my head around the fact that I was now a cat owner. Bernie had been so cute sitting on my lap that I'd convinced myself I needed a cute little boy cat to make my house a home. But the weight of the box as I carried it inside said this wasn't Bernie. Unless Kat had given me more than one cat after all.

My first thought was to drive straight back to her place and switch cats. But if I took the cat back, she might decide not to help me—or worse. With her skills, she wasn't exactly the best person to have as an enemy. Not if I wanted to have any kind of online life.

A plaintive, "Meow," echoed from inside the box. It couldn't be too bad, could it? Maybe Kat had given me the big white cat with no ears. He was sweet. Yet the box didn't feel heavy enough for that old boy.

I set the box down on my coffee table, had the presence of

mind to close all the windows and doors, then opened it a crack. All I could see were two huge eyes. At least there was just one set.

"Meow-ow-ow," the cat wailed.

I opened the box a crack more. Two yellow-green orbs sat in the shadow of the cat's sandy and white face. Kat had given me the British shorthair cross—and its pupils were wide with fear. "Oh, you poor darling."

I sat back on my haunches, biting back disappointment but trying to look on the bright side. This was still a young cat. I could bond with it and love it, right? A cat was a cat. They ate, slept, kept your property a rodent-free zone and curled up on your lap when watching television in the evening. All good.

I reached in to pat it, but the cat shot past me and shimmied up the curtains.

"Meow-ow-ow." It hung there, swinging, its claws fastened deep into the fabric. Then it scrambled further up onto the pelmet.

I pulled over a chair and reached up for the cat, but my ceilings were too tall. It was wearing a bright blue collar with the name 'Cora' written on the leather in thick black ink.

Cora. Cute name. A girl cat, then.

I called to her. "Cora, Cora, come down," but the poor thing edged further away.

"Puss, puss, puss! Come here, little one." I held out my hand, but Cora's you've-gotta-be-kidding-me look said no. I stepped back off the chair. "I'll guess you'll come down in good time."

It was then that I noticed the note in the box.

*Dear Ruth,*

*Thank you, thank you, thank you for adopting a cat. I've given you Cora, instead of Bernie, as she's the one most needing a forever home. She's gone to two homes before this, but they didn't work out. She needs somewhere now so she can learn to be a pet. Another month and it might be too late. She has a lovely purr and loves a cuddle, but keep your hands away from her if her pupils dilate.*

*Kat x*

*BTW she's called Cora because she's got a small, grey heart-shaped mark on her chest. You can name her whatever you want, but I think Cora suits her.*

I sat down on the sofa and watched my new little cat leap off the curtains with one loud, floorboard-shaking thud and dive under a chair on the other side of the room.

Cora needed time to adjust—I knew that—but why had her previous two attempts at adoption failed? And what happened when her pupils dilated?

I shifted in my seat.

"Meow-ow-ow!" Cora wailed from across the room. The tip of her tail flicked back and forth, peeking out from under the chair.

I rubbed my now sweaty palms on my jeans. What had I done?

Cora seemed happy hiding, so I nabbed my laptop and Kat's USB stick and sat down at the kitchen table. My stomach churned as a memory leaped out of nowhere. The last time I'd done any kind of computer-based investigating—if you could call it that—was when I'd worked for Bradley.

I'd met him when he asked for help from the museum where I was working, to identify some stolen Roman artefacts. I fell for him hard, and he persuaded me to leave the museum and come and work for him. You'd think I'd have learned after my experience with Paulo. Once again, I gave up everything for a guy, and once again, I was burned.

Heat rose in my face. Had I really been that gullible? I'd acted like a stupid, love-struck teenager and given up a good job on the promise that he'd train me to investigate art theft. He gave me some of that work—in a low-key way—but he told me I was hopeless at fieldwork, and I mainly got to do screeds of paperwork and make him coffee.

I realised he just wanted to keep me near so he could have sex on a whim.

But then he got bored. One night I dropped some paperwork at the office after hours and found my sleaze of a partner making out with a half-clothed Cassandra on his desk.

I may or may not have snuck back later and deleted some important files and poured red wine into his open laptop. I admit nothing.

I smirked at the memory, but then sobered. It was my pattern—fall too hard, then give up my life for some guy who then two-times me. Like I told Shona, I needed to find my own path before I looked for a man. That way if the relationship went south, I wouldn't lose everything.

I glanced around the room. There was no sign of Cora. I'd put her litter tray, food and water in the laundry where she could find them easily. I knew enough about cats to know you can't make them do anything, so I ignored her and focused on Rossi instead.

Curiosity bubbled through me as I brought up the images of the threats to Rossi on my screen. Working with Bradley had taught me that a PI can easily make enemies. Sometimes threats were just people venting, but it was too strong a coincidence to ignore.

Kat must have worked fast to take these photos after news

of Rossi's murder broke. Or had she already taken the images for her records?

From what I could read, Rossi had no idea who had sent the threats or why. But the images of the journal and note-book intrigued me. There were all kinds of notes and appoint-ments, and I only recognised some of the names. Rossi had dealings with lots of different people.

An entry in the diary dated five months prior, particularly intrigued me. A list of names and scribblings about threats were listed next to a doodle of a lightbulb.

*Elouise*

*Paul and Donna Farrow*

*Xavier Kingston*

*Rick Smythe*

Below the names, Rossi had written, *If so... why now?*

My heartbeat quickened as I sat back in my chair. What did my dead dad have to do with threats to Aldon Rossi's life?

# Chapter Twenty-Four

My brain raged in overdrive as I drove into town to get pizza for Kat. How could Dad have anything to do with this? He'd been dead for nearly four months. The diary entry was about a month before he died, but there were other notes after Dad passed, including a newspaper obituary that made a lump bigger than one of Joe's donuts form in my throat. How could Dad have been part of this if he was dead?

I stopped at a traffic light and scrunched my hands through my hair. Nothing made sense.

Who had threatened Rossi? They had to be the murderer, didn't they?

I tapped the steering wheel, waiting for the lights to change. At least it was now pizza o'clock and time to get some answers from Kat.

A wonderful aroma pervaded my little red Mini as I loaded in the takeaway pizzas. My digestive juices were turbocharged, but so was my anxiety, which made for a weird mix of simultaneous hunger and queasiness.

Shona had been jealous when I rang and told her how Kat was helping me.

"I want to be there," she'd said.

"Then come. Kat won't mind as long as we bring food."

"I've got theatre group tonight." I could hear the disappointment in her voice. "You have to tell me *everything*."

"Of course." Although I wasn't sure what to do if I found something that implicated Paul Farrow.

Anticipation churned as I put the Mini into gear. I needed answers and in my gut I knew that Kat could help. But then the phone rang.

"Sorry, I have to cancel," Kat said when I pulled over and answered. "Prof gave us a massive assignment and I'll need to keep working on it until late. I'll look at the files later and call you if I find anything." Her voice faltered—a slight hesitation. "How's Cora?"

"She was hiding under the bed when I left." I kept my tone light.

Another brief hesitation. "You're not mad?"

Honesty was best. "I was disappointed you didn't give me Bernie, but I'm sure Cora will come round."

The relief in her voice was palpable. "Thank you."

Her words warmed me. "Have you always loved cats?"

"When I was growing up, Mum and I rescued stray kittens."

"Sounds like a cool thing to do," I agreed.

"When she died, I had to stop. Dad didn't like it and took a litter away."

"To a shelter?"

"I'm not sure." Her voice took on a haunted tone. "But then I ran away and started rescuing cats again." Her sparkle returned. "It makes me think of Mum."

My eyeballs burned and were in danger of badly leaking. I

wanted to hug the girl. "That's a lovely way to remember her. She'd be proud of you."

I hadn't been close to my mum, but I was to Dad. Could I remember him by doing good, like Kat? Although she was a bit young to be a crazy cat lady—a nineteen-year-old *goth* crazy cat lady with a genius IQ. I liked her already.

Something bleep-bleeped in the background on her end. "Hey, I gotta go," she said. "Talk later. Promise."

And she hung up.

I looked down at the two large pizzas on my passenger seat. What was I going to do with all this food? Would Elouise like them? Bridget? I didn't know where the barista lived.

I was pondering this when I noticed a group of six teenagers hanging out in a rotunda in the small park across the road.

Could I?

Should I?

Would I?

The town hated me. These kids would scream and run a mile if they saw me. But what did I have to lose? Teens were always hungry, right? Especially boys. And people always underestimated kids. They saw stuff, but people hardly ever gave them credit for what they knew. It was worth a shot, so I picked up the pizzas and drinks, got out of the car and sauntered over to them.

A tall, fair boy of about sixteen—their leader?—squinted at me as I approached.

"What ya doing, grim reaper?"

My steps faltered. This was a hugely bad idea. I should go back *now* before I made more of an idiot of myself. But then I straightened and tried to still my breathing. This could work.

"Comin' to take us to hell?" a shorter, dark-haired kid snarked.

"Actually, I'm bringing you pizza."

I grinned at their open-mouthed astonishment. Their eyes regarded the boxes with both hunger and suspicion.

One girl whispered, "Is it poisoned?"

Her friend shook her head. "It could be cursed."

"I bought this to eat with a friend, but they cancelled on me, and I don't want it to go to waste."

I kept my voice casual despite the hundred million moths fluttering in my stomach. Butterflies were too pretty for what was going on in my gut.

I sat down in the rotunda, set the pizza boxes on the bench, and flipped open both lids. "Dig in."

The kids exchanged incredulous glances. When I was a teenager and out with friends, we wouldn't have turned down free pizza, unless it came from some creep. But would I have taken it from a proclaimed harbinger of death? And what stranger invaded a group of teens and sat with them?

I shrugged internally, held my head high and hoped these kids liked to live on the edge.

The leader licked his lips as he stared at the food. I could almost see his thoughts and digestive juices wrestling with each other.

"These guys do great pizza." I reached out for a piece.

"No!" he said.

I pulled back my hand.

He pointed to another piece. "Eat that bit."

I rolled my eyes. "I'm not trying to poison you."

"Eat," he said.

I shrugged, reached for the wedge of pizza he indicated, and took a large bite. "Mmmmm," I groaned as I wiped pizza juice from my chin with the back of my hand. "This is good."

The shorter dark-haired kid broke first. He pounced on a piece of the meat-lovers pizza and bit into it. When he didn't dissolve into smoke or start to sparkle in the leftover sunlight, the others dived in like starving seagulls.

"If we die," a red-haired girl said as she chewed, "we are totally haunting you."

I laughed. "Okay, but you know I'm a vampire?"

Another girl almost choked at my joke and her friends slapped her on the back until she caught her breath.

*Note to self. Don't kill any kids.*

I held up both hands in surrender. "Seriously, I'm not cursed, nor am I any form of undead. When I was a kid, my idiot cousin made up some stupid stuff and it stuck." If these kids really believed in my supposed curse, there was no way they'd be eating my pizza. "I'm Ruth, by the way."

It turned out that the fair-haired leader was Malcolm, the shorter dark-haired kid, was Seth, and the redhead was Caitlin. They all looked about sixteen. The other three hung back and didn't say who they were.

"So, if you're not cursed," said Seth, "why did that guy die in your shed?"

"I have no idea. That's what I'm trying to find out."

"You didn't kill him?"

I shook my head. "I'd just found out that Rossi went to the same school as my dad. I wanted to find out more about what Dad was like back then. Like when he was your age. I had no reason to kill him. The opposite, really."

The teens gave each other wide-eyed looks that said they'd never considered the possibility someone as old as me could have had a dad who was once their age. Kids liked to live in the moment.

I continued. "I was wondering if any of you saw anything strange happen the night Rossi died. The last time anyone saw him was right after the business bash." I grinned at them. "Or was that past your bedtime?"

Malcolm and Seth rose to that like the proverbial red rag to a bull. "We were around." Seth pointed to himself, then Malcolm. "Just hanging."

"See anything?" I tried to keep it casual and not pressure them. Let them tell their story.

Malcolm frowned, thinking. "Just that dairy farmer dude, heading down the road, looking pissed."

"Paul Farrow?"

Malcolm nodded.

"He was angry?" I asked.

"Yeah, and drunk."

"Did you see him get in a car?"

Both boys shook their heads.

"Rossi played golf with my dad sometimes, so I know what he looked like." Malcolm added. "Rossi argued with someone else—I couldn't see who it was—but then got in the car and drove away."

"The other person or Rossi drove away?"

"Rossi."

"Did anyone follow him?"

Malcolm shook his head. "Don't think so."

Seth elbowed his mate in the ribs. "There was that car that pulled out right after him, remember? It looked like they were in a hurry and they went in the same direction."

I leaned forward. "Did you see what kind of car it was?"

Seth shook his head. "It had those really bright, halogen headlights. Dad won't let me get a car with those 'cause he hates them. He says other drivers can't see properly."

"I don't suppose you know what time this was?" There was hope in my voice.

Their estimate set it around thirty minutes after I left the celebration.

"Thanks, that helps." Only a little, but I wanted to encourage them. Several avid eyes followed the bottles of cola and ginger ale I plonked onto the bench. "Would you be willing to tell Larsen—the tall, blonde woman cop—what you told me?"

Malcolm grinned and elbowed Seth in the ribs. "Seth will."

The dark-haired boy's face flamed. It looked like Legs-to-Breasts had a fan.

"Great." I patted the bottles. "These are yours if you want them. I'll catch you later."

I hummed to myself as I headed back to the car. These teenagers actually *talked* to me and *ate my pizza*. Maybe this wasn't impossible. Maybe I could regain some small-town favour and stay. And maybe, just maybe, the bright lights of the car were a clue.

Excitement thrummed though me at the thought of clearing Joe and Shona's names as well as mine. But that was replaced by a small, stabbing fear.

I glanced back over my shoulder at the group of teens, who were taking turns swigging on the soft drink, and prayed none of them would get food poisoning tonight.

# Chapter Twenty-Five

It was late, the clock had just struck eleven, and I was curled up on the sofa, a steaming cup of hot chocolate cradled in my hands. I had almost given up hope of hearing from Kat when my phone erupted into life, cutting through the silence of my dimly lit living room.

"Ruth, it's Kat. Sorry for the late call, but you need to hear this."

I sat up straighter, alert. "What's up?"

"Okay, so, diving deep into Rossi's archives, I found something odd. He's been tracking the Farrows' finances for decades. Like, obsessively."

Decades? My eyebrows knitted together. "But why? Did you find anything incriminating?"

"Not really. There's a surge in income early on—apparently Donna inherited some money."

"Nothing suspicious?"

"No embezzlement or wrongdoing as far as I can see."

I screwed up my face. "He must have been looking for something important."

She hesitated. "There was one thing—an email from Rossi to Paul Farrow. Rossi wrote, 'I know what you did in '83.' And Paul replied, 'Then you know I did nothing other than get engaged to Donna.'"

"Neither said what the *thing* was?"

"Nope. Nothing. And most people didn't even have computers back then so there's not much online."

"So, there's history there but we don't know what it is?"

"Correct." Her voice sparked with hope. "But I'm sure I can find out."

"Any sign the Farrows could have sent the threats?"

"Nope. Paul was pretty open and direct. There's actually two sets of threats: the emailed ones and the paper cutout ones. I think they could have come from different people. But whoever sent the emails covered their tracks well."

My grip tightened around the mug. "And my dad? Anything on him?"

"Just emails about you. Nothing sinister." Her tone softened. "Ruth, this stuff… I know you're aware this isn't exactly legal."

A cat-sized lump formed in my throat. "I know. But we can't stop now… unless you feel you need to? I'd understand if you did."

"Like I said, Aldon Rossi was good to me. And I won't get caught. I'm too good. It's worth the risk to give Cora a good home."

"Just… be careful, Kat."

"I will. And I'll keep digging, but Ruth, promise me something?"

"Anything."

"If I do get caught, and I go to jail, will you look after my cats?"

. . .

I stared into the remnants of my hot chocolate, sleep now feeling like a distant dream. The case had morphed into something more than clearing my name. A desire for justice burned deep in my belly. Rossi had been a two-timing slimebag, but no one had the right to take his life. And good people were standing with me, taking serious risks to help piece together a puzzle that spanned decades.

And the Farrows… they were lovely people, but Donna's migraine tablets muddied Paul's alibi. If she was zonked out, how could she have been sure what time he came home?

And what had happened in '83?

Maybe it was time for another chat with Elouise Rossi. She might have answers—but I'd need to ask her in a way that didn't reveal Kat as my source.

A thought began to form. Paul and Donna had invited me to help with the milking one morning. It was too late to call and ask if I could go tomorrow. But the day after might work. It was worth a shot.

Truth lurked in the shadows. If only I could find the light.

# Chapter Twenty-Six

The shimmering dawn blanketed the rolling hills in a red-gold glow as the cows milled around in yards near the milking sheds. It was a cold morning, but gratitude hugged me and squeezed warm joy right through me. This beautiful part of the world was my home.

A magpie chortled on a nearby fencepost, seemingly grateful for the morning too.

Then I remembered why I was there.

What did they say? Red sky in the morning, shepherds' warning. Today the sky was crimson.

"Lovely, isn't it." Bridget stood at my shoulder. "You'd see that view from your place, wouldn't you?" She nodded in the direction of my block.

"If she's ever awake in time," Shona scoffed.

"You're not a morning person?" Bridget asked.

"No. She. Is. Not." Shona's lips twitched. "But now she's a cat owner, she'll have to get up and feed it."

I rolled my eyes. "I told you I've changed since I moved to Pelican Bay. I'm usually up by seven."

"I've been up for two hours by then," Bridget boasted.

"You are not real," I said with a laugh. The expedition to the Farrow farm had become just that—an expedition. I'd texted Shona, who'd wanted to come. She told Bridget, and Joe said the barista could start late that morning. The Farrows agreed 'the more, the merrier'. Which was probably true as far as laughter went, but not so much for productivity. If it wasn't for their two farmhands we'd probably still have been there at lunchtime.

Milking had been happening for about half an hour before I got there. I'd slept through the first alarm, but jumped up at the second bleep, bleep, bleep. The warm weight of Cora left my ankle in an instant and the young cat sprinted through the house to hide. I didn't see her again before I left, but I made sure she had food and water and a clean litter tray.

I'd arrived at the farm to a yard full of cows, an armful of overalls and a warm hug of welcome. The overalls, and the boots that came with them, were useful when the cow in the bail in front of me lifted its tail and deposited a huge, steaming cowpat right next to me.

"Whoops," said Donna, pulling me back with a laugh. "Occupational hazard."

"Did you get that in your hair?" Shona beamed, a twinkle in her eye.

I shook my head. "You've got some on your cheek."

"Eww!" She wiped off the offending manure with her sleeve.

"At least cow manure doesn't smell like cat or dog poop," Bridget said.

"What about bird poop?" Shona suggested. "A pickpocketing parrot pooped on Ruth's head in Paris."

"Say *that* fast ten times." Bridget's tone was dry, but there was laughter in her eyes.

"Now that's a story I need to hear." Donna dodged another tail-lifting explosion of cow manure. "Cow dung is much more earthy and herby. But then I'm used to it," she said. "Who wants to have a go at putting the milking cups on the udder?"

I put up my hand. "I will."

I was wearing gloves, which was just as well as the gravel rash on my hands hadn't quite healed. I stood close to Donna, eyeing the hooves of the large cow in the bail,

"Hold it here," she said, holding her hand out flat with the four cups dangling down either side of her hand. "Then use your other hand to guide the cups onto the teat. Like this." She eased each cup onto the udder. They made a deep hissing sound as they sucked on the teats and began pulsing.

She shuffled across to the next cow. "Have a try. Arwen won't kick you."

"Arwen?" The cow cooperated as I slipped the cups onto her teats.

Donna laughed and nodded towards her husband. "He loves Tolkien. That year all the cows were given names from The Lord of the Rings. We take it in turns." She pointed back to the pen where a bunch of calves waited for their mothers. "That lot all have Star Wars names. The heifer at the front is Leia."

"Can I have a go?" Shona stood at my shoulder, her voice eager. "I can't believe I've never done this before. I've known you guys forever."

Donna led her to the next cow, and she successfully completed the task.

"That's right! Well done!" Donna said.

Bridget took her turn as Donna released the cups from the other cows.

I smiled at our host, pleased that I wasn't totally incompetent. "You're a good teacher. And the cows seem happy."

"We don't over-milk them." Donna shrugged. "Lots of dairies milk all the cows twice a day and say that's better, but because we leave the young calves on them, we milk less. Our yield is lower but the cows are healthier, and the milk is of infinitely better quality. It's also organic—we don't use chemicals on the place—so we can charge a premium for our products. Our cows don't get sick and we rarely get mastitis. We wean the calves at five months, and the boys are raised for beef and the best of the girls become part of our breeding herd."

"Good to be a girl then."

"Yeah." Donna sighed. "But it's better than sending them as babies to be raised for veal. That's one meat I'll never eat." Then she nudged me. "Go on," she said, handing me the milking cups. "Try another one. Claire won't kick you."

"Let me guess," I said, edging closer to the cow's warm side and lifting the cups onto the teats. "Outlander?"

Donna chuckled. "Exactly. Not that I get much of a chance to read." She nodded at Paul again, who was shooing the cows already milked out and manoeuvring others in. "We watch the TV show." She grinned at me, her eyes taking on a misty, dreamy quality. "I'd love to go to Scotland one day. There's a farm there pioneering this kind of farming. I'd love to see it firsthand."

"Yay for Scotland." Shona stuck a fist in the air.

I nudged Donna's arm. "Hoping to see Jamie Fraser?"

Donna laughed as Paul came up behind her, wrapped an arm around her shoulder and waggled his bushy eyebrows. "She doesn't need him, she already has a red-blooded fella."

Donna hushed him, but her cheeks had a faint pink tinge.

I wanted that kind of relationship one day. Married for who knows how many years and my husband still able to make me blush. Paul and Donna certainly loved each other and were there for each other. But would Donna lie for him? Love—especially lifelong love—was a powerful motivator.

A shudder juddered through me. I hated that Aldon Rossi had died. I hated that he'd died in my shed. I hated that my reputation scared little kids. But I especially hated the creeping feeling that Paul Farrow had killed Rossi.

After the milking shed had been hosed down and the calves reunited with their mothers, we all rinsed off our rubber boots, pulled off our overalls, and headed up to the house for a quick cuppa.

My stomach rumbled as Donna put a heaped plate of scones in front of us.

She laughed. "Dig in. We worked you hard this morning."

I obeyed, adding a large dollop of both jam and cream onto the still-warm scone.

Shona did the same. "You're allowed carbs when you've done some hard work, aren't you?"

I giggled. We'd been watching Paul, Donna and their farmhands work hard, but only got our own hands slightly dirty.

"What's your background, Bridget?" asked Donna. "When we've dropped into the café you've always been too busy making coffee for a proper chat. Is that a US accent?"

Bridget grinned in Shona's direction. "See, I work hard. How about a raise, boss?"

Shona shot Bridget an in-your-dreams look, but the barista didn't seem perturbed. She turned back to Donna. "I grew up on the New South Wales south coast. I went to live in LA for a while, before coming back to look after Mum, so I still have traces of that accent. Mum died a couple of years ago. I travelled around for a while then ended up in Pelican Bay."

"I'm sorry, love." Donna gave Bridget's arm a quick squeeze. "What happened?"

She shrugged. "I'd rather not talk about it." Shona had mentioned a while back that Bridget's mum had died of some type of liver disease, and her dad wasn't on the scene, but she didn't know any more.

An awkward silence hovered over the group.

Bridget broke the tension by taking a bite of scone and groaning with pleasure. "This is delicious. Way better than the supermarket stuff. People should be breaking down your doors to get this."

We all took her lead and praised the scones and cream.

Donna's cheeks flushed again. "We have people who regularly drive down from Adelaide for our cream. And we always have artisan producers clamouring for our milk."

Paul mumbled something about it all coming to an end.

"Things have always worked out." Donna took her husband's hand and laced her fingers through his. "They'll work out this time too."

He harrumphed from across the table. "Larsen wants me to go down to the cop shop later this morning. She said she has something to show me."

"Do you know what?" Donna asked.

He shook his head.

"Do you want me to go with you?" There was love in her eyes as she regarded him.

He held her gaze then looked away. "Nah. She'll be right.

It didn't sound too serious. Just poking her nose into other people's business, like she does."

Donna shifted in her seat, and let his hand go.

I almost volunteered to look after their shop for a couple of hours so she could go with him, then remembered I'd promised Shona that we'd talk about everything I'd already discovered. She hated being left out of the action. FOMO was real.

But I could help another time. "If you ever need to have someone watch the shop, I'm happy to help if I'm free. But I can't do it today."

Donna's faded blue eyes lit up as she smiled. "That's kind of you, Ruth. We sometimes close when my migraines are bad. We'd pay you, of course."

"Great. Let me know." It was work and it was helping someone. Bonus!

I suddenly realised I hadn't asked about 1983 yet—the whole purpose of this visit. But how could I bring it up? I couldn't ask Paul about Rossi's email, or he'd know he'd been hacked. My dad was probably the best starting point.

"You knew my dad back in the day, didn't you?"

"He was a good man," Donna offered. "True as they come."

"He was a card shark," Paul said, with a twinkle in his eye. "He was bright and into all the mathematical stuff. Could count cards and did a few of us out of our hard-earned cash. Even Rossi."

A smile played on my lips. "My parents hosted card nights with friends when I was little. Dad never cared much for other social events."

"No. He was quiet, right enough. Would always help out a mate." Her expression softened—as if her gaze had drifted to some distant memory.

"I stumbled on an old journal of Dad's. He hinted that something significant had happened in '83, but left out the details."

"What old journal?" Shona and Bridget spoke at the same time.

I sidestepped the question. There was no journal.

Paul and Donna exchanged a sideways glance and my heart skipped a beat. Had I hit a nerve?

Donna intertwined her fingers with Paul's again. "A lot of things happened that year. I saw the light and dumped Rossi for the man of my dreams." She squeezed his hand, and he squeezed back. Her voice took on a dreamy quality. "We got engaged at Vivonne Bay on Kangaroo Island." She turned back to me. "And your dad and the rest of his family moved to Queensland." She let Paul's hand go. "Anything else, love?"

Paul shook his head. "That's the important stuff." But his eyes drilled into mine.

I swallowed and turned to Donna. "I didn't know you and Rossi were an item."

"Yeah. We were all friends back then. This one here," her eyes filled with warmth as she tilted her head towards Paul, "had wanted me to see the light for a long time, but it took me a while."

I turned back to Paul. "Was that what broke the friendship? From what you said the other day there didn't seem to be any love lost between you and Rossi, not just because of the land deal."

The tall man grunted and caught his wife's gaze. She nodded almost imperceptibly before he continued. "That was a part of it. He didn't like losing."

"Even at cards." Donna gave my arm a reassuring squeeze. "But Aldon respected your father. Everyone did."

That rang true. And Dad must have thought well enough of Rossi to ask him to try to find me.

I wanted to delve deeper, but Paul stood abruptly. "I'd better be getting back to it, so I can get into town." He nodded in the direction of the farm sheds. "Thanks for your help this morning, ladies. You're all naturals."

My laugh was genuine, but overshadowed by the questions swirling in my mind. "I'm a bit too scared of cows I think, but thanks. And thank you for letting me see what milking was like."

We all rose, and the others thanked Paul and Donna, too.

"Our pleasure." Paul kissed his wife then excused himself and headed for the door.

"You're welcome, Ruth." Donna's embrace was unexpected, her warmth enveloping me in a comfort I hadn't realised I'd missed. Mum had never been the huggy type. Dad was… had been. But that was so long ago.

"Hang on a minute." Donna strode over to another shed as we walked outside and came back with tubs of cream and ice cream, which she gave to each of us.

"You shouldn't…" I started to say, but Donna shook her head.

"Your morning's wages." She winked at me. "Now to get the café open. No rest for the wicked!"

I sighed as I waved goodbye to the others and drove away from this kind and hardworking couple. Paul and Donna were lovely people, but they were wrapped up in the middle of this mystery and I needed to find out how, and why. Paul hated Rossi with a passion, and there was obviously more history there than winning the girl. And Rossi had been investigating Paul and Donna's financials, since forever. There had to be more to the story.

I drummed my fingers on the steering wheel. If they were all friends together back then, maybe Elouise Rossi could help.

# Chapter Twenty-Seven

I found Cora under my bed, a small wary shadow, her pupils dark pools in the dim light. She took a couple of steps forward to sniff my finger—which I'd dipped in tuna juice—but then retreated. Kat said that this was her third attempt to find Cora a home, so I guessed it would take her time to adjust. I left some of the tuna on a saucer next to her water and headed out to see Shona.

I breezed into Joe's Café. Bridget must have cleaned herself up in record time because she looked calm and collected as she frothed milk for a customer's cappuccino.

"Hey, Bridget. Is Shona here?" I glanced around the café. At least there were a few customers today. A forty-something couple in the far corner looked at me suspiciously, and a man in his sixties was reading a newspaper in the alfresco area. I blinked. For a moment I thought he was my dad.

*I miss you...*

Bridget shook her head. "Not yet. Can I get you a coffee? The usual? Or the other usual?"

I grinned. "The usual usual."

"Double-strength macchiato coming right up." Bridget could brew any coffee to perfection. She also had a brilliant memory. It made her really popular with the customers.

"Did you enjoy this morning?"

"It was great. I hadn't been on a dairy farm before. Glad I didn't get kicked." She handed me my coffee.

I took a sip. "Mmmm. How did you get to be so good at coffee?"

She laughed. "Practice. I've been doing this for years. Mum had a café back in Bega. And Joe buys his coffee beans fresh. It makes a difference."

"Yeah." I took a deep sip. "Heaven." I glanced around. "It's still quiet."

"Yep. It turns out that murder is bad for business. Who knew?"

I shot her a dark look.

"What was that about your dad?" she asked. "You mentioned 1983. He lived here?"

"He grew up here, with his mum and dad and little sister. But he moved to Brisbane with the rest of the family around then. He left me the house in his will."

Bridget looked like she was going to ask something else, but then a woman in her twenties walked in with a toddler and ordered hot chocolate with marshmallows.

I took it as a win that neither the woman nor the kid screamed when they saw me. Things were looking up. But when I took my coffee and sat down at a table near the door, the forty-somethings shared a glance, then left. I told myself they were nearly finished, but they'd only eaten half of Joe's cake. Nobody did that.

For a moment I was back in the schoolyard, when none of the cool kids would let me sit with them because of 'death germs'. I squeezed my eyes shut. Did people genuinely think

I'd killed Aldon Rossi? Were they staying away in case I cursed them, or did they just take joy in being mean? I inhaled my coffee and decided to feed my sorrows with cake.

I checked my phone again ten minutes later. Still no Shona. No message either. Had something happened? I realised I was bouncing my foot and stopped, but I couldn't halt the slow churning in my stomach. She was only a few minutes late, so yes, I was overacting, but she usually called if she wasn't going to be on time. And there was a murderer among us. I was about to ring her when Elouise Rossi swung through the door.

"Elouise," I called out to her.

"Hello, Ruth."

"Are you staying for coffee? Come sit with me if you like."

The older woman smiled, but there was uncertainty in her eyes.

"Shona will be here soon. She'll have all the latest gossip." It wasn't untrue.

Elouise's smile hit her eyes this time. Most of the town knew how good my super-caring, super-extroverted friend was at talking with people and hearing the latest 'news'.

"Okay." She ordered at the counter, then sat down, poured herself a glass of table water and filled up my glass too.

"How are you doing?" I asked.

She shrugged. "Up and down. Still in shock, I think. Aldon was a no-good cheating scum, but I still spent over forty years with him."

I told her about my Italian ex-fiancé, although I didn't mention the Mafia connection. What would that do to my reputation if it got out?

"I didn't know how to feel when the police said they

believed he was dead," I said. "Paulo lied to me, he'd been cheating behind my back, but you don't stop loving someone overnight."

Elouise nodded. "Exactly. I'm sorry that happened to you —you're so young. When I remember the happy times with Aldon, I want to grab that knife and give the killer a taste of their own medicine. When I remember how he betrayed me, I want to help them stab him. Does that make me a horrible person?"

The vehemence in her voice made me shift in my seat. Paul Farrow wasn't the only one who could have killed Rossi in a murderous rage. But would rage drive a small, sweet woman like Elouise to follow Rossi to my shed?

If she'd just grabbed a knife in the moment and stabbed Rossi at the celebration, I'd have believed it. People did bad things when they were mad. But while Aldon's stabbing was almost certainly deeply personal, the fact that whoever took Joe's knife had followed Rossi added a premeditated element. It wasn't like they'd stolen the knife to make lunch and then said, "Oh, look. How fortunate. I have a knife in my bag right when I want to kill someone."

Elouise must have seen my thoughts on my face because she pressed her eyes shut and let out a deep sigh. "I didn't kill him, if that's what you're thinking."

"No. I…"

"It's okay." A small smile played at the corners of her lips. "I would suspect me too. But I have an alibi."

"Alibi?"

Bridget set Elouise's coffee and cake on the table, but there was still no sign of Shona. She'd be mad at missing this.

"I didn't tell you the other day, but I saw red when Aldon panted after that Briscoe woman, so I went to see a friend."

"A friend?"

"A male friend."

"You were having an affair, too?"

She shook her head. "Not before that night."

"Who?" It was none of my business, but I was curious.

"Do you know Len Philips, the butcher?"

I leaned forward. "Len?" Even though I'd only been in town a short while, the butcher was one of the people you got to know quickly. He was a good-looking widower, a little younger than Elouise.

She had the grace to blush. "There was nothing going on… until that night."

As with Paul and Donna, I told her that I'd found some diary notes Dad had written when he was young, and that he'd said something big had happened in 1983.

Her eyes widened and there was a flicker of something there. Surprise? Fear? She let out a long, slow breath. "I didn't know Rick kept a diary. He was more into maths and science than writing."

I shrugged but didn't say anything. If the silence technique was good enough for Larsen, it was good enough for me, although it was hard not to fill the void with words.

Eventually Elouise took a deep breath and spoke. "Aldon and Paul were best friends. They grew up together and did stuff together all the time. Until…"

"What happened?" I leaned closer.

"It was one of their stupid poker games. They played a lot." She reminisced, echoing Paul Farrow's comments. "Your dad was brilliant."

"What was he like?" I couldn't resist asking.

"Smart, nerdy, kind. Always in his books, but he had a good heart. He'd help anyone. He had a thing for Donna at one stage and helped her through a bad time." Her expression softened. "And like I said before, he was good-looking. We went on a couple of dates. Don't worry, nothing happened." She winked at me. "Nothing more than kissing, anyway."

I screwed up my face and laughed. "The thought of either of my parents having a romantic life makes me queasy."

She chuckled. "Yet you're here. That couldn't have happened otherwise."

"There's that," I conceded. "Go on. You were saying Paul and Aldon played poker."

"Paul didn't have a lot of money. All he ever wanted was to be a farmer. He didn't come from a land background though, so it was important to learn the technical side and get a job. Back then you didn't have to pay university fees, but if you lived down here you really needed to go and stay in one of the uni colleges or flat with other students in Adelaide. Even if you commuted, you needed money for practicals and placements. He enrolled in agricultural science but got to the point where he was so desperate for cash, he tried to make money from poker." Elouise sighed. "It was a mistake."

"He kept losing?"

"Yes. Rick tried to dissuade Paul, but when he wouldn't stop, he tried to teach him how to count the cards." She shook her head. "It wasn't Paul's strength." She took a big spoonful of Black Forest cake and swallowed, a look of ecstasy on her face. "This is so good."

"Paul lost big time?" I prompted.

"Yes. One night Paul lost several hundred dollars to Aldon. He didn't have that kind of money, but he said he was good for it. There was some heirloom opal necklace his great-aunt had left him recently. There weren't any girls on that side of the family, apparently." She took another spoonful of the cake. "Aldon said he had some connections and could sell the necklace, as it was worth a lot more than the debt. Paul agreed, but the price Aldon got was lower than Paul thought it should have been."

Understanding dawned on me. "Paul said Aldon screwed him over. He thought Aldon had cheated him?"

Elouise nodded. "Aldon told me he got a reasonable price for it. He had it checked out by some expert, but she said the opal wasn't real. The setting was gold, so it was worth something, but the stone was just a high-quality fake. It was worth only a little more than the actual debt."

I sighed. "Poor Paul."

"I hated it. They'd been like brothers, but Paul kept saying Aldon cheated him. But he didn't. Aldon gave Paul fifty dollars of his own money back as he knew Paul was doing it tough."

"Fifty dollars?" My voice squeaked, my heart raced and the room swam. I could feel Aldon Rossi pressing that fifty-dollar note into my hand.

*Paul killed Rossi.*

It had to be him.

My chair made a loud scraping sound as I pushed it back and leaped to my feet. "I... er... just remembered, I need to be somewhere."

"Are you okay?" Elouise drew her brows together, her gaze holding mine.

"Yeah. Fine. Gotta go. Sorry."

# Chapter Twenty-Eight

I snatched up my bag and careered out of the shop, smacking right into Shona. At least it wasn't Dan this time. I steadied her before she fell. "I know who the killer is. Come with me to see Larsen."

"What? Who?" She reached for my arm, but I was already sprinting down the footpath towards the police station.

"I need," I puffed to the desk clerk when I reached the station, "to see Detective Larsen." I wheezed in another breath, which told me I also needed to get fitter and eat less cake. "Larsen," I breathed again.

"She's not here." The clerk regarded me with caution, like he was wishing he had a taser on his desk.

"Anyone." My breath was slowly returning as Shona joined me. "What about Gary Stone?"

"I'll see if he's available."

"What's going on, Ruth?" Shona was also out of breath, but not as bad as me. "Who murdered Rossi?"

Before I could reply, Gary appeared in the corridor. "Ruth, what's wrong?"

"I…" How could I say it? Paul and Donna were friends.

He ushered Shona and I through to his desk. Several officers glanced at us before getting back to their work. He asked us to sit. "Can I get you a water?"

I shook my head.

"Yes," Shona said.

He filled two cups at a water cooler and gave one to Shona and put the other one in front of me. "I think you could do with this too. Tell me what's wrong."

"Paul Farrow killed Rossi," I blurted.

"No!" Shona rose out of her chair.

"No," said Gary, in a matter-of-fact voice.

"Yes! The fifty dollars Rossi pressed into my hand." I gulped in another breath.

"What?" Shona frowned in confusion.

"Ruth," Gary began, but I interrupted him.

"I need to get this out before I forget the details."

I told them both about the animosity between Rossi and Paul Farrow, how Paul thought Rossi had swindled him, how Rossi had given him fifty dollars as a consolation prize. I stood and began pacing back and forth. "Rossi was managing the sale of the farm out from under Paul and Donna. Paul had access to the knife, and he must have snapped and—"

"Ruth." Gary stood, put his hands on my shoulders, and pressed me gently back down into my seat. "Paul didn't do it."

Shona breathed a relieved sigh.

I screwed up my face. "But he must have. The fifty dollars…"

"We've never been able to find that."

"It's real," I pleaded. "I wouldn't make that up."

Gary's voice was steady. "I'm not saying you did, Ruth. The thing is, Paul's got an alibi."

"He can't have."

Gary looked around at the other officers. No one was paying attention anymore, so he leaned forward and lowered his voice. "I'm not showing you this, right? It's evidence. I'd get in big trouble if—"

"Show us already," Shona broke in.

He chuckled and hit some computer keys, turning the screen slightly so we could see. A series of CCTV videos sat in rows on his screen. He clicked on one that looked like it was near Aldon Rossi's office. Paul Farrow was staggering down the street, obviously blind drunk. Paul stopped, yelled something, then threw the bottle, smashing it on Rossi's shopfront door. The time stamp was twelve thirty a.m.

Gary turned to me. "Rossi was last seen alive and well at eleven thirty p.m. He died in your shed around twelve forty-five, right?"

I nodded.

"The knife nicked his aorta. He was barely alive when you found him."

I shuddered, remembering how I'd tried to save him. "Yes."

"He would have needed to have been stabbed just before you got there. The killer could still have been nearby."

A creeping cold started at the base of my neck and seeped down my arms. "They could have taken the fifty-dollar note."

"Yes. And they could have been in the shed while you were there. They could have killed you if you hadn't left the shed to get your phone."

Blood rushed in my ears. Had the murderer been watching me? I was suddenly grateful for Dan's security system.

"Paul Farrow couldn't have got to your place in time to do this," Gary continued. "He could have barely got back to his car given his state of inebriation. Larsen questioned him this morning and he admitted he'd thrown the bottle and slept in his car before going home."

Shona frowned. "So… Donna lied too?"

Gary's face softened. "We spoke to her about it, and she admitted she could have been wrong about the time. Those migraine tablets really bomb some people out. My mum takes them and she once swore she cooked a turkey in the middle of the night." He shook his head with a wry smile. "All she'd made was Vegemite toast."

We laughed.

His voice sobered. "Mum was annoyed, mind. She had a migraine that day too, but Donna had apparently bought the last packet of tablets from the pharmacist. She had a script, but they'd run out. I ended up taking Mum to the hospital at Victor Harbor for a pethidine injection."

"That's awful, Gary." Shona put her hand on his arm.

I ran my hands over my face to try and wipe away fatigue. "If Paul couldn't have done it, who did?"

He gave me a small, sweet smile and shook his head. "We still don't know."

"I'm an idiot."

"No, no." He stood and so did Shona and I. "It was pretty good deducting really, but that's why this is police work." He began to usher us towards the door. "We get to look at all the evidence." His tone was only a little condescending.

"Thank you for showing us." I turned to Shona. "We'd better go. We still haven't had lunch and I can't keep you from café duties forever."

She grimaced, then winked. "I've done pretty well in avoiding it today."

"Hang on," Gary said. "There is one more thing." He left the room, then returned with a clear plastic evidence bag containing an old, blue plastic satchel in one hand and my broom in the other. "When forensics searched your place, we found these inside your chimney. We cleaned the bag up and checked it out, but the contents were all from the 1980s. It looks like it belonged to your father. I don't know how it got in there, but there's nothing of interest to the investigation."

"Thank you." I reached out and took the bag from him.

He held up the broom. "Any reason this was in the chimney?" His raised eyebrows said it all.

I caught Shona's gaze and we burst out laughing. Gary squinted at us, but neither of us bothered enlightening him.

Shona reached out and touched the package. "*This* was in the chimney?" Her voice was tinged with reverence.

I clutched the bag to me. "Want to check it out with me?"

She nodded vigorously.

"Ring Bridget and see if she can stay at the café for the whole afternoon. You're coming home with me."

# Chapter Twenty-Nine

We sipped our hot drinks and stared at Dad's old schoolbag. It sat in the middle of my kitchen table, still sheathed in the plastic police evidence bag.

Shona frowned at the package, as if willing it to speak. "How did you get into the chimney?"

I scooped some froth off my cappuccino and licked the powdered chocolate from my spoon. The macchiato had had its turn earlier at the café. Now I craved milky froth. "Dad must have hidden it for some reason."

"All those years ago?"

I gave a slight shrug. "Got a better suggestion?" I hesitated another moment before reaching out and dragging the bag towards me.

But when I touched the plastic, it was as if Dad was standing behind me and the room was filled with the delicious scent of barbecuing sausages. I could almost hear his sardonic chuckle and see the twinkle in his eye as he flipped another sausage and snuck a small piece to the dog. My throat tightened, the memory—or whatever it was—was so vivid.

Then his hand was on my shoulder. Warm, encouraging… present.

"Are you okay? Where did you go?" Shona's voice was kind.

Dad's presence vanished as quickly as it had appeared, leaving me with an acute sense of loss.

"I felt Dad again. Like he was here."

She gave my arm a quick squeeze. "This is part of him. Of course you'd feel like that."

I shook my head. "You didn't smell them?"

"Smell what?"

"Barbecued sausages."

She laughed softly. "You think your dad's nearby when you smell barbecued sausages?"

"We used to have a barbecue on Sunday afternoons in summer." A soft smile curved on my lips. "We did it all the time in Brisbane around the swimming pool, but even in England… Don't you remember? You came over a lot, with your brother and your mum and dad. Sometimes it would be other friends. He always wore that boxing kangaroo apron when he cooked."

I paused, my feelings winding and twisting like lantana inside me.

"It was as if he was here for a moment. His hand was on my shoulder. I could smell the smoke and taste the sausages."

Shona blinked. "Yeah, I remember. Your mum kept telling him off for giving Happy too many sausages." Happy was a whippet cross that we dog-sat for a while when we lived in England.

"That dog would eat anything she could get her paws on," I agreed.

Shona patted my arm, gave a little wave, and called out to Dad. "Hello, Mister Smythe."

I groaned. "He's not really here, Shona. It's all just…" I ran my hands over the plastic parcel in front of me. "Memory."

She rolled her eyes and smirked. "Some people never believe."

"I'm a realist, okay?"

"Whatever you say." She laughed and pointed to Dad's schoolbag. "If he's cooking sausages, it sounds like he approves of what we're doing, anyway. Would you like to do the honours? Or shall I?"

"Let's do this together."

But my hands trembled as I picked up the scissors to open the evidence bag. Why had he hidden the bag? What secrets lay inside? What if it was something bad? I hesitated, my fingers hovering over the smooth plastic, before taking a deep breath and cutting.

A few minutes later we had the bag's contents strewn out over the table. Some of it was schoolwork.

"Ugh! Differential equations!" I showed Shona the pages and pages of mathematical scrawl.

"I did higher maths in senior school," she said.

"Brain!"

"Not really," she scoffed. "I promised to do it on the condition I could also go to drama classes. Best bargain I ever made." She shrugged. "Dad was an engineer too, remember?" Her eyes sparkled. "I sucked at it though. So much so, they let me swap it for art in my final semester. I had bad dreams about it for years afterwards."

I gave a small shudder. "Maths anxiety dreams are a thing. I knew I wanted to study archaeology, so maths wasn't that important to me, although I could do it. I did enjoy statistics."

"You are officially weird," Shona said.

I picked up the book. "I understand some of this, but I didn't love it. Not like Dad did."

She sighed. "Feels like a long time ago."

"It was." I ran my hands over the yellowed paper in front of me. "Not as long ago as this was written."

I learned a few things about Dad that day. His handwriting had once been neat and precise—it was more scrawly by the time I left home. He was a hard worker—and brilliant—but I already knew that.

Overall, I was a bit disappointed. I'm not sure what I expected, but it was as if he'd tossed his entire senior school year into the chimney and thrown in some university texts. I put aside a couple of smallish textbooks that had been scribbled in, along with a yearbook and a hardcover journal, to read later.

"Maybe it was a symbolic act," suggested Shona when I raised the issue. "School is over—"

"But there's some uni stuff in there too."

I leaned my elbows on the table and rested my chin on my hands, staring at the pile of schoolbooks and willing them to talk to me. "There's something I'm missing…"

My frown deepened and I picked one of the books off the table.

"You don't think he was just rebelling against his parents by going up on the roof and stuffing something solid down a chimney?" asked Shona.

"Maybe." I shrugged. "I don't know what he was like back then, but while he was always scatterbrained, he usually did things for a good reason. They didn't move to Brisbane until late 1983, which was the year all the other things happened."

"Right… So?"

"So, he couldn't have stuffed his bag in the chimney until then because the family would have needed to use the fireplace. They would have found it."

Shona tilted her head as if deep in thought. "Makes sense. But no one lived here after that? Your grandparents didn't rent the place out?"

"I have no idea. Probably. I guess we could find out."

"If he hid the bag deliberately," Shona chewed on her lower lip, "it would mean there's something in there he wanted to keep secret."

"Most are Year 12 books, except…" I picked up two textbooks and a workbook and flicked through them. The first contained a heap of formulas—mostly advanced calculus. "These are all university-level maths, other than this one." I lifted an Ancient History paperback text and flicked through it. Various passages were underlined but it was otherwise unremarkable."

"I didn't know your dad was into history."

"When I was a teenager, we sometimes watched the History Channel together, but I thought he only did it because I loved old civilisations." I paused, revelling in the memory, then checked inside the front cover. "It was published in 1982—an earlier edition of the one I used as an undergraduate." I placed the book back down then flicked through the maths books some more, staring at formulas that were several levels beyond my understanding. But around the top of some of the pages of the workbook was lettering that looked familiar.

"Look at this." My heart quickened as I showed Shona.

"Looks intense. Your dad was brilliant."

"Yeah, he was. But look around the edges."

"Random letters and numbers?"

"I think it's some kind of code."

"Code?" She looked perplexed and I told her about how Dad used to teach me to break ciphers, when I was a kid.

"Holiday fun then?" Her wry sarcasm was obvious.

"I really enjoyed it. It was a place Dad and I could connect. Once we cracked the code, we'd eat ice cream and I'd tell him everything about my life and he'd tell me how amazing I was." My eyes began to burn.

She gave me a gentle punch on my arm. "You *are* amazing."

"You and Dad are the only two people who ever thought so."

"Rubbish. You're smart, beautiful and kind. All key qualities of amazing."

I changed the subject before things got too mushy. I loved my friend, but compliments made me squirm. "But why hide the bag in the chimney?" I tapped my chin, deep in thought. "His parents—my grandparents—could easily have sold the place. And like you said, there could have been tenants. And tenants would have wanted to use the fireplace."

"Maybe he thought he could come back here and get it," Shona suggested. A smile flicked over her lips. "Maybe he tried to get it out, but it was stuck, and he decided to leave well enough alone."

I screwed my face up in thought. "There's another option."

"What's that?"

"Well, the bag is obviously old. It's discoloured and the plastic is perishing around the edges. But does it look to you as if it's been exposed to the elements for the past forty years?"

"Where are you going with this?"

"The police cleaned it up, right? They would have checked for prints and all that kind of stuff. But if it had been in the chimney for forty years, wouldn't the plastic have perished by now?" My thoughts tumbled over each other. "What if Dad hid this bag at the back of a cupboard all that time, and only put it into the chimney…"

"When?"

"Recently. Sometime not long before he died."

"But why would he do that?" my friend asked.

"Because he was hiding something." I stared at the pile of books, then picked up an exercise book brimming with stray pieces of newspaper clippings stuffed between the pages. There was part of me that wanted to stop—a niggle that said the more I looked, the more I might find things I *didn't* like. But this was about *Dad*. And the archaeologist in me—the questioning mind he'd always encouraged—couldn't let it go. Nor could the daughter who had always loved her father and wanted to know everything about him.

I let out a deep sigh and handed the book and news clippings to Shona. "How about I make us another hot drink? Then we can look through these for clues."

# Chapter Thirty

I tapped my leg with my fingers, surveying the news clippings, when a small wet nose sniffed my hand.

"Meow!" Cora jumped onto my lap and butted me with her head.

"You really do have a cat," Shona said. "I was thinking she was a figment of your imagination. Although the stinky litter tray in your laundry does say otherwise." She screwed up her face and pinched her nose with her fingers.

"Ha ha." I rubbed Cora behind the ears. "Hello, little girl."

"Meow."

"It's the first time she's come out of hiding since I brought her home."

The young cat started purring.

"Wow," Shona said. "That's a rich purr for such a small kitty."

"Like chocolate liqueur." I hummed to myself. I had a cat, and she had a lovely purr. It was all going to be okay.

I smoothed my hand over Cora's silky ears again, and she leaned her head into my hand, demanding more.

Shona reached out and scratched Cora under her chin. "She's a darling. Just needed some time."

My heart went out to the little cat. "She's had a couple of homes already. They didn't work out for some reason." I shrugged. "Maybe she needed a quieter life?"

"She should get that here," Shona agreed.

Cora leaned in for another caress of her ears, her purr rising to a new crescendo, and I ran my hand absently down her silky fur. Then there was a sudden knock on the door behind me.

"Hey, ladies." Dan's resonant voice boomed from behind the screen door. "Can I come in?"

Before I could say anything, Cora bit me on the hand then tore through the house.

"Ow." I nursed my hand against me as Dan opened the door.

"Are you okay?" Shona asked.

Frank gave one loud woof, slid past Dan, and scrambled on the spot as he tried to get traction on the slate floor. Then he tore through the house after the cat.

"Frank, NO!" I sprinted after the cat and dog. "Shut the door!"

"Woof."

"Meow-ow-ow!"

"Yip!"

I reached my bedroom to find a confused Frank backing out from under my bed. I dived for him and snatched his collar just as a cat paw reached out from under the bed and whacked him hard on the head three times.

"Meow-ow-ow!"

"What the—?" Before Dan could finish, I handed him Frank.

"Get him out of here."

"His nose is bleeding," Shona said.

"Take him through and check him. I'll be out in a moment." My hand throbbed as I bent down and looked under the bed. "Cora."

She sat staring, eyes wide and pupils dark, whisking her tail backward and forward. Then to my surprise she gave a plaintive, "Pruuurp," crawled forward and rubbed her head on my uninjured hand. I tickled her under the chin and she edged out from under the bed, gazing up at me like nothing had ever happened. Before I could stop her, she started strutting down the hallway towards the kitchen, tail high and purpose in her stride.

"She's coming your way," I called to Dan and Shona. I hurried down the hallway after her. Dan was sitting on one of my kitchen chairs with Frank in his arms, while Shona cleaned Frank's nose with some cotton wool and water. When the dog saw Cora, his eyes widened and he backed further into Dan's arms. Cora gave the dog a disdainful glance and began washing herself.

Dan rubbed the dog's ears. "It's okay, mate. I won't let the bad cat get you."

I bristled, hand on hip. "Bad cat? She wasn't expecting a dog."

His eyes crinkled at the corners. "Sorry, I forgot you'd asked Kat to help you. You obviously bowed to the pressure."

He nodded at Cora, who had stopped washing and was whisking her tail back and forth again.

"I've only been here for a few months, but it's a thing in this town," he continued. "Someone needs some online research done or their computer fixed? Kat will do it for a 'price'." He laughed as he made air quotes and gestured towards the cat.

Frank followed his gaze then looked away, avoiding Cora's eyes.

Shona giggled.

I frowned at both of them. "You could have warned me when you ate my food the other night."

"Sorry." He laughed as he glanced at Shona, whose giggles had morphed into serial snorts.

I glared at him in mock annoyance. "Liar."

Shona grabbed a handful of tissues and blew her nose, managing to get herself under some kind of control. "Not sorry, either. I thought if you had a pet you might stay in Pelican Bay."

My heart, gut and everything else twisted inside me. I should be mad my best friend was manipulating me—again—but it still meant something that I was *wanted*.

"You told me that today is the first time she's come out of hiding? She's doing okay." Shona's tone was reassuring.

"She doesn't look as if she's that fazed by the trauma," said Dan. "How's the hand?"

"Lemme see." Shona reached for my hand.

I let her look but pulled back when she touched the bruised area near the two small puncture wounds. My gravel rash was just beginning to heal—now this.

"It's not too deep, just a nip. Let me clean it." She rushed to the sink, washed her hands and tended to my hand just like she'd cleaned up Frank's nose. Then she dabbed the wound with iodine.

"Thanks." I pulled back my hand and held it to me. Her ministrations had turned the wound into a hot poker that jabbed in time with my heartbeat.

Dan screwed up his face in sympathy. "You might want to go to the doc and get antibiotics and a tetanus shot."

I huffed out a laugh. "Still on them from the other day when someone ran me off my bike." I held up my hands.

He groaned. "Ruth, I'm sorry—"

"You don't have to keep apologising. I'm teasing. It was more my fault than yours. I didn't look. And I'm okay. And…" I waved my hand in the direction of the newly installed security sensors. "You've done all this."

"You did bring it up." Shona's eyes sparkled, the way they always did whenever she was giving me a hard time about Dan. "The accident, I mean. Strange that Dan ran you off your bike, and into you at the pub, and on the plane, you fell on top—"

I cut her off before she could say anything else about me, Dan, accidents and fate.

"Why are you here, anyway?" I turned to Dan with a small frown on my face.

He rubbed Frank's ears, laughter in his eyes from Shona's earlier inference. Then he reached into his jacket pocket and pulled out a small CCTV camera. "I had another couple of these and thought it might be good for you to have extra footage of your back porch and the shed where Rossi was killed. Just in case."

"Just in case," Shona agreed with a wicked gleam in her eye.

"Uh, thanks." An inner glow spread through me and I gave him a genuine smile. "You didn't have to do any of this."

He held my gaze for a long moment, warmth in his eyes, just as Frank reached up and licked his chin with a big slobbery kiss. He pulled back. "Away, dog."

I giggled. "That dog loves you. Want some tissues?" I plucked a box off the bench and handed them to Dan. Our fingers brushed for the barest moment, and the bolt of electricity was there again. What was I? Some kind of Dan Rivers superconductor?

But the reaction was real, and visceral. I was attracted to him. There was a part of me, a deeply buried part of me, that would like nothing better than to run my lips along that strong jaw, feel the warmth of his breath on my skin, and…

*Stop!*

I couldn't think like that. Not until I got my life together. And even then, how could it work? We wanted different things. He was leaving for Europe soon. I looked away and tried not to envy the small dog with the huge fluffy tail, snuggling deep in Dan's arms.

# Chapter Thirty-One

"Feel safer?" Shona grinned in the direction of Dan and the work he was doing outside. Frank was whining, tied up outside for his own safety—not Cora's—and Dan was mounting another CCTV camera in the corner of the back porch. He'd already placed one in the back shed. He was reaching up from a ladder and I couldn't help seeing an inch of tanned, bare skin as his shirt hitched up over his belly.

Shona followed my eyes and her grin widened. "Safe probably isn't the word of choice here."

I let out a huff and half-whispered, "Okay, he's eye candy, but nothing's gonna happen."

Shona tossed her hair. "There's always Gary, I suppose."

"No!" I raised my voice for emphasis.

She nodded sagely. "*Too* safe."

The door banged open behind us. "What's too safe?" asked Dan.

"Ruth was just saying how we can't be too safe, given there's a murderer on the loose."

I kicked at her under the table and connected with a glancing blow.

"Ow," she mouthed.

"Well, I'm about done here," Dan said. Frank whined outside. "We'll be off."

"Thank you so much, Dan. I *will* pay you for this."

"There's no rush. Whenever you can, but just for the hardware." His lopsided grin lit up his face. "For the labour, I'd settle for another dinner sometime."

"I can do that." The words slipped out of my mouth before I could stop them. A warmth spread through me at the thought of a dinner with Dan. Alone.

"I… um… next week sometime?" My voice squeaked.

Shona snorted.

A broad smile lit up Dan's face and the warmth in his eyes made my pulse quicken. "I'm free Thursday. I fly out on Friday."

Fly out? The warmth drained from me as reality hit. I found myself speaking automatically again—for a different reason. "Um… yes. Thursday is fine."

Dan, the perceptive scoundrel, smirked. "Just to Sydney for business this time."

"Yeah… okay," I stammered, trying not to show my relief.

"Okay, right. It's a date then," he said. "I'll bring the wine."

"It's a date," Shona mouthed.

"Bye, ladies."

Cora had sauntered back to the kitchen and Dan bent down and held out his hand to her. She butted her head against his fingers and purred.

"I think she likes me."

"She does." I nodded, surprised by the sudden show of affection from my scaredy-cat-turned-surprise-feline-socialite.

It was then her pupils dilated. Hadn't Kat said something about that? It might have been okay, but then there was a huge bang outside as a couple of large squabbling birds clattered onto the tin roof of the porch.

Cora jumped.

"Meow-ow-ow!" she screamed and leapt in the air. Dan fell back on his haunches as the cat attacked his work boot. He scrambled to his feet, but Cora kept holding on, sinking her teeth again and again into the tough leather.

"Woof. Woof. Woof." Frank joined in the fracas, straining at his rope, willing to give his life for the sake of his master.

"Help. Get it off me. Get it off me!" Dan shook his leg again, but the cat remained attached, savaging the shoe.

"Cora." I tried to shoo the cat off, but she was determined to do whatever she could to subdue the threat of Dan's foot.

"Help!" He hopped on one leg, shaking his leg, boot and the half-grown cat in the air, but Cora held on.

I caught Shona's eye and we both dissolved into outright laughter. This ex-soldier, now security expert, taken down by an attack-cat that was barely more than a kitten.

"Where did you say you served?" I asked. "Afghanistan? Syria? Just as well the enemy didn't use kittens."

"Very funny." He shook his leg again as Cora held on tight, terrorising the boot with her teeth. "Just… call off your cat!"

# Chapter Thirty-Two

Dan and Frank left, and a saucer-eyed Cora sat quivering under my bed. A bunch of the news clippings had fallen on the kitchen floor in the chaos and Shona picked them up and plonked them onto the table in front of me.

"Is this why Cora couldn't settle into a new home?" My voice wavered as I addressed my friend. "Tell me it'll be all right."

"It will be okay. I can feel it," Shona's tone was warm and reassuring.

"What if it's not?"

"It's only her first day out of hiding. Give her time. It's traumatic to be chased by a dog." She filled up the kettle and switched it on. "Want a cup of tea?"

I shook my head. "Still have my coffee." I pointed to my mug. "I don't think Frank triggered her attack mode. She got a fright when they arrived. She was scared and nipped me. Any scaredy-cat could have done that. But that attack on Dan's boot was something else."

Shona's eyes sparked with amusement. "Did you see his face when he couldn't get rid of her?"

I giggled at that. "That was pretty funny." But the ache in my chest didn't go away. "Can I live with this cat? Can I have friends over? What if she hurts someone?" I scrubbed my hands over my face. "One minute she's Hallmark sweet and the next she's Cujo crazy. Do cats get psychosis? Was she traumatised at birth?"

"Give it time," Shona urged. "Maybe talk to a vet. It will be okay."

"How are you always such an optimist?"

She beamed. "I believe in goodness. Things work out."

I regarded my friend, wishing I could share in her sunshine. Then I took a sip of my coffee and made a face. "Ugh! Cold coffee is evidence of evil." I went to the sink and poured it out then fired up the espresso machine, before sitting down again at the kitchen table. "Let's look at these news clippings."

Each yellowed article heightened my sense of connection with Dad—they were a snapshot into his world forty years ago—but they also left me puzzled. What had he seen in these that had made them worth keeping? There was a story about the opening of a new community centre, and another about the renovation of the local cinema… but nothing was interesting until I saw one about a young woman.

"Here's one about an accident," I told Shona. "A girl was knocked off her bike in a hit-and-run. Rose Mathers. They never found the driver."

Shona reached over and took the article from me. "The driver wasn't related to Dan, was he?"

I shot her my best deadpan look.

Her expression sobered as she read. "Poor thing." She

lifted her eyes to look at me. "Could it have been Rossi? Maybe the family wanted revenge?"

"Maybe. Could it have been Paul?" I told Shona about the email from Rossi to Paul Farrow and the significance of the year.

"But if that's right," Shona argued, "Paul did something, not Rossi. If the motive was revenge, Paul should have been killed, not Rossi. Unless Paul was trying to cover up the crime and killed Rossi to keep things quiet." She shook her head. "But it's a long time ago and the CCTV shows Paul didn't kill Rossi."

"Whatever happened in '83 may not have anything to do with Rossi's death." I closed my eyes and rubbed my temples. We were going around in circles.

Shona picked up the article and stared at the photo of Rose again. "She looks vaguely familiar." She handed the photo back to me.

I studied the image but came up blank. "Maybe we've seen her in another photo?" I placed the clipping back on the table.

She continued to sort through the news stories. "These are all just things that happen in a small town. A local band performance, the opening of the bridge, a local cake competition."

I snatched that article away from Shona. "Why would my dad keep an article about a cake competition?"

"Who won?" Shona asked.

"Donna." I handed her the clipping. "Donna said Dad was a friend."

Shona waggled her eyebrows. "Maybe he wanted to be more than friends."

"You think so?"

"He's a young bloke and he's interested in the results of a

cooking competition? And he's not Joe," she added with a smirk. "I know men can be great cooks, but your dad was a science geek who liked barbecuing sausages, not baking gâteaux. I can only think of one reason he'd keep that clipping. A woman!"

"It's weird to think of Dad like that. The only woman he ever showed any interest in was Mum."

"Our parents had hormones too." She picked up another of the articles and read it. "This one is about a robbery—some jewellery heist. They caught one of the guys that did it, but at the time of writing, the other was still missing." She looked up at me, a question in her eyes. "I wonder if they ever got him."

I shrugged. "Probably skipped the country."

She scanned the last of the old news stories. "Here's one of Paul Farrow and Rossi. Must have been when they were still friends. Their team won the local Under-19 Aussie Rules competition."

I gazed at the photo of the two beaming, mud-covered young men and filled Shona in on what Elouise had told me about the break-up of their friendship.

"That's why I thought it was Paul," I said. "He had motive on several fronts, opportunity, and the means to do it."

"But he alibied out, so…"

"We're back to square one."


I lay down on the bed, leaving my arm dangling over the side. Shona had left a few minutes ago and I needed peace to process things. Within a few minutes I felt the tickle of whiskers and the soft rub of silken fur as Cora nuzzled my hand. I caressed her behind the ears, and she fell into the touch, purring deeply.

"You're a terrible beast." A giggle rose in my chest at the image of Dan trying to get Cora off his boot. I snorted at the look of fear in his eyes. But then I remembered how careful he was not to hurt her.

I let out a long, deep sigh. I liked Dan a lot.

"Meow?" Cora jumped up on the bed and then onto my belly. Her claws kneaded back and forth as she began her chocolate liqueur purr. Then she flopped down on her side and rubbed her head against my hand, her purr getting louder with each caress of her ears.

"What are we going to do with you?"

"Meow." She sounded so innocent, but was there a gleam in her eye? She rolled over onto her back and lay next to me, batting my hands with her soft paws.

"Sorry-not-sorry, eh?"

"Meow."

I'd need to talk to Kat about her. I was going to see her tomorrow anyway, after I helped Joe at the engagement party.

I rubbed Cora's ears again, but her pupils dilated, and I pulled my hand away.

"Best give you some space, then?"

Cora purred. "Meow."

My mind drifted to the Kingstons' party. I hadn't been introduced to Xavier Kingston, but I didn't like the way he'd treated Elouise at the business do. Maybe I could look around and find out something at the party. But who was I kidding? My ex, Bradley, would have said I had no idea what I was doing. I wished I didn't agree with him.

Cora patted my face with her paw, then nuzzled in close to my neck. I closed my eyes and willed myself to relax and enjoy the comfort of my warm, purring cat. But I couldn't shake the feeling that time was running out. Someone killed

Rossi and they were still out there. We needed answers and we needed them soon.

# Chapter Thirty-Three

It was Saturday morning and time to help Joe with his catering extravaganza for Fiona Kingston's engagement party. My phone said seven o'clock, but I wasn't ready to get out of bed yet. I arched into a languid stretch, which was soon echoed by the warm mass of kitten-cat curled against my leg.

The phone rang, making me and Cora jump. Who would ring at this time of day?

"Joe? What's up?" I was looking forward to getting the pay for today, so I hoped the event hadn't been cancelled.

"Can you come earlier? Bridget got here early, but she threw up. Probably one of those 24-hour stomach-flu bugs. Not good for business if guests get sick after eating my food."

"Okay. When?"

"Can you get to the café by eight thirty? We'll finish the prep then take the van and the coffee cart to the Kingston's place."

"No problem." Eight thirty still gave me plenty of time.

"Hi, Ruth." Shona's voice echoed in the background on Joe's phone.

"Is Shona still off to her koala gig?" I asked Joe.

"Yes." His tone was terse.

"You said I could take any acting gig if it was local." Shona's muffled words sounded thin in the distance.

"Yeah, but this isn't acting, and with Bridget sick, I need your help.

"It's better than nothing. And you promised."

There was silence.

"I'm going now."

Longer silence.

"If that's how you want it to be."

Even longer silence.

The door slammed.

I swallowed hard. I hated when my friends fought.

There were a few more seconds of silence before Joe spoke again.

"Apologies for that." Tension reverberated down the line. "I need to go and see if another of the casuals can come in early."

"It will be okay, Joe."

"Of course it will." His sarcasm said he wasn't convinced.

My whole body ached by the time the party was in full swing. The same jazz quartet that had been hired for the business celebration played happy music, as the sparkling glitterati milled in and out of a huge marquee. The house was beautiful, and the gardens were exquisitely manicured. The Kingston property oozed class as well as cash.

For a fleeting moment I found myself missing the bright lights of Europe. Paulo had done things in style, and we'd had some amazing parties. Probably one reason why my young, impressionable and lovesick self, had made the dumb decision to leave everything for him.

I shook myself. This was not time to reminisce—I had work to do. It wasn't looking like I'd have any time to find out more about Xavier Kingston. It was mid-afternoon and I was starving, so I leapt at the chance to take a breather when Joe suggested it.

"Take a break, Ruth. Tara can make the coffees."

"Thanks!" I made myself a quick macchiato and scooped some leftover canapés onto a small plate. Then I found a wrought iron garden seat and sank onto it, glad to relieve the pressure on my feet.

The food had gone down well so far—platters and platters of Joe's special canapés that almost melted in your mouth. People didn't seem to mind that I was there, although I did get, "Where's Bridget?" from a few of the locals, along with an accusing, "Bridget always remembers my order."

I tried not to bristle. Bridget's superpower may have been a photographic memory, but I could make great coffee, too. Joe's beans made it easy. At least I wasn't hassled by the curse thing. Lots of Kingston's guests were from out of town and several of the locals were 'people of influence' or professionals who wouldn't want to appear superstitious, but I did see a couple of hesitant looks when I was serving. At least Ed-the-vet smiled and said hello.

When my lunch was finished, I slipped into the house for a bathroom break. I did what needed doing, splashed water on my face and was ready to face the world—and a hundred guests—when the itch to explore began to twitch. I was in Xavier Kingston's house, he was on Aldon Rossi's list, and he'd been at the business celebration and could have taken Joe's knife. I didn't have much time, but this might be my only chance to check him out.

Not that I had a clue in heaven what I was looking for.

Joe and I had met Xavier Kingston in his office that morning, so I knew where it was. If Joe could have afforded to lose this gig, I think he'd have pulled out of catering when the sale of the Farrow farm became public. But he was a businessman and had to pay the bills. I shuddered when I remembered the tension that had radiated off Joe in Kingston's presence. In Joe's eyes, Kingston had sold out his friends.

I tiptoed down the long, stately hallway. Xavier and his wife were outside enjoying the party so it couldn't hurt to have a quick look, could it? If I got caught, I could make something up. Joe would have my back.

My pulse quickened as I slipped through Kingston's study door, easing it shut with a soft click. I stood there, gazing at his old mahogany desk, with absolutely no idea what to do next.

Bradley was right. I sucked at fieldwork.

*Desk. Begin with the desk.*

Butterflies jazzed in my stomach in rhythm to the music outside and my heart slammed bass beats against my chest wall. I edged closer to Kingston's desk, my eyes scanning for the smallest clue. Paper scraps or glue could be evidence of the threatening letters received by Rossi. If I could find anything to indicate animosity or a secret deal between Kingston and Rossi, I could tell Larsen.

Elouise's theory—that Rossi was extorting Kingston and others in the town—nagged at me. It felt increasingly plausible. Knowledge is power.

I took a breath to settle myself then edged towards the paperwork stacked neatly in manila folders on the desktop. One folder caught my eye. It was labelled 'Kingston Hill', the official name of Paul and Donna's farm. I opened the folder, but it just held formal documents—the letter of offer and other legal stuff. What was next?

I needed something more personal, like evidence of blackmail. Had Rossi found something that he'd used to make Kingston sell the farm to Claire Briscoe? I made a mental note to ask Kat about it tonight.

I opened one of the desk drawers to find a large diary nestled inside. A small note of triumph flickered inside me. Like Rossi, Kingston liked ink and paper. You didn't have to be a computer expert to read it. I ran my fingers over the soft leather and flicked through to a couple of weeks before Rossi's death, but the only detail that caught my eye was a meeting scheduled with Rossi on Monday afternoon, barely hours after I'd been due to see him.

Probably just coincidence.

Before I could think any further, footsteps echoed down the hallway and stopped abruptly outside the study door.

My eyes darted for a hiding spot. Options were few. Beneath the desk? Far too conspicuous. My heart hammered as I edged towards the door. Hiding behind it when it swung open was a gamble. Maybe I could say Joe sent me to look for some paperwork.

The handle twisted, then stopped. An unfamiliar woman's voice floated through the wall, speaking to whoever was at the door. I assumed it was Kingston. He huffed and his footsteps retreated. I clutched at a shelf until my wild heartbeat resumed a steadier rhythm. That was too close. I needed to get out of there, now.

I swung towards the door but bumped the bookshelf as I moved. A small, framed photo slapped over face first on the shelf. I righted it, recognising Kingston, Rossi, Paul and Donna Farrow, and Dad, but I didn't know who the others were. I took a photo with my phone, just in case it was important, then slowly turned the door handle and peeked out. There was no one around. I was heading for the back door when an elderly woman stepped in front of me.

"Hello." Her voice had a tipsy lilt and she swayed a little.

Had she seen me coming out of the office?

She was petite, about five foot two, with short, straight white hair, a Betty White smile and a long, blue velvet, lace-trimmed dress that matched her eyes. She held a tall cut crystal glass, filled with clear liquid and ice that clinked against the glass with each unsteady gesture of her hand. A slice of lime sat precariously on the rim, looking like it could fall at any moment.

So did the old woman.

"Hi," I replied, taking a step closer as she swayed. "Great party."

"Yes." She hummed as the musicians outside bashed out an old 'big band' number. Then she stepped close, the heady scent of gin dancing through my senses as her body swayed towards me. Who was she? Kingston's mother?

"Do you know where Benjamin's gone? I can't find him." She leaned even closer and spoke with a conspiratorial whisper. "It's our engagement party, you know."

Recognition clicked. This was definitely Kingston's mother. I'd heard she had some kind of dementia. Benjamin Kingston, Xavier's father, had passed a couple of years ago.

"It's Fiona's engagement party, Mrs Kingston. Your granddaughter."

The old lady gave me an admonishing smile. "Don't be silly. Fiona is only ten. She can't get engaged." She started humming again and took a long sip of gin.

"Right then, I'd better go and help make coffee." My

heart went out to the older woman, but there was nothing I could do or say that would help.

"Bye, dear!" She waved, words slurring as she wobbled and turned to go. I reached out to steady her. There'd be no drunk grannies with broken hips on my watch. Her warm, gin-soaked breath made me glad there were no open flames nearby, and I wondered if alcohol had caused her dementia.

She leaned on me as I guided her through the house.

"Where would you like to go, Mrs Kingston?"

"Call me Olivia." Her singsong voice emphasised the 'liv' in her name.

"Okay, Olivia. Is there somewhere you'd like to sit? Can I get you a coffee or tea?" She waved her empty glass in my direction, and I took it from her and put it on a hallway table. The passageway opened into a large living room, and I led her over to a soft leather sofa. But instead of sitting down, she giggled, grasped my hands and slurred. "Want to play whing-a-whing-a-whoshie?"

She was stronger than I thought. She pulled me out into the middle of the room by both hands and spun in a circle. "Whing-a-whing-a-whoshie, spockets full of poshey. A tissue, a tissue. Whoshie falls down." She pulled down hard with both her hands as she tried to fall to the floor in a fit of giggles, pulling me with her. I managed to stay on my feet and hold her up.

"What's going on here?" Xavier Kingston stood in the doorway.

"Um… I came inside to use your bathroom, but Olivia—your mum—looked unsteady on her feet so I brought her in here to sit down. Then she grabbed me and wanted to play."

Kingston blanched. "What game?"

"Whoshie," Olivia slurred. "Whoshie fall down." She

giggled again. This time Kingston caught her before she could fling herself to the ground.

"Whoshie fall down." She suddenly put her hands over her face and began to shake. Was she crying? Xavier pulled her tenderly into his arms and rocked her against him. "It's okay, Mum. Everything is okay."

He looked over his mother's head towards me. "Thank you, Miss…"

"Smythe. Ruth Smythe."

"Thank you for helping my mother, but I'm sure you can be of more use to Joe outside."

I shivered as I made my way to the door, summarily dismissed. Whoshie had to be Rossi, right? Was Olivia retreating into her childhood days or had she seen Rossi die? Had Xavier Kingston killed Rossi?

I was so caught up in thought that I nearly missed the buzz of my phone in my pocket.

"Hey, Kat."

"Can we meet at your place tonight? My internet is down."

"Sure."

"Can we have burgers? But only from Kenny's. They have the best salsa."

I laughed to myself. Kat didn't waste words. "I'll see what I can do. If you get there before me, you'll need to use the spare key." I told her where it was and gave her the code for the alarm. I also told her that I'd found some old notes and news clippings that I wanted to get her take on, but I didn't give her the details.

"Thanks. See you tonight." And she was gone.

It was just as well I'd thrown Dad's bag and its contents into my car boot this morning. Kat's curiosity might have got the better of her if she'd found the bag. I'd get her take on the news clippings, and maybe some of the notes, but not Dad's code—if it was a code. That was something to cherish between him and me. I couldn't bring him back, but I could discover what was in his head and heart, even if it was forty years ago.

Olivia started bashing out some old wartime song at the top of her voice. How could that frail old lady have been in my shed when Rossi was murdered? I couldn't conceive of any reason in the universe why she would have been there in the middle of the night watching her son kill Rossi.

I joined Tara outside and together we took orders and created cappuccinos, macchiatos and almond chai lattes, but it was hard to focus. Olivia might have heard about the murder from Xavier. Everyone local knew about it. But why did it make her cry? Who was Rossi to her? Was he a close friend of the family?

I couldn't wait to get home and see what Kat had found online.

# Chapter Thirty-Four

By the time I'd helped Joe clean up at the Kingstons' place and pack everything away back at the café, the line outside Kenny's Burger Place stretched well along the footpath. I texted Kat to see if she'd settle for a lesser burger, but I didn't get a reply, so I'd opted for fish and chips instead.

I thought I heard someone call my name, but when I turned around I didn't see anyone, so I kept going. The smell made me salivate, so I stole a chip or five from the packet as I drove home. Potato was the best comfort food, especially when deep-fried to perfection.

All of that made me late, and I gazed up at the darkening sky as I crunched down the path towards the house. There was still a faint pink tinge on the horizon, and stars twinkled in the crisp, clear, autumn evening air.

But when a shooting star blazed across the star-scape, it set off a deep pang of sorrow. Was life just a bright flare of light like that meteor? One moment of un-take-backable violence, and it's gone?

I rolled my shoulders, trying to ease away the tension. It

didn't matter if it was me or Gary or LTB, someone needed to find out who killed Rossi. It wasn't just about my reputation or proving my innocence or the innocence of my friends. That was important, but something deep in me wanted to make things right—or as right as they could be after this man's light was snuffed out.

Even if he wasn't a good person—even if he had been doing bad stuff to people—he didn't deserve to die.

My mobile bleeped. It was Joe.

JOE L.

Have you heard from Shona? She was due
back over an hour ago.

No. Have you called her?

Yes. No answer.

Have you tried her friends?

I couldn't get hold of them all, but she's not
with anyone I've spoken to.

Fear snagged around my heart. I texted back.

She's always forgetting to charge her
phone.

I know, but... I've got a bad feeling.

I'm just home. I'll try her myself. Call me
when she gets home.

I was so deep in thought as I stepped up onto the back porch that I didn't realise until I reached for my keys that the house was dark, the back door wide-open, and Kat was nowhere to be seen.

"What the—?" My breath caught as I took a tentative step forward.

A shadow moved beside me, and a hand clamped over my mouth. Before I could scream, Dan's voice whispered in my ear. "Ruth, it's me."

His soft breath against my ear made me shiver. He took his hand away from my mouth but stayed close, holding my arm. He held his finger to his lips, cautioning me to be silent.

"Dan? What the hell?" My words were a harsh whisper.

"Shhhh!" He pulled me deeper into the shadows. His warmth radiated through his shirt, and I could feel the vibration of his voice as he spoke. "I think there's someone in there."

"Why are *you* here?"

"I was out to dinner and the backup alarm triggered on my phone."

"Backup alarm?"

"I'll explain later. I need to check inside."

"Kat should be in there."

"What?" Dan's hand tightened on my arm.

"She was helping me… research. The internet has been playing up at her place."

He stilled and swore under his breath. "Wait here. Stay in the shadows."

"What are you going to do?"

He pulled something out of his jacket.

"Wait, is that a gun?"

He didn't answer. "Stay right there. I'm going to check inside. Lydia and Gary will be here in a minute."

Lydia… Of course that was who Dan was having dinner with. I tried to ignore the twang of my heartstrings.

He edged towards the door and stood to the side, nudging

it open with his foot, his gun at the ready. Then he slid through the opening into the house.

"Be careful," I whispered into the darkness.

There was a shuffling inside the house, and I strained to see, shivery ants crawling up and down my arms.

"Aaaaaahhhh!" An awful shriek blared from inside the house.

"Dan!" I took a step forward, but before I could do anything else, a large ringtail possum with a baby on her back galloped out of the house and sprinted for a gum tree. The terrified creature scrambled up the trunk, only stopping when she was safely out of reach.

Dan stepped out of the house, putting his gun back in a holster, just as a car turned into the driveway. Headlights glared and I covered my eyes. I thought it was a police car, but I couldn't see for sure.

"Kat's not here. The house is clear." Dan's steady tone calmed me. He was okay.

I stepped towards the door. "What about her stuff? Her computer?"

"I don't know. I'll see if I can turn the power back on." He disappeared into the dark at the side of the house,

Lydia Larsen and Gary Stone got out of the police car just as the lights flicked on inside. Dan reappeared and met the two police officers on the porch.

"There's been a break-in," he told them. "Kat Mackenzie was apparently here earlier, but she's not here now."

I tried to call Kat but there was no answer. When I put the phone away, Dan and the police were already inside but I still hesitated in the doorway.

"It's okay, Ruth. It's safe." There was something in Dan's tone that made me hesitate again. It wasn't safety I was worried about—I was scared what I might find.

I swallowed hard when I saw the mess. My home had been ransacked. Every drawer and every cupboard had been opened and the contents dumped on the floor. There was no damage as such—not like the slashed sofas and cushions you see in the movies—but it was bad enough. All the cushions had been cast off the sofa, my study had been upturned, and the sheets ripped off my bed.

The intruder had been looking for something specific, I was sure of that, because in the middle of all the mess I found my laptop among some rubble on the floor just inside the back door.

I picked it up and cradled it to me. It was obvious from the empty chip packets and cola bottles on the coffee table that Kat had been here. But where was she now? Had she been kidnapped?

I turned to Dan, trying to keep the annoyance out of my voice. "Why didn't the security system stop them?"

"It did. That's why we knew to come. Whoever it was disabled the main alarm, but not the backup." A small, smug smile ghosted on his lips.

"I've been out all day helping Joe at Fiona Kingston's party. Kat had my spare key. Maybe she didn't lock up."

He shook his head. "The back door was jimmied open."

I glanced at the door and noticed the splinters near the lock. "She should be here." My eyes widened. "You don't think someone's taken her, do you?"

Dan frowned and called Larsen over. I explained my concerns.

Larsen's eyes narrowed. "Kat is a hacker. She was working with Aldon Rossi. What was she doing here?"

"I... um..."

Dan stepped in. "When Ruth found out her dad had hired Rossi to find her, she naturally wanted to know more.

She asked Kat over to pick her brain and do some research on the relationship between her Dad and Rossi."

My eyes sent Dan a silent, "Thank you."

His equally eloquent raised eyebrow replied, "You owe me."

"That had better be all it was," Larsen said. "You do know that hacking as a means of breaching privacy is an offence with possible jail time?"

I made my expression as innocent as I could. "We weren't hacking into anything."

Joe texted right at that moment.

JOE

Nothing from Shona?

How could I have forgotten to ring her?

The police are at my place. I've had a break-in.

You okay?

Yeah. I'll tell the cops about Shona.

I looked up from my screen. "That was Joe. Shona still isn't home. She didn't come back from her koala gig in Adelaide today."

"Koala gig?" Larsen screwed up her face in confusion.

Dan filled her in. "Acting assignment."

"Oh?" Her tone was cool. "When did she go missing?"

"Today. This evening."

She pursed her lips. "Then she's not a missing person."

"A murder happens on my property. I get broken into. Kat is gone. Now Shona disappears. You think that's a coincidence?" My voice quivered. "You need to look for her."

"Could she have stopped to catch up with friends?" Dan's question was reasonable.

"Joe is trying to get hold of them, but Shona would have called."

Larsen sighed. "Try to call her."

I dialled Shona but there was no answer. I glared meaningfully at Larsen, who sighed again, gave me a long I-don't-believe-you-look, and turned to Gary.

"When you've finished here, go have a chat to Joe Leventis." She turned back to me. "Have you tried to ring Kat yet?"

"Yes." Heat crept up my neck at Larsen's penetrating gaze.

"I suggest you do so again before we put resources to it."

I pulled out my phone and called Kat. To my surprise her thrash metal ringtone blasted from outside the back door. We all turned to see her standing in the doorway with a brown paper bag that smelled delicious and had 'Kenny's' written on the front in big red letters.

She stared around the room. "What's going on?"

# Chapter Thirty-Five

Kat stepped inside and closed the door behind her. A knot in my stomach unravelled. She was okay.

"There was a break-in," I told her. "Looks like they may have taken your computer." I regarded her carefully, not sure how she'd react to that kind of devastating news.

"Oh no! Your laptop was new, wasn't it? I've got mine here." She patted the bag hanging off her shoulder. "I take it everywhere with me. Did they get the clip—?"

I cut her off before she could say too much. "I've got my laptop. It was near the door, but I'm not sure why." While I'd told Kat about the newspaper clippings, I didn't want Larsen knowing that the contents of Dad's schoolbag could be relevant after all. Not until I'd processed everything. The police had had their go. I breathed a prayer of thanks that I'd shoved the bag in the boot of the Mini. Next time I'd take my laptop too.

"I think they might have dropped it." Dan took my computer and examined it. "They may have seen me arrive and were in a hurry to leave."

My eyes strayed to the floor near where I found the laptop. Cat fur. I'd forgotten about my cat! "Where's Cora?"

"Cora! Cora!" I couldn't see her anywhere.

"Who is Cora?" Larsen frowned. "How many people were actually here?"

"Cora is Ruth's cat." Dan's foot twitched.

Another patrol car arrived, there were footsteps and Constable Jones tramped in through the door.

"Shut the door," I yelled.

She stood there looking confused.

"I don't want my cat to get out."

Jones grinned and closed the door behind her, but the latch fell apart. She must have seen my harassed look because she propped a small side table against it to hold it shut.

Larsen sighed deeply. "Go and check the perimeter, Jones."

"Detective," Jones nodded, undid her makeshift doorstop, and disappeared into the night. I rushed over and wedged the door shut again.

"She hasn't been here long enough to know it's home," Kat explained.

"She could have got out before we got here. The burglar left the door open."

"Crap." Kat scanned the room, blushing and looking away when she met Dan's eyes. It looked like her crush hadn't gone away. "We need to find her."

Alarm flashed over Dan's face at the possibility of being co-opted into cat-finding duties. "I'll just check the security footage. Can we power up your laptop?"

I hesitated only slightly before turning on the computer and logging on. I trusted Dan but didn't want the world to know my password.

Then Kat pointed. "There she is!"

The young cat strode into my living room, took one look at the house full of strangers, then tore straight back into my bedroom. I only saw her for a moment, but that brief microsecond was all I needed. Her white paws were stained red.

Cora had blood on her paws.

"Blood." I pointed to where Cora had disappeared down the hallway. "She has blood on her paws! There could be DNA."

Kat ran after Cora, but Larsen looked at me as if I'd gone crazy.

"There's blood on Cora's paws," I repeated. "She might have attacked the burglar. There could be DNA."

"I don't think that little cat—"

Larsen was interrupted by Dan's loud laugh guffawing from where he sat at the kitchen table. He pointed to the computer.

"What?" I asked.

"Come and see." He turned the computer screen to let me see CCTV footage of my back doorway.

There was a grainy black and white image of a person wearing black clothes, gloves and a balaclava, leaving the house with my computer under their arm. Then a shadow soared through the air towards the intruder and landed on their head. The small cat bit at the intruder and raked at their neck with her back claws. They flailed at the cat, dropped the laptop and ran off into the night. Cora strutted around, fur fluffed up, before flicking her tail and sauntering back inside.

Dan's eyes crinkled as he grinned up at me. "You didn't tell me you had your own security system. That's one crazy cat." His foot twitched again, but his voice said he was impressed.

"See." My voice was urgent as I spoke to Larsen. "There's still blood on her paws. Can't we use that for DNA?"

Larsen and Gary Stone looked at each other, then Larsen spoke. "It's not worth the resources. I'm not running DNA from a cat's claws, especially from an attempted burglary."

"But the burglary could be linked to the murder." I stopped as an even worse thought blared loud in my mind. "It could be linked to Shona. She hasn't come home and—"

"There's no point. It will be contaminated by," Larsen glanced at Gary, "all kinds of matter."

"She's a clean cat. She washes herself all the time," Kat insisted. "She'll be under the bed, but we can coax her out."

"She could be licking the blood off right now." My voice was pleading. "Can we swab her paws or something and then work out later if it's going to be useful? If we wait any longer, it could be too late."

"The resources…" Larsen was beginning to waver.

"Stuff the resources." I gulped in a breath and tried again. "Rossi was killed in my shed, and now I've been burgled, and Shona hasn't come home yet. If there's any chance these things could be related…" My voice trailed off as I pleaded with the detective.

There was silence in the room.

"She wouldn't have washed it off by now?" There was doubt in Gary's voice. "Any DNA could be pretty degraded."

"I don't know. But I know there was blood on her paws."

"She did have a good go at whoever it was. And she does use her claws." Dan lifted his jeans leg to show us the cat-claw sized gouges in his work boot. "This happened yesterday."

Larsen let out the deepest sigh. "Okay, go get the cat." She turned to her offsider. "Get the CSI technician back here."

"Thank you!" Then I hesitated, looking around the room. "I may need some help."

. . .

Dan and Larsen stood to the side as Kat squirmed under the bed, trying to reach Cora. I hadn't got around to getting a cat crate, so we had to make do with the box Kat had sent her home in.

"Someone needs to hold this." I tried to hand the box to Dan, but he pushed it away.

"Don't look at me. I'd need danger money to go near that thing."

I gave him my best are-you-for-real look. "Okay. I'll hold the box if you block her escape."

His eyes squinted into a grimace. "And put my life on the line?

I caught Larsen's gaze for a moment and noted the briefest of eye rolls. I shot her a knowing smirk. Who would have thought we'd bond over Dan?

"She's just a small domestic cat, isn't she?" Larsen laughed.

He shook his head. "You saw the video footage."

"You were Special Ops. Pararescue," Larsen's voice was dry. "It's just a cat."

I glanced at Dan, stifling a laugh. "Kittens can be scary."

It was Dan's turn to roll his eyes. "Okay, but can I get a blanket or something? It would help stop her slipping through my legs."

At least he'd decided to be helpful. "Blankets are in there." I pointed to the bottom of the large chest of drawers in my room.

"Why can't we just close the bedroom door?" Gary looked around.

"There isn't one." I pointed to the empty space. "Low priority for me in fixing this place up."

Dan snared an animal-print blanket and stood in the

doorway. He gave a shaky grin. "My will is in the top drawer in my office."

I laughed. "Man up, flyboy!"

He shot me a dark look. "You owe me. Especially if I lose my eyes."

"Ready, everyone?" Kat called from under the bed. "I'm going to try to catch her, but if she runs, wrap her in the blanket then drop her in the box." She wriggled further under the bed. "Here, sweet Cora."

"Meow-ow-ow."

"What are her pupils doing?" I asked Kat.

"Dilated, but it's dark under here."

"Pupils?" asked Larsen.

"Her pupils dilate before she attacks," I said.

Larsen grimaced. "What kind of pet cat is this?"

"One straight from hell," Dan answered.

"Okay, I've nearly got her." Kat's words were muffled under the bed. "Get ready."

"Meow."

"That's a good girl."

A loud purr began emanating from under the bed.

"You really are a darling, aren't you?" Kat murmured. "Ready, Ruth? I'll just grab her scruff and try to ease her out."

"Cat whisperer." Dan spoke in a regular kind of whisper.

Kat didn't reply but kept murmuring sweet somethings to Cora. "Good girl. That's it… come out with me." And in a moment she had Cora out from under the bed and in her arms. "Sweet girl… Ready, Ruth? You'll have to close the box quickly. She won't like it."

"Ready."

She lifted Cora towards the box.

"Meow-ow-ow." The cat began to struggle and Kat held her gently by the scruff.

"It's going to be okay, girl." She placed Cora in the box. "Now, Ruth."

I was ready, I swear I was, but right at that moment the voice of the police CSI tech boomed in the doorway. "Detective Larsen?"

"Meow-ow-yow-yow!" Cora leapt up and over my shoulder before I could close the box. Dan dived for her, but she fled straight over his head and into the hallway.

"Catch her," called Gary.

"Shut the back door," I yelled.

We sprinted out of the room and down the hallway. Someone had already shut the door and Cora was in the living room hiding under the sideboard.

"Let her be," Kat clutched my arm. "She's scared."

Larsen crouched down and peered under the sideboard, focused on the cat. "Here, kitty, kitty, kitty."

Cora let out a depths-of-hell growl.

Dan raised his eyebrows and mouthed, "See!" in my direction.

I tried hard not to smile.

"Let me try again." Kat tried to push in front of the detective.

But Larsen wasn't deterred. She stood up, went to the laundry and came back with a broom. This was my new life. The local police knew my place well enough to know where to get cleaning gear.

"Okay," she said. "Let's do this. Operation, Catch a Kitty." She angled the broom under the sideboard. "Out you come, little one!"

# Chapter Thirty-Six

Larsen's attempt to catch Cora had been an epic fail. It was like a scene from an old Three Stooges movie—I used to watch them with Grandad when I was a kid. Dan and Gary diving for the cat, falling on their backsides and knocking heads, Kat yelling at them to stop, Cora smashing a bottle of red wine in my kitchen and wrecking the room even further. Sanity finally prevailed and when Larsen let Kat work her magic it only took her ten minutes to have Cora purring again.

While Cora didn't like being put in the box and began attacking the cardboard as soon as the lid was closed, thanks to a whole roll of duct tape we were able to secure her for the drive to the vet.

Dan drove. The CSI tech, who we now knew as Trent, sat in the front with him to maintain chain of evidence, and Kat and I sat in the back with Cora, just in case it took two of us to hold the box closed. I shuddered at the thought of my attack cat getting loose in a car. But the box held secure, and we made it to the clinic.

"You were had. Let's face it," Dan whispered beside me as we trooped into the vet clinic behind the tech. "You thought you were getting Simba, but Kat landed you with Scar." He chuckled to himself. "Although I guess both are predators."

I shrugged, my lips twitching upwards. "I was pretty desperate."

"Obviously." His eyes crinkled. "Cora's another name for Persephone, isn't it? Queen of the Underworld?"

"She was scared." I gave him my best I-can't-believe-you-said-that glare, but was secretly impressed that he knew his classics. I turned and glanced behind me. Kat was walking, head down, deep in thought. I slowed so she could catch up.

"You've got a gift," I said to her.

She shrugged. "Animals are like people. You treat them well and they'll treat you well in return."

Dan scoffed. "I was nice to her, and she attacked my boot."

Kat frowned. "She must have felt threatened."

"Yeah, right. When I held out my hand to let her sniff me and rubbed her ears?"

"I think she attacked you because of the noise of the magpie clattering on the patio roof. It gave her a fright." I stretched to relieve my tired muscles. It had been a long day. "At least we have Cora and we're here."

'Here' was a small vet clinic owned by Ed, who quickly ushered us inside.

"Come in, everyone. Hello, Ruth."

"Hi, Ed. Where's Doug? Asleep like we should be?" I flashed a warm smile, remembering the sulphur-crested cockatoo who knew my name.

"Indeed, he is." He glanced at the box. "Hopefully this won't take long."

Ed had once owned a large district veterinary hospital,

but sold the business with the idea of retiring and travelling. But then his wife died of cancer, and he needed something to do, so he opened a small clinic under his house. He was a local through and through, and even though he was supposedly semi-retired, he had plenty of work and was still the first contact the police had for after-hours emergencies.

Not that cutting a cat's claws was usually an emergency, but the circumstances made it so.

Trent had to witness the collection of the samples by a professional, or collect them himself, and Cora needed to be sedated before anyone could swab her claw folds and take nail samples.

But it was all so calm and simple when we got to Ed's. Kat held Cora while Ed gave the cat a sedative injection. Cora gave a soft spit in protest but that was all—she was soon sound asleep on the warm rug on the surgery table. The technician went to work swabbing Cora's claws, taking both dry clippings and wet swabs stored in vials of saline. It looked like there still was blood there. The technician also took swabs from Dan, Kat and me because our DNA could still be on the cat's claws. Larsen said they would run the samples, but they would be low priority unless more evidence could be found to link the break-in to the murder.

I stroked Cora's silky fur as Ed went to get something to reverse the sedative. "She's pretty when she's not being Catzilla."

"Yes, she's got flecks of grey through her fur. She's actually a tortoiseshell." Ed nodded. "Quite a light one."

"Aren't tortoiseshells evil? I read that somewhere," Dan said. Kat glared at him.

"This one is," muttered Larsen.

Ed laughed. "Some can be cranky. I had an associate once who swore the darker the coat, the crankier the cat."

"She's a good cat!" Kat stepped forward and ran her fingers through Cora's fur. "I called her Cora because there's a heart-shaped patch of grey, right over her heart. See?" She lifted Cora's front leg and pointed, glaring at each of us. "She may be cranky, but she's got a good heart."

No one dared contradict her.

I ran my hand through Cora's soft belly fluff and found... a lump?

"Ed, what's this?" I didn't like the feel of it.

"What's up?" The vet put his glasses back on.

"There's a lump here. At the back of her belly, near her leg."

Ed frowned as he felt the young cat's belly. "You're right. In her groin." He looked up at me over his glasses. "You're observant."

"What is it?"

He felt the lump again. "It feels like an inguinal hernia."

"That doesn't sound good?" I said.

"It's not. There's a spot in the groin where all the blood vessels and nerves run out from the belly area into the leg." He traced the path with his fingers. "It's supposed to close over not long after a kitten is born, but sometimes it doesn't close properly. People can get them too. You can be born with them, or it can happen because of trauma—especially with men. I got one lifting a foal a couple of years ago." He rubbed his lower belly. "It swelled up in a large lump and I had surgery to fix it." He stepped back from the surgery table. "It's pretty common. You young blokes need to watch out. It's worse when you herniate into your scrotum."

Dan, Gary and Trent shuffled uncomfortably where they were standing. I caught Larsen's eye, and we both snorted at the same time. It was our second moment of bonding that night. At this rate we'd be BFFs by morning.

"Can we fix it?" Kat asked.

Ed felt the lump again. "It's large. I'll see if I can reduce it." He massaged the lump a few different ways, stopped, seemed deep in thought, and then tried again. "These ones in the groin are often harder to reduce than the umbilical ones and more likely to strangulate."

"That's when bowel gets caught in the hernia, isn't it?" Kat asked. "And the blood supply gets cut off."

"That doesn't sound great." I shook my head. This wasn't looking good for Cora.

"Aha! There she goes." The lump disappeared.

"Hey, doctor genius. You've fixed it." Kat clapped her hands.

He let out a long breath. "Without surgery it will keep on happening."

"And then?" I had a bad feeling about the answer.

"It could be painful. If it strangulates and a loop of bowel gets trapped, it could kill her."

We all looked at the fierce little cat lying on the table, beginning to twitch now that Ed had given her an injection to reverse the sedative.

"An operation would be expensive?"

"I'd try to keep costs down, but it can take a while. So unfortunately, yes."

"And the other option is to wait until she's in pain, or it strangulates, and put her down?"

Ed inclined his head. "Or do it sooner. It's hard to tell if she's in pain now. And if she's a difficult cat and attacks people..." His voice tailed off with his shrug.

I frowned, still stroking Cora's soft, silky fur. I knew *sooner* meant now. "Could pain be why she's difficult? If she had sudden jabs in her groin, could it make her attack people?"

"It's possible. We all get grumpy when we're sore and it could be partially strangulating—that can give sharp, deep pain. But there are lots of animals who suffer pain without attacking people."

"If I went ahead, would you do the surgery?"

Ed nodded again. "Although my receptionist is away this week. It's not something you can do when the nurse has to answer the phones."

"I can help." For all of Kat's super-tough, don't-give-a-crap exterior, cats were her kryptonite. Her eyes pleaded with Ed. "I can answer the phone and I can even do some nurse stuff. I've helped you with my cats after hours before. I know what to do."

"Well, it's up to Cora's owner. She'd be footing the bill."

All eyes turned to me.

"Please." Kat's eyes pleaded with mine. "She attacked the intruder. She defended your home. That has to count for something."

That was true, but did she defend my house out of loyalty or psychosis?

"And the patch over her heart. It's a sign. She might be a bad cat sometimes, but she's got a good heart." Kat was clutching at straws now.

All eyes were on me as I ran my hand along Cora's sleek fur. She lifted her head at my touch then relaxed down again. There wasn't much money left in my bank account. Not until the next part of my inheritance came through, or until I got regular work. But would anyone in this town give me a job? They were all too scared I might make them drop dead. Being considered a harbinger of death puts a dampener on your employment prospects.

There were lots of other cats in the world. Nice, friendly cats that sat on your lap, head-butted your hand and purred as they slept by your feet at night. Cats that didn't bite your hand and savage your friends. Cats that needed a loving forever home. My thumb still throbbed where Cora had latched onto it. Why would I spend non-existent money on a cat that was the devil incarnate?

Cora was half awake now. I caressed her silky ears, unable to say the words I knew I must. Just then the little rogue turned and lay her small round head in my hand. She rubbed her face against my fingers, looked up at me through half-closed, sleepy eyes and emitted a soft, "Meow," followed by her signature chocolate liqueur purr.

My eyes misted over. "Oh, you beast." I knew when I was beaten. "Okay." I turned to Ed. "Do the surgery."

There was a collective sigh around the room. They all knew I'd been close to making the other decision.

To my great surprise Dan leaned in and whispered in my ear, "I'll pay half."

I nearly kissed him.

# Chapter Thirty-Seven

Ed suggested leaving Cora at his clinic until Monday, when he'd do the surgery. That way she could be kept quiet, and I'd have a chance to get my destroyed house back together. Dan dropped both Kat and me back at my place, but I was surprised when he got out of his Jeep.

When I asked why, he shrugged and said, "I need to fix your back door. And the wires on the alarm."

"But it's the middle of the night. I'll be fine." But a shudder juddered through me when I looked at the prised-open door.

"It won't take long, and I'll be out of your hair."

I glanced at my watch. It was half past twelve, but it seemed a lot later—or earlier. Kat excused herself with a smile at Dan, a faint blush on her pale cheeks and a lowering of her eyes as she went to her car.

My stomach growled, a loud rumble that made both Dan and me laugh.

"Sorry," I said.

"When did you last eat?"

"At Xavier Kingston's party this afternoon." I thought for a moment. "Plus a few hot chips after I bought them in town tonight, but they'd be beyond eating now." I frowned, there wasn't much food in the house, then I brightened. "Cheese on toast?"

Dan's smile lit up his face. "Sounds brilliant."

"Coffee, tea or…" I honestly didn't nearly say 'or me'. Honestly… I only hesitated for moment before saying "Something stronger?"

There was laughter in Dan's eyes, but it was paired with something more intense. I couldn't escape the feeling that the 'or me' option would have been taken up instantly.

"Something stronger would be great," he said.

I turned away from him to cover the flush that rose up my face. I needed to get it together. It was okay for Kat to have a crush on this man, but it wasn't how I rocked. He'd done a lovely thing in saying he'd pay for half of Cora's surgery, but I couldn't let that weaken my resolve. If Dan and I had a fling, I'd dive in too deep and run off with him overseas. Then I'd get hurt when he became tired of me. Either that or I'd stay here as his one-time conquest. Neither of those options worked for me.

But he helped me clean up the kitchen disaster, and found another bottle of red in the cupboard while I got the toasted cheese on the way. Wine and cheese probably weren't a great recipe for good dreams after all that had happened today, but I needed to wind down and calm the worry that niggled in my gut when I thought of Shona.

I closed my eyes and sent up a quick prayer. If there was a God, I wanted him to be looking out for my friend.

*She'll be fine.*

*She'll be fine.*

*She'll be fine.*

Maybe if I said it to myself enough times, I'd believe it.

The toasted cheese was ready and Dan downed tools and joined me as I poured us each a large glass of wine.

Toasted cheese is supposed to be comfort food, but I didn't feel comfortable. Even if Shona was still mad at Joe, she would have returned *my* calls or texts. I only nibbled at the food and barely sipped at the wine as Dan and I sat together in lost-in-thought silence.

"I should ring Joe," I said, after offering Dan the last of the toasted cheese.

"Still worried?" His voice was edged with concern.

I nodded. "It's not like her."

I stood and reached for my phone but before I could dial, the screen lit up. "It's Joe." My hand shook as I accepted the call and put it on speaker. "Is she okay?"

There was a moment of silence on the other end of the phone and something like a sob. *No.* My legs wobbled. I sat down heavily in my seat as the coldest of shivers surged through every part of me. "Joe? What's happened?" Dan edged closer and put a steadying hand on my shoulder.

There was silence for a moment then Joe's voice broke. "She's gone, Ruth. The cops found her car, but she wasn't there. They think she's been… taken."

My breath caught. My pleading eyes met Dan's. This couldn't be happening.

He gave small nod and squeezed my shoulder.

"Hang on Joe, I'm with Dan. We're coming over."


Joe opened the door for us wordlessly, then sat down on his living room sofa with his face buried in his hands. I sat down next to him and put my arm around him. "They'll find her.

She'll be okay." But my words felt hollow, and I could smell the dank sweat of Joe's fear.

My stomach clenched and the toasted cheese churned. There'd been a murder in my shed, my house had been broken into and now Shona was gone. Was she lying dead, like Aldon Rossi? Or was she out there somewhere, alone and scared?

"There's no chance she broke down and went to get help?" I could tell from Dan's tone that he didn't believe that, but it was worth asking.

Joe lifted his head. He was as pale as his famous cream cheese icing, but his eyes were puffy and rimmed with red. "They don't think so. They found her keys a couple of metres away from the car. There are no obvious signs of a struggle so she might have known whoever it was."

"Could she have gone off with a friend?" My voice was tight with worry.

"She wouldn't have left the car open. Especially not with the koala suit inside." Joe's head sank into his hands again. "It's my fault. If I hadn't given her a hard time about the koala thing, she would have come straight home. She wouldn't have been driving back late."

"It's not your fault, Joe. People fight." I managed a grin. "You guys do fight, but you're pretty good at making up."

Joe acknowledged that with the smallest of smiles. "She can't be gone. I love her so much."

"She knew," I shook my head, "*knows* that."

"I'm not sure that coming home earlier would have made any difference, mate." Dan's voice was low, and compassionate. "If someone wanted to take her, they would have found a way."

Joe looked up from his hands and held Dan's gaze. "You're in security. Tell me the truth. What are her chances?"

Dan opened his mouth as if to say something, then looked as if he'd changed his mind. "Honestly, mate. It's not good. But until…"

"Until they find a body?" Joe's voice broke.

"Until they find a body, which they haven't yet." Dan inhaled deeply and scrubbed his hands over his face. "And from what I know of Shona, she won't make it easy for them."

"If she got away…?" My voice trailed off.

"The police will find her." There was assurance in Dan's voice.

"If she got away, the person who took her will be looking for her," I added.

"And then the police will catch them." Dan nodded.

I grasped Joe's hand, trying to hold it together for his sake. "We're here for you, Joe." Then I drew him into a deep hug. His body shook as I held him, and I blinked back my own tears. Shona couldn't be gone. She couldn't.

I pulled back when Joe's phone rang.

He answered. "Yes… no… Thank you, Detective." Then he hung up and let out a loud breath. "They've done a sweep of the area and there's no sign of her. There are tyre marks nearby, but it's in a spot where people often stop to turn around. And they're going to convene a search of the bushland at first light, near where her car was found."

We all sat in silence, lost in our own thoughts as Joe's clock struck two.


My thoughts tumbled around inside me as Dan drove me back to my place. My brain screamed the apocalypse, fearing news of the coming terror.

Dan pulled up in my drive, then got out of the car and followed me inside.

He must have seen my surprise. "I want to check that it's clear."

Fear quivered through me, and I folded my arms around my body. Even with the break-in it hadn't occurred to me until now, that whoever took Shona might also want me.

Dan went inside and the lights flickered on in the house. I waited in the doorway, listening to the sounds in the cool of the night. There was the rustle of leaves in the breeze, the hoot of a tawny frogmouth, the hiss of a possum and the eerie baying of a fox, but there were no human sounds of danger.

"It's okay, Ruth. You can come inside."

I shuffled in through the back door. My glass of red wine sat, almost untouched on the kitchen table and I picked it up and downed it in three large gulps.

I offered the bottle to Dan. "More?"

He shook his head. "Mind if I make a coffee?"

I should have offered to make it for him, but I was spent. My limbs sagged, heavy like wet sandbags, but it wasn't the I want-to-sleep-now type of tiredness. My body was heavy with fatigue, yet my nerves were electric and on edge. I put the wine bottle aside. "I'd better have decaf. I'm going to have trouble sleeping as it is."

Dan looked around the kitchen. "Where?"

I pointed. "There's some in the top cupboard."

It was nice to be waited on. Dan moved easily around my kitchen, discovering a packet of ginger nut biscuits I'd forgotten about in a cupboard. He put some on a plate and set my coffee down in front of me. I nibbled at the biscuits, but I still couldn't eat much, and I soon stood up and began pacing.

"We need to find them, Dan... whoever did this. If we find whoever killed Rossi, we'll find Shona."

"Ruth, it's—"

"Dangerous, I know. But I have to do something." My eyes burned and I blinked back tears. "Standing by isn't an option."

"The police are on it."

"And what good has that done?" My voice was laced with sarcasm. "What have they done so far? Suspect me, Shona and Joe? News flash—we didn't do it." My voice trembled, betraying every effort to sound composed. "I can't believe she's gone. Maybe I *am* cursed. Everyone I care about ends up leaving, dying or shutting me out." I turned away from Dan and smeared away my tears with the back of my hand.

Then he was there, his presence solid at my back, guiding me to face him. He pulled me close and I wept into his chest, my sobs raw and ugly as his strong arms held me. I clung to his warmth as all my grief for Shona, and for everything else that had unravelled, poured out.

His hand stroked comforting circles on my back. "You're not cursed, Ruth. You know that's crap. We'll find her." His breath was warm against my hair, and he smelled of earth and coffee.

I pulled back and dared to meet his gaze, finding blue eyes creased with concern. "You can't know that. What you said to Joe earlier…"

"I'll do whatever it takes to find her, Ruth. Know that." He drew me in again and hugged me hard as if to squeeze away my tears. He held me like that for a few long moments then leaned back, his gaze intense. "Larsen's good at her job. I know she can be prickly at times, but she won't stop until she finds the killer." He wiped the tears off my cheeks with his thumbs. "You've got good people on this case."

Gratitude merged with a surge of longing, and I had to avert my eyes before I revealed too much. Or did something really stupid, like kiss him. Instead, I pulled back, patted the wet patch on his chest and spoke in a small voice. "Sorry for snotting on you."

He laughed as he ran his hands down my arms, squeezed my hands and let me go. "I've had much worse than snot on me in my time. I think I'll survive."

I grabbed some tissues and blew my nose, then met his eyes with a faint smile. "Thank you."

"There's just one other thing."

I waited.

He pointed over his shoulder with his thumb in the direction of the door. "I managed to jury-rig the lock on the back door, as you know, but I'll need to get more materials tomorrow to fix it and the alarm."

"You don't need to—"

"I want to," he cut in. "I've got the time and it's no trouble. But..." His cheeks flushed a faint pink and he stuffed his hands in his pockets, as if he knew I wouldn't like what was coming next.

"But what?"

"With what's happened with Shona you don't have anywhere else to stay, do you?"

"No, but that doesn't matter."

"There's a murderer out there, Ruth."

"I'll be fine."

"Maybe, but until I can fix the door properly, you're not staying here alone. I'm sleeping on your sofa."

I lay motionless in the quiet of my room, sleep a distant hope. I'd argued with Dan, but he'd insisted on staying, and in the end we'd pulled the living room back together and I'd set him up on the sofa with blankets and a pillow.

His nearness brought both comfort and temptation. I did

feel safer with him there. I could take care of myself, but two were always better than one when real danger lurked. Of course, there was the other kind of peril. A silent voice, treacherous and alluring, suggesting how much better it would be if Dan and I were together, wrapped in a warm embrace here in my bed. My lack of a bedroom door meant that if I called out to Dan, he would hear me. And if I said yes, I didn't think he'd say no.

I rolled over onto my side. I hated myself sometimes. Here I was fantasising about a man while Shona was out there... somewhere. If she wasn't dead, she was lonely and afraid. I had to find her—whoever took her had to be the same person who killed Rossi, right? It was too much of a coincidence otherwise. If I could find Rossi's killer, then I might be able to find Shona. But would I be too late?

It was about an hour later, when I was finally drifting off to sleep, that I had an idea.

# Chapter Thirty-Eight

The morning sun warmed my skin, rousing me from sleep. I blinked. What time was it? But before the thought could fully form, a shard of ice pierced my drowsy mind.

*Shona!*

Shona. Was. Gone.

But how could she be? It wasn't possible. I'd seen her two days ago. I'd heard her in the distance yesterday when Joe rang me.

I wrapped myself in my robe and shuffled towards the kitchen, the remnants of sleep clouding my vision. I squinted at the sofa, taking a moment to register the neatly folded blanket next to the pillow.

Dan.

He'd stayed the night.

On my sofa.

Nowhere else.

My cheeks warmed as a wave of awkwardness mingled with gratitude washed over me. His presence had been a comfort, nothing more. Dan was good and Dan was kind. There was a murderer on the loose and he wanted to keep me safe. But butterflies danced in my belly when I remembered how he'd comforted me in his strong embrace. At least he had to come back and repair my door and alarm.

Unless he'd already fixed them.

I glanced at the back door—the handle was still jury-rigged—and tried to ignore the small jab of joy that flickered inside me. I continued my bleary-eyed shuffle through to the kitchen. Clarity, I decided, was dependent on large amounts of caffeine.

I sat at the table, eyes closed and inhaling the aroma. This was good, fresh coffee. Yes, I owned it. I was a coffee snob.

The coffee had just started to clear the morning fog from my mind when I noticed the note peeking out from under the vase in the centre of the table.

It was from Dan.

*Hey Ruth,*

*I've gone to help with the search for Shona. I'll call you if we find anything, but I'll be back to fix the alarm and door later.*

*Dan.*

A small smile curved on my lips for a moment before grief crashed around me.

My vibrant, brimming-with-dreams friend was missing.

It didn't feel real. Shona had too much life. She was the one who wanted to be an actress—who sometimes called herself a show pony—but who had the heart of a saint. In my mind's eye I could see the bounce of her hair as she tossed her head, and her eyes light up as she devoured Joe's cream-drizzled lemon myrtle and poppyseed cake. A life force like Shona shouldn't be gone.

Couldn't be gone.

But look at Dad. He'd had so much brilliance, but his early departure showed how short life was.

Suddenly Dad was present again, enveloping me in his warmth. It had to be my imagination. When I was little, I'd snuggle close in his arms and feel safe and warm, 'like a possum in a nest'. I longed to go back in time and relive that moment forever. I couldn't—he was gone—but it didn't stop the wanting.

"Dad, if she's with you, please look after her."

There was a lessening of the warmth, like the night before when Dan drew back from the hug to look at me. Then I *felt* words—not spoken, but present, deep inside me.

*She's not dead.*

The sense of warmth and of Dad's presence vanished as quickly as it had come.

I shook my head. It had all been too much. Was I losing it or was my subconscious telling me what I knew deep down? Shona wasn't gone.

I rang Dan to find out if there was any news, but hung up before he answered. It was probably bad to distract him. I put the phone back down onto the table, only for the screen to light up with his number almost immediately.

"Have they found her?" My words were a hoarse whisper.

"No luck so far. It's highly possible that whoever kidnapped her took her by car." He paused, the silence heavy. "At least we didn't find a…" His voice tailed off.

"No body is a good thing."

"She could be anywhere, Ruth. There's thick bushland around here. And the road leads here or back to Adelaide." His voice hung with weariness. He could only have had a couple of hours of sleep—although his military background probably meant he could cope better than most. "We're going out again soon," he continued. "I'll keep you posted. I'll get to your place late afternoon to fix the door properly and tend to the alarm. You'll be okay until then?"

"Of course I'll be okay." But then I realised my response probably sounded too sharp. This wasn't really the time to play the hyper-independent female. "Sorry, I really appreciate you doing this. I think I'll go around and see Joe. Or is he there, too?"

"He came down here, but Lydia wouldn't let him be part of the search. It would be pretty bad if he found—"

"She's not dead, Dan." The conviction in my voice surprised even me. I wasn't sure how to frame my experience earlier. He would think I was crazy if I told him I thought Dad had spoken to me from the grave—more than once. It was probably just my mind playing tricks on me, but the words resonated inside me.

*She's not dead.*

*She can't be.*

Dan hesitated. "If you're right, then Lydia and Gary will find her. Promise me you'll lie low. If you go out, don't be on your own."

Right then my phone began beeping—there was another call on the line. "Gotta go, Dan. Someone's calling." I quickly switched calls and Joe's familiar face filled the screen.

"Are you okay, Joe?"

"They still haven't found her." The defeat in his words made my chest feel tight.

"I'm coming to your place." The thought that had drifted into my mind before I fell asleep still made sense. "I've got an idea where we can look."

# Chapter Thirty-Nine

I wish I could say butterflies danced in my stomach as Joe and I drove to Xavier Kingston's place, but the sensation was more like a swarm of dragonflies rampaging inside my belly.

"We have to be careful, Joe. Don't let on we're looking for clues about Shona."

Joe ran a hand over his pale, unshaven face. "Tell me again why you think Kingston's got Shona?"

"I'm not saying he has, but…"

"But?"

"It doesn't feel right. He was on Rossi's list and—"

"And he has motive," Joe said.

"He does if Rossi was blackmailing him. What if Shona found out something?"

Joe stared straight ahead as he drove, shoulders set, knuckles blanching as he gripped the steering wheel. "If he's hurt her, I'll kill him."

I swallowed hard. I didn't want Joe arrested for homicide. His knife was already implicated in Rossi's murder, and he still was on the suspect list, for sure. The last thing he needed was another display of anger.

I'd thought of going to see Kingston myself, but I'd read too many novels where a young woman investigator rushes into danger alone. This wasn't a book, it was real life, and I was no hero. I didn't want to be TSTL—too stupid to live— even though we needed to find Shona. Taking Joe with me was a calculated risk.

Although if Kingston had hurt just one hair on Shona's head, I could easily join Joe in murder.

I took a deep breath and presented my logic. "We don't know that he had anything to do with any of this, but what are the chances that a murder, a kidnapping and a burglary all happened in a sleepy small town a few days from each other? The burglary happened on the same property as the murder— my place—and it's my best friend who is missing. The odds that these things are unrelated are a gazillion to one. And like you said, if Kingston is being blackmailed, he has a motive. Rossi might have been asking for other things as well as the sale of the property."

Joe gripped the steering wheel tighter.

I continued. "Cora had heaps of blood on her paws and claws, so she would have scratched my house invader badly. If we go to Kingston's home and say we left something behind, we could look around for anyone with deep scratches."

"But why would Kingston ransack your place?"

"Lots of people knew that Shona and I were asking ques- tions about Rossi's murder. And I'd mentioned that Kat was going to be at my place. And everyone knows she does computer-based research."

"They could have been targeting Kat?" Concern creased Joe's face.

"I don't know, but she went to stay with her brother in Adelaide last night."

"What did she do with all her cats?"

I gave him a wry grimace. "She took them over to Ed's clinic. He's boarding them for a couple of nights."

"He's too kind, that man."

"He has a soft spot for Kat, I think. But she says she'll help him out at the clinic as payment. If she ever gives up on computers she could have a career as a vet nurse."

"Hacking into the finances of people who don't pay their vet bills?"

"Ha! Ed's too law-abiding for that."

"Sure he is… but is Kat?" It was good to see even a ghost of a smile on Joe's face. Kat's skills were obviously well known in this town.

We sat in silence for a few moments. The closer we got to Kingston's home, the faster thoughts whizzed through my mind.

"You need to be careful, Ruth," Joe was first to speak.

"I can take care of myself."

"Just because you're good at that Krav-Jitsu stuff, it doesn't mean they can't get you. Rossi was fit, and he'd have had some self-defence skills in his line of work, but someone still killed him."

I shivered. "If we see something suspicious, we don't say anything, right? We get out of there and call the cops."

He shrugged.

"I mean it, Joe. We don't do anything stupid."

He was silent again for several long moments. "Okay. But if we find Shona, we're getting her out of there, no matter what."

I let out my breath with a whoosh. "Agreed."

•  •  •

We were five minutes from the Kingston mansion when I suggested to Joe that it was time to call them. He pulled over, dialled, then put the phone on speaker.

Fiona Kingston answered, her voice warm and smooth like mulled wine. "Hello, Kingston residence."

Joe's voice in contrast was as rough as a night out gone wrong. "Hi, Fiona. It's Joe. Ruth and I think we might have left my milk thermometer at your place yesterday. We're in the area. Can we swing by to check?"

My hand fell on the cool steel of the thermometer in my tote bag. It was a good lie, because a milk thermometer was essential for great coffee making, but small enough to hide in my handbag so I could pretend to 'find' it.

"Sure. Drop in. I haven't seen it but that doesn't mean it's not here."

The welcome we got at the door was cooler. One of Kingston's goons opened it with a scowl on his face and a sneer on his lips.

I couldn't resist a snarky, "Good morning to you, too," as I scanned his face and neck for wounds. It was a cool early autumn day, but he was wearing a heavy jacket with a high collar that screamed, *I'm hiding something*. The dragonflies in my gut buzzed overtime. I didn't trust this man. He reminded me of a gangster I met in Paris once.

"Kitchen only." He eyeballed Joe, then me, before ushering us through to a room rimmed with gleaming stainless steel appliances and sleek, dark granite countertops. A huge professional-level stove sat next to a double-door refrigerator large enough to hold a banquet's worth of food. Large windows on the northern side flooded the room with natural light, but it was the aroma of freshly baked cookies cooling on the benchtop that made the kitchen feel like home.

"We won't take long," Joe said. "We may have left the thermometer in here or it could be near the marquee."

The man stood close with folded arms, looming over us like a low, dark cloud. He obviously had no intention of letting us wander freely around Kingston's house.

"It's okay, Peter, I'll take it from here." Fiona Kingston floated into the kitchen wearing a blue and white apron that was dusted with flour and smeared with cookie batter.

Peter tensed. "I was told—"

"I'm telling you it's okay. Go help Dad and the groom with that horse."

Peter hesitated then pushed past us, muttering to himself as he strode outside. Fiona turned to us, her voice swiftly morphing from commanding to gracious. "Sorry about that. That was rude. I'm staying with Dad for a few days. Mainly to help out with Gran." She gazed back down the hallway, with warmth in her eyes. "My fiancé is still in bed. He was up late watching the soccer."

"Is Olivia okay? We had a chat yesterday."

"Just more confused than normal, poor thing."

As if on cue, Kingston's mother shuffled into the room and clutched onto her granddaughter's arm. Her face lit up when she saw me.

"Want to play again?"

Joe raised an eyebrow. I'd told him about Olivia's whing-a-whing-a-whoshie game yesterday.

"I'd love to, but maybe later." I watched as Olivia artfully pocketed a large cookie that had been cooling on a rack on the bench.

Fiona and I shared a knowing smirk. She'd caught her gran's sleight of hand, too.

"Do you mind if we look in the drawers?" I asked.

"Someone might have washed the thermometer and put it away by mistake."

"Sure. If it's not here, I'll check Gran's room." She winked. "It's amazing what we find up there."

"Congrats on your engagement, by the way." Envy and admiration flicked through me. Fiona was a little younger than me but miles ahead in life—career, love, you name it. She was also beautiful and appeared to care about people. I wanted to dislike her, but I couldn't.

The woman smiled, a genuine light in her eyes. "Thanks. And thank you both for catering so well yesterday."

"Joe was the mastermind, I'm just the hired help."

"Have you seen my fiancée?" Joe blurted.

Fiona blinked, clearly thrown off by his bluntness. I braced for what was next.

"Um… should I have?"

The old lady shook her head, her face twisting with sadness. "No fiancée."

Joe looked like he'd swallowed something sour, his hands raking through his hair in frustration. "Sorry. That was abrupt. I'm just… Shona didn't come home last night. They found her car abandoned. I'm trying to track her movements… Thought maybe she might've come here after we left yesterday."

That was a good thought. Shona could have gone home before she vanished. Her kidnapper could have snatched her, then dumped her car and koala suit out of town. But that scenario would need two people.

Fiona's response mirrored her earlier warmth, but was now tinged with concern. "I wish I could say yes, but she hasn't been here."

While she was talking to Joe, I'd slipped the milk thermometer from my pocket into a drawer.

"Look, here it is." I held the thermometer high.

The old lady's eyes sparkled as she winked at me and tapped the cardigan pocket that contained her stolen cookie. "Secrets," she whispered.

"Glad you found it!" Fiona beamed a wide smile before turning to Joe. "Let's hope your fiancée is as easy to find." I'm sure she meant to comfort, but her words totally messed with Joe. His face paled, his jaw set hard and the pulse on his temple throbbed fast.

"I need air." His voice strained with forced calmness. "And I need to see your dad. Is he around?"

"He's down at the stables. Would you—"

But Joe was already striding out through the door and onto the well-travelled, gravelled path towards the horses.

# Chapter Forty

"Joe... wait!" Fiona and I hurried after him, but he didn't stop. "Think this through!"

"What's he going to do?" Fiona's worry echoed mine.

"I don't know." My inner dragonflies were swarming. I'd seen what Joe could be like when he was protecting the people he cared for.

I sprinted to catch up with him. "Cool it, Joe," I puffed as I reached for his arm. "You need to think first."

He shrugged me off, slowing only marginally.

Fiona appeared beside me, hardly puffing. "I'm sorry if I said something wrong, Joe. I can't imagine how hard it must be for someone you love to go missing."

Joe stopped and turned to her. "Someone took her. She's out there..." His voice cracked. "I just need to know if anyone has seen her, okay?"

"Joe." I stepped between him and Fiona and put a hand on his chest. "Steady. We've got the milk thermometer now. Let's go. We don't know if anyone here *has* seen Shona."

He exhaled, the tension in his shoulders easing slightly. I breathed easier too.

But that all changed once we reached the stables.

The old sandstone buildings sat in a u-shape around a compacted gravel courtyard. The pungent aroma of hay and manure filled the air and Xavier Kingston was intently testing a horse's hoof with large metal callipers. Another man—possibly a groom—held the horse. And that man had several large scratches on his neck.

My breath caught in my throat.

Joe stopped dead next to me, his face bright red, then he lunged for the groom. "Where is she?" He lifted his fist. "What did you do with Shona?"

"Joe, stop." I tried to pull him away, but he just shrugged me off. The horse startled, and kicked out, a hoof just missing me. Fiona dived in and grabbed the halter and tried to quieten the animal.

The goon, Peter, and Kingston ran to help the groom. There was yelling and then someone, either Joe or Peter, collected Kingston in the face.

Kingston pulled back, cradling his bloody nose, while Joe held fast to the groom's arm.

"He took Shona!" Joe's voice was raw. "What did you do to her?"

"We don't know that, Joe." I tugged at his arm, trying to pull him off the groom. "This isn't the right way."

"I'm not letting him go until he tells the truth. Who took her? Who killed Rossi?" he yelled in the groom's face. "Was it you or your slime-bag boss, or the no-neck henchman over there?"

Fiona inhaled a sharp breath. The horse she was holding backed away before she put a soothing hand on its nose again.

"I don't know what you're talking about." The groom shook his head.

Joe pushed him away and turned to Kingston, who was putting pressure on his bloodied nose. "You're selling the Farrows' farm from under them. Why did you kill Rossi?"

"I didn't kill Rossi, and I don't know anything about Shona. Did something happen?"

Joe stepped up close to Kingston, breathing in his face. "Don't give me that crap. Shona disappeared late afternoon, yesterday. While we were packing up here. After *both* of you left the party."

"Don't threaten me." Kingston gestured to his nose. "This is assault."

Joe gestured towards Peter. "It was his elbow, not mine."

"It wasn't deliberate," I insisted.

"You're as bad as he is." Kingston turned on me. "You come here, abuse my trust. Try to get Mum to say something she shouldn't. And you were snooping in my study."

"I wasn't."

"I saw you come out. Why were you there?"

Before I could reply, another voice spoke behind me.

"Hello?"

I swung around, my mouth wide open like one of those clowns in a sideshow alley. It was Ed, the vet. "What are you doing here?"

Ed smiled at me. "Hello, Ruth. We meet again." He gestured to the horse Fiona was still holding to the side. "Lame horse." He surveyed the group. "I couldn't help over-hearing."

I suspected anyone within a kilometre would have heard.

Ed continued, his voice calm and matter-of-fact as if he was talking to a spooked animal. "Both of these men," he looked in the direction of first the groom then Kingston, "were here at the stables late yesterday afternoon, helping a sick horse. It had colic last Saturday but had another bad bout yesterday."

"Saturday?"

"Late Saturday night. After we left the party."

The swarm of dragonflies buzzing in my gut fluttered to a standstill. "You mean when Rossi was killed?"

"Yes, when Rossi was killed." Kingston pulled his hands away from his face. His nose was swollen and bleeding. "I may have hated the bastard, but I'd never ruin my life by killing him." He frowned as he looked towards the goon and the groom. "Or having him killed."

"Peter was here on Saturday night when Rossi was killed." Ed offered.

"Dad is always here for his horses." Fiona's voice held a wistful tone. I wondered how many times the horses had got in the way of father-daughter time.

"We were here until two in the morning," Ed said. "I told the police that."

My face flamed. If I'd known that, I wouldn't have dragged Joe down here and had us both make idiots of ourselves.

Kingston spun back to me. "That's why you were in my study, wasn't it? Looking for *evidence*." He spat the words out, looking first at Joe, then me. "I'll get him for assault and you for trespassing."

"Hang on," Ed said. "That's a bit rough."

"I didn't hit you." Joe pointed at Peter. "He did."

Anger flashed in Kingston's face. "First Rossi blackmails me, then *she*," he pointed at me, "snoops around, then *he*," he jabbed his finger in Joe's direction, "breaks my nose. Like hell I'm going to let that go."

"Why was he blackmailing you?" I didn't want to make Kingston madder, but the question slipped out of me.

"It's none of your business, you stupid—" He stopped and pulled out his phone. "I'm calling the police now."

"Wait." I pressed my eyes closed. This was getting worse, except… something had been niggling at the back of my mind. "When was Shona originally meant to be back, Joe?"

"About five thirty."

"And you rang and spoke to Shona's friends— the ones she sometimes catches up with when she's in Adelaide —when?"

"About six thirty, after I couldn't get hold of Shona."

"And you contacted her other friends?"

"Everyone I knew."

"So, if she didn't catch up with anyone she went missing before five thirty?"

He thought for a moment, then agreed. "Yes."

I turned to Ed. "Was Peter here for the *whole time* you were here yesterday?"

"He was to begin with, I think, then he left."

"What time?"

"Probably around five thirty,' The vet inclined his head. The flicker of recognition in his eyes said he saw my reasoning.

I glanced in Fiona's direction. "I don't see you hurting Shona, but—"

"I was with my fiancé all afternoon and evening."

"She was," said Kingston.

I swung back to the groom. "How did you scratch your neck?"

The man grimaced. "The horse with colic grazed me as

she tried to kick me. She was in pain," he added, as if to excuse the animal.

"Okay. If Peter left at five thirty, then he couldn't have intercepted Shona. But…" I paused, thinking. "If Kat left my place a bit after six, Peter could still have ransacked my home."

"Don't be stupid." Kingston's voice held the faintest ring of uncertainty. Sometimes the way people talk is like music. There's the melody line they want you to hear but there are other notes that sit underneath the tune—a bass line that helps you know what they're really saying. I knew he was lying.

I eyeballed him. "You heard me talking to your mum and sent your goon to break into my house to see what I knew."

"You can't prove that." Peter shifted on his feet.

I smirked at him. "You're wearing that jacket with the high neck. That's overkill for this time of year, isn't it? Take it off."

He shook his head, but his hand reached reflexively to the back of his neck.

"I'm not listening to this any longer." Kingston started pressing numbers into his phone.

"So, if the cops compare the DNA on my cat's claws to Peter's DNA, we won't find a match?"

Kingston froze, his finger hovering over the dial key.

"You can't get DNA that way." His voice was shaky.

"We did, didn't we Ed?"

The vet inclined his head, regarding me with a bemused half-smile. "The police brought the cat in to get tissue samples late last night, after I left here."

"You call the cops about this," I gestured to Kingston's still-bleeding nose, "and my snooping, as you called it, and I'll happily tell them whose DNA they need a warrant for."

I turned to Joe, who was looking at me with something akin to awe. "I wonder if Peter has committed any other crimes?"

"Hmmm." Joe scrunched up his face and tapped his chin, as if thinking deeply.

"I didn't hurt Rossi or Shona." Kingston took a step towards me, but Joe blocked him from getting closer.

*Those* words felt true. "So why did you send Peter? Why search my place? What did Rossi have over you?"

Kingston stood silently, his face dark with thunder, a storm ready to crack and sizzle.

"Mum." Fiona spoke softly. "And me."

# Chapter Forty-One

"Be quiet, Fi," Kingston warned, but his daughter ignored him.

"Many years ago, Gran was in an accident. She's always had a problem with alcohol and had been drinking. She hit a young woman and killed her."

Another piece of the puzzle fell into place. "Rose Mathers —Rosie? I thought your mum was talking about Rossi when she was playing the game, saying Rossi fell down. But it was this girl, Rosie."

Fiona blinked away tears and stepped closer to her dad, laying a hand on his shoulder. "That was years before I was born. Dad suspected back then but didn't ask any questions. It wasn't done to talk about that kind of thing." She lifted her arms in an open-palmed shrug. "Granddad paid off the girl's family somehow and I didn't know anything about it until recently, when Rossi began blackmailing Dad to sell his mistress the farm. We didn't know what to do other than go along with Rossi for now. As Rossi thought Dad had been driving, we tried to keep it that way. To drag Gran through the courts now, even if she was declared medically unfit, would be awful."

"The accident happened in early 1983, didn't it?"

Fiona nodded. "Granddad told Dad about a year before he passed away, but he'd already suspected. If the truth got out now, we figured Dad might get into trouble for helping cover it up and my political aspirations could go south quickly. Dad can be a bastard in business, but he loves his family."

"Sounds like a motive for murder," Joe said.

Kingston's face reddened. "We didn't—"

"I believe you." My eyes narrowed. "But you did something, didn't you?"

Kingston shook his head.

My voice was desperate as I pleaded with him. "I get why you want to protect your mum. I'm just trying to find Shona before it's too late." I held his gaze. "Imagine if it was Fiona who was missing."

Kingston shook his head. "Before Rossi died, I was looking for ways to… retaliate. There were rumours that he'd done some bad things in the past, but I couldn't find anything concrete." He paused, licking his lips. "And then I overheard you yesterday. You were talking on the phone and mentioned the notes and clippings you'd found."

"But how could that help? Rossi was already dead. Someone took care of your problem for you."

"You were talking to Mum, and I thought you might know what happened. I didn't want you to blackmail me, too. If I could get your dad's notes and maybe your computer, there would be no evidence. So, I sent Peter to look." He swallowed hard. "But I didn't do anything to Rossi or Shona."

"Dad didn't do anything. I did."

We all turned and gaped at Fiona.

She blinked, hesitated, then spoke. "I didn't kill him. I'd heard on the grapevine that Rossi was getting some threatening emails. I decided to amp it up a bit."

"You sent him the cut-out letters?"

She looked at me quizzically. "How did you know about that?"

I didn't reply, but instead asked a different question. "Why? What were you wanting to achieve?"

"Just to scare him, I guess. If he thought he was in danger he might leave, take his stupid property developer mistress with him, and forget about Pelican Bay." She shrugged. "It wasn't the best thought-out plan." She touched her father's arm. "You didn't hear from Rossi at all after he left back in the eighties, did you?"

Kingston shook his head. "Dad asked Rossi to disappear, paid him some money, and he did. The trouble only started when he returned."

I rubbed my hands over my face, thinking, then turned back to Fiona. "You said you heard that someone was sending Rossi threatening emails. That's what gave you the idea?"

She nodded.

"Can you remember anything about that? Where you heard it?"

She screwed up her face and shook her head. "Just in town. At the pub, I think. General scuttlebutt."

My sigh was deeper than the Southern Ocean. "If you think of something, please let me know."

"We need to find my fiancée," Joe said.

I regarded Fiona. "As long as your dad doesn't press charges against us, I won't say anything about your gran, or the letters." I turned to Kingston. "Do we have an agreement?"

His nod was faint, but anger still flickered in his eyes. I

couldn't fix that, but at least his nose had stopped bleeding. "And you need to pay for the repairs to my place."

Ed coughed. I'd almost forgotten he was there.

"How does all this sit with you?" I asked him.

It was good we had a witness, even if Ed was an old friend of Kingston's. I was sure Xavier Kingston could be ruthless, so it was even better that the person in the know was the preferred vet for Kingston's treasured horses.

Ed tilted his head to the side, thinking. "The girl your mum killed, Xavier."

Kingston nodded.

"Rose," I said. "Rosie. She had a name."

Ed inclined his head. "Does Rose's family know what happened?"

"Her parents did," Kingston said.

"You paid them for their silence?"

Kingston nodded again.

"They were happy with that?"

"They accepted it. They were desperate for money. Rose had a half-sister—same mother, different fathers—who was going through a hard time. They wanted to help her."

Ed thought for a moment. "So a whole lot of innocent lives are caught up in all of this." He stroked the grey bristles on his chin. "Unless it comes out that you're lying, and there's more to this, I can't see how any good would come from putting Olivia through the mill. Not after forty years." He raised a bushy eyebrow in Xavier's direction. "That do you?"

"Yes." The tension in Kingston's shoulders eased and his daughter took his hand.

"Now that the truth is out, can the sale of the farm be stopped?" I asked.

•  •  •

"That was impressive." Joe squeezed my shoulder. "You've missed your calling. You're almost as scary as Legs-to-Breasts."

The adrenalin had kept me going until we reached the car and my knees turned to cooked lasagne. I sagged against the car, resting my head against the cool metal. I waved my hand to acknowledge his words.

"You okay?" There was concern in his voice. "Sorry I lost it there."

"Just give me a moment." The world spun as a tsunami of fatigue washed through me. I gulped in a deep breath and let it out slowly. Once I'd regained my equilibrium, I turned back to him and grinned. "It was kinda fun."

"And they're going to try and stop the sale." He grinned back at me, but both our faces changed when my phone rang. It was Dan. I answered quickly and put the phone on speaker so Joe could hear. They'd found no sign of Shona, but he was on his way to my place to fix the door and the alarm.

"Do you want to come?" I asked Joe. "I'll need to get my car from your place, but you're welcome if you want company."

He shook his head, checking his phone for any messages. "I keep thinking Shona's going to just turn up at home with some outlandish story, you know?"

I nodded. I did know.

"It's crazy, but…"

"You want to be there if she does?"

Joe's eyes glistened as he shrugged.

I hugged him, fighting back my own tears. "We'll find her, Joe. I don't think she's dead. Whatever has happened, wherever she is, Shona will never give up."

# Chapter Forty-Two

It scared me how much I was coming to rely on Dan. All those weeks of avoiding him since flirting on the plane had taken a drastically different turn in the last fortnight. After running me off my bicycle—okay, maybe that *was* my fault—Dan had put in a security system, fixed my broken door, and held me in his arms as I sobbed all over his shirt. He'd become a friend, like Shona had suggested, and even though I was still attracted to him, we seemed to have found an equilibrium. For now.

But my heart still skipped a beat when—having repaired my door and the alarm system—he said it was late and suggested getting a meal at the pub.

"Um… yeah." My face warmed. Eloquence had always been part of my charm.

"Great. Do you mind if I have a shower? I've got a change of clothes in my car." And he sauntered out the door to get them.

Clothes in the car? Did that mean he'd been planning

this? Or did he often do that on days when he did messy work?

I needed to stop second-guessing everything and get ready. A few minutes later, I also needed to stop thinking about the fact that Dan was standing naked under my shower a few metres down my hallway.

*It's not a date.*

We were just two friends having a meal together, like he often did with Lydia Larsen. But my breath caught when he emerged from the bathroom freshly showered, wearing dark blue jeans, a crisp, white button-down shirt, and sexy half-smile on his lips.

I gawked for a moment before looking away.

*Danger, danger, danger.*

My sudden urge to run my fingers through his ruffled, damp, dark hair would have been very unwise. But when I went to get ready, I took extra time to wash and apply makeup.

I put on black jeans and a silky turquoise camisole that matched my eyes, and offset it with an equally silky waterfall jacket. I wasn't trying to attract Dan—it was only that I didn't want to look out of place next to this striking example of manhood.

At least that was what I told myself as we drove into town in his Jeep.

Normally on Sunday night the pub was buzzing—not as busy as Saturday, but still humming along with great food and the occasional live artist. But there was a more sombre mood tonight. The word about Shona had obviously got around. When I entered, the hum of conversation was replaced by one or two jeering expletives.

It felt as if every eye in the universe drilled into me, ready to expose my evil core.

Suddenly Hannah was at my side, taking me by the arm and leading us towards what was becoming my regular booth in the back corner.

"Don't pay any attention to them," she said. "You're always welcome here." But before we reached the booth, harsh words made me freeze.

"You've killed our Shona now!" A rough-looking man I recognised as Jim Stephens, a local sparky who had done some work for me, took a couple of steps in our direction. "Come to curse us all, have you?"

His mates giggled and nudged one another in that idiotic way only stoned or drunk guys can.

"Neanderthals," Dan murmured under his breath. He touched my arm and gestured back towards the door. "Let's go."

"How do you do it?" Jim took a few more steps and angled himself between us and the exit. "The dark arts? You make up a potion with mandrakes, or something?"

One of his friends sidled up behind him. Then two more joined them. "Look at those eyes," the first friend said. "That colour's not natural. She's cursing you right now, mate."

"Oooh." One of the other men waved his fingers in the air. "Spooky."

"Go home, witch," a woman called from another table.

"That's enough," Bruce warned from behind the bar. "Calm down, everyone. The next person to insult Ruth gets chucked out. And Jim, the bar is closed for you, mate. Go home."

Jim ignored him and lurched closer. "First Aldon Rossi and now Shona. It's not safe to be anywhere near you. Go away. We don't want you here, Ruthless-the-Killer."

He jabbed the air with his finger three times to punctuate the last three words. I took half a step back, more from revulsion than fear. Jim was now only a couple of steps away. His breath was a toxic blend of meat pie mixed with so much cheap whisky, you could have lit a match and powered the pub's kitchen for a month. If that wasn't bad enough, a group of people crowded close behind us. I had nowhere to go.

Dan stepped between me and Jim. "Leave, mate, before you regret it." His voice was even, but I could hear the steel behind it. I wasn't sure if this side of Dan attracted me or scared me. Probably both.

Jim leered at him. "She's got you under her spell, fella. You don't mind dying? She's that good in b—?"

"Leave," said Dan. He tensed and clenched his fists.

"Don't. He's not worth it." I caught Dan's arm and pulled him back. He could whip Jim and his idiot chorus in a second —possibly really hurt them—but I didn't want him to get into trouble and I didn't want there to be a fight in Hannah and Bruce's bar.

More people shifted forward to see the show. Someone catcalled from the other end of the room and others jeered. My mind flashed back to when I was in the schoolyard, surrounded by taunting kids. They poked their fingers at me, laughed at me and screamed if I touched them. That wasn't going to happen here. Not anymore.

Jim sniggered.

I'd had enough.

"Shut up." My voice was soft, but sure. "Shut up!" I amped up the volume and the ring of people around me hushed, but the larger crowd still murmured, some spoiling for a fight.

I stomped up onto a chair and then onto a table. "SHUT UP!"

A glass shattered in the kitchen. Someone swore, then... silence.

"Ruth?" Dan's voice was low with warning. I ignored him.

"You—all of you." Every eye focused on me as I gestured around the room. "You should be ashamed of yourselves. Shona is *missing* and all you can do is make stupid accusations about something that's not even real."

I took a deep, deep breath and told them some of what I'd told Larsen.

"When I was a little kid, I was naughty and threw my hat into the meerkat pen at the zoo. My cousin Karl thought it would be funny to tell me and the other kids of school that the meerkats died of stress. There was nothing wrong with the meerkats. They were fine, but I believed him and so did the other kids. I got the nickname," I glared at Jim, "you seem to like so much."

I swallowed hard before continuing.

"And then my best friend died. She got viral hepatitis. She picked it up on holiday—nothing to do with me—but I thought I'd killed her because she got sick soon after I hit her with a softball. Then Grandad slipped on a sea wall, broke his hip and got a blood clot on his lungs. It was a horrible accident, but the kids at school started whispering again. My gran died six months later. She already had serious health issues, but Mum blamed me and said she died of a broken heart. We went to the UK for a couple of years—that was where I met Shona. Everything was fine there, but when we returned my neighbour, Mrs J, died when she was showing me how to glaze ceramics. Her family said later that she'd been having chest pains for six months, but hadn't gone to the doctor. It wasn't my fault, but I believed it was."

Emotion gravelled in my voice and I cleared my throat.

"My stupid reputation, made up by my moronic cousin, took on a life of its own. That's what my sister was referring to when you," I glared at the Gone Potty group sitting at a nearby table, "overheard her and started spreading the word about me. Thank you very much for that." The group members turned to each other and began whispering.

I was running out of steam, but I summoned one last surge of energy.

"I expect stupidity from school kids, but not from *adults*." I spat out the last word. "This has nothing to do with me. I didn't cast any spell. A man has been murdered because somebody in this town wanted him dead and did something about it. And my best friend was kidnapped, and I think that was because she wanted to find out who killed Rossi, because she loves Joe, and she loves me, and she loves this town. I think the murderer thought Shona *knew* something."

The room was largely silent now. There was a shifting of feet, a shuffling of chairs and lots of averted eyes seemingly fascinated by the beverage on their table.

"Shona, who you all know and *love*, is *missing*. She could be dead, but something in me says she's still alive out there somewhere. Scared. And all *you* can do," I eyeballed Jim and his friends, "is act like a mob of obnoxious, superstitious, chicken-livered halfwits. If you had another neuron in your brains, it'd be lonely."

The room was silent—all eyes on me. Jim still stood sneering in my direction, but two of his mates had sat down nearby at the bar. I stood straighter.

"I won't let them stop looking until they find her. I'll sit on the doorstep of the cop shop if I have to. But I can't do anything for her unless you all shut up about stupid curses. You're scared—we all are—but you need to stop being jerks and actually help me."

My legs wobbled and Dan reached up to grab my hand and steady me. I grasped it hard, relishing his strength.

"So, if any of you have heard anything—anything at all

that could be relevant—tell the police. If you don't want to talk to them directly, tell me or Dan or Joe. Please just do *something that can help*."

My legs wobbled again, but this time I was done. Dan helped me slide back down off the table and I sank onto a chair. I sat there, head in my hands, until the silence surrounding us morphed into muted conversation, and the people who had pressed close to watch the commotion drifted back to their seats.

"You okay?" Dan had taken the seat beside me, and his warm hand rested on my back. "That was pretty impressive."

I was trembling, but I shot him a shaky smile. "It felt good." It had certainly been my day for giving it back to people. I steadied myself and rose to my feet. "Let's get out of here."

# Chapter Forty-Three

Aglow to the west lit the soft twilight as Dan and I walked along the boardwalk, enjoying the gentle breeze in the cool autumn evening. Neither of us spoke—we were both lost in our thoughts. A flock of seagulls squabbled out on the water, only to be interrupted as a large pelican flew in and landed splat in the middle of the group. The seagulls flew squawking in every direction.

I giggled. "Bird police."

Dan laughed too, then was silent again for a few moments before he spoke. "Feeling better?"

"Yeah. It's peaceful down here."

"You know they're just a mob of dropkicks, don't you?"

I shrugged. "They're scared, like we all are."

"You don't strike me as someone who scares easily." Our hands brushed for the briefest of moments, setting off a flutter in my chest.

I huffed out a laugh. "It depends on what the danger is."

*Like my attraction to you.*

For a minute I thought I'd said that out loud, but Dan didn't react, so I was safe.

"That childhood stuff," he continued. "That kind of thing can get into your soul. It's good to know that you don't believe it anymore."

When I didn't reply, he stopped and looked me in the eye. "You were pretty convincing in there."

"Of course I don't believe it." Even I could hear the ring of uncertainty in my voice.

"But?" The rotten man could see right through me.

I glanced up at him, a soft smile on my lips. "Everything I said in there was true. There was a logical explanation for everything that happened." I paused, gazing at the squawking gulls. "But sometimes it's hard to get childhood things out of your... soul, like you said." I rolled my shoulders to release the tension that was creeping back. "Sometimes I feel as if there's something wrong with me and it really *is* my fault."

Dan's deep blue eyes held mine. "None of this is your fault. Not Rossi. Not Shona. None of it."

"Not even my Mafia ex-fiancé?" I quipped, reminding him of the dinner conversation the other night.

"Ha!" His eyes narrowed and there was a hint of teasing in his voice. "I'm not sure about him."

I laughed.

"He cheated on you, didn't he?"

"Yes, he did." I tried to keep my voice light. "But his family—or hers—got to him before I could."

"I'll bear that in mind."

*What did he mean by that?*

I kept it light. "Like I said once before... maybe you should be scared to hang around with me."

"I'll take my chances."

"So did Shona."

Dan turned to face me and looked me in the eyes. "We'll find her."

I nodded and blinked back my tears. A stray strand of my hair blew across my face and he reached out and tucked it behind my ear, sending soft shivers from the base of my neck, down my spine, along my arms—through all of me.

His gaze deepened its intensity.

"They're beautiful, by the way."

Another stray strand of hair blew across my face. This time I pushed it away.

"What are?" I had no idea what he was talking about.

"Your eyes. Jim said he didn't like them, but they're beautiful. Blue in some light, other times they're turquoise like the Indian Ocean, with flecks of gold. Like they can't make up their minds if they want to be blue, turquoise or hazel."

I laughed a little to cover my embarrassment. "So even my eyes are confused?"

"Ruth." He cupped my face with his hand, caressing my cheek with his thumb.

I leaned into his touch. I shouldn't do this—it was a bad idea. The timing was off. He was leaving soon. But I was mesmerised by his gaze, drawn to him like the moths to the streetlight above us. Dan was kind, and good, and hot—a rare combination. I wanted—needed—to kiss him right now. But even as I gazed at him, and my eyes flicked to his mouth, a huge bogong moth tumbled out of the sky and smacked me dead in the middle of my forehead.

"Ah!" I pulled back as the insect flopped to the ground, exhausted, still buzzing and fluttering in circles.

God... or the universe... or whatever... was using bugs now to bring me to my senses?

"Ruth…"

But before Dan could say anything else, a breathless Hannah caught up with us. "Come back to the pub, guys. People are talking."

# Chapter Forty-Four

The chatter in the pub was louder than when we left—the room buzzed like a hive of swarming bees. I took stock of who was still there. Jim and his cronies had left—no doubt kicked out by Bruce—but the rest of the crowd remained.

"Everyone is recounting what happened the night Rossi died, and last night when Shona disappeared." Hannah gestured to a man standing by us at the bar. "Bill, tell them what you told me."

Bill, a local artist and Aboriginal elder, scratched the back of his neck. His eyes darted away—discomfort clearly on his face. "I saw Shona stop for fuel at Mount Compass."

"When?" asked Dan.

"Just after five o'clock, I'd reckon."

I leaned closer. "Did she seem okay? Not upset or anything?"

Bill shifted from one foot to another. "She was talking to that redheaded woman—Rossi's mistress." He glanced over at a table where Paul and Donna sat engrossed in deep conversation. "Shona seemed upset—preoccupied, like—but she drove south and Briscoe, or whatever her name is, took the road north towards Adelaide."

"Did you tell the police?"

Bill shook his head. "I didn't know she was missing 'til I got here." He gestured to the people around us then lifted his eyes, his face earnest. "I would have said somethin' sooner if I'd known."

"I'll call Lydia and get her to come down here." Dan clapped Bill on the back. "Thanks, mate. We know she was okay then. The police can follow up with Claire Briscoe and talk you through the details. If you can think of anything else, let us know."

Bill nodded. "I will." He gave me a sad smile. "Shona was a good woman. Always kind to Mari and me."

"*Is* a good woman." My voice was firm. "We'll find her. Alive."

"Ruth, come over here." Vivien, the ringleader of Gone Potty, beckoned us over.

"This apology better be good," I muttered to Dan as we pushed through the crowd towards their table. Vivien gave me her chair and pulled over two more for her and Dan to sit on.

I gave her my best forced smile and waited.

She turned to the group of ladies, each holding a wine, beer or soft drink, then back to me. "We didn't say anything."

"What do you mean?" I asked.

"We didn't tell anyone about the killer thing."

"You were right there."

"Yeah, well, we heard your phone call with your sister—and it all sounded strange—but I just asked everyone here and they didn't say anything."

I raised my eyebrows. "You expect me to believe that? A group like this is made for gossip."

"Look, you don't know her, I think, but have you heard of Emma Cooper? She used to live in this town."

I shook my head.

"It was about three years ago that one of us—she who shall not be named," Vivien glanced over at a blonde woman who had turned a bright shade of puce, "overheard Emma talking to a bloke down at a pub in Victor Harbor."

The blonde woman broke in. "I thought Emma was having an affair, but I didn't ask her about it, I told Peta." She nudged the dark-haired woman next to her. "And Peta told her husband, who told other people, and it got out of hand." She swallowed. "It turned out that the man was a literary agent who was going to take on Emma's romance book. But then Emma's employer got wind of the supposed affair and she lost her job. Emma's husband Rodney got done for assault after he punched the agent, thinking he'd had a fling with his wife."

"It was a complete balls-up," Vivien interjected. "Mess upon mess. Emma and Rodney stayed together but they ended up moving to Sydney and she never got her book published. We felt awful." She glanced around the group. "I can't say we've never gossiped since." Amusement flickered in her eyes. "But we don't work on rumour. We have a code. We made a rule that we need to confirm our sources before we spread any gossip. And if it will really hurt someone, we won't share beyond the group."

I couldn't help a half-laugh. "Wouldn't it be better not to gossip at all?"

Her eyes sparkled. "We've gotta be realistic here. The gals come to pottery club because they want to have a chat." She turned to a curly-haired, olive-skinned woman on the other side of the table. "Megan here tried to talk to you yesterday, didn't she?"

I frowned, thinking. "When?"

"I was standing in the line at Kenny's burgers," Megan said. "I called out, but you didn't stop."

I looked at them sheepishly. "I was in a rush and left to get fish and chips."

Vivien nodded. "Whoever spread the rumour about your… death thing, it wasn't us."

I thanked Vivien and her friends, my mind racing as Dan and I stood to leave. I wondered what would have happened if I *had* talked to Megan or Vivien or any of the others. But a lot of people had been in the pub that night, and only a couple of tables were close enough to have heard the details of my call. Who had spread the rumours, and why?

We talked to a few other people, without any further revelations, when Bruce appeared at my elbow with two large cardboard food packs that smelled distinctly like fish and chips. "Here you go, guys. It's on the house."

"I'm not hungry," I managed to get out, a second before my stomach gave a loud and embarrassing rumble.

Both men laughed and Dan took the two containers from Bruce. "Thanks, mate. It sounds like it's needed."

"Hannah's let the cops know that people are talking. Gary Stone will be down soon to chat to Bill and others."

I added my thanks and followed Dan back outside in the direction of his Jeep. If we could talk through everything I'd discovered so far, maybe he'd see something I missed.

# Chapter Forty-Five

We ate the fish and chips in my living room and washed it down with a half-bottle of Pinot Grigio I found in the fridge.

"Bruce does great chips." Dan's eager eyes lit up as he nabbed another handful and put them on his plate.

"The best," I agreed, my mouth half-full. Then I took a sip of the delicate, fruity white wine. "Thanks for tonight."

"What for? Leading you into a lynch mob?"

"Ha ha! No." I looked at him over the rim of the glass. "For supporting me when I told them where to go."

"Any time."

A faint warmth flushed in my cheeks. I blamed it on the wine.

"Some other men I know would have told me to get off the table and not make a fuss."

"They would be dropkicks." Mirth flickered in Dan's eyes. "Mind you, when I was in the forces, I was trained to assess the situation and avoid unnecessary danger. I figured it was safer to let you talk than try to stop you." His grin widened.

"You know… land mines… enemy snipers… Ruth Smythe when she's mad."

I threw a chip at him.

He pretended to duck, but then caught the chip in his mouth. He had great reflexes.

I narrowed my eyes and raised an eyebrow. "I won't miss next time."

He laughed, his infectious smile making my heart flutter as I mirrored his expression. It had been a long twenty-four hours and all I really wanted to do was crawl into his arms, rest my head on his shoulder and lose myself in his warmth. But I'd lost myself too many times, in the arms of too many men, so I dragged my mind to a different subject. "Do you mind talking through what we know about Rossi and Shona?"

He hesitated.

"Talking about it can help." I swallowed hard. "I used to do that with Shona."

His face softened. "Sure. As long as we take anything useful to Lydia."

"Agreed. I'll go and get Shona's whiteboard. And I really should ring Kat to see if she's okay."

Dan cleared up the plates as I phoned Kat. She was fine— still at her brother's place in Adelaide but would be back tomorrow to help Ed during Cora's surgery.

Dan called Lydia, to find out if there was any news, then Joe rang to see if I was okay after our visit to Xavier Kingston's place. His voice was slurred, and I could tell he'd been drinking.

"We'll find her, Joe," I told him. But the optimism in my voice felt hollower tonight. The chances of finding Shona alive were plummeting with each hour she was missing. I knew that, but I couldn't give up hope.

"What was that about Xavier Kingston?" Dan asked when I ended the call.

I'd deliberately avoided saying anything to him about the visit Joe and I made to the Kingston's place.

"Ruth," he asked again, warning in his voice. "What happened?"

I let out a long, deep breath, and told him.


I stood writing notes on Shona's whiteboard while Dan sat on the sofa, arms folded, huffing like a student on detention.

"You shouldn't have gone there, Ruth." He leaned back in the seat with a distinct frown on his face.

"Joe needed to do something. Larsen wouldn't let him join the search and I thought we'd be okay. Get in, check for scratches on bodies then get the hell out of there." I gave Dan a sheepish grin. "Probably should've realised Joe would go ballistic."

"We should tell Lydia about the car accident."

I'd vacillated over telling Dan about Olivia's accident. I had in the end, but first I'd made him promise not to tell the police. "We can tell her if it matters to the case. Have you met Olivia Kingston?"

"The sweet old homicidal drunk? No."

"That's a bit mean."

"She killed a girl, Ruth."

"I know, but she's not with it. Dementia. She wouldn't know what was happening if the police questioned her."

"It's the rest of the family. They shouldn't get to cover that kind of thing up."

"Yeah, I know. But I didn't know what to do at the time. I didn't want them having a go at Joe or having me arrested for snooping. And a lot more people would be affected if it came out."

Dan relented. "We can talk about it tomorrow. Let's look at the list again."

I went through everything I knew with him.

"Paul and Donna Farrow had motive because of the sale of the farm. Paul had access to the knife, but CCTV cleared him of everything but a minor property damage charge."

Dan grunted.

"Donna took the bomb-you-out-of-your-brain migraine tablets so she couldn't have driven into the town, got the knife, driven home and killed Rossi in my shed. Elouise had motive and opportunity, but she's got an alibi." I told him about Elouise's dalliance with the butcher. "The other people who had opportunity to take the knife were Bridget and the girls who helped with catering, but I can't see how any of them have motive."

"I rang Lydia when you were talking to Kat," Dan said. "She's talked to Bill about Claire Briscoe. Her alibi checks out. She was at a meeting with a client forty-five minutes later and couldn't have kidnapped Shona."

"She had no alibi with Rossi," I added. "But no motive either. Why would she want him dead if he was helping her?"

Dan rested his head against the back of the sofa, eyes closed, thinking. "With what happened tonight at the pub…" He tailed off. "If the Gone Potty group didn't spread the gossip about you, then whoever did could have just been gossiping, or—"

"They could have been deliberately trying to throw more suspicion on me."

"Yep." Dan ran his hands through his hair, making it stick on end, and I had to resist the urge not to smooth it down. "Who else was at the table with you guys that night?"

I tried to think back. "Me, Shona, Hannah, Bridget. There was another table nearby, celebrating, but I can't remember who was there. And a middle-aged couple—I think they were tourists. I vaguely remember them talking about writing and laughing about blue whales. I thought it was weird as you mainly get southern right whales down here."

"You've got a good memory."

"Most of the time. But usually only for useless trivia." I hesitated for a moment then sat down beside him. "I can't see Hannah or Bridget having any reason to kill Rossi or kidnap Shona. Hannah likes everyone and Bridget's only been in town for a few months. There's no obvious connection between her and Rossi." A smile played on my lips. "Maybe she forgot his coffee order and to keep her perfect record, he had to die?"

Dan snickered. "People have been killed for less."

"I'm sure Lydia has done background checks on all of them."

"I assume she would."

I tried to stifle a yawn—unsuccessfully. It had been a big day, and an even huger twenty-four hours. "Any chance you could ask her if there was anything off?"

Dan half-laughed, half-groaned. "She can't tell me private stuff about people."

"You guys used to be an item, though." I tried not to blush as I said it. This was diving back into personal territory, but I couldn't say I wasn't curious.

"A long time ago." It was as if a 'do not trespass' sign had been nailed to Dan's chiselled jaw, but I couldn't help myself.

"But on the plane…"

He sighed. "Okay, we were giving it another go. We'd been back together for about four weeks, then I had business in Brisbane and Lydia was at a training course on the Gold

Coast. We went out for drinks then decided to take the weekend and spend time together on Moreton Island."

"But?"

"It didn't work, for the same reason we didn't work before. She's beautiful, smart, driven…" He smirked. "All the things I like in a woman." He paused, as if searching for the right words. "But for some reason we work better as friends than lovers."

I waited, trying to push down intense curiosity.

"We fought, we made up." Dan's small smirk left me in no doubt as to what 'made up' meant. "We fought, made up, and so on, until I woke up the morning of our flight home and realised it was all too hard. We liked each other, we were attracted to each other, but for me anyway, something was missing." He let out a long breath. "That morning I'd decided to break things off with her when we got back to Adelaide. Before I met you." He quirked a half-smile that made him seem younger and more vulnerable than his years. "I wanted you to know that."

"Thanks for telling me." I held his gaze then looked away as warmth flamed my face. Part of me had wondered if Dan was a *player*. He was in a relationship when I met him, yet he flirted with me. Was he like every other unfaithful scumbag I'd dated? Not that I was dating Dan, of course, but it was the spirit of the thing. Now it sounded like he wasn't a player, and that made me like him even more.

There was obviously a lot more to the Dan and Lydia story, but that could wait for another day. He didn't have to tell me this much. But there was one thing that still niggled at me. "Why didn't you tell her straight away? She obviously thought you were still together when you were on the plane."

"I wanted to, but I wasn't sure how she'd respond. And

she'd be stuck next to me for a couple of hours on a plane instead of having space to process."

I was quiet as I considered his words. If I'd been Larsen, I'd have wanted to know the relationship was over, ASAP, but I could also see his point. There were few things worse than being stuck in a confined place with someone you'd just broken up with. Been there. Done that. Tearstained shirt to prove it.

He reached out and took my hand. "I'm glad we met, Ruth."

"I am too," I laced my fingers through his. Forget Cinderella's slipper, it was as if our hands were made to fit. Desire warmed me—a strong current, pulling me towards Dan like a riptide. But the battering of my heart against my chest wall wasn't just because of attraction, it was panic.

Fight or flight? Flight won.

I'd spent a lot of time on Australian beaches growing up and knew the best way to survive a rip wasn't to fight it. You swam parallel to the coast until you were free of the pull and could swim to shore. That was my tactic now.

Before I could do anything stupid, I gave his hand a small squeeze, eased my fingers out of his, then stood and yawned. "It's getting late."

Dan stood too. Was that a flicker of regret on his face?

I touched his arm. "I really appreciated your help tonight, but if I don't get some sleep, I'll be useless tomorrow."

"I could…" His eyes flitted towards the couch. "Stay."

I knew I was a goner if he spent the night here again.

"It's okay. You fixed the door and the alarm. I'll be fine. I don't need twenty-four-hour protection." My words came out a little too fast.

A slow grin spread across his face as he considered that thought.

Heat rose in my chest, then travelled up my neck and over my face.

"Well, Ruth Smythe." His voice was low and his breath was warm as he bent and brushed my cheek with his lips. "Let me know if you ever change your mind on that one."

And with that he sauntered to the door and out into the cool autumn night.

# Chapter Forty-Six

I woke to a bloodcurdling scream.

"Wha—?" I jolted upright and fumbled in the dark for my bedside lamp. It wasn't there. Where was I? I wasn't in my bedroom.

*What?*

I sat up, heart hammering and breathing fast. I groped around me. Where was my mattress? I was on some kind of sofa. My sofa? I was on my sofa in my living room. My heart resumed a steadier rhythm.

Now I remembered lying down, listening to music after Dan left, drinking in his woodsy scent that was still on the pillow he'd used the night before. The sofa was comfortable, and I was tired. But if I'd fallen asleep, why weren't the lights on?

The scream rang out again just outside the window, followed by a thumping on the iron roof of the porch. Adrenalin spiked again and I lurched to my feet—until I realised what it was a moment later.

Possums!

I sank back onto the sofa to the sound of more clattering and screaming. If the possums felt free to have a rooftop rave party, there was no one out there. I was safe.

But why were the lights out? I was sure I'd at least left a lamp on.

My foot hit something hard. My phone. I picked it up and saw the message announcing a local power outage.

I let out the rest of my breath. Everything was okay. I could resume normal programming and head to bed properly.

I switched on my phone torch and took a couple of steps before the lights flicked on and the refrigerator began to hum. The power was back on, and I could go to bed and sleep.

The problem was, I was now wide awake.

I'd read once that before the industrial revolution and electricity, people often had two sleeps. They'd go to bed early, then wake up in the wee hours, write their books, poetry, or whatever, then go back to sleep. Thanks to my possum friends and my anxiety over Shona, I was awake like those pre–industrial revolution people and didn't see myself getting to sleep anytime soon.

The kitchen beckoned and I boiled the kettle and made some tea, mixing a teaspoonful of honey in with the lemon myrtle and camomile blend my Aunt Izzy had sent me as part of a care package. She was a psychologist, so she was probably right when she said it was more calming than coffee. I still preferred my double-strength macchiatos, along with the occasional cappuccino, but even I knew that wasn't the best brew to have at 3am.

I made a mental note to ring her and thank her. She'd said she wanted to come and stay for a visit, but I hoped all this Rossi stuff would be over before she did.

I sipped the tea and added a little more honey. Something was bothering me about this murder case, niggling at the back of my mind.

I padded back into the living room, popped on some gloves, then reached up into the chimney and pulled out the bag with all Dad's notes and numbers. I was glad I'd taken it with me in my car, otherwise I'd have lost it forever. After the break-in, the chimney—its old resting place—seemed the best place to hide it when I was here. I left the plastic covering and my gloves in the fireplace and extracted the exercise books and newspaper clippings without getting soot everywhere. A major feat!

I shuffled through the papers, clippings and photos until I found the one I was looking for—the newspaper article about Rose Mathers' accident. That was what was niggling at me. Rose looked familiar, but I just couldn't place her.

I flicked through some old Polaroid-style photos, trying to match the people with their older counterparts. Everything clicked when I picked up a photo of Donna. The young Donna looked very different from the older, farm-work-weathered version. She was slender with smooth skin and gorgeous,— long fair hair, but I'd recognise those sparkly eyes and that cheeky grin anywhere. Rose had dark hair but the same eyes and the same grin.

I shook my head. Someone had mentioned that Donna had a half-sister. I rifled through more of the photos. Nothing. I picked up the yearbook and flicked through the images. I was about to give up when I found it: a photo of the two girls, obviously taken on a sports day. Rose was the younger. There was a caption, 'Sisters win three-legged race'.

Blood pounded in my ears. If Donna and Rose were sisters, that could explain the payment into Donna's account.

It hadn't been a family inheritance—it was blood money. I swallowed hard and wondered if Donna knew where the money had come from and why.

Xavier Kingston hadn't said anything about the Farrows, but it could explain why his parents had put Paul and Donna in charge of the farm. It had worked out well and made them a profit, but it could well have been part of the agreement.

Until Rossi blackmailed Xavier Kingston into selling.

I chewed my lip. What if Donna had found out? The problem was, if she realised one of the Kingstons had killed her sister, wouldn't she want to take her revenge on them, not Rossi? But if she'd found out he was blackmailing the Kingstons and making them sell…

I flicked through more of the old Polaroids. There was another of Donna leaning into a young Aldon Rossi. That wasn't surprising. Donna had said she'd broken off the relationship with Rossi before she got together with Paul.

Also in the picture was another dark-haired teenager who looked longingly in Donna's direction. I caught my breath. *Dad.* He was so young, yet he wore his trademark dark-rimmed glasses. It had to be him.

There were so many thoughts churning around in my mind. I pressed my eyes shut and tried to think. I needed to talk to Donna about Rose and speak to the Kingstons again about coming clean about the accident. It could have a bearing on the case, after all. I'd talk to Fiona and her dad in the morning and share my fears with Larsen. Would the Kingstons retaliate with assault and trespassing charges? I hoped not.

I shuffled the papers back together, looking again at the 'code' Dad had written in the margins of his uni maths book. I didn't think it could have anything to do with Rossi, but I found my phone and took photos of any page that had the code numbers and letters. Some of it was doodles. Was Dad writing notes to his university sweetheart?

Then I remembered that photo and the look of longing in Dad's eyes as he stared at Donna. Had she studied maths at uni? Was the code a message to Donna?

# Chapter Forty-Seven

When I arrived in town at lunchtime the next day, everything was abuzz. Monday morning made mourning a luxury few had time to deal with. Life went on. People went out to do their thing, leaving only a few of us with pain that stabbed, jabbed and sliced so deep you could barely breathe. I still sensed Shona was out there, alive, but then I still felt Dad's presence beside me. How could I trust my intuition when I wanted something so badly?

The fragrant scent of fresh bread from a local bakery made me think of Joe. The café was closed, but he'd assured me he wouldn't sit at home and mope—he'd mope in town. His words, not mine!

My stomach rumbled and I powered down the street to the pub. I was relieved to see Joe's ute parked out the front. Hopefully he was focused on food, not alcohol.

"Hey, Ruth." Hannah waved from behind the bar.

"Hey." Was it only the night before that I'd stood up on the table and told half the town where to go? A couple of locals nodded to me, and one older woman glared, but the reaction was in a different league to what it was last night. A frisson of pleasure swept through me. It was always good to stand up to bullies.

"Ruth!" Joe raised his hand and called out to me.

"Hey." I slid into the seat across from him. I was pleased to see he had a plate of steak and chips in front of him, although it didn't look as if he'd eaten much. He offered me a chip from the plate, but I shook my head. "Ate too many last night. Any news?"

He looked at me, his eyes dark and haunted. "They found another knife."

"What?" My voice was a shrill, strangled squeak.

"With blood on it. Larsen rang and asked me if I'd had another knife like the one that killed Rossi. I said no." Tears wet his face. "I don't know what's happening, Ruth. What if it's Shona's blood?"

Dread reached out, seized my heart and squished it in both fists. "It won't be her blood, Joe. It can't be." I reached for his hands and squeezed. "Where did they find it?"

"In the bushland when they were searching for her. Someone saw the glint of it in the sun. It was sitting half under a rock in a gully."

"They should be able to find out if it was Shona's blood pretty quickly. She has an unusual blood type, doesn't she? AB negative?"

"Yeah. Larsen said they'd call me when they found out if it was her type or not. We don't have to wait for DNA testing."

"You know that if there's another knife, this changes everything. The knife the murderer stuck into Rossi's chest might not be your knife. This one they found could be yours. You were chopping meat, right? What if the murderer took your knife as a decoy, hoping to put the blame on you, and used a different one to kill Rossi?"

Joe rubbed his hands over his face. "You're making my head hurt."

"It doesn't put you in the clear. You could have had two knives. But other people could have had them too. How easy were they to get?"

He tilted his head, thinking. "I get my knives straight from the supplier. They're expensive, but I heard the company had a Black Friday deal last November."

Someone cleared their throat behind me, and I turned to see Megan from Gone Potty. She was sitting in the booth behind us with Bridget.

I regarded the barista. "Feeling better?"

"Much."

"I couldn't help overhearing you," said Megan. "Can we join you?"

I shrugged and Joe nodded. "Sure."

Megan moved around from her booth and sat down with us, as did Bridget, who gave Joe a long, strong hug. "I'm so sorry," she said.

"Thanks, Bridget," he mumbled.

Bridget winked at me. "I heard you told Jim and his loser buddies where to go last night."

I grinned. "News travels fast in this town."

"You're not wrong," Bridget said. "I've only been here a few months, and I've heard stories about everyone."

Megan gave us both a scolding look and leaned towards us. "There was a short, sharp Black Friday sale late last year, where a premium knife range was half price. Half of our pottery group bought a set, including moi." She lifted her hand in a small wave. "It was a great deal and we told others about it, so…"

I groaned out a sigh. "So anyone could have bought them?"

Megan nodded so hard I thought her head could have fallen off. "Yep."

"If someone took Joe's knife," I mused, "this whole thing was premeditated with a capital 'P'. If someone was enraged at the party, stole the knife, and followed Rossi to whatever he was doing in my shed, that's one thing. A blend of premeditation and in-the-moment rage."

The others nodded.

"But if someone bought the knife last November, then stole Joe's knife to implicate him, that takes planning."

"Yet," Joe added, "Rossi was stabbed several times, wasn't he?" His voice broke a little. "Shona said using a knife was personal."

I squeezed his arm. "So, less likely to have been used on Shona. Someone was planning to kill Rossi for a while." I took in a deep breath and turned to Megan. "Have you told the police about this?"

She shook her head. "I didn't realise it was important, but I will now." She turned to Joe. "I'm not sure why, but I think Shona will be okay."

He managed a lukewarm smile. Any encouragement was better than none.

I got up to order lunch. "I'm going to do everything I can to help make that happen."

My shepherd's pie sat heavy in my belly as I headed to Ed's veterinary clinic. I'd normally have no problem devouring my food, but today I could only eat half. This new knife made everything more complicated. Especially as it was found on land not far from where Shona went missing… I tried to tell myself it didn't mean much. Her car was found at a place where cars often stopped and turned. Anyone could have stopped there and gone for a walk in the bush. But it hung over me like Damocles' sword, ready to fall and devastate me forever.

I blinked my eyes shut. *She's alive. I know she's alive.*

I needed a distraction and Cora's surgery should be over by now, so I'd decided to go and see how she was doing.

Despite her attack-cat tendencies, in the short time I'd owned Cora, the small feline fiend had managed to wrap her soft, furry paws around my heart. I liked that she was feisty and willing to take on the world head on. Maybe she *had* been in pain, as Ed thought, or tough times had scarred her young life. I got that. There were times I'd have liked to savage more than ankles, so maybe we were a good pair after all. At any rate, I hoped she'd be okay.

While I was still on my way, Larsen rang to ask me Joe's whereabouts on Saturday, and if everything had been okay between the two of them.

"They had a fight that morning," I admitted. "But it wasn't serious. Just a relationship hiccup thing."

There was a moment of silence on the other end of the line.

"And Joe was at Kingston's party all afternoon?"

"Yes. By the time we got back to the café and cleaned the coffee machine it was almost dark."

"Did he seem normal to you? Upset?"

"Same as always. A bit grumpy, but that's just Joe. And worried he'd messed things up with Shona." I hesitated for a moment. "I did find out something yesterday that could be relevant. It's about Xavier Kingston and his mother."

"When you and Joe went down there yesterday to harass them?"

"We didn't harass—" I stopped. "How did you know?"

"Because they came down to the station this morning."

My heart beat faster. I hoped Joe wasn't in trouble. "They told you about Olivia?"

"Yes."

"That she was driving Xavier's car when she hit Rose Mathers?"

"Yes."

"What's going to happen to her?"

"It will be investigated, and she could be charged, but I doubt she's competent to stand trial."

"What about Xavier and Fiona?"

"That's none of your business, Ms Smythe. But we're looking into the circumstances. By the way, do you know how Xavier Kingston got his black eye and broken nose?"

"Um… not sure on that one. I think he accidentally made contact with his goon's elbow."

Larsen coughed. "Joe is lucky Kingston isn't pressing charges."

I swallowed. "Good."

I told Larsen what Megan had said about the knife, and she agreed to look into it.

"Rose Mathers was Donna Farrow's sister." I tried to push for more information.

"I'm aware of that."

"It could be relevant."

"You know I'm not at liberty to discuss the case." Her shut-down said our conversation was over.

I tried again, desperate for anything that could help me find my friend. "Is there anything more about Shona? Joe told me you found a second knife."

I could almost hear her thinking. "Nothing more. As next of kin, Joe will be informed if there are any more developments." Larsen hesitated again. "Be careful, Ms Smythe. There's still a murderer out there. Stay out of this and let the police handle it. We don't need you disappearing too."

I probably should have listened to her.

# Chapter Forty-Eight

Larsen had done it again. She'd told me not to do something. It was like when I was in Year 2, and we were told not to go behind the school shed because there were dangerous things dumped there. What did we all do? I'd never had any desire to explore behind that shed, and nor had most of my classmates, but we all trooped down there and got into big trouble afterwards.

I immediately turned around, strode back to my car and drove to the place where Shona had been kidnapped.

It wasn't just rebellion. I missed my friend and I suddenly longed to be close to her—wherever she was. The nearest I could get was the last place she was known to be.

I pulled off the road, got out of the car and looked around.

The place looked so… ordinary. Shona's car had been taken away and the police had long left the scene of the crime. A pair of ravens picked at the remains of a burger in a Kenny's wrapper and the cool autumn wind blew an empty, sweet potato chip packet end over end down the road. It reminded me of a tumbleweed in an old Western, setting the scene for the gunslinger to make their entrance.

Except it wasn't a gunslinger. It was Claire Briscoe who pulled up in her gold BMW and waved. She called me over, while sitting in her car in all her well-coiffured, redheaded, nip-and-tuck, designer-clad glory—and smiled.

Fight or flight? I froze. But then I remembered that Claire had an alibi for Shona's disappearance and little motive for killing Rossi. I set my shoulders and walked towards her car.

"I'm sorry about Shona. I talked to her not long before she…" Claire gestured at the roadside. "This is where it happened?"

I could only nod.

"Anyway, I wanted to pay my respects. Do you know if you're staying in town once this all dies down?"

I found my voice. "I don't know anything yet."

"Understandable." Claire nodded, her face framed with sympathy.

Maybe she wasn't as evil as we all thought.

"But here's my card. If you do decide to sell, I'd be really interested. My number is on the back." She held out a small business card.

I automatically reached to take it, then stopped and looked askance at her and the offered card. How could she do this now? I'd thought she'd stopped out of sympathy, but all she'd wanted was to get her grubby little hands on my property. I bet she knew Rossi was blackmailing Xavier Kingston.

I let my hand drop, shivering as the cool breeze strengthened. "No thanks. I've decided to stay."

. . .

Ed's vet clinic had a much more cheerful atmosphere. When I walked in the door there was a cacophony of meows, along with a cornucopia of smells.

"Hello," I called.

"Hey, Ruth," Kat called. "In here."

I walked towards the sound of my friend's voice. She was cleaning out the litter trays of several cats I recognised from her place.

Ed appeared beside me and beckoned me to follow him. "The surgery went well."

The knot in my stomach loosened. "Can I see her?"

"Certainly. Come through." He started towards the room across the hallway, but before I could follow, he stopped and turned back to me. "Any more news on Shona?"

"Nothing. Other than they've found a second knife."

"Have they now?" He rubbed his chin. "That's interesting."

"It has blood on it. They're testing it to…" I swallowed. "See if it's Shona's."

"I'm sorry, Ruth." There was compassion in his dark brown eyes. "You fear the worst?"

I shrugged, but my eyes burned and my gut twisted into a knot. "What if it *is* my fault?"

"How can it be your fault?" His voice broke through my thoughts.

I was silent.

"I was there at the pub last night. You said that your death reputation is all a beat-up."

I nodded. "It is. But…"

"But sometimes you still wonder if there's truth to it?"

I shrugged, not daring to speak. Last night's victory over Jim and his ring of drunk dropkicks had felt amazing, but the news about the knife had thrown me. As I'd said to Dan, no matter how often I denied it, there was still a gossamer thread of guilt that wouldn't go away, like a spider spinning the filaments of a new web each time the old one was torn down.

Ed closed his eyes and leaned back against the wall for a moment. What was he doing? Sleeping? Thinking? Praying? All of the above?

He opened his eyes and looked sideways at me, regarding me for a few moments. When he did speak, his voice was gentle.

"You say there's been a pattern in your life, where people have died and others have made sport out of that?"

I nodded.

"That's pretty cruel."

"Like I said, my cousin started it. I don't think he meant any harm—he just wanted to torment me—but it took on a life of its own."

"Including in your own head?"

"I don't believe it, but sometimes it sneaks up on me, like one of Kat's cats stalking a mouse."

Ed inclined his head and stroked his beard, looking for all it was worth like a slightly overweight Obi-Wan Kenobi—the Alec Guinness version, not the Ewan McGregor one. If he'd told me to 'use the force', I wouldn't have been surprised.

But what he said did surprise me. "I can't promise you that everything will be okay with Shona, but if there's one thing I've learned in my years on the planet, it's to flip the question. Don't just ask why," he made quotation marks in the air with his fingers. "Ask, what now." Again he made air quotes. "That's what I had to do when my wife Jenny died."

"I'm not sure I understand."

"When bad stuff happens, I ask myself what I can do about it. Even this Ruthless-the-Killer thing. That's what they called you, right?"

I nodded.

"What if the worst-case scenario were true and you really do attract death somehow?"

My breath caught. "No one's ever asked me that before. Not without it being an accusation."

"I don't believe it's true, but sometimes we need to confront our demons head on." He gave me a wry glance. "Do you believe in God? A higher power? Fate?"

"I don't know." I was honest.

"Well, I do. What if there's a purpose behind your problem? I don't believe you're cursed, and it's completely unfair that you got this reputation." He shrugged. "But given it happened, what if you could use it for good?"

"I'm not sure I understand." I shook my head, trying to press pause on the emotional tumble dryer that was spinning on a mental fast cycle.

"I've only known you a short while, but I can see that you are a determined young woman. You love your friends—deeply—and you're kind. You're willing to spend money you don't have on a cranky cat you've only owned for a few days." He smiled at me, his eyes warm and encouraging. "It seems to me that you're the kind of person who, when she sees a problem, will do something about it. Maybe all the bad experiences made you into that kind of a person."

"I'd rather not have had the bad stuff." An ache built in my chest—a solid, heavy, tangible pain. I wanted to run from everything, find somewhere new where no one knew me, and kiss this dump-truck full of cow crap, goodbye. I wanted the world to leave me alone. I wanted Shona to be home with Joe and everything to be okay again.

But if I ran, Claire Briscoe would get my land.

"I think my 'what' is linked with 'who', Ed." I looked up

at the kind older man. "I might not be able to find out who killed Rossi, but I have to try. I have to help Shona."

I closed my eyes and let myself feel the ache in my chest until it began to ebb, like a snowball melting on warm sand.

"Right," Ed said, when I opened my eyes again a short while later. "Let's go see your cat."

# Chapter Forty-Nine

Ed said I could take Cora home, but she looked so warm and bleary-eyed wrapped up in her blanket and heating pad that I decided to leave her with him overnight. He was right upstairs if anything happened. That would let me focus on the next part of my mission. I needed to talk to the pharmacist.

Even though bonk-your-client-Bradley had said I sucked at fieldwork, I knew I needed to be thorough. I didn't really think Donna had killed Rossi, and I didn't see how she could have hurt Shona, but I still had to check out her claims about the migraine drugs.

Carey LaCour was around the same age as Ed, but looked more like a movie star than a pharmacist. His silver-fox vibe radiated wealth. His grey hair was cut short in a trendy style, his clothing was good quality, and he gave me a wide, super-white, even-toothed smile.

The pharmacy business must be doing well.

"What can I do for you, Ruth?"

Did everyone know me? One way to get known by

everyone in town is to have your childhood reputation get out. At least Carey didn't back away from me as if I was carrying the plague. "Yeah... er... I want to ask you about migraine drugs."

"You're suffering from migraines?" His smooth brow rose, and I realised something odd. His face had no wrinkles. Botox? Why would a chemist use Botox? Did he give himself the injections?

"No. Not me. I'm... asking for a friend."

*Great one, Ruth.*

"I'm just wondering how much someone would be bombed out after taking Migradone, and for how long."

"You're referring to the murder, aren't you? The police were in here the other day, asking the same thing. You know I can't disclose patient information."

I nodded. "I know that. I'm just asking generally. I looked Migradone up on the net and it said that it sometimes made people drowsy, but not always. Is that right?"

"Well, speaking generally of course..."

I nodded quickly. "Generally is good."

"People rarely react the same way to any of these medications, even the prescription ones like Migradone. I know a teacher who takes it and doesn't feel drowsy, but she can't mark any of her students' papers when she's taken one." He flashed a charming smile. "Mind you, it depends on what other medications people are on. Migraines can often cause nausea and if the patient takes an anti-emetic—that's a tablet to stop them vomiting—then migraine medication could easily knock them out."

"Like Gary's mum," I muttered under my breath.

"As I said, I can't give specific comments about specific people."

"What about this one? Migradone."

"That's one of the few migraine meds that still contain opiates. We have a doctor in town who still prescribes it, but it's not common. That's why we sometimes run out of it."

"Thanks. That helps." I gave him my best happy-customer smile. "Just one more thing. Did you run out of Migradone on the Saturday Rossi was killed?"

Carey hesitated. "Yes. I sold a packet that morning to a customer who had run out. I remember because three different people came in that day with scripts. That doesn't happen often. It must have been a bad week for migraines."

"Mum used to get them. It was more hormonal for her."

"You're lucky you don't get them, then."

"She had lots of headaches, not just migraines. She never would take her blood pressure meds."

The pharmacist grimaced.

I gave him my thanks again before slowly wandering back to my car. My mind was in overdrive. Donna could easily be telling the truth. Paul had said her migraines made her queasy, so she could have been on both meds. I vaguely remembered her saying that she reacted to the preventative migraine drug so she might have needed a good dose of the treatment.

A wave of grief smashed through me. This didn't bring me any closer to finding Shona. If she was dead, the murderer could have buried her anywhere. If she was alive and being held against her will, she could still be anywhere. It still didn't feel like she was dead, but that could have just been false hope.

My mind was miles away when I walked slap-bang into Dan—again.

"Woah!" he said, grabbing my shoulders and steadying me. "Are you okay?"

"Um, yeah." To my shame my thoughts of Shona were

displaced immediately by the feel of Dan's warm hands on the top of my arms. I took a step back. "Sorry, I was thinking."

His smile was warm and kind. "Shona?"

"Am I that easy to read?"

"She's the main topic of conversation everywhere you go today. And she's your best friend, so…"

"I've just been to the pharmacy to double check about migraine meds."

His eyebrows rose slightly, and I was expecting another lecture about being careful, but he seemed to see the wisdom of not going there.

"Did Donna check out?"

"LaCour couldn't tell me specifics about anyone, but he said different drugs in combination with others can make people sleepy. And everyone is different."

Dan nodded, then took me by the arm. "Want to go for a walk? I've got something to tell you—and something to ask."


We walked in silence for a few minutes. Grief about Shona hung over me like a wet wool blanket, weighing me down and stealing my joy, yet when I was around Dan the soggy weight of sorrow shifted. He was like one of the happy pills LaCour could supply if you had the right script—an addictive pill that no doubt could destroy your life if you relied on it to wash away your pain.

"I had a late lunch with Lydia before," Dan said.

My emotions clanged inside me like the small aluminium dinghy clap, clap, clapping against the side of a nearby private wharf. It was stupid to worry. They were just friends.

*Like Dan and I are just friends.*

He continued. "We were talking about Shona's disappearance and Lydia said that it has now been declared a major crime, and CIB have sent someone more senior down here. Expect to have to tell other people about Rossi and your… background." He shot me a rueful look. "I thought I'd better warn you. Lydia said the guy heading up the investigation is a bit of an arse. She had some funny stories to tell about him."

"Okay." I didn't like the sound of that, but there wasn't much I could do about it.

"There's another thing. The security company over in Rome want me to head over earlier to do this job. I'll be leaving for Europe in just over a week, not flying to Sydney."

The dinghy clanged against the wharf again, even louder than before.

"How long for?" *I'll miss you.*

"Three to six months. And I'll miss you too," he said with a roguish gleam in his eye.

"Did I say that out loud?" Heat rose up over my face.

"Indeed, you did." A lottery-winning smile spread across his face. "And that leads to a whole host of things I'd like to talk to you about later, when we have time. But right now, there's something else I need to ask you. A favour."

"You've done so much. Anything."

"Would you look after Frank for me while I'm away?"

"What?" My voice squeaked. I didn't know what I'd expected him to say, but it wasn't that.

"Nikki Golding—the woman who lives next door to me —was going to take him, but now her sister in Maitland has cancer and she'll be spending a lot of her time up there." Dan's pleading, puppy-dog gaze was on a par with Frank's. "I know I can trust you and I'll pay you."

"What about Cora? You've seen what she can do. I don't want her to eat him."

"I'm sure they'll settle. Frank likes Nikki's cat. And I think Cora likes Frank a lot better than she likes me."

I wasn't so sure, but how could I refuse? Dan had done so much for me.

"Could you give it a go? I could bring him over for a trial run sometime. Tonight, even."

"Sorry, Kat's coming over tonight. Research."

A small frown formed on Dan's face. "Be careful, Ruth."

"What?" I smirked, deliberately deflecting. "I promise I won't fall for any more of Kat's adopt-a-cat blackmail attempts."

He gave me a dark look. "You know that's not what I meant."

"It's fine. Kat's just helping me with research. Nothing illegal. Well, not very illegal. Nothing unsafe. Don't worry."

Dan let out an exasperated sigh. "I don't want whatever happened to Shona to happen to you. The thought of it…" He trailed off, his eyes clouding with concern.

"I know. And thank you. Truly." My voice softened. "But Kat is staying the night. Double girl power. And some guy I know recently installed a cool state-of-the-art security system." I tried to lighten the mood with a grin. "Although I'm sure Kat would love you to drop around."

His cheeks turned pink. "Might be a good reason to stay away."

I chuckled, the tension easing slightly. "Her ears turn red every time she talks to you. She's got it bad."

"Ruth. I'm serious." The quiet intensity in his voice made me shiver. "You need to be careful."

I shifted from one foot to the other, my own frustrations bubbling up. "Look, I appreciate everything you've done for me. I really do. You've been so good to me. But you're not my… keeper." I swallowed hard, stopping myself from saying 'boyfriend' just in time. "You have to trust me to do stuff."

He huffed and turned away, both hands stuffed in his

pockets. The distance between us suddenly felt vast. "They could come for you." His voice was tight—barely more than a whisper.

"Kat and I aren't stupid. We'll lock the doors and if anything happens that isn't… right… we'll call you, okay?" I reached out, my fingers hovering near his shoulder but not quite touching. "I promise I'll—we'll—be careful."

"Right, then." He straightened—his body still angled away from mine. "You know best." And he stalked off along the boardwalk, leaving me gaping, as the dinghy clanged against the wharf three more times.

A knot formed in my stomach as I watched him go. I'd only known Dan a short time, but I'd never seen him this agitated. His intensity unsettled me, and for a moment I wondered if his fears weren't entirely unfounded.

# Chapter Fifty

Joe rang that evening as Kat and I huddled around her laptop on my kitchen table.

My hand shook as I stood and pressed answer. "What's happening?"

"It's not her blood." His voice broke.

My knees wobbled and I sank back in my chair. "Do they know if it's human blood?"

"I'm not sure. I think they're doing more tests." His voice cracked again. "All they told me is it's not type AB, so not Shona's."

"So we still don't know if it's your knife?"

"If it was mine, then my prints would be all over it."

"They could have been wiped off the handle." I thought further. "If someone wanted to frame you, and the knives are identical, it would make sense for them to hide your knife to misdirect the police."

"That's true," Joe said.

"So, if the traces of blood on the knife belong to an animal, the odds are high it's your knife."

"I suppose so."

"They didn't say how long further tests could take?"

"I didn't ask. I was too grateful it wasn't Shona's blood."

"I am too, Joe." I paused desperate to find words of reassurance. "They'll find her. We'll find her."

There was silence for a moment on the other end of the line, then Joe coughed as if to clear the emotion from his throat. "Thanks, Ruth. For everything."

While I'd been talking, Kat had been tapping away on her computer at a frantic pace.

"What are you looking for?" I asked her, when I hung up.

"So far I've found fifteen people who bought those knives in that sale."

"How did you do that?" I hesitated. "Maybe you shouldn't tell me."

Her eyes lit up. "I used the logins I already had from Rossi's work. So far, I've found that Donna Farrow, Elouise Rossi, Bridget, Vivien and half of her Gone Potty crew bought the knives."

"Rossi was investigating Gone Potty?"

Kat shook her head, "No, but they are a great source of local gossip." A small smile played on her lips as she typed some more. She was enjoying this far too much.

"This is so illegal," I sighed.

"I'm good if you are." Her eyes shone with professional pride, mixed with a hint of naughty kitten. "All the private stuff is from files I'd already accessed for Rossi. And I'm keeping my search to the things we really need."

"Right now, I'd risk anything if it could help us find Shona." I wished I knew what I was doing. I was like one of Kat's kittens, finding a stray strand of wool and teasing it out to see what unravelled. Other than that, there was very little plan.

I took our freshly emptied pizza boxes over to the sink, then walked over to Shona's whiteboard to add some notes. "Half the town could have bought the knife used to stab Rossi, right?"

Kat shrugged. "Not quite, but lots of people."

"I'm just thinking. With these being high-end knives, do they have serial numbers? Individual ones, I mean." There was hope in my voice.

"I doubt it, but I can check." Kat began tap, tap, tapping on the keys again. After a few minutes she said, "Sorry, doesn't look like it."

A soft sigh escaped me. It was time to change our focus. "I'd like to go back to 1983 and find out what else happened back then. Here are the newspaper clippings I found." I laid the yellowed papers on the table next to her. "Can you check local papers for other stories?"

"Only if someone has archived something online. Or mentioned it in a blog or something. There wasn't really an internet back then so it's possibly only big stuff."

I sat down across the table from Kat to give us each more space and opened an old journal that was part of Dad's chimney stash. He'd filled it with copious notes. Who knew he was such a meticulous record keeper? I guess he'd needed that skill for his research work. I flicked through more pages and discovered a padded sleeve in the back that contained a clear, plastic ziplock bag with more news articles.

"What are those?" asked Kat.

"Some more of what I gave you." I shrugged. "They must have been important, or Dad wouldn't have kept them."

She pushed back from the computer, engaged in a distinctly feline stretch, and shuffled her chair around to my side of the table. "I can look if you like."

"Sure."

She took a long sip of her cola drink and began to sift through them. "It looks like he taped some of these to a board."

She held up a clipping with yellowed sticky tape attached. As she did, another small newspaper article flitted down onto the table.

"What's that?" I asked.

Kat picked up the clipping. "It was stuck to the back of this one." She held up a longer article about a new extension being built at the local high school.

"What does it say?"

She frowned as she read the text, then handed the article to me. "Something about a robbery. Some rich people who lived in Victor Harbor had their jewellery collection stolen. It happened in July 1983."

I skimmed through the article. "It must have been big. It made headline news." I sifted through the other clippings. "I'm sure I saw another robbery one." I found it and compared it to the article Kat had discovered. "This one is a follow-up, six weeks later. They caught one guy but they never found his partner or the loot."

"If your dad had two of these articles, it could be important," she said.

"He was obviously following the story." I gestured to her laptop. "Can you find out anything else about the robbery? Who were they? Where were they from? Especially the guy who wasn't caught. Like how old would he be now? Could he be living here in Pelican Bay?" The thought sent a small shudder through me. What if he came into Joe and Shona's café every day?

She frowned. "It's pre-internet, but I'll see what I can do." And she headed back to the other side of the table and began searching.

I scanned both news stories again. Could Paul be the thief? Is that what he did in '83? But I didn't see him as the robbery type, even if he was desperate. I shook my head to dislodge the cobwebs building there.

"Did I tell you about Olivia Kingston?"

Kat stopped typing and looked up. "No, but it's all over Pelican Bay."

I half-groaned. "Who spread the news?" It was supposed to be this big secret.

"I don't know," she answered. "But once something gets out in a small town…"

"You know the girl who was killed, was Donna's sister, Rose?"

Kat nodded.

"When did Donna get that inheritance?"

"Hang on, I'll check." She hit some keys. "There was a large payment into her account in April."

"That's a couple of months after Rose died. It fits with the money Kingston paid the parents." I frowned, thinking. "Nothing that happened around the time of the heist? No sudden windfalls?"

Kat began typing again, focusing intently at the screen, then shook her head. "Nothing that I can see."

"Ah ha!" She leaned around her screen so she could see me. "Someone made an online mood board about the robbery a while back."

"Someone?"

"Bronwyn Donaldson. I'll find out more about her in a second. She did this about five years ago. Looks like she scanned in some articles and uploaded them to social media."

"Why would she do that?"

"People do it to keep everything together, really. And sometimes to ask people for help if they want to find out stuff. You can keep that kind of thing private, but maybe they didn't know that, or didn't see the need."

I moved around to stand behind her, then pointed to one of the images on the screen. "Click on that one."

Kat did as I asked.

"Harry Carter, from the south coast of New South Wales," I mused as I read the article. "He was part of the robbery, but he went missing. The cops thought he'd escaped the country with the loot."

Kat clicked on another image. "This one is from a national paper." She screwed up her face. "All it says is that there was a major robbery, and two men were involved. One was apprehended but Harry Carter was still at large. The jewellery was never found."

"See what you can find out about him and the other bloke who got arrested. Also, about the woman who put up these clippings. Why did it matter to her? Was she the one who was robbed?"

Kat tapped away at the computer again.

I chewed on my lower lip. "At least we know that Rossi, Paul or Donna weren't involved in the robbery."

"Unless they were hidden partners?"

"I don't think so. Given the first guy, Eric Nisbett, outed Harry, I doubt he'd have kept the identity of anyone else secret. Not unless it was their employer, and neither Rossi nor Paul Farrow could have been that back then. They weren't much more than kids."

We both frowned at the screen.

"Let's have a break," I suggested. "Coffee?"

"Hot chocolate?" Kat flashed a hopeful smile.

I chuckled. "Sure. But I need caffeine to keep me awake."

• • •

I sat opposite Kat at the table, sipping my macchiato while she devoured her hot chocolate, and opened both my notebook and Dad's old university workbook.

"What's that?" Kat asked.

I hadn't intended to show them to her—I wanted to keep the code to myself—but Shona was gone, and I was desperate. "I think this is some kind of cipher."

I held out the workbook and told her about the games Dad and I used to play. She handed it back to me and I studied the numbers again.

"Oh my goodness." I let out a squeal. "Those are dates."

"Dates?" Kat stood, walked around and peered over my shoulder.

"Yeah, I've looked and looked at this, but I've just seen it. The numbers in the margins are dates in reverse." I turned to Kat. "Do any of the dates correspond to any of the newspaper articles?"

Kat picked up a bunch of the clippings and sorted through them, handing several to me. "These do."

I looked at the earliest article closely. "Someone's underlined some letters in pencil. It's faint, though."

Kat grabbed her phone and shone the torch on the old articles. My whole body vibrated. Dad was speaking in code from beyond the grave. I wrote the letters and underlined punctuation in my notepad, but then sat back in my chair.

BLFPMLDLHLHRRHXFNVULIWILIILMHBLF.
SVWIRMGPMLDDRGSSVSZW.
R'OOZODZHYVGSVIVULIBLFWLMMZ.

"They're nearly all consonants mixed with an occasional 'I' and 'O'." I couldn't keep the disappointment out of my voice.

"Hang on, I'll do a search on ciphers." Kat moved back to her laptop and began tapping away again. After a couple of minutes, she looked up. "What about an Atbash cipher? That's—"

"I know what it is. Thank you. It's been so long. I'm rusty." An Atbash cipher reverses the alphabet. An 'A' becomes a 'Z' and a 'B' becomes a 'Y' and so on.

I substituted the letters then played with the words. My breath caught when I read it. I wasn't sure it would help solve Rossi's murder, but it gave me a glimpse into Dad's heart. I read the words out to Kat.

"YOU KNOW ROSSI IS SCUM FOR DROPPING YOU.

HE DIDN'T KNOW WHAT HE HAD.

I'LL ALWAYS BE THERE FOR YOU, DONNA."

"Sounds like he loved her." Kat's words were hushed.

For a moment I wondered what it would have been like to grow up with the warm-hearted Donna as my mum rather than my own hypercritical mother. But if Dad had got together with Donna and had a family, I'd never have been born.

Like it or not, Mum was part of me.

I stared at the words, tapping my finger on the table. There was still something that bothered me.

"Donna said she broke up with Rossi, not that Rossi dumped her. They told me when I was at the farm one morning." I lifted my eyes to Kat's. "Why would she lie?"

I closed my eyes and tried to think. "I'll give Elouise Rossi a call."

# Chapter Fifty-One

Twenty minutes later I was in Elouise Rossi's lounge room, another hot drink in my hand and many questions on my mind. I'd called her straight away, but she'd said she didn't want to talk on the phone. Kat was happy to stay and keep going with her research, so I jumped in the Mini and drove straight over to the Rossi residence.

Whisky and Soda had greeted me with their trademark wiggling bottoms, wagging tails and snuffly licks. Now the dogs sat either side of me on the sofa with their heads on my lap. I wasn't sure if they were adoring me or watching over me, guarding their mistress. Possibly both. Whisky, on my right, groaned with pleasure as I fondled his soft, silky ears. Soda sighed and nudged my hand, demanding ear rubs too.

Elouise took a sip of her steaming brew then set it down on the table.

"Aldon and Donna were together, but I was the other woman." Elouise's lips turned down at the painful memory. "Aldon began hanging around me, being really attentive. I didn't feel right about it because Rosie had only been killed in the accident a short while before. Donna was going through a hard time. But he could be really charming, you know?"

I nodded. I'd have used the word slick rather than charming, but they say beauty is in the eye of the beholder.

"I gave in, and we got together. I should have known that if he was the kind of man to cheat on his girlfriend, he would cheat on me later on." She sighed deeply. "Love is blind."

"What happened with Donna?"

"She hit rock bottom." Elouise cast her eyes downwards. "It was awful. Rick—your dad—was a stalwart though." She gave me a half-smile. "He had a thing for Donna. Everyone knew. She liked him, but just as a friend. And later she fell for Paul."

I nodded. "I found some photos from around that time. In the yearbook." I didn't mention the code I'd cracked.

"I discovered later that Aldon had gone about the whole thing badly."

"What did he do?"

"They were living together in a small flat. He went there and told her it was over. She needed to get herself together, stop being weak." She looked up at me, shaking her head. "Can you imagine? She'd only lost her sister a month before."

"So that was around March that year?" The more I heard about Aldon Rossi, the more I disliked him.

"Yes. Aldon tossed some money on the table, told her it was for the rent, and walked out." She bowed her head. "I felt terrible. Donna and I had been friends."

"Did she talk to you about it?"

Elouise shook her head. "She found out about us when she saw Aldon's car in my driveway, one Saturday afternoon. It was years before she would even speak to me. It was horrible."

My mind raced. All this gave Donna even more reason to hate Rossi. "But you stayed with Aldon?"

She shrugged. "We do daft things in the name of love."

I couldn't agree more with that. My own list of romantic disasters said it all. "Love can be like an addiction." I sighed. "You keep on hoping the next pay out will make your life better."

There was sympathy in Elouise's eyes. "You're too young to be that cynical." She furrowed her brow. "Aldon was a bastard. I heard later that he didn't give her nearly enough to cover the bills. She had to borrow money before she got that inheritance."

The ghost of the earlier conversation I'd had with Elouise, about Paul Farrow, came to life, niggling at my subconscious like a kid tugging on her parent's sleeve.

"How much did he give her?"

"Fifty dollars."

"Just like with Paul," I breathed.

"I guess it was his thing." Elouise nodded, seemingly surprised at the connection. "Is it important?"

My breath caught, and my heart thump, thump, thumped against my chest wall.

"Are you okay?" Elouise asked.

Soda lifted her head, looked at me with concerned brown eyes, and whined.

"I'm sorry, Elouise. I have to go." It seemed like I was always doing that to the poor woman.

I almost tripped over my body-wagging, four-legged escorts as I stumbled towards the door.

*It couldn't be.*

Donna was on the migraine tablets—they bombed her out. She couldn't have killed Rossi. I could see the box in my mind's eye. Migradone. The last box sold by the pharmacist that day. I saw myself knocking it off the table, the sealed foiled tablets falling out, me picking them up putting them back in the box and handing them back to Donna.

"Oh crap, crap, crap." I remembered clearly now. All the tablets were inside the foil. None of them had been taken.

I tried to slow my breathing. This didn't mean anything. She could have had other tablets there, couldn't she? But she'd said she'd run out and had bought the last pack.

My stomach gripped hard inside me, a tight ball of pain. Why would she lie? Donna might have a motive for killing Rossi, but surely there was no way she'd hurt Shona. Donna *loved* Shona.

Unless the kidnapping and the murder were unrelated after all. But how likely was that?

My mind was in overdrive as I jumped in my Mini and threw it into gear. I let out the clutch too quickly and the donut-shaped mag wheels did a wheel-squealing, smoke-billowing, acrid-rubber-smelling burnout before I drove as fast as I could towards Paul and Donna's farm.

# Chapter Fifty-Two

I sat parked on the verge outside the Farrow farm and caught my breath. What was I doing? This was a murderer I was dealing with. I breathed in and out several times to settle the racing thrum of my heart. Shona could be in there. Scared. Hurting. Dead.

I couldn't accept the last option—she *had* to be alive— but if Donna had killed Rossi, I was contemplating barrelling onto a murderer's property. My phone was in my bag. I'd call Larsen. She might think I was an idiot, but she was smart. She wouldn't ignore me.

I dialled three times.

No answer. Just voicemail.

Then I rang the regular number for the local police station. Gary answered and I poured out my concerns about Donna to him. I could almost hear the cogs turning in his brain. I'd done this to him before.

"Ruth, I know you're concerned about Shona, but you have to leave this to the police."

I've never dealt with 'condescending' well. "I am leaving it to you. That's why I called. Shona could be hidden on the farm."

"You were down at the station saying almost the same thing, but about Paul, the other day. You were sure he was the killer and he alibied out."

"I know, but—"

"That was after talking with Elouise, too. I'm worried she's putting ideas into your head."

"No. I approached her. Rossi—"

"We'll get his killer, Ruth. And we'll find out what happened to Shona. I'm really sorry. You know that."

Dark spots clouded my vision. "Not as sorry as you'll be if you don't believe me."

"You're out of line, Ruth."

"She's not dead. I know she isn't. Please, please come out to the farm. Look around."

"You know we can't do that without a warrant."

"Then get one."

"Ruth... we'd need real proof."

I closed my eyes and squeezed away my tears. "Please, Gary. Get in touch with Larsen. Tell her to call me, okay?"

"Ruth..."

It was no use. I hung up and rang Larsen's mobile again, leaving a message this time asking her to call me back. What was the point of having a direct number to a cop and them never answering?

Who else could I call? Dan? I dialled his number, and my heart did a flutter at the sound of his resonant voice, but I realised almost immediately that I'd only reached his voicemail.

I left a message similar to the one I'd left for Larsen and tried to stop my crazy brain from imaging them together. Candlelit dinner. Candlelit... other things.

*Stop!*

What they did—or didn't do—was their business. I had to think. I got out of the car and wrapped my arms around myself as I stood in the cool autumn night air. A half-moon hung low in the sky, framed by fluffy clouds. It would have been a lovely night for a stroll on the boardwalk. With…

*Let's face it, you want to be with Dan.*

Something rustled in the undergrowth near me. Snake? Blue-tongue lizard? There was the faint lowing of cows in the distance and something else, a loud, squawking call. Some night bird, a bat, or a possum maybe. But I found myself edging towards the fence, bending the wires back, and slipping through the trees that bordered the farm.

I checked my watch. It was just after ten o'clock. Not late by European standards, but past the bedtime of most Aussie dairy farmers. The heady smell of cow manure hung in the night air as I crunched as softly as I could across the gravelled yard towards the farm's outbuildings. If I could just look—make sure Shona wasn't here—I could let the Donna thing go, at least until I talked to Larsen and told her my fears.

I shuffled forward. "Ow!" My foot kicked a stone and I stumbled, swearing under my breath and hopping on one leg until the pain eased. I put my foot down gingerly, testing it. My big toe throbbed, but it could bear weight. I slid closer to the building and hid in the shadows, waiting to see if anyone had heard me.

Everything was still. Everything was quiet.

Until my phone rang, loud and clear in the crisp, cool night air.

*Crap, crap, crap!* I fumbled for it, declined the call and turned the phone audio to silent. I sat there for a moment longer, but nothing stirred.

Dan's name flicked across the screen in a silent notification. He'd left a message. I turned the phone's volume to low and pressed it hard to my ear. It wasn't the time to worry about brain tumours.

"Hey, Ruth. Sorry about this afternoon. What's going on? Please call me."

I took another deep breath and typed an answer.

I'm at the Farrow farm—looking for Shona.
Please come. Text me when you get here.
I'll come to you.

DANGER DAN

What the hell, Ruth?

Donna lied about the migraine meds.

Is she there with you?

No. But I have to look around.

Get out of there now, Ruth.

But Shona... And no one knows I'm here.

Get out now. If she's the murderer you're in danger.

Okay, I'll go back to the car. I'll wait for you.

Don't wait. Go home. I'm still 30 minutes away.

Are you with Larsen?

No. Why?

I couldn't reach her. I'll wait in the car.

I turned off the screen and gazed up at the silver stars massed above, breathing a prayer into the cool, dark night. At least now Dan was coming. I trusted him. He'd believe me. He'd make Larsen search for Shona.

I'd taken one step through the darkness in the direction of my car, when I heard a metallic sound like the sliding of a bolt.

"Put your hands up where I can see them and turn around."

I turned and came face to face with Donna, her shotgun pointed right at me.

# Chapter Fifty-Three

"I thought it had to be you." Donna's hands were steady as she pointed the gun at my chest. I couldn't say the same for my knees. They shook so hard I had to grab onto the shed wall to steady myself.

"What do you mean, me?" Indignation rose like a tidal wave, smashing all caution aside. "You killed Rossi. Where's Shona?" My voice was as cold as the galvanised steel I leaned against.

"Don't try to put that one on me. You killed Rossi and I don't know what you've done with my Shona. Now you're after the jewellery." Donna shook her head. "Shona trusted you. I can't believe you'd do this."

"What?" My mouth gaped.

"I know you know where it is. I don't care about Rossi—I hated that low-life and I'm glad he's gone—but Shona? She's your friend." She swallowed, lifting her shotgun higher. "She's like a daughter to me. You *took* her, and now you're trying to steal my jewels."

"*Took* Shona? *Your* jewels?" Did Donna mean the ones

from the robbery? My heart raced and my mouth seared dry. "That's insane. I know about the heist, and I know you're mixed up in this, but I have no idea where the *stolen* jewels are. And I was still working when Shona went missing." I looked around for anything I could use to defend myself, but I couldn't see far in the darkness. How long ago had Dan texted? Five minutes?

Donna shifted her feet, but she was still pointing the shotgun in my face.

"I do know," I continued, my voice rising, "that you lied about taking the migraine tablets. The packet hadn't been opened. Why would you do that if you hadn't killed Rossi? And you said you dumped Rossi when you were young, but he dumped you. Why would you lie? And you ordered a knife online exactly the same as Joe's. The knife that killed Rossi." I paused to catch my breath. "And Elouise told me about the fifty dollars!"

"Fifty dollars?" Donna screwed her face into a frown.

"Elouise *told* me." I tried to slow down enough to get the words out clearly. "She said that when Aldon broke up with you, he left you a fifty-dollar note for his share of the rent and bills."

"That little creep was always cheap."

"You don't deny it?"

"Deny what? That I was too broken and ashamed to want the world to know Rossi dumped me? That I wasn't strong enough to stand up to him and at least make him pay his fair share? I had enough pitying, prying looks after Rosie died. I couldn't take more."

"So, you deny that you killed Rossi and stuffed a fifty-dollar note in his pocket as part of your revenge?"

"What? No. I mean, yes." She shook her head. She lowered the shotgun slightly. "You didn't kill Rossi?"

"No. Why would I kill a PI I hardly knew?"

"Bridget said—"

"Bridget? What's she got to do with it?"

"Nothing." Donna shook her head. "She said she heard someone say you and Rossi had angry words at the business celebration. Something about your dad."

"What?"

"I heard her tell Larsen."

"But that's not true. Rossi and I made a time to talk on Monday and Elouise gave me an open invitation to have dinner with them to talk about Dad. Who said we had angry words?"

"I think she said it was Xavier Kingston."

I screwed up my face and tried to remember. It had been loud in the community centre, with the music and the buzz of the crowd. Kingston must have misheard my conversation with Aldon and Elouise. No wonder Larsen kept hassling me.

"Well, Kingston heard wrong. Can I put my hands down now?"

Donna nodded slowly and dropped the weapon to her side.

I lowered my arms, rubbing them to get the circulation going. "Why did you think I knew where the stolen jewels were?"

"Because I asked your dad to hide them."

"You did what?" My mouth gaped like a beached mullet gasping for breath.

Donna sighed and gestured to the tractor shed door. "Let's go inside. It's cold out here."

I was still a little wary of her and her shotgun, but she put it down on an old wooden table as soon as we stepped inside. I was pretty convinced now that she hadn't hurt Rossi or Shona, but I didn't have a clue what was really going on.

She turned on the shed light. We sat in two plastic chairs next to the table, bathed in an insipid fluorescent glow.

"If I tell you this, it will be up to you what you do with it, but your dad's name will be at stake," Donna warned. "Okay?"

I swallowed hard and nodded. Dad could never do anything really bad, could he?

"You seem to know most of it anyway. It was all a complete balls-up," she said. "Paul had lost money to Rossi, gambling. I had some cash coming from an inheritance from some distant Aunt, and I offered to pay the debt." She shook her head. "Paul wouldn't have it. He said he had a family heirloom—a necklace. It wasn't worth a huge amount, but it would pay his gambling debts and maybe some of his uni accommodation fees. Rossi said he had contacts and that he'd sell it for him."

This matched with what Elouise had already told me about the opal necklace, but I kept quiet to see what Donna would reveal.

She sighed. "I moved back in with Mum and Dad after Rossi and I broke up, and I stayed there for a few months. They were still doing it tough after we lost Rosie. I was too. Paul and I just started dating. I really liked him, but it was all pretty new. Back then my family lived on this property, in the small house near the west fence, doing maintenance work for the Kingstons."

"But my dad...?"

"I'll get to him in a second." She patted my arm. "Paul and Rossi had been best friends for a long time, but that so-called heirloom made it all fall apart. Rossi came back saying it was worth a lot less than it really was. It all got ugly, and Paul accused Rossi of stealing from him."

"Did he?"

"Possibly. But Rossi might have had trouble selling the 'heirloom'," she lifted her fingers in air quotes, "because it was hot. It was part of the stash of jewellery that had been stolen and everyone would be on alert for the pieces."

"What? How did Paul get it?"

"He found it. We were walking around the property and Paul was telling me about his dreams of being a farmer and breeding an elite dairy herd. He always had ambition and heart, but no money. There was an old water tower down near the southern fence. Not far from the back of your block. There'd been an old house there, but even then it was burnt out ruins. The tower was still standing. Paul got curious one day, climbed up and then looked inside."

"And found the jewels?"

Donna nodded. "He didn't tell me at the time, but something changed in him after he went inside the tank. I went back later and found them." She gazed at me with a bemused half-smile on her face. "I've never seen anything like it. On one hand, jewellery and gems—bits of cold rock—on the other, more riches than I could ever dream of knowing."

I thought I understood. "The robber—Harry Carter—came back, didn't he?"

She stared intently at the table, eyes veiled. "It was a few days later. I'd go up there just to look at the jewellery. I wore gloves because of fingerprints, but I'd hold the pieces and imagine they were mine. Harry found me there just as I was coming out of the tank. We struggled. He pulled a gun on me, but…"

"But?"

"Your dad turned up. He called out and distracted Harry.

Harry was going to shoot him, but I wrenched at the gun and tried to stop him…" She swallowed hard. "He fell and hit his head. Died straight away."

"You didn't tell anybody? It sounds like self-defence to me."

"That's what Rick said. He told me to go to the police. They would understand. But if I did that, they would have known Paul sold the necklace and that Rossi was involved too. Selling stolen goods is an offence, last I heard." Her lips curved in a small, momentary smile as she gazed vacantly at the shed wall. "I didn't give a damn about Rossi, but I couldn't do it to Paul."

She turned back to me.

"Your dad was my rock after Rossi dumped me. I knew he was sweet on me and I'm ashamed to say I encouraged him, even though I didn't feel that way about him. I liked the attention and it felt good to have someone on my side. He knew I was protecting Paul, but he still agreed to help me. He helped me dump the body in an old roo pit and then I asked him to take the jewellery and hide it somewhere I'd never find it. I never wanted to see it again."

"And he agreed?"

She ran her hands through her hair. "I should never have asked him. It wasn't fair to Rick. He took the whole lot and promised it wouldn't be found. I regretted it almost immediately, and begged him to give it all back, but he said they were bad for me. My 'precious'." She smiled at me through her tears. "Although later he said I was more like the dragon, Smaug. Rick was a tragic Tolkien fan, like Paul." She closed her eyes and sighed deeply, as if reliving the whole experience. "He was probably right." Her eyes were troubled as she held my gaze. "I went back to the tank several times just to remember what it was like to hold those rotten jewels, even though they were long gone."

I let out a long, slow breath. I'd wanted to know more about Dad, but this? Could I see him hiding a body and a stash of jewellery, all because of love—unrequited love at that?

"He never talked about it?" Donna asked.

I shook my head. "He never mentioned Pelican Bay. I was overseas for ten years, too. I didn't know this place existed until after he died." I squinted at her in the flickering light. "But what about the night of Rossi's murder? You lied about the migraine tablets. Why?"

Donna seemed to have shrunk in size with her confession. Now she deflated further.

I waited as the silence hung around us, wanting her words to fill the void, not mine.

"I didn't want to go to the dinner. I didn't trust myself not to scream at Rossi and make a scene." She shivered and rubbed her arms, then stood up and began pacing back and forth. "But he came over that night. He said..." her voice shook, "that Paul must have found—and taken—the jewellery. Paul didn't have the imagination to be part of a robbery, but he'd set Rossi up by getting him to sell the necklace. Rossi got that bit right, but he thought Paul must have killed Harry and got rid of him." She looked at me with wide, haunted eyes. "But Paul's denial had finally convinced him. And if Paul hadn't done it, then it must have been me."

She sat back down in her chair and covered her face with her hands, then looked up at me with red-rimmed eyes.

"I lost it—I really did. I screamed at him about how he'd dumped me right when I'd needed him. Abandoned me with no money and no hope. I told him I wanted him to go to hell. I went to my purse, took out a fifty-dollar note and threw it in his face. You know what? The cheap bastard smirked and stuck it in his pocket."

She pressed her hands on the table, as if trying to still her shaking.

"He said that if I gave him the jewellery stash, he might be able to stop the sale of the farm. But if I didn't, and there happened to be a human skeleton found when the developers rolled in, then Paul and I would both go down for murder."

I squeezed her arm. "I'm sorry, Donna."

"I was so angry, Ruth. I told him I couldn't give him what I didn't have. I wanted him to die. He was going to take everything away from us. Everything in me screamed, 'Kill him!'" She glanced at her shotgun. "I picked up the gun and told him to get the hell off my property. I came so close, I aimed at him. I nearly pulled the trigger, but I didn't kill him. I fired a shot above his head as he ran."

"I think I heard that. A bit after midnight?"

She nodded. "Not long before the storm hit."

I pressed my eyes shut. Her words rang true.

"You have no idea where your dad hid the jewels?" There was pleading in her eyes and her voice. "We found out today that the sale of the farm is on hold because of some loophole. If I can find them, Paul and I could sell them and make a counter-offer."

I frowned at her. "But they're not yours to sell."

"We could still lose everything." Her eyes flicked down to the shotgun again, then back to me. My pulse spiked and my muscles tensed. I had reasonable reflexes and could probably get to the gun before her, but she was stronger than me. Could she have killed Rossi anyway? Followed him and stabbed him out of spite?

I held her gaze for a moment before saying in a slow,

gentle voice, "Just like you said to Rossi—I can't give you what I don't have."

She dropped her head. "I'm sorry. I'm just desperate, that's all." She gestured in the direction of the house. "This is such a mess, and Paul…"

"Does he know? About you finding the jewellery, and Harry's death?"

She shook her head and wiped the tears from her cheeks with the back of her hand.

There was a soft cough behind us and we both jumped and turned. Paul stood in the doorway, staring at Donna, his eyes dark with sorrow.

"I do now."

# Chapter Fifty-Four

It broke my heart to see the tough-as-nails Donna crying, but Paul went to her and wrapped her in his arms.

I blinked back my own tears and walked out into the night. Life may have continued to throw all kinds of rubbish in the direction of Donna and Paul, but they'd work it out—together. Whatever happened, they'd be okay. A wave of longing surged through me. I wanted that for myself someday—someone I could trust who would be with me no matter what.

I just had to fall for the right kind of man.

As if on cue, I got a text from someone I was in grave danger of falling for, even though I still suspected he was absolutely the *wrong* kind of man for me.

DANGER DAN

Are you okay? Traffic stopped. Some kind of major accident. Not sure how long I'll be.

Talked with Donna. All good. Heading home now.

I pressed send, and tried to ignore the disappointment that settled over me now there was no excuse to see Dan tonight.

I scrolled through the screen and began walking in the dark, towards my car. There were three missed calls from Kat. I tried to call back, but her phone went to voicemail.

Unease shifted through me. It was stupid. She'd probably just gone to the bathroom.

I hung up and tried again.

No answer.

My finger hovered over the screen. Kat's messages could be important.

I scrolled down and pressed dial on her first voicemail message, but all I could hear was a buzzing of music in the background. I let out a breath. Kat had just bum-dialled me —several times it seemed. I grinned to myself. She may be a techno-whiz goth-girl, but she wasn't infallible.

I reached my car and groped for the keys in my pocket. The cows were mooing in the distance—a low-grade, shifting restlessness like the niggle that wouldn't shift from my mind. I believed Donna. She had motive and opportunity to kill Rossi and she had lied about the migraine meds, but I could *feel* the truth in her words. I hated that she'd used Dad, though. He was always too kind—and naïve—despite his brilliance. That was how my sister had kept us apart for so long.

The cool breeze strengthened. As did the niggle. I could understand Rossi running from Donna. But why my place? You couldn't see it from here. If he was in danger, why didn't he go straight back to his car?

I shivered as I pressed the remote key.

Nothing happened.

I tried again.

Nothing.

Then a third time—but the remote, or my Mini, was dead.

I bit back panic, trying not to be spooked by the inky blackness. I fumbled the keys and dropped them twice before I managed to open the door. Relief flooded me as I slid into the driver's seat and slammed the door shut beside me.

I tried my key in the ignition just in case the problem had been with the key fob, but everything was dead.

Unease prickled through me. I made sure all the doors of my car were locked, then I picked up my phone and called Dan.

He didn't answer so I left a message, hoping I didn't sound too pathetic. "I'm still at the Farrows' farm. My battery is dead. Can you come?"

I gazed at the screen for a few moments, willing him to call, but there wasn't an immediate reply. He was probably still driving, so I tried Kat again.

No answer.

She couldn't still be in the bathroom, could she? The wind was getting stronger and I jumped as something banged onto the roof of the car. I turned on my phone torch, only to see a pinecone roll down the windscreen. It was followed by leaves and other debris, then by the slap of an empty chip packet against the glass. A sweet potato chip packet.

*Get a grip, Ruth!* I stared at it for a moment, my brain trying to compute. It was the same brand I'd seen tumbling down the road near where Shona had been taken. Slow, cold fingers traced their way from the back of my neck down to the base of my spine. I checked the door locks again and took in a deep breath to steady myself. It was a coincidence, nothing more. The police would have bagged the chip packet as evidence if it had been near Shona's car, wouldn't they? It couldn't have been hers as she prided herself on her love of real potatoes.

Unlike…

A memory flooded in.

Unlike Bridget, who didn't eat nightshades.

I scoffed at myself. It was a flimsier conclusion than the soft plastic packet that flicked off my windscreen into the night.

My heart blam, blam, blammed against my chest wall. It was silly. Bridget didn't know Rossi. Why would she kill him? Donna had said Bridget told Larsen that Xavier Kingston heard me arguing with Rossi. But when we'd all eaten together at the pub, Bridget said she'd noticed I was pally with Rossi and had asked me about the appointment. She'd also said she didn't remember much about who came in the kitchen, or what happened that night. It was all a blur because we were so busy.

Bridget never forgot *anything*.

I flushed hot then cold. That was just after she'd talked with Larsen. I remembered the day we'd all joined in with milking. I'd been looking towards the horizon, and Bridget had mentioned that my house was in that direction, and that I must love the view. But you couldn't see my place from there. And Bridget had never been to my home.

Or so I thought.

I shone my phone's torch into the night. There was no one there. I tried Larsen again, but she still wasn't answering. There was no point ringing Gary, so I tried Dan again, but the call went through to his voicemail. Had he got my first message?

I scrolled through my missed calls again and pressed play on Kat's next message.

"Ruth! Ruth!" In my mind's I could see her bouncing in

her chair with excitement. "One of the news articles in the plastic bag is from 2023. It talks about the history of the area, including the unsolved crime. It's proof that your dad put at least some of the clippings together recently. And guess what." Her words tripped over each other. "There were underlined letters on that one too. I used the same key and it said, 'Returned to sad water'. I'm not sure what it means, but I thought you'd want to know."

The second message made my gut claw into a ball.

"Ruth, ring me as soon as you get this. Remember how that article said Harry Carter was from the South Coast of New South Wales? I did some digging, and it turns out he's from Bega. So is Bridget. Bronwyn Donaldson is her mother. She put that mood board on social media. Bridget is Harry Carter's daughter. And get this, she spent several years in the US and studied computer networking and security. She could be the hacker."

There was a pause.

"Someone's here. Is that you, Ruth?"

Then… silence.

# Chapter Fifty-Five

I sucked in deep breaths, trying to push away the panic. A car pulled up in front of me, and I raised my hand to block out the glare of the super bright headlights. It wasn't Dan's Jeep, nor did it look like a police car. Fear prickled through me. Fight or flight? Stay in my car or get the hell out of there?

I was going to stay there, locked inside the Mini, until I saw the gun, silhouetted in in the hand of what appeared to be a woman of medium build. She stooped to pick up something from the ground then strode in my direction.

"Crap. Crap. Crap." I fumbled at the lock, flung the door open and sprinted for the fence line, but I'd only taken three steps when my head exploded.

Stars and coloured lights blazed as white-hot pain consumed me. I fell to the ground, my fingers digging hard into the soil beneath me. The earth smelled of grass and manure. Where was I? The farm?

I lifted my head and tried to stand, but pain and nausea smashed through me.

*Breathe.*

I reached back to touch warm stickiness on the back of my head. Had I been shot? I hadn't heard a shot. Why wasn't I dead?

A strong hand grasped the back of my shirt and pulled me roughly to my feet, sending fresh waves of pain searing through my skull. Bridget's soft Aussie-American twang whispered in my ear. "Keep quiet." She shoved me back towards the road and pushed something cold and hard into my ribs.

The gun.

I stumbled, turning my ankle on a baseball-sized rock. Was that what she'd hit me with? I reached for it, but I was too slow. She kicked it away.

"Move, now." She shoved me forward, propelling me towards her car.

"New car? Don't you know those headlights aren't safe?" I said, channelling Seth's dad. "They can blind oncoming traffic."

"Shut up." She glared at me and shoved me into the passenger seat. "Get out your phone."

I complied.

"Now turn it off, take the SIM out and break the SIM in two."

I did as she said.

"Now put it in the glove box."

I obeyed her. "Won't someone trace it?"

"Not when it's turned off. Not easily, anyway." She screwed her face into an unpleasant smile. "Waste not, want not. That will give me some extra pocket money. And you won't need it where you're going."

Nausea welled again and I brought up tonight's pizza on the car floor.

"Hope this *is* your car," I muttered under my breath.

That wasn't a good move, as Bridget spun me around roughly and wrapped duct tape around my wrists. "Insurance against that Krav-Ninja crap. You say anything else, and I'll cover your mouth too." She nodded to the mess on the floor. "That might not work out so well for you if you're throwing up."

I managed a nod and wished I hadn't tried. It gave a whole new meaning to the term 'splitting headache'. It felt as if an axe had cleaved open my skull into random-sized parts. Two? Ten? Twenty? Who's counting?

I twisted my wrists in some futile reflex aimed at feeling the back of my head and making sure no brains were oozing out. Then again, brain leakage would mean I was dead. Pain was good. Pain meant life, which meant my brain was intact, at least for now. For that I was grateful.

We weren't on the road for long before we pulled into my drive. My chest tightened when I realised Kat's car was still there.

"No!"

"What did I say about talking?"

"Leave Kat out of it." The pain still throbbed with every movement, but my head was clearing.

"Too late, Nancy Drew. You should have thought of that before you asked others to be part of your little quest."

"Nancy Drew? Couldn't you at least call me Buffy? She's a lot cooler."

"That would make me a vampire."

"If it fits." I shrugged, then regretted it as white-hot pain raged again. "What is it you want?"

"You really aren't very bright, are you? I want the jewellery and I want revenge. You're going to help me get both."

My heart thumped a rapid staccato beat. "I don't know where the jewellery is."

"So you told Donna." She smirked. "Let's say I don't believe you."

Vertigo spun as I tried to make sense of what she was saying. "You were there?" I had to keep her talking.

"Just outside. My car was parked further down the road. You need to be more careful with locking your car. I disabled your battery." She sniggered. "It was so much fun to scare you like that."

I balled my hands into fists, twisting against my restraints, testing for any weakness, but I tried to keep my face neutral. I couldn't—wouldn't—give her the satisfaction of seeing my fear. "I know you killed Rossi." That much was clear.

"But where's Shona? If you've hurt her…"

Bridget's eyes blazed. "I'm the one who has been wronged here. My father. My inheritance. My life. Everything was taken. Mum died last year with cirrhosis because she drank herself to death. I had to leave work to care for her."

She waved the handgun in circles as she spoke. I flinched when her finger slid close to the trigger. If my hands weren't tied, I'd back myself against her. But bailed up like this there was nothing I could do. I bowed my head as a suffocating fatigue pressed around me, stealing my breath, destroying my hope and threatening my resolve. I willed it to leave. I had to stay strong.

"It was the not knowing that was hardest on Mum." Bridget's voice wavered. "If you know someone is dead, or has betrayed you, you can move on. If you don't know, it eats at you until there's nothing left inside. Most people thought Dad had nabbed the stash and moved to Costa Rica." She shook her head. "Mum never believed it."

"What changed? Why come here now?" The longer I could keep Bridget talking in the car, the more there was a chance that someone would come. Except Dan would go to the Farrow farm. He wouldn't come here. The cavalry would be too late.

"I did some investigating. Someone had sold a necklace that was part of Dad's stash. It wasn't easy, but I found out it was Rossi and I assumed he killed my dad. But then I found out he'd been doing his own investigation."

"You were the other hacker."

Her eyes gleamed. "No one suspects the barista of having IT skills. Rossi hired that stupid goth kid to stop me, but I'd got most of his records by then anyway. Enough to know he suspected Paul and that your dad was part of the picture too. I went to the Farrow farm to confront Paul that night, but he wasn't home yet. Rossi had arrived before me. I didn't hear everything that was said, but it was funny when Donna chased him off. When I followed Rossi to your place that night, I figured he'd worked out where it was."

"But why kill him if you thought he knew where to find the jewellery? And why a knife rather than a gun?" I gestured to the weapon in her hand.

"I like knives," her eyes gleamed and her nostrils flared. "So I stole it from Joe. I already had one at home, but two is even better. Popped it into my bag when no one was looking. A lucky accident, really. When I cornered Rossi in your shed, he denied knowing where the stash was. Donna had told him your dad had hidden it. He had thought as much, which was why he'd made the appointment to see you, but she confirmed it. He said you must know where it was."

She grimaced. "His words rang true, but then he started making all these comments about Mum. He'd done his research, and she was nothing but dirt-poor, alcoholic trash. I told him to stop, but he went on and on about it. I think he wanted to distract me, so he could run, but I saw red. None of this was fair on Mum—or Dad. None of it! So I stabbed him." She sniggered. "The knife worked out well because it created a host of suspects. Especially as Joe had that fight with Rossi."

I swallowed back bile. How could she be so nonchalant about taking a life? I glanced out into the night. There was still no sign of Dan or Larsen. My only hope was to keep Bridget talking for as long as possible.

"Why the second knife? I assume you planted it in the bushland?"

"It seemed like a good way to confuse the cops." She shot me a sick grin. "It worked."

"I'm sorry about your Dad… and your Mum. It must have been hard for you." I truly did have sympathy for that part of her story. I'd believed my own dad had rejected me and it had devastated my life. I could see how her dad's disappearance could have shattered hers.

She grimaced. "Sorry? What good does sorry do? Dad goes to get the loot and they kill him and cover it up. Mum kills herself with drink." She swallowed hard. "Once I've got the jewellery, I'm going to deal with Donna. Then I'm going to deal with you. You get to pay for your father's sins."

# Chapter Fifty-Six

Bridget lifted the gun and pointed it at me. "This is where you tell me where the stash is."

"I told you I don't know."

She scoffed. "I don't believe that."

"I really don't." I tried to make my shrug nonchalant, but I was stiff with fear and did a weird jerky shoulder twitch.

"You can't even lie properly." She gestured to the car door. "Out."

"Wait… You were still in the shed when I found Rossi?"

"I thought about killing you too, but I needed to know where you'd hidden the jewellery. And it was much more fun to implicate you, Joe and Shona. Then your sister told the world about the hilarious Ruthless-the-Killer thing. Must have been great fun growing up with no one wanting to be near you and people dropping dead everywhere."

I swallowed hard. "None of that was true."

"You admitted it in the pub last night. You said people died around you all the time." She let out a short laugh. "No matter, because if you don't cooperate, it's going to happen all over again."

She opened her door and eased herself out, all the time keeping her gun trained on me. Then she walked around to my side and yanked the car door open.

"Move."

I eased myself out of the car and stood, but instantly regretted it. Pain pulsed through my head with each thud of my heartbeat and flashes of bright light cut across my vision. I had some form of concussion—that was obvious—but I hoped I didn't have a fractured skull or one of those subdural haematomas they were always talking about on medical dramas. I sent up a prayer and silently vowed to watch less television.

I tried to think through the pain. I'd told Kat to reset the outside alarm after I'd left, but she was so hyper-focused on her research she could easily have forgotten. Was she inside waiting innocently for me? How could I warn her? I took a deeper breath—that was probably my only tell—but Bridget dug her gun into my ribs. "Too late, fancy Nancy. She's already indisposed."

My stomach lurched. "What have you done?"

Bridget said nothing but marched me around to the back porch and shoved me towards the door. "Don't worry, the alarm's off. Humans are the reason ninety-five percent of security systems fail." She simpered, pleased with herself. "Kat let me in not long after you left. I could have killed her but thought you might need some extra motivation."

I stumbled over the doorstep and my knees hit the floor. The jarring sent stars and pain searing through my head again, but when my vision cleared, I looked to my left into the living room. Kat was gagged and taped to a chair with duct tape. And next to her, also restrained and gagged but very much alive, was Shona.

Tears filled my eyes as I clambered back to my feet and surged towards my friend. My voice caught. "Are you okay?"

She nodded. Her eyes were round with fear, her hair was mussed up and her face grazed and dirty, but there was fight in her eyes.

I blinked my tears back. If it took more than a sociopathic nutcase to beat Shona, I wouldn't let one beat me.

"Right," said Bridget. "Now, the jewellery. If you don't tell me where it is right now, I'll kill your friends." Her matter-of-fact tone made me shudder. She was totally screwed up, but that just made her more dangerous.

I forced a swallow, trying to unstick my tongue from the roof of my mouth. I just wanted my friends to be safe, but I knew that even if I could give Bridget what she wanted, she'd kill us anyway. There was no good reason to leave us alive. All I could hope for was to stall… but for how long would that work?

I shuffled back a couple of steps in the direction of the kitchen. If I could get to the bench, I might be able to trigger the silent alarm Dan installed. I'd thought it was overkill at the time, but now I wished he'd put one in every room.

"Don't even think it." Bridget pointed the gun at me again. "I disabled that switch earlier. With Kat's help, of course. No one is coming. I made sure an accident would block the road for a long time."

"You caused the accident?"

"A chemical spill." She smirked and lifted her shoulders in a small shrug. "I'm good."

*You're the opposite of good.*

I blinked at Kat. I thought I'd seen a slight shake of her head when Bridget mentioned the switch. Did that mean she'd done something? Had she managed to set off the alarm? Was the cavalry coming after all? The pain in my head had subsided slightly, making thinking easier. I had no idea where the jewellery was, but I had to get Bridget away from Shona and Kat.

My eyes fell on Dad's bag, the one that had been sitting in my chimney for no more than six months. What if he had hidden the jewels somewhere around the same time?

I remembered what Kat had said. The article dated 2023 had held a code. *Returned to sad water.*

"I know where the jewellery is," I blurted out. "It's in the old water tower."

"Good try. I heard you and Donna, remember. She said they were there, but your dad hid them somewhere else." She shook her head. "You can do better." She lifted the gun and casually pointed it at Shona, who flinched, but didn't make a sound. "Rossi thought it was in your shed."

"Think about it." My voice was insistent as my words spilled out. "Dad came back here six months ago. He left a bag of old school stuff hidden in my house. He'd written some codes in parts of it. We used to play ciphers when I was a kid, so I was able to decode them. I found something that mentioned the water tower and Dad and Donna meeting. But Kat found another phrase that looked as if it had been written more recently. *Returned to sad water.* I think it means he put the stash back in the water tank."

"Stop wasting my time." Bridget jagged the gun from Shona to Kat and back again. "Just tell me where the freaking jewels are."

"I have told you. It makes sense." I strained against the duct tape confining my wrists. My breath was ragged, and the sour taste of bile filled my mouth. "Why would I lie? I think

Dad came back, hid the bag, and then hid the jewellery in the one place Donna thought it wouldn't be."

I wasn't sure if I was right. But it was plausible—so plausible that I'd begun to believe it. It was the kind of thing Dad would have done.

"Okay." Bridget shrugged. "But if it's not there then... too bad." She gestured towards my friends.

My eyes stung as one by one I met their gaze. Shona gave me an almost imperceptible nod.

"Let's go," Bridget said, and shoved me out through the door.

# Chapter Fifty-Seven

The beam from Bridget's torch cut through the night, slicing side to side as she marched me through the bushland that ringed the back of my property. The wind had stilled, and the crisp notes of snapping twigs rang loud and clear as we crunched along the overgrown path. My skin tingled with cold, but I shivered for a different reason. Bridget wasn't concerned about the noise because there was no one to hear. I was at her mercy.

Everything sounds louder at night, and I wondered if she could hear the whirring of my thoughts or the thrash metal thrum of my pulse in my ears. My theory about the water tank had one big problem—the police would have searched that area after Rossi's death. If the stash was there, wouldn't they have found it? That would have depended on how thoroughly they searched the area and how well the jewellery was hidden.

Theoretically the police should have risked looking in the rickety old water tank, but its rusty rungs and creaking wood might have put them off. I didn't know and I didn't care—as long as I could get Bridget away from my friends.

I stopped to catch my breath—and delay as long as possible. "One thing I don't get. Why take Shona?"

Bridget scoffed. "She'd texted me, asking me who used the knife after I washed it the last time. She'd remembered I was the last to use it. Problem is, that's when I took it. She still hadn't twigged it was me yet, but she was getting close. She was doing that stupid koala thing. I pretended to be sick, so I didn't have to work, and waited for her on the way home. I knew she'd stop if I pretended to have a mechanical problem."

"But why didn't you…" I stopped before I said the worst thing.

"Kill her?" Bridget scoffed again. "And lose leverage over you? There'd be time for that later."

A wave of nausea washed through me. I needed to get away and save Shona and Kat.

"Hurry up." She pushed me forward through a break in the fence and into the Farrow's land. I tripped, jarring down onto my knees again. Bridget had gone back to the car and exchanged the handgun for a rifle before we left, and she prodded me in the back with its long barrel.

Pain seared through my head again, but it wasn't as bad as before.

*Probably not a fractured skull then.*

*I might live if she doesn't kill me.*

"Get up."

"I'd have better balance if you untied my hands."

She just laughed. "You won't be worried about that in a minute."

Her tone filled me with a creeping coldness, and I wrenched my wrists within their restraint. My self-defence teacher had said that if you can hold your wrists at a slight angle when you're tied up, you have more room to wriggle out of the restraints. I'd had the presence of mind to do that, but this was duct tape. I'd seen experiments on TV where they towed cars with duct tape. What hope did I have? I'd been working at it out of Bridget's sight since we left the house but all that effort had given me was raw wrists and burning shoulders.

We reached the clearing where the water tower stood near the ruins of the old house Donna had told me about. It was strange that the tower had survived, but the house had been destroyed when the fire burned through here. An old guy at the service station had told me that the bushfire had skirted what was now my house, and Kingston Hill had been mostly spared too. A miracle, they'd said. But that had been over sixty years ago—ancient history for this area.

I took in a deep, shaky breath. It would take another miracle for me to stay alive long enough to enjoy my home.

Bridget nudged me forward with the gun in my ribs and made me walk past the water tower.

"Aren't we going to look in the tank? Where are we going?" A death march pounded in my chest.

"You don't know where the jewellery is, or you would have told me." Bridget's eyes gleamed in the moonlight, giving her a ghoulish stare. "I'm taking you to one of the Farrows' roo pits." She paused for emphasis. "Like your father took my dad."

My stomach twisted and I swallowed back more acid bile. My voice wavered. "I know where the jewellery is. I told you."

She sneered. "I know what you said, but I could tell you made it up. You just wanted to try to save your friends."

I didn't miss her emphasis on the word *try*. Even if I helped her, she was going to kill us.

"Please… just look."

She looked over at the old tower then turned and regarded me. "You get it."

I tried to still my breathing, but it came out fast in short, sharp bursts. The tank sat on a tall, rickety wooden platform about eight metres off the ground. There were two rusted iron ladders, one up to the tank platform and the other up the side of the tank itself.

"I… can't."

"What do you mean, you can't? You've just pleaded with me to find it. You want to die now, instead?" She pointed to a trail that led deep into the bush.

I shook my head and squeezed my eyes shut. "I don't… I can't… do heights."

"Too bad, Nancy Drew. It's your choice. You die sooner then." She gestured to the track. "Move."

It was then that I heard a noise. It was faint, distant, in the cold night air. A man, then a woman, calling my name. "Ruth!"

My heart leapt. Had Kat managed to get a message out? Had my friends been saved? I straightened, locking eyes with my enemy. "They're coming."

Her predatory smile was smug. "We'll see. I might have set a small trap at the house. That old wiring can cause a fire so easily."

"Please don't hurt them."

"And I might have to do some more damage first. This town killed my dad. Everyone should suffer for it." She pointed to one of the struts holding up the tank. "Over there."

"What are you going to do?"

She didn't answer, but pulled out her roll of duct tape and slapped a length over my mouth. Then she taped me to the post.

"Ruth!"

"Ruth!"

I struggled against my bonds. The voices were distant, but it was Dan, for sure, and Larsen.

"Plan B," said Bridget, holding up her rifle. "The tower is as good a place as any to shoot from. I've got great night vision and there's enough moonlight. Then I'm going back to make sure that fire starts. That should give me enough time to get away."

Bridget started to climb. I strained at my ties, my tears tasting of salt in the back of my throat. There was nothing I could do. I would die and so could my friends.

Maybe it was my imagination again. Or maybe being close to death meant the veil between this world and the next was thin. I didn't know, but once again I felt Dad's presence. Not a warning like it had been with Rossi, but a warmth. A strength. I couldn't see him, but I could breathe his scent.

*Ruth!*

Was he really here? Was I going mad? Maybe, but a wave of resolve washed through me. Shona hadn't given up. I couldn't give up either.

*Help me!* I didn't know who I was asking. Dad? God? The universe? I'd take help wherever I could. I struggled hard against my bonds. The tape was tight, but Bridget had wrapped the duct tape in a big loop around me and the post. If she'd wrapped it around the strut first, and then me, I'd have had no chance.

"Ruth!"

"Ruth!"

I strained again. I couldn't let her hurt them. Not Dan, the kind guy with warm eyes and a killer smile who'd become my friend. Not Legs-to-Breasts either. I'd grown to respect the Valkyrie warrior. I couldn't let Bridget hurt her.

I strained backwards on my tiptoes, pulling myself up and away from the post. The tape moved a little. Then I bent my knees in squats to try to work the duct tape up and down and away from where it was stuck to the post. Splinters bit into my arms, but it worked—except my knees were shaking so hard they gave way, and I slid down the strut.

I stilled when Bridget swore as she clanged up the rusted ladder and pulled her hand away from the railing. Good, she must have cut herself. I hoped she'd get tetanus.

*Please, please, please.* I pressed my eyes shut. My hands could touch the ground now and I groped behind me for a rock, or anything I could use to cut the tape.

Bridget had reached the top of the first ladder and was sidling around the tank platform to the other. I realised what she was doing. She would be up high and largely hidden from Larsen and Dan when they broke into the clearing. She'd get a clear shot before they could find cover.

I reached again and my hand snagged a rock. My breath caught when I realised it was sharp—probably slate. I worked it clear of the soil then tried to manoeuvre it between my fingers and my wrists, then between my wrists and the post.

"Aah!" My voice was muffled by the gag, but I couldn't help crying out when I cut myself.

"You'd better not be trying to get away," Bridget's voice rang out. "You know I'll shoot you if you run."

I tried again and caught the edge of the tape. I sawed hard and the restraint gave way. My wrists stung as I freed my body and then my mouth.

Larsen and Dan were getting closer.

Krav Maga said that the best defence was to run if you could. My first instinct when I got free was to run, hide and call out a warning, but the clearing was wide and there wasn't much cover away from the ruins of the house. Bridget was right—I'd be dead in a second. If I hid under the tower and called out to Dan and Larsen, Bridget would simply climb down and shoot me.

The only other option was to stop her myself, or at least slow her down. It took one long moment before I grasped the roughened ladder, closed my eyes and started to climb.

Vertigo swirled around me, making it hard to be silent.

*I can do this. Mind over matter. Fight over flight.*

Larsen and Dan called again. They were almost at the clearing. I closed my eyes and leaned briefly against the ladder before moving silently upwards.

*I won't fall. I won't fall. I won't fall.*

I was only a few metres off the ground if I did—that was all—but when I reached the platform, my fingers clung hard against the metal tank. I tried to ignore the spinning as I started up the second ladder after Bridget.

"Ruth!" Larsen entered the clearing.

Bridget was just above me, taking aim. I called out a warning and lunged for her ankle at the same time as she fired. The bullet went high, hitting a tree. Larsen and Dan dived for cover.

"Get out of there, Ruth," called Dan.

I tried. They couldn't shoot if I was in the way—I guess I hadn't thought that through—but I couldn't move. My feet felt glued to the rung of the ladder.

Bridget kicked down at me, just missing my head with her boot. I grappled for her ankle again and the edge of her boot caught my cheek. Pain exploded in my face, and I swung outwards, holding on with one hand. I think that was why her bullet missed me.

Larsen and Dan rushed forward, flanking the water tower on the left and right. My ears were ringing from the shot. Bridget kicked at me again and this time I caught her ankle. I yanked hard and she crashed into me as she fell. Somehow, I managed to hold on as she hit the ground with a thud.

I clung to the ladder, trembling, as more police surged into the clearing. Some ran to Bridget, who was groaning on the ground. Dan called out to me, but I couldn't hear what he was saying. All I could do was hold on and close my eyes as the world whirled around me.

"Ruth."

I heard him this time; the adrenalin must have been fading. My head was pounding, and the world was still spinning.

"You're okay. It's safe. Shona and Kat are safe. You can come down now."

I shook my head and another wave of pain flashed through me. "Get Shona and Kat out of the house. Bridget set a trap."

"It's okay, they're safe. We found the incendiary device. Kat knew where it was."

I rested my head against the cold, rusted rung and looked down at Dan briefly. Big mistake. I closed my eyes again. "Don't. Like. Heights."

"You've just fought off a murderer, Ruth. It's only a few metres," he encouraged me.

"Can't." I pressed harder into the ladder.

His tone softened. "Come on, I'll talk you through it. Just take one foot at a time down onto the platform."

I shook my head again but managed to move my foot off the ladder and onto the platform. The world swam around me, and I pressed every bit of me into the cold metal of the tank wall. How long had it been since Shona had talked me down off my own ladder? It felt like an eternity. In reality, it was less than a month.

"That's it, you're doing great. Now edge around towards me." Dan had climbed part way up the first ladder. "Here, I'm coming to get you. I won't let you fall." His voice was calm and steady, like he was talking to a spooked horse.

I reached the top of the first ladder, but I couldn't let go of the tank.

"Crouch down if you have to." Dan's voice was soothing. "Then edge back to the ladder. I'm right below you. You won't fall."

I did as he said, but I was shaking so hard I could barely hold onto the railings. I pressed my eyes shut as I eased over the edge onto the rungs of the ladder, testing it first with one foot then the other.

"It's rusty." My voice trembled. "What if it breaks?"

"It won't break."

The rung held, but that was the moment I slipped.

"Aargh!" I slid downwards, cannoning into Dan. His arms grabbed me as we both fell with a loud "oof" onto the ground below.

We lay there for a moment, the wind knocked out of us, my back to his front.

"Are you okay?" he asked, his arms tightening around me.

My breath was quick and shallow. "Yeah. I think so." I slid three-quarters off him, then reached out to touch his cheek. "You?"

"Yeah." He shuffled back up until he was sitting then drew me into a desperate hug. "Thank God you're okay."

I clung to him, my fingers digging hard into his shoulders, tears wet and salty on his shirt.

"They're really safe?" I mumbled against his chest. "Shona and Kat?"

He leaned back so he could look at me. "Paramedics are checking them, but I think they'll be fine." He ran his fingers through my hair, sending warm goosebumps across my skin. My head still hurt where I'd been hit, but Dan's touch was better than any opiate.

"You shouldn't have gone after her like that." He gestured to Bridget, who was now being lifted onto a stretcher. She had an IV in her arm and was rambling about her father. Maybe she wouldn't say too much about Dad's part in all this—probably a vain hope.

I met his watery gaze, blinking back my own tears. "She would have killed you. Both of you."

I half expected him to tell me off again, but he didn't. He enveloped me in his arms again, drawing me close. I squeezed my eyes closed and buried my face against his shoulder, revelling in his warmth and strength. He breathed into my hair and whispered, "Thank you."

Maybe it was just reaction, but my overactive sense of the ridiculous took over. In the safety of his arms and the close crush of our bodies, a realisation sparked a giggle. "I fell on top of you again."

Dan pulled back and looked down at me. His eyes crinkled with amusement, which morphed into a low chuckle, that rumbled into full-bodied laughter. My giggle became a snort and I fell against him, losing all control. We clutched each other, tangled together in laughter and relief, not caring about the puzzled glances of passing police.

# Chapter Fifty-Eight

A few days later I sat on my back porch with Joe and Shona. It was a beautiful autumn day, warm with clear blue skies and not much wind. We could see for miles down the valley. Cora sat on my lap, kneading her claws into my leg. Her excessive grumpiness seemed to have taken a back seat to her quest for love, but I was careful to keep my hands well away whenever I saw her pupils dilate.

I let out a deep, contented sigh. It was so good to relax with my friends—I was never going to take that for granted again.

"Wait, what's that?" Shona breathed as she pointed to something in the backyard. A small, spiny, round, brown animal was tottering across the grass. "An echidna!"

We all held our breath as the little creature stopped for a moment, sniffed the air, then waddled its way towards some bushes. Cora leaned forward, whiskers twitching, but then decided that whatever it was, it might be sharp and best left alone.

"I can't believe she's got an echidna on her property."

Shona turned to Joe, who gave her a warm smile. "I want an echidna."

"I'll see what I can do," he drawled with a grin.

Right then I reckoned Joe would do almost anything for Shona. He hadn't left her side since she'd been found and taken to hospital for observation.

"Kidnapping a wild animal rarely goes well," I argued, before realising what I'd said.

"Point taken," Joe said. We both turned to Shona, who was gazing in the direction of the echidna, with unfocused eyes.

"How are you really going?" My voice was soft as I refilled first her glass, then Joe's and mine, with wine.

Bridget had kept Shona in the shed of an abandoned property just outside of town. Most of the time she'd been blindfolded as well as gagged, although she'd been given food and water. The doctors had admitted her to hospital overnight, then released her with antibiotics for her cuts and bruises and a referral to see a psychologist. She was mostly back to normal physically, but her face was pale, and she looked pinched around her eyes.

"Huh?" She turned her focus back to me. "I'm fine." But her smile was superficial as she took a sip of the wine.

I might have bought it if I hadn't known her so well.

"Really." She sat taller in her chair and put her glass on the outdoor table.

"You're not sleeping," Joe said.

She sighed. "Thanks for telling the world."

"It's not the world. It's Ruth."

I reached out and took her hand. "I'm here if you need to talk. *Any time.* Call me, even if it's at two in the morning."

"I really will be okay." A smile played at the corners of her lips. "No experience is wasted for an actor. I'm thinking of auditioning for a role—in a film that's going to be shot in South Australia later in the year."

"You didn't tell me that." Joe gave her a surprised look.

"I just saw the role this morning. It's a suspense/thriller." Something flickered in her eyes. "Someone's kidnapped."

I regarded my friend. "Are you sure you want to do that?"

"I think so. I really do feel okay, but you know…" She winked. "Method acting."

I mustn't have looked convinced because it was her turn to grab my hand and squeeze. "I'll be fine. It will help me process—if I get the role, that is. Will you help me make an audition tape? If they're interested, they'll call me back for a face-to-face audition."

"I can do that," Joe offered.

She shook her head. "It's okay. Ruth's good at that kind of thing."

His face fell. I didn't think he liked the idea of Shona doing this project, but he'd told me earlier he wanted to be a bigger part of her acting world, given their fight the morning before she disappeared.

She beamed her old sunshine smile at her fiancé. "But you could help with the lighting."

"Sure." He straightened in his chair, picked up his phone and started searching YouTube.

Shona swung to me, her face even more animated. "Remember how we made those movies at school?"

"How could I forget?"

"Bad Nuns," we both said in chorus.

"That I gotta see," Joe said.

"There were others but that one was the best." I flicked my eyes in the direction of the shed. "I don't know if I still have a copy."

"We got into so much trouble over it at school." Shona

was positively bubbling. "But I know for a fact that Sister Agnes watched it more than once."

"I'll have a look when I go through all my stuff," I offered. "Better still, you can help me."

Her eyes lit up. "I'm in."

"So…" Joe swivelled in my direction and changed the subject. "I hear the mayor wants to give you a bravery award."

Heat rose in my face. "I wasn't brave."

"Yes, you were. Legs-to-Breasts suggested it," Shona said.

I shook my head to dismiss the thought. "I was terrified all the time."

"But isn't that what courage is?" Shona's gaze was warm. "You even climbed up the water tower. If you hadn't tackled Bridget, she would have shot Larsen and Dan, killed you and burned your house down with Kat and me inside."

"She was some super crazy chick." Joe's voice turned deadpan. "I really can pick my employees." His expression brightened. "Speaking of which, Ruth, if you'd like some shifts, they're yours. We're opening again on Monday."

"Thanks. As long as I don't drive away your customers." I didn't think barista work was my ultimate goal, but it would be good to have *something* to keep me afloat financially while I waited for the rest of my inheritance. And while I worked out what I wanted to do with my life. "I don't want my reputation putting people off your café again."

"I wouldn't worry about that." Joe's eyes sparkled.

My brow furrowed. "What do you mean?"

"You haven't been into town yet, have you?" Shona's eyes lit up the way they did when she had a secret that she was desperate to share.

"What? I'm having lunch with Kat tomorrow and getting in some supplies."

"That's right." She gave me a knowing nod. "For your big date with Dan."

"It's not a date. I'm just making him dinner to say thanks."

"I believe you." Her tone said the opposite.

"He's leaving." I held my voice steady, trying to convince myself. "I like him a lot, but I don't need an international impossibility complicating my life."

Shona's eyes crinkled. "I get it. But don't miss out on something good just because things have gone bad in the past."

I huffed a soft laugh, raised my wineglass and took a sip. "Bad is nowhere in the ballpark, my friend. Catastrophic is much closer."

But something fluttered deep inside me when I thought about what taking a risk with Dan might mean.

I waved to Kat as I entered the pub the next day. She was sitting in a booth at the far end of the front bar, and I had to manoeuvre past people at other tables to get to her.

I wasn't expecting Vivien from Gone Potty to reach out and touch my arm as I passed. "Well done, Ruth."

Then there were other well-wishers gathering around me and patting me on the back. It was the total opposite of the other night. Too much so. Heat rose in my face as I pushed through towards Kat. This kind of attention was the last thing I wanted.

Well, maybe the second-last. I lifted my eyes and saw Jim, the sparky, on the other side of the room with his mates. Our eyes met and he gave me the finger, followed by the sign of the devil, followed by an even ruder gesture.

I let out a deep sigh. Some things never changed.

"Hey." I held Kat in a bear hug before letting her go and telling her lunch was my treat.

When we sat down, her first question was, "How is Cora?"

"Pretty mellow," I told her.

Mine was, "Did you—we—get into trouble with the computer stuff?" Larsen hadn't said anything, but I didn't want Kat taking the blame for something I'd asked her to do.

"Nope." She sat tall in her chair, her face more animated than I'd ever seen it before. "The information we found out about Bridget was discovered in a legitimate way—no hacking —and I was able to show Larsen the traces Bridget left within Rossi's system. It will hold up in court."

"Did we leave any traces?"

She raised her left eyebrow and regarded me coolly.

I snorted. "Of course you didn't."

She leaned back in her chair, folding her arms with a satisfied smile. "Now you understand."


Lunch went quickly and I soon found myself at the markets looking for fresh ingredients. I thought I'd give beef Wellington another try tonight.

I was heading back to the car when Lydia Larsen fell in step beside me. "How are you, Ruth?"

"Okay." I shrugged as nonchalantly as I could. I still felt super nervous around Larsen, even when she was being nice to me. 'Ruth' was a step up from 'Ms Smythe', but I had the feeling she didn't want me to call her Lydia anytime soon. I held up my arms, which had been covered with splinters and scrapes. "Healing up. Head's good too. Any news on Bridget?"

"She's having a second surgery on her ankle tomorrow."

I winced. "That would hurt." I'd heard that Bridget had broken ribs and a smashed-up leg, but in truth I wasn't feeling sorry for her. It's one thing to hurt me. But try and kill my friends? That's something else again. "Then she'll go to jail?" Hope rang in my voice.

"She's currently undergoing psychiatric assessment."

I opened my mouth to ask more questions, but Larsen changed the subject. "I wanted to let you know that the jewellery has been returned to its rightful owners."

"That's great." It turned out that I was right about the location. Dad had taped the jewellery high up on the side wall of the old water tank. You could only see it if you went inside the thing and shone your torch on the right spot. It wasn't surprising that the police missed it when they were searching for the knife that killed Rossi.

"The good news is that even though your father hid the stolen goods, and helped cover up a man's death," guilt squirmed through me at her disapproval, "the owners have decided to still give you the finder's reward."

My mouth dropped open. "Finder's reward?"

"Yes." She flashed a white smile. It was the first time I'd seen her looking anything less than stern, other than when she was laughing with Dan. "You're ten thousand dollars richer. Don't spend it all at once."

She walked on, leaving me gaping on the footpath, but it wasn't long before a *squee*, welled up inside me. In my head I was doing Julie-Andrew's-style pirouettes on the pavement then swinging my hips in a bad rendition of the Macarena. But I kept the celebrations internal. Many in the town already thought I was weird. Why confirm it?

I swallowed a laugh as I buzzed back to the car. Ten thousand dollars wouldn't last long, but I could pay my debts and buy plaster and paint for the walls. And of course there was tonight's 'thank you' meal for Dan.

Life was looking up.

# Chapter Fifty-Nine

I grabbed the bottle of wine off the kitchen bench, poured myself a glass, and took a large gulp. This wasn't a date, so why was I so nervous? It was just a thank you dinner for a guy who'd supported me through a tough time. Dan really had gone the proverbial extra mile for me, with the security system he still wouldn't let me pay for.

He was a good guy. The best.

A friend.

But there was a traitorous part of me that wanted him to be much, much more.

I took another gulp of wine then set the glass down. I wanted to steady my nerves, not drink myself to oblivion before he got here.

I stared down at the glass as it sat on the benchtop. Maybe one more sip.

"Hic." My whole body jolted. Hiccups.

*Uh-oh.*

"Hic." I jolted again.

I checked my watch. Dan would be here any moment.

I wracked my brain for cures. Holding my breath sometimes worked.

I sucked in a deep breath and held it, but my body jolted again.

"Hic."

Then I tried drinking a glass of water from the furthest away point of the rim. That *always* worked.

"Hic."

I looked out of the back door. No sign of Dan. Then I ran to the front. No sign of him there either. I breathed a sigh of relief as I headed back to the kitchen.

"Meow-ow-ow." Cora gazed up at me with wide, puzzled eyes.

"Hic."

A bell rang and I clutched the kitchen bench. He was here? My hands jerked and I knocked over the glass of wine just as I realised it was the alarm on the oven, not Dan. But now the kitchen floor was covered in red wine. I snatched up fistfuls of paper towels and mashed them onto the bench and the floor, where they pooled like the aftermath of a murder scene.

The irony didn't escape me.

Not only was I fresh out of a murder investigation, I was quickly killing off any chance I had of impressing a man I didn't want to impress anyway.

I was officially insane.

I shook my head, wiped up the rest of the wine and realised I'd spilled some on my clothes.

Knee-length boots and black skinny jeans replaced my more casual blue jeans and cream sandals. What if Dan thought I was coming onto him?

*It's not a date.*

I hesitated for a moment, then realised that at least the wine drama had cured my hiccups.

*Knock. Knock. Knock.*

He was here!

I smoothed down my top, stood tall and walked towards the door with my best version of calm.

"Hey." I opened the sliding door. "Come in."

Dan rocked a pressed white shirt, dark brown leather jacket and blue jeans the colour of his eyes. "Hey." There was a breathless tone to his voice. His gaze flicked over me, and his lips quirked upwards into an appreciative smile. "You look nice." He held out a bottle of wine.

"Thanks. Um… come in." I took the wine as Frank strained on his lead, eager to sprint past us into the living room.

"Meow-ow-ow!" Cora launched herself at Dan's leg.

A fire crackled in the hearth as Dan and I sat in companionable after-dinner silence, each nursing a glass of wine. It was the first time it had been cool enough to set a fire since the police had removed Dad's secret things from my chimney, and I was mesmerised by its flickering warmth.

Cora sat on my lap, casting suspicious glances in the direction of Dan and Frank.

"She's not going to attack again, is she?" Dan's frown mirrored Cora's look of suspicion so exactly I had to cover my mouth to suppress a laugh.

"She only savaged your foot *once*," I said in mock exasperation.

"What about Frank's nose?" He rubbed the dog behind the ears and Frank gave a small groan of pleasure.

"It's a tiny scratch." I grinned at the dog, who was now

sitting comfortably on the sofa on the other side of Dan. "Seriously though, I'm glad he's okay. I was impressed with his attempt to defend you." I gave Dan a mischievous wink. "Good to know someone in the family isn't scared of kittens."

Dan muttered, "You'll keep." But the twinkle in his eye, the gravel in his voice and his lazy stretch back on the sofa made the threat feel more like a promise—the good kind that sent warmth flooding through every part of me. "At least that cat is another level of security for you," he drawled. "I don't need to be worried about you getting into trouble while I'm gone."

"Ha ha! I can handle myself."

"Yeah." He rubbed his left leg, feigning a groan. "I'm still recovering from that self-defence class. And all the times you've fallen on me since I met you. I'm worried what will happen if I'm not there to catch you."

"You knocked me off my bike."

"Not my fault. But I picked you up again."

"You did." I tried to resist flirting with him, but I failed, holding his gaze for more than a long moment before I looked away. "Anyway, the danger's gone now." *One kind of danger.*

Dan's face sobered as he raised his glass. "Here's to life."

I clinked my glass against his. "Life." I took a long sip.

"And to beef Wellington." He raised his glass again. "It was delicious."

"It was a little overcooked. I'm still getting used to my oven." I made a face. "I'll never be up to Joe's standard."

Dan waved my humility away. "Don't sell yourself short."

"Speaking of Joe… You know how I said Shona was auditioning for that movie role?" I'd given Dan an update on Shona earlier in the evening, but something was bothering me.

He nodded. "Yeah."

"I mean, she might not get the role, but if she did, could it traumatise her? Make her worse? It's a suspense movie about a kidnapping."

He stared into the fire for a moment before speaking. "It could actually help her." He lifted his eyes to mine. "Narrative therapy helps PTSD, and acting can be a form of narrative therapy."

I looked at him quizzically. "Speaking from experience?" He didn't talk about his time in the military much.

He stared at the fire for a few seconds more before shaking his head seriously. "Yeah… the attacks from your cat have been pretty traumatic. I think I'm damaged forever."

"Ha ha." I rolled my eyes. If he didn't want to talk about dark stuff it was okay with me. I was still jumping at shadows after everything that had happened with Bridget, so I couldn't imagine what fighting daily in a war would do to you. "I was talking about acting. Although you don't strike me as a thespian. Somehow, I can't see you under stage lights."

He straightened on the sofa. "I'll have you know I was in a band."

I laughed. "Now that I'd like to see. You can sing? Guitar? Keys?"

"I used to sing and play guitar."

"What kind of music? Rock? Thrash metal?" I paused, amusement sparking in my voice. "Folk? Wiggles cover band?"

His ears and neck flushed red, and he rubbed the back of his neck. "Jake and I were in an Alice Cooper cover band." He spoke quickly and it wasn't much more than a mumble.

"Alice Cooper?" My voice was half squawk and half laugh. "That's a bit retro, isn't it? Not to mention bad for chickens."

He laughed. "Our band didn't last long and Cooper didn't

really bite the heads off chooks. It was all an act." His lips curved into a reminiscent smile. "My gran was—is—into him. Back then her favourite song was *Cold Ethyl*. I think it was a rebellion thing with her church group." A soft smile played on his lips. "But I think her all-time favourite is *You and Me*. She said it reminded her of Grandad."

"Your gran sounds cool. She's still alive then?"

"Yeah, but in the US." A distant, wistful expression fell over Dan's face. "I call her sometimes, but it's been too long since I've seen her."

"Do I get a demonstration?"

His eyes crinkled at the corners and he raised a suggestive eyebrow. "Depends on what kind of demonstration you want."

It was my turn to blush. "Of your singing, I mean."

"I'm too rusty, I've eaten too much," he stretched out his legs and rubbed his belly, "and I don't have a guitar. It's my security blanket. I can't sing without it." He must have seen my face fall, because his voice softened. "I'll play you something when I get back from Europe."

I met his gaze for a moment but looked away to try to hide my blush. "So… you said three to six months?"

He shrugged. "I honestly don't know how long this job is going to take."

He reached out a hand towards me, but I pushed Cora off my lap and stood up. "I'll get coffee."

"Meow-ow-ow!" Cora wasn't pleased, but she jumped back up on the sofa beside Dan.

Frank whimpered, side-eying the cat and licking his lips.

Dan caught my hand and tugged me down on the sofa next to my cat. "Protect me!" There was mock fear in his voice.

I giggled and nudged Cora off the sofa and onto the floor.

She turned to glare over her shoulder at Dan before stalking away with a twitch of her tail.

Frank jumped down to follow her.

I realised Dan was still holding my hand—or I was holding his.

"Dan…"

"Ruth…"

He squeezed my fingers. My heart began to race.

"I don't know where I'll be long-term, but tonight…" He ran his thumb over the back of my hand, his touch sending warm shivers through me.

Flickering firelight danced across his face, highlighting his stubbled jawline and sensual lips. Behind his laughter lines was an ingrained knowledge of pain that both aged him and gave him a youthful vulnerability. I was on dangerous ground.

My grip tightened on his fingers. Dan was hot and Dan was kind. I wanted to reach up and caress his cheek, to melt against him as his warm lips claimed mine. I wanted to breathe in his scent and revel in the press of his arms around me. I wanted to feel his breath on my skin, his hands roaming, caressing, tangling in my hair. Heat rising, kisses deepening, passion growing—giving ourselves to each other until the dawn light bathed us in the promise of a new day.

But Dan was leaving in that new day.

He was leaving tomorrow.

The old me would have gone for it. But that me had shed too many tears. I'd given too much to too many guys who'd promised the world then walked out of my life, leaving me squashed like roadkill on the romantic roadside.

It nearly killed me to pull back. "I can't."

Dan looked away and let go of my hand.

The sense of loss was acute. "It's not… that I don't

want…" I took a deep breath and tried to find the right words. "You've been such a good friend to me."

He screwed up his face. "Ouch. Friend-zoned." There was a catch in his voice and he whooshed out a loud breath. "It's probably time I should go." He made to stand. "Thanks for dinner, Ruth."

"Wait." I leapt to my feet, grabbed him by the shoulders and pressed him back onto the sofa. "That's not what I meant." Heat rose in my face again. "I do *like* you. *A lot*. It's just…"

"Just what?" His gaze was open and earnest. I *really* liked this man.

I let his shoulders go and slumped back down on the sofa beside him, closing my eyes and resting one hand on his knee. "I just can't do flings. Not anymore. And that's all we can be." I opened my eyes a crack and peeked at him sideways. "Isn't it?"

He put his hand over mine. "Flings can be fun." He wiggled his eyebrows at me.

I couldn't help laughing. "Yes, but they can also hurt when they're over and you're someone who dives in too deep."

He hesitated for a moment. "You could always come with me." The lift of his brow said he was more than half serious. "I can find someone else to look after Frank."

I shook my head. "I need to be here." I gestured around the room. "I've got a chance of a fresh start and it looks like the town doesn't hate me anymore." A wry smile played on my lips. "Well, most of them. And you're the take-on-Europe hot-shot security guy, not someone who wants to settle in a quaint coastal town." I couldn't quite keep the wistfulness out of my tone. "We want different things."

He held my eyes for a moment—was that a flicker of uncertainty? Then he gave me his now trademark lopsided smile. "It would have been good." His tone was low and husky.

I countered with my best nonchalant shrug. "Maybe." But I couldn't help grinning.

"I'll be back," he offered, with a twinkling gleam in his eye. "But by then you'll probably be engaged to that cop, Gary."

"No. Way." My reply was quick.

Dan laughed and squeezed my hand. "What did you say about coffee?"

We sat talking for about another half hour before Dan looked at his watch then stood. "I'd better go." He reached down and ruffled Frank behind the ears. "Be good, buddy." There was warmth in his smile as he turned to me. "Thanks for agreeing to look after him."

The little dog whined and tried to jump up into Dan's arms.

"Hang on," I said. "I'll pop him on the lead, otherwise he won't let you go."

We walked to the door. Frank was straining on his lead, standing on his hind legs, scraping at Dan's jeans.

Dan squatted and smoothed down Frank's fur around his face. "Why is leaving a pet always hard?" The little dog whimpered, instinct telling him something was wrong.

My heart caught—I wasn't the only one who was going to miss Dan. I squeezed his shoulder. "Because they love us— just as we are."

"Yeah. I didn't even want a dog."

He stood again, close enough for me to feel the warmth of his breath. I lifted my eyes to his and swayed towards him just a little. He cupped my face in his hands and placed the softest, sweetest, tenderest kiss on my lips.

"See you around… friend." His tone was teasing, and his eyes crinkled with amusement as he spoke, but I was suddenly desperate to take the *friend* line back. I opened my mouth to speak, but he was already out of the door.

And I stood there like an idiot and let one of the kindest, most attractive men I'd ever met, walk out of my life. Maybe for six months… maybe forever.

# Chapter Sixty

The wan dawn light filtered through the curtains as I paced up and down the hallway, blinking away my lack of sleep. I shouldn't have had coffee so close to bedtime—that was the problem. Of course, the feel of Dan's lips brushing mine and the memory of my stumbling 'friend' comment had nothing to do with my complete inability to rest.

I pulled my robe tight around me.

Cora had been pressed into the crook of my knees as I slept. When I stirred, she'd opened one bleary eye, given me a you-have-to-be-kidding look, and curled up and gone straight back to sleep.

But I needed to do something—*anything*—to keep my mind from racing.

I let Frank out of his dog crate, took him outside to do his business, then set to cleaning the kitchen. Once that was done, I made myself a coffee and sat on the back porch.

My hands wrapped around the warm mug as I breathed in the fragrant aroma. Frank leaned against me, his large, sad eyes making me ache inside a little more.

I let out a deep sigh and caressed the small dog's ears. "I miss him too."

Frank gave two feeble thumps of his tail, echoed my sigh, and shifted to lay his head on my lap. His forlorn gaze focused on the horizon. Could dogs get depressed? Frank had lost three owners—Jake's wife, then Jake, and now Dan was gone too. For now.

I glanced at my watch. He'd be boarding his plane soon, flying high to his high-flying security role. I'd be nothing but a faint memory to him in a couple of weeks. A girl he liked and almost took to bed, pushed from his mind by the sassy, rich, blonde musician, actor or nuclear scientist he was protecting.

There was still a war raging in me.

I told myself I'd done the right thing. My track record with men was abysmal and I needed to draw my own line, not in the sand but in the soil under my feet here in South Australia. I needed to find *me*. Work out who I was and what I wanted from life before I could be a good partner for anyone.

On the other hand, letting Dan walk away left a deep, empty ache inside me.

"It can't be helped, Frank." I scrunched my fingers through his soft fur. At least he was a reminder that Dan would be back some day. Unless I got a call that said to put Frank on a plane to Paris, or Rome, or Barcelona. Anything was possible.

My eyes fell on the back shed. It beckoned to me, bathed in what was now bright morning sunshine, telling me it was time to stop being a wuss and sort through my things. If I wanted to make a life for myself here in Pelican Bay, I had to start there. I plonked down the coffee cup, nudged Frank back onto the ground and strode towards the shed.

I threw the door open before I could wimp out, stepped inside and nearly tripped on the pottery wheel. I regarded it, not sure what to do with it.

Make pottery?

That was what you usually did with a pottery wheel.

I eyed it where it sat. I'd barely been able to look at it when Mrs J died—especially when Mum blamed me for bothering her to death. It had sat unused for eighteen years and I didn't know if it still worked.

I could sell it. Or donate it to Gone Potty.

But I'd need to see if it still worked first.

An urgency filled me. I wanted—needed—to try. The wheel was heavy, but I hefted it into my arms and hauled it up to the house. Aunt Izzy wasn't arriving until after lunch, so there was time.

Then I dressed and scooped up my car keys.

"Come on, Frank."

The little dog wagged his tail.

"Let's go and get supplies."

An hour later, I was back with clay, sculpting tools and glazes from the craft shop. Vivien had caught me in the act and invited me to use Gone Potty's kiln and join their group. I wasn't sure if I was ready for full commitment, but I thanked her.

Now I pulled on old clothes, found a stool, laid out a tarp on my back porch and set the wheel on top of it. Then I plugged the wheel into a wall socket.

No sudden explosions.

No black smoke.

No reason to stop.

I pressed the pedal, and the wheel began to turn.

Even better.

I grabbed the clay, cut off a piece and wrapped the rest in a moist cloth before putting it back in a sealed container.

All my energy—physical and emotional—went into kneading that clay.

Not in any version of any universe would I have suspected Dad could have helped cover up a killing—even if it had been for the best motive. And then there was Bridget, who had so much rage she actually did kill.

I'd known rage. In my mind's eye I saw the face of my sister—beautiful, blue-eyed, perfect Sarah. Sarah who ran our father's office with a keen eye and a cast iron fist. Sarah who had systematically edited my existence out of Dad's life. I was absolutely, totally, devastatingly angry with Sarah when I'd discovered what she'd done, but I never would have killed her.

Or would I?

Every bit of angst I'd ever had went into that clay. Like Bridget, my father had been taken away from me. Like Bridget, people who I thought cared about me had let me down. Like Bridget, I thought I deserved better.

It shook me to realise that I was very much like Bridget, except I was taking my rage out on clay rather than on people.

I kneaded, and kneaded, and kneaded. Frank and Cora sat either side of me, watching with fascination as tears rolled down my cheeks and mixed with the clay. I wiped them away and smeared clay on my face. I didn't care. Clay was in my hair and clay was on my clothes—some even found its way up my nose. Clay was everywhere.

As quickly as it began, the energy dropped out of my pounding. The clay was ready. I carved off a smaller piece, plonked it on the wheel and sprinkled on some water. I eased my foot onto the pedal and the wheel began to spin. The clay came alive under my hands. Joy surged as my fingers slipped up and down the forming vessel. I could still do this.

I began to cry again. Like this pot on the wheel, I could remake my life. It was possible. I couldn't turn back the hands of time, but I could move forward. Find a new way. The Ruth way.

Deep down, I knew the key was letting go. It was casting off the bitterness and the feelings of isolation. It was acknowledging my mistakes and the mistakes of others. Mistakes that I'd let define me.

I wiped my face with the back of my hand again, smearing on even more clay. Giggles gurgled out of me. Clay was good for the skin, wasn't it?

There was a knock, knock, knock on the door. Aunt Izzy! Her plane must have been early. She'd insisted on hiring a car and driving herself from Adelaide airport. I laughed at myself. I bet I was a sight, but she wouldn't mind. She was a psychologist and was probably used to people having clay-covered meltdowns.

Cora ran for the bedroom and Frank barked and spun in circles. I ran to the door, opening it wide without stopping to look through the peephole or check out the CCTV feed.

"Aunt Izzy!"

Dan stood there, his jaw dropping as he took in my full-body mudpack.

He recovered quickly. "New beauty routine?" The scoundrel's eyes danced and he made a strangled, choking sound as he tried to hold back his laughter.

I stood there, gaping in my patented beached mullet style. Frank made up for my lack of words with loud, joyful yelps, leaping at Dan's legs.

"You're supposed to be on a plane," I managed to squeak out.

He frowned. "Yeah, about that. I was at the airport when I got a call to say my contract had been delayed for six weeks." But then his face brightened. "It means that I can spend some more time here." His eyes took on a teasing gleam. "And it seems Pelican Bay now has a hot clay spring. Who knew?" He snorted at his own joke. "What on earth have you been doing?"

Heat rose in my face. "Just testing out an old pottery wheel." I tried to nonchalantly toss my hair away from my face, like Shona did, but a long strand stuck to a glob of clay still wet on my forehead and dangled down between my eyes.

Dan's eyes crinkled—the sod was still laughing—then he reached out and tenderly tucked the strand of hair behind my ear. His finger caressed my cheek in the same action, and I wondered if he could feel my shiver.

"There is one thing I need to ask." His feet shifted and it was his turn to redden.

My heart began to thud. What was he going to say? Ask me on a date? I shouldn't have been so firm about the friend zone.

"I know it's only for a few weeks, but could I have my dog back?"

I looked at Dan for a moment, then without a word walked into the kitchen, gathered up Frank's lead, bowl and bed and put them inside the dog crate.

"Thank you." Dan's eyes held true gratitude. A half-smile played on his lips as he took Frank's things. "See you around, Ruth."

Then, dog in one arm, crate in the other, he strode down my garden path towards his Jeep, leaving me blinking in his wake.

It was just at that moment another car pulled up.

Dan acknowledged my visitor with a nod as he slipped into his car.

"Aunt Izzy." I ran to greet her, almost knocking her off her feet with my hug.

"Ruth!" My favourite aunt in the whole world wrapped her arms around me. "I told you, call me Izzy or Isobel. 'Aunt' makes me feel like I'm a hundred years old."

I grinned. "Old habits."

Izzy gazed back at Dan's Jeep as he beeped the horn and took off in the direction of the coast. "Who was *that*?"

I ignored her and grabbed her case. "Come on in."

She looked towards the road again, then turned back to regard me in all of my clay-covered glory. Her eyes sparkled as she looked me up and down. "I can see we've got some work to do."


It was a couple of hours later. I'd cleaned myself up and taken Aunt Iz—I mean, Izzy—for a quick drive to show her what Pelican Bay was like now. She'd only been ten when she lived here with Dad and my grandparents. We popped in to see Joe and Shona, but when we got home, my aunt decided to rest. That suited me as I needed to clean up the pottery wheel.

The weather was coming in cooler now and I realised I'd have to find a better spot for the wheel if I wanted to use it regularly. It would be too cold and wet to house it on the back porch in winter, and it was too heavy to move every time I used it. The best place to create a studio would be the big shed, but I didn't know if I could cope with that, given every-thing that had happened. Maybe the smaller, second shed? It was either that or use the third bedroom, but that would bring more mess inside. And there *was* mess. I'd managed to get clay everywhere, not just on me, and it took a while to clean everything down.

In the meantime, the wheel would have to go back where it came from. But as I dragged the contraption towards the porch steps, something moved under my hand.

I bent down and traced my fingertips around the rim of the wheel's tabletop. A small metal container sat tight against the metal casing of the motor, held on by a strong magnet. I prised it off and turned it over in my hands. It was a similar colour to the metal, so I hadn't noticed it when I cleaned up. How long had it been there? It looked reasonably new. I traced the edge until I found a small lip and used my thumb to click the container open.

Inside was a small USB thumb drive, with one word written on the casing in Dad's handwriting.

*Ruth.*

I sat back on my haunches and stared at the small object in my hands. Why would Dad hide a USB on an old, disused pottery wheel?

"Are you there, Ruth?" Izzy called from inside the house.

"Yes, just cleaning up." I snapped the USB back inside the container and slipped it into the pocket of my jeans.

She peered through the door. "Is everything all right?"

"Yep. All clean now. Could you help me take the wheel back to the shed?"

"Absolutely."

But even as we hoisted the wheel between us, the USB burned in my back pocket. Dad had gone to great lengths to hide it. Was this to do with the missing plans Sarah had spoken about?

Something had been going on with Dad before he died—something more than hiding a stash of jewellery in an abandoned water tank. I had no idea what, but until I could find out, I didn't want anyone else to know about the USB I'd discovered—a USB that was marked with *my* name.

The adventures of Ruth, Shona, Dan and the gang continue in **Mostly Dead (Book 2 of the Ruthless-the-Killer Mysteries).**

*When Dan is accused of murder, Ruth will risk almost anything to clear his name, but as the mystery surrounding her father deepens, she's not sure who she can trust.*

To find out more about my books and stay up-to-date with new releases and special offers, sign up for my newsletter at **www.susanjbruce.com/newsletter/**.

And if you'd like some entertaining *Dead Ahead* bonus content (two short stories written from Dan's point of view) you can find them at: **dl.bookfunnel.com/hrs3 zouls3.**

# A Note From the Author

If you enjoyed reading about Ruth, Shona, Dan and the gang, I'd love you to leave a review. Tell the world about *Dead Ahead,* and help other readers find great stories.

Remember, this book is written in 'Aussie', and we sometimes spell things differently down-under, but if you do find a spelling or punctuation error, please let me know at susan@susanjbruce.com.

# Afterword

Thank you for reading *Dead Ahead*. I hope you enjoyed the twists and turns and fell in love with Ruth, Shona, Dan and the rest of the crew in Pelican Bay.

The idea for *Dead Ahead* came from a character I created for a short story, many years ago.

In *Ruthless the Killer*, Ruth comes home to Australia for her father's funeral, after being exiled from her family for ten years. Facing her relatives makes her confront her childhood reputation as a jinx, and in the process she discovers that her exile is not all it seems.

Ruthless the Killer is essentially a poignant and funny, short women's fiction, but for years I had a question running around in my mind: *What if Ruth, with her history, was thrown into a murder mystery?*

*Cue diabolical laughter*. In every mystery series I've ever read, bodies seem to turn up wherever the sleuth goes. Cabot Cove syndrome, anyone? I hear real estate is cheap in Midsomer!

So why not *go there*?

I wanted to write a mystery series with heart and humour. Ruth has to solve mysteries in each book, while wondering if she has any part in making the deaths happen. In the meantime, she's becoming embroiled in a meta mystery surrounding her dad and trying hard not to fall in love.

I'm going to revisit that original short story sometime this year, and update it to make it consistent with the series, so stay tuned for that.

One of the excellent things about being an author is that you get to spend time in worlds you love. *Dead Ahead* is set in one of my favourite regions—the Fleurieu Peninsula of South Australia—and Pelican Bay is (very) loosely based on the township of Goolwa.

However, just as a movie or television show creates a world from scouting various locations and bringing them together to make up a fictional place, I've done that with Pelican Bay. All of the people, places and local businesses in Pelican Bay are fictional, and *any* resemblance to anyone alive or dead is purely coincidental.

I have grounded the story with some real-world localities. Lydia Larsen works out of the Victor Harbor CIB, for example, and Mount Compass and Adelaide are mentioned, but I've used some artistic licence with distances.

My rule is that if something bad happens in a place, the location is either extremely vague (like 'the road from Mount Compass'), or completely fictional.

That includes dairy farms. There are lots of ethical dairies in Australia and quite a few organic ones too, but as far as I've been able to discover, there are none in South Australia quite like the farm I created for Paul and Donna. If I'm wrong and there are farms like theirs local to Adelaide, it's my error. But I salute all those who make ethical and sustainable farming a priority.

Bringing together a book like this takes a team and I want to thank everyone who helped birth *Dead Ahead.*

The members of my writing group, Literati, who have been a constant stream of encouragement over many years. Special thanks to those who provided insightful beta reading comments on the manuscript.

The Wednesday and Friday morning writing sprints crew… I couldn't have got these words down without your constant encouragement and accountability. You are amazing.

My editors: Serena, who stepped in at short notice and provided the copyediting polish the manuscript needed, and Marc who patiently proofread the myriad of changes I made.

To Genny, my final pre-publication 'beta-reader'. To Fiona and Janet—incredible authors who let me pester them with all kinds of questions. And to the online writing community as a whole, thank you so much for your generosity and collective wisdom.

And last, but never least, Marc (again) my greatest supporter and encourager. Thank you for your loving patience, wit, wisdom, and the neck and shoulder rubs that helped me keep going. This would have been so much harder without you, babe!

And to you, my readers. THANK YOU for reading Dead Ahead. You're part of the Pelican Bay family now and I hope you'll enjoy the series as it unfolds.

You're going to love what comes next…

# About the Author

Susan J Bruce is a former veterinarian who writes mystery and suspense stories with heart.

If you love stories where characters discover courage they didn't know they had, you'll like Susan's books. If you like some romance and humour along the way, you'll find her new Ruthless-the-Killer mystery series suitably binge-worthy!

Susan is a self-confessed animal addict and creatures regularly run, jump, fly or crawl through her books. Susan's writing group once challenged her to pen a story without mentioning any animals—she failed!

Visit Susan at www.susanjbruce.com.

 facebook.com/suethebruce

 x.com/suethebruce

 instagram.com/suethebruce

# Also by Susan J Bruce

Running Scared

Peck Pocket